WALL OF FAME

Quest for her Father

ISBN 9789490077228

© All rights reserved Dif Books Inc, New York, NY, 2012
Dif Books Inc is part of Brighter World / Dif Books BV
Rotterdam, The Netherlands
www.difbooks.com
Design: Burger & Jansen
Translated by: Barbara Backergray
Original title: Wall of Fame, in het spoor van haar vader
Printed by: Cushing-Malloy, Inc.

Read the blogs of Dutch on:
www.iamdutch.com

Authors and publisher of Dif Books support the Flying Pig Foundation
www.flying-pig-foundation.org

WALL OF FAME

Quest for her Father

By Dutch

For those who fight against social and economical injustice in the world.

PART 1

1.

Traffic was heavy as it zoomed by on Central Park West. Jens had attempted to hail a cab several times. It was rush hour and therefore pretty hard to stop one of those yellow monsters. New York cab drivers consider driving to be a matter of life and death. He threw back his long hair and lit a cigarette. Now he definitely wouldn't get a cab any time soon. Smoking had practically become a capital offense in his home country. However, the stricter the rules became, the heavier Jens smoked.

A middle-aged woman with two miniature Pinschers crossed to the grand old trees on the opposite side of the street. So many dogs had watered the trees that it was a miracle they were budding again this spring. The woman, who was at least twenty years older, looked thoughtfully at Jens and greeted him with a vague smile.

He inhaled deeply, feeling his adrenaline level slowly come down. It had been pretty high during the past hour. He'd had a meeting with Brigitte Friends, a pop singer who, although she wasn't on the Forbes 400, was definitely worth over one hundred million dollars. The walls of her guest bathroom were covered from floor to ceiling in gold records.

Jens had received a call a week ago from one of Friends's personal assistants. He initially assumed a friend of his was playing a trick, especially when he was immediately transferred to the star herself.

Brigitte Friends was famous for avoiding publicity. She gave interviews only when she released a new album or kicked off a tour. The interviews were generally no more than superficial chitchat lasting at most fifteen minutes, to which reporters were often invited in groups of two or three.

Brigitte seldom talked about her private life. Her standard line was that she was extremely boring, that she preferred spending her evenings watching soaps, and that she hated being in the spotlight everywhere she went. The only reporter who had ever really tried to delve into her past hadn't found out more than that she was from Europe and estranged from her family. She had adopted her artist name Friends since—as she said regularly in interviews—her friends were her real family.

Jens had reservations when he first talked to Brigitte. Why would a star like her personally invite a guy like him over to talk? She said she wanted to get acquainted, to find out "whom she was dealing with." She was looking for someone to write her biography. Jens had immediately said yes. His friends were probably tricking him or they were organizing a surprise party. Either way, he wouldn't disappoint them.

The Brigitte impersonation was first-rate. She had a distinct voice and he couldn't imagine, off the top of his head, which of his female friends would be able to imitate Friends's wonderful gravelly sound. The longer the conversation lasted, the more he wondered if it really was a joke. What if this was for real? However uninteresting Brigitte Friends may be, any publisher would still pay a hefty advance to acquire the rights to a book about her.

"May I ask what kind of book you have in mind?" Jens had asked. She said she would rather explain in person.

"Very well," he replied, adding warily, "An unusual request from someone who's known for avoiding publicity. You do realize who I am and what I do?"

Brigitte knew. She gave a rapid and perfect summary of his résumé, much better than Jens could ever do himself. He would go on and on and get lost in details while at the same time being so modest that in the end you still wouldn't have learned anything about him.

Jens Jameson was born in Boston and raised on Cape Cod, the Mecca for writers, poets, painters and other artists who were attracted to the place where Tennessee Williams, Truman Capote and Norman Mailer had found inspiration.

He had gone to Boston College, where he majored in journalism.

7

However, his heart hadn't been in it. He wanted to be a writer, although he hadn't decided on a genre yet. He was drawn mostly to nonfiction. Now, at age thirty-eight, he had written three books. Two of them hadn't made it to a second printing but the third was a modest success.

His first book dealt with the New York punk scene at the end of the seventies. It had resulted in an argument with the manager of the Ramones, who didn't like the way Jens had portrayed the band. The second book was a portrait of the London guitarist Steven Curtain. Jens had been convinced this guy would be famous. Despite being severely autistic, Curtain composed the most unusual melodies. Later he was accused of plagiarism. He and his guitar subsequently ended up in an institution and were never heard from again.

His most recent book was about Jenna Long, a forgotten pop star who had had hit after hit in the seventies. After a tumultuous career involving lots of drinking and drugs, she had retreated to Cape Town, where she had set up a small business with township youth making trendy sandals from car tires. Jens first met her while she was fundraising for her project in the States. He was impressed with her and suggested writing a book about her life. They could split the profits, which could end her financial problems.

For three months Jens stayed in a small corrugated iron hut in Jenna's backyard. A single light bulb hung from the ceiling and he had one outlet, enough to charge his laptop. The book was a success and even though he had to split the money, he had been able to live off his half quite comfortably for roughly six years.

But now his reserves had pretty much dried up. His little one-bedroom apartment in Tribeca cost a fortune in rent each month and he paid child support for his daughter Barbora. Life in New York isn't cheap for a bachelor who doesn't like cooking and who likes to party from time to time.

Brigitte Friends's apartment was on the ninth floor. She opened the door herself, after the doorman had let him into the building. She wasn't what he expected. In her clips, Brigitte was a sexy bombshell with heavy make-up, provocatively scant clothing, long blond hair and big, dark brown eyes. The little girl in a ponytail standing before him wore glasses and absolutely no make-up. She was clad in faded jeans, a sparkling white t-shirt and well-worn sneakers. She thanked him cordially for coming. He followed her into the living room, where he was introduced to Nora, her personal assistant. Nora took his coat and went off to hang it in another room.

The apartment was minimally decorated in a modern style. No exaggerated design furniture, but nevertheless quite a few luxury brands. The furniture was the opposite of the classical style of the apartment itself, with its countless details in the doors and ceilings. Despite this juxtaposition the whole was in perfect harmony. Jens asked Brigitte who her interior designer was and he wasn't at all surprised when she proudly told him she had chosen everything herself.

He sat down uneasily. *Just a sweet, regular kid*, he thought as he sank into a de Sede chair and glanced around. Brigitte sat on the sofa, kicked off her sneakers and folded her legs Indian style.

"I read your book about Jenna. I like your writing." She spoke with the slightly raspy, sensual voice he had heard on the phone. "Did you enjoy working with her?"

"Jenna's extraordinary. I couldn't have found anything negative to write about her if I tried, not even when I was forced to hang out with her for three months in the slums of Cape Town."

"I envy her. I wish I could do what she does."

"What makes you think you couldn't?" Jens was genuinely surprised.

"I don't have the guts. I might think of stuff like that but when it comes down to it, I'm a coward."

"It can't be easy to perform for ten thousand people, though."

"Oh, that's a piece of cake. I don't actually see any of them. Just my own band. I stare into the light and all I see is a big black void. I don't hear anyone. Sure, a wall of screaming, applause, some whistling, but if anybody yells 'You suck,' I don't hear it."

Jens had never thought of it like that. And he was amazed that she spoke with such candor, considering he was a complete stranger.

"It would be scarier to sing just for you, right here. I used to get really nervous when I had to play in the small clubs where the audience could almost touch me."

She shuddered at the memory.

Nora entered, holding a tray with a cappuccino, a glass of water and a white wine. It was almost five—the time Jens usually had his first

9

alcoholic drink of the day. He was slightly taken aback when Nora put the wine in front of him, gave Brigitte the cappuccino and took the glass of water for herself.

"Cheers," he said.

"Cheers." Brigitte laughed impishly at Jens as he took his glass. "I had a background check done on you. I hope you don't mind."

Jens did mind. How did she know what kind of wine he drank and when? Had she hired a detective?

"Have you been delving into my private life?"

"Well, it's a habit with Onkel Gerard, my manager. He always checks out anyone we do business with."

"I'm not sure I want to do any business with Onkel Gerard." His voice betrayed his annoyance.

"Come, come, Jens Jameson. Isn't it your job to delve into people's private lives? At least I'm straightforward about it."

"You can't imagine the idiots who show up at the door or try to intrude on Brigitte's life in other ways," added Nora, taking a sip of her water.

Jens held his wine up to examine it against the light. He sniffed the glass and took a softly slurping drink, rolling the wine around in his mouth before swallowing. Not that he was a wine connoisseur—he either liked it or he didn't. This one was divine.

"I rarely drink wine like this." A jab at whoever had checked him out.

"I don't drink at all. I just wanted to treat you to something special to make up for the background check."

"Well, it does help." Jens took another sip. "And did you discover anything interesting?"

Brigitte sipped her cappuccino and smiled sweetly.

"Not really. And that's fine. You were married. You have a fourteen-year-old daughter named Barbora. You wrote three wonderful books. You rent a small apartment on Jay Street. No criminal record. You don't do drugs. Your friends are normal. The occasional date—nothing steady. You're almost broke and you write really well. That's pretty much all I need to know."

"Sounds hopelessly boring when you put it like that."

"Nothing wrong with that." She laughed. "You know my reputation."

The rest had been chitchat. He referred to her research a few more times and in the end they had both laughed about it. Nora was constantly called away by a ringing phone in the next room. It sounded like one of those old-fashion dial phones, which seemed out of place in these surroundings. Jens didn't mind, though; Nora obviously didn't feel as friendly toward him as Brigitte did.

"She's just trying to protect me from everything and everyone out there," said Brigitte as Nora left the room yet again.

"Shall we get down to it—the biography?"

"Yes." Brigitte's mood quickly changed. She considered how to say what she wanted.

"You probably did some background checking yourself before you came here." She gave a short laugh. "I'm aware there's little to say about me. On the other hand, there's nothing less to say about me than about any other artist." She paused to catch her breath. "Nobody's familiar with my past for the reason that nothing is actually known!" She waited for the remark to sink in. "I don't know everything about my past and I've reached a point in my life where I'd like to learn more."

She got up, walked over to a smooth white sideboard and pushed one of the panels. A drawer opened without a sound. She took out a photo and gave it to Jens. As she stood beside him, he smelled a subtle perfume he couldn't identify. As with wine, he only knew if he liked it or not.

The photo showed a woman with a baby on her lap that he would never have recognized as Brigitte. The moment she gave him the picture, she touched him lightly. She gazed intently into his eyes, as if that would tell her if she could trust him. Jens met her gaze questioningly and she nodded, satisfied, as if this was exactly the reaction she had expected.

Jens turned the picture over to see if there was anything on the back. A date and a town he didn't recognize. However, the photographer's stamp mentioned Amsterdam. He turned the picture back over to see if he could detect anything Dutch in the background, but it was taken in a studio.

"You and your mother, I presume?"

"Yes, that's my mother. I haven't had any contact with her in fifteen years. The last time was when I was fifteen, before I ran away from home."

"Were you born in the Netherlands?"

"Yes, but I'm an American citizen. My mother moved around a lot and I've lived all over."

"And your father?"

"Well, that's the big question." Brigitte returned to her place on the sofa, though she sat on the very edge. She put her elbows on her knees and supported her head with her hands. "I never knew my father. And you know how it is with us bastards." She laughed, looking to see if Jens got her little joke. "Little girls grow up and want to know who their father is."

"Aha," said Jens. "And why—?"

She interrupted him. "—haven't I hired a private investigator to find out who my father is?"

"Exactly."

"I did." She leaned back and crossed her legs. "He didn't find anything. He worked for months and sent a whopper of a bill."

"Well, making a child is a pretty intimate event. Your mother won't tell you anything?"

"That's the gist of it."

"And what do you think I can do?"

Brigitte gazed silently at Jens for a while. Her eyes betrayed insecurity, hope and despondency, all at once. She swallowed a few times.

"I don't know. Maybe you'll find something, maybe you won't. Consider it a journey into my past, to find out who I am—who I am now as well. Does that sound silly?"

"No. Anyone would want to know. And you have the luxury of hiring somebody to find out for you."

"Does that bother you?"

"I'm no private investigator. I really want to write this book, but we do have to discuss what I can and can't write. I'm not a ghostwriter. If that's what you want, you'd better find someone who will just do what you want—who writes what you want to read."

"I'm not as stupid as I look," Brigitte said fiercely. "I chose you because I believe you're stubborn enough to really delve into the story and make it special."

Jens had looked at her again. He hadn't expected such a strong reaction. He was beginning to like her. He had only begun seriously listening to her songs a few days ago—he didn't really care for that genre of pop music.

"I'm sorry, but you have to realize that I must have the freedom to tackle it my way."

"I suggest we talk more some other time," said Brigitte. "This was just a chance to get acquainted. Take your time to think about it."

Jens sensed she might be having second thoughts. "I don't have to think about it. I like you and I believe you're interesting enough."

"Onkel Gerard will want to draw up a contract . . ."

"I'll be waiting for it."

Brigitte got up and left the room. Jens assumed the meeting had come to an end, but she came back a minute later with a bottle of wine. A Chardonnay Three Sisters Vineyard 2006. It must have cost at least two hundred dollars. She poured him some, even though he hadn't emptied his glass yet.

"Maybe you can take the bottle with you. Nobody here drinks it and it would be a waste to throw it out."

Jens was amazed at this multi-millionaire's frugality. "Keep it for the next time I'm here."

"But wine won't keep once it's opened, will it?"

Jens felt terribly guilty. This pop idol was his financial savior and he had spoken scornfully about her because her music wasn't taken seriously in his circles. He had pigeonholed her as just another diva. Now he was telling her about vacuum tops for opened wine bottles.

They had remained in the living room a while longer. She drank two glasses of water and he drank three more glasses of wine. She wanted to know all about his daughter, his time with Jenna Long, and the New York nightlife. He had invited her to go out with him and said bluntly, "Nobody will recognize you the way you look right now." When she took that the wrong way, he had scrambled to find so many compliments that she blushed. It was a confusing encounter. When he left, so little remained in the bottle that neither of them mentioned it.

Back on the street, he savored the first drag of smoke in his lungs and the effect of the nicotine on his body. *I don't know what I did to deserve this, but I just hit the jackpot. I'm definitely going to party tonight!* He set off

13

walking and felt the wine gradually sink to his thighs and calves. He threw down his cigarette and finally managed to stop a cab by recklessly jumping out into the street.

2.

Onkel Gerard's office was on a floor of a prestigious office building on W 57th Street near Broadway. Jens sat in one of the tasteless but expensive leather chairs in the waiting room. Displayed on the table were expensive coffee table books and magazines that looked like they had never been touched.

For the past week Jens had been busy researching Brigitte and Onkel Gerard, whose actual name was Gerard Schöteldreier. In his business, with a name like that, anyone would have taken an artist name or alias. Schöteldreier got his nickname when he discovered the 15-year-old Brigitte Vermeer in Hamburg, Germany, where he was co-owner of a café on the Reeperbahn. It was located in the middle of the red-light district, although Jens couldn't find anything linking the Musik Café Das Schwere Hertz to the sex industry. The age difference between the 15-year-old runaway and the then 48-year-old Schöteldreier immediately gave rise to questions, so he presented himself as her uncle—hence his nickname.

The information Jens uncovered wasn't general knowledge, yet it had been amazingly easy to acquire. His request for information about Schöteldreier's management company at the Chamber of Commerce resulted in his age and full name. A colleague who spoke German googled him and learned that his hometown was Hamburg. Thanks to a local correspondent for an American newspaper he occasionally wrote for, Jens had gotten a pretty good picture of Gerard Schöteldreier.

It wouldn't take him long to put together Brigitte's biographical timeline. Apparently no one had ever taken the trouble. Investigative journalism used to be an important part of the profession; nowadays there was barely time or money to do much more than collect data off the Internet.

Despite his age—sixty-three—Schöteldreier could be found at every party in New York. Also at those in Los Angeles, London and Paris. His favorite drink was champagne from the most expensive house. Aside from Brigitte he also had a few other starlets under contract. They brought in less money than his cash cow but they did help him stay in with the tabloids.

The man seemed untouchable on the scene and only had one enemy—Frank Johnson from *Entertainment Inside*, a seedy pulp magazine that unfortunately couldn't be ignored because it had a circulation of three million a week nationwide. It was a mystery where Johnson got his mud. Every week he came up with new painful exposés. Particularly at his home base New York, Johnson was a hated figure with every star, agent and record producer whose dirty laundry he aired. Nightclub owners had tried to ban him from their establishments but Johnson had sued them, winning every time. With freedom of the press, discrimination of homosexuals—although it was doubtful he really was one—or some other argument, Frank Johnson's lawyer always got legal redress. He left exasperated judges no other choice than to fine club owners and demand compensation. For a while, this was a better source of income for Johnson than his day job. And it was obvious; he wore the most expensive Rolex watches, Armani suits and Prada shoes.

Schöteldreier made Jens wait for more than thirty minutes. Evidently the pecking order was being established. The first contract he had sent left Jens just enough room to write some sweet little story. And even that would have to be authorized by Onkel Gerard.

Jens had been furious. He had a double hangover. Subsequent to meeting with Brigitte, he had treated his friends and partied late into the night. The contract came special delivery the next day. He read it with a throbbing headache, his heart banging with excitement, and then tears of disillusionment had welled.

He called Brigitte but Nora answered. Brigitte wasn't in, she said, but she would give her the message. He couldn't work with such a contract, Jens had said. Either Schöteldreier had drawn up something completely different from what he and Brigitte had discussed, or they had totally misunderstood each other. He left his cell phone number and stomped furiously into the first bar he stumbled upon to drink away his frustration.

Winning the lottery but losing the ticket—that's how Jens felt as he sat

on the stoop of that bar with his cigarette. The
had also reached the New York food-service in
ing despondently, convinced that Schöteldreie
gitte out of her foolish plan. His iPhone did
private number. He looked at it despondently, an
anyway. When he heard her voice, he jumped up and begā.

"This is Brigitte. Are you upset?"

"No, dear Brigitte, I'm not upset. I just let myself get carried away yesterday. Your plan isn't possible, not like that."

"What do you mean *not like that?*"

"Well, that you would trust me with writing your life story. Trust just doesn't belong in this world anymore."

"You're drunk and you're being sentimental."

"Sorry. I was drinking away my defeat. I'm not drunk, just disappointed."

"I haven't seen the contract. As far as I'm concerned, we don't need one but Onkel Gerard insists on having something on paper."

"Okay, but I'm not acquainted with Onkel Gerard. So is it going to be a battle between lawyers?"

"Just send me a contract. Tell me how you want it. I trust you."

Brigitte was apparently being addressed by someone next to her— Nora or perhaps Schöteldreier. Her vexed response was clearly audible: "This is what I want."

Then to Jens, "I didn't think you'd give up so easily. I'm a bit disappointed as well."

Jens had thrown away his cigarette and he moved his jaws quickly up and down and from left to right to mask his delayed speech.

"I haven't given up. I only said I can't work with such a contract."

"Nora informed me you had canceled. That you no longer wanted it."

"Well, it must be hard having so many people around you who have their own ideas of what you should or shouldn't do." He felt cowardly, because he had in fact already given up on the idea of a book.

"You're quite the diplomat," Brigitte had said before hanging up.

After the phone call, Jens had walked over to Broadway and then four blocks uptown to his literary agent's office. Jerry Walker was pretty much useless. He had never gone out of his way for him. It was always

o came up with new ideas. It was always Jens who made the
ions for the cover, for the book presentation and for the promotion
mpaign, limited as he was by the lousy budget Walker made avail-
ble. He also had to do much of the work himself, such as preparing
snacks and opening wine bottles at promotional events. But in New
York it was a big deal to even have a literary agent who said he believed
in you, even if he didn't mean it. And anyway, within Walker's small
firm Jens had connected with people who really did believe in him,
people who had become friends, like his editor Ellen Jacobs. She
rewrote Jens's texts better than he ever could have put them on paper.

Ellen was twenty-seven. At first glance, with her glasses, her hair in a
bun and a stuffy suit, she seemed the type of woman who might change
into a bombshell if she would let down her hair, take off the glasses and
open her blouse . . . However, she wasn't at all sexy in that way. Her
glasses hid a monobrow and an unnerving gaze due to a defect in her
eye muscles. And at five-seven and 130 pounds she wasn't the volup-
tuous secretary of the average male fantasy. But Ellen was sweet, like-
able and extremely capable. Jens loved her. She had a perfect sense of
humor; she was rarely serious if it didn't involve cracking a text, as she
would say. At times she was Jens's best friend. Except when a woman
temporarily came into his life. Then it didn't work. Ellen was posses-
sive, even though they had never shared a bed.

She was surprised when Jens came storming into the office without
an appointment.

"Jens, you've been drinking and you stink," was the first thing she said.
Jens looked at her pathetically, so she added, "Nothing serious, I hope?"

"I need an advance." Jens sat down in a chair across from the desk.

"How would you feel about fifty thousand dollars?"

It was a joke, of course, but Jens didn't blink. "No, I need at least double that."

Jerry Walker spotted Jens at Ellen's desk as he crossed the office. He
approached him, his hand extended, exuberant.

"Ah, there's our successful author!" And then in a Mork-calling-
Mindy voice, "The top man from the Walker stable calling home base."
He was the only one laughing.

"Jens wants a hundred-thousand-dollar advance." Ellen loved getting her boss riled up. Even if it was about a mere hundred dollars, it never failed.

"Ha, ha, ha!" Walker said, as believable as possible.

"I also need a lawyer who can put together a contract," said Jens.

Walker grabbed a chair, glaring at him.

"Come on," Jens continued. "It's not as if it's coming out of your own pocket."

"Yeah, yeah. Bring me the story first—if you're serious, that is."

Jens shrugged. "I could go elsewhere. I only came here because I like working with Ellen."

"I believe in you, Jens. I've invested in you, man. Tell me what you have." Walker spoke loudly as they walked to his office, which was absolutely chaotic. Manuscripts were piled from floor to ceiling. They found a place to sit among the books, binders and contracts. Paper bags with half-eaten sandwiches, empty wine and water bottles, boxes with leftover pizza slices and ashtrays were scattered everywhere, as well as coffee cups with cigarette butts.

Jens cleared his throat. "An authorized biography of Brigitte Friends, all the way, with her deepest desires, pain, loves, a complete revelation of her rough past, a hunt for the father she has never met, maybe even reconciliation with her mother from whom she's been estranged since she was fifteen. She's letting me draw up the contract. Complete author freedom."

Jens had already lit a cigarette while he gave this summary. He sucked hard, letting the smoke press deeply into his lungs.

Walker had sighed. He realized he had just been handed the golden ticket. This was the absolute top, he knew, and he thought of all the publishers he could play off one another for this book. He grabbed the phone and called the Walker Agency lawyer, who would draw up the contract with everything Jens wanted.

Brigitte's manager Onkel Gerard was ready to see Jens. A secretary ushered him to his spacious office. The man was on the phone and the discussion could have been about a deal involving millions of dollars but just as easily about his grandson making the baseball team. Except that Jens knew the man had never been married and had neither children nor grandchildren.

"Sorry to keep you waiting," said Schöteldreier.

"It doesn't matter. I expect this meeting won't be that important and that we can get right to signing the contract."

Schöteldreier ignored the remark. He was a big man. He may at one time have been a blond, blue-eyed German but now he was gray, wrinkled and his eyes were dull. Only the lights in his pupils indicated that somewhere deep down this man still had passion. Whether this passion stemmed from an original mind or a criminal mind wasn't yet clear to Jens. Either way, he would never trust him. He knew that ten seconds into the meeting.

Schöteldreier wore a tailor-made suit with a red bow tie over a white shirt with light blue stripes. He gave Jens the once-over and clearly disapproved of his appearance. Jens wore warm boots lined with rabbit fur all year round, along with tight-fitting jeans, a t-shirt and a leather jacket. He wore his long hair in a ponytail and he shaved his beard every ten days, mainly because by then it started to bother him. He hated shaving, barbers and buying clothes. His personal care was limited to showering once a day and brushing his teeth twice a day.

"I would like to make a few amendments to the contract."

"Mr. Gerard, or however you want me to address you, it's a pretty simple contract, founded on trust. Trust between Brigitte and me. Don't ask me what that trust is based on. We only know each other from one hour-long meeting a few days ago. But there was a connection. I'm sure you've experienced it, that sense of . . . you know . . . I trust this person. That's it. I had a hard time explaining it to my publisher's lawyer as well, because as you can see, it's a big risk for them too."

Schöteldreier hadn't expected this cascade of words. "I don't see it that way. . . . What's the risk for them?"

"They will give me an advance of my fee and they'll pay tens of thousands of dollars' worth of expenses."

"But our risk is many times bigger."

"Why's that?"

"Something like a book—a biography—can result in tremendous damage to her reputation. That's our risk. That can cost millions."

"You mean there's a lot to hide?" Jens feigned surprise.

Schöteldreier smiled.

"Come, Mr. Jens, you know that certain trivialities can spell disaster for a star."

"Such as?"

"Have you begun your interviews yet?"

"I mean, give me an example. Apart from Brigitte."

"Something in someone's past. A misdemeanor. Drug use. Political activity."

"Oh come on, we live in modern times, Mr. Gerard. Besides, it won't be that kind of book."

"Just call me Gerard." He put on his heavy horn-rimmed reading glasses and scanned the contract again, including the notes in the margins. He growled at every one of them. "These are our lawyer's comments. He doesn't understand this contract."

Jens waited patiently until Schöteldreier had reached the end of the text, which he had written himself, based on a concept by Walker's lawyer, who had also been extremely unhappy with the result. But he had stood his ground.

At one point Jens studied contractual law in the States. An American contract is an average of ten inches of paper in various binders. Personally, he preferred Japanese contracts, in which everything was said on a single sheet of paper, in a maximum of five hundred words. In the end, it's about the essence of what both parties agree to. That's how Jens had drawn up this contract. He would write a book about Brigitte. He had the freedom to describe her life to the best of his abilities with respect for all journalistic and ethical standards. He promised not to harm Brigitte with the publication, neither personally nor professionally. It included just about everything from the eighty-page contract Schöteldreier had sent him.

"Brigitte has arrived at a difficult point in her life. I have to protect her," said Schöteldreier.

"I realize that what she wants is an inconvenience to you. Still, everyone can arrive in a phase where certain questions must be answered. Brigitte wants to find out more about her father. About her background. She's interested and so is the rest of the world. I don't feel the need to practice sensational journalism, and that's why she chose me. She read my book about Jenna Long and she concluded that I would be the right author for her biography. It was a good choice. So come on, just sign the contract and let me get to work."

Schöteldreier was exasperated. The meeting wasn't going as he had expected, mainly because Jens Jameson wasn't what he had expected. He was determined, smart, and refused to be pushed around. So Onkel Gerard changed his tone.

"Okay, if this is how you're going to word it, I want a few guarantees of my own. I mean regarding what you write about me."

"What sort of guarantees?"

"I have a say about what you write about me."

Jens exhaled heavily. *So that's what this was all about. Gerard Schöteldreier would rather keep his past secret.*

"The story is about Brigitte and the people in her life. I don't intend to invade anyone's privacy if it doesn't serve the greater story, but I can't make any promises. You'll just have to trust me, Gerard."

Schöteldreier looked at Jens again and then rode his chair to the printer, which produced a clean contract.

Jens took his pen from his pocket. "I would like Brigitte to sign the contract."

Schöteldreier gave him a weary look. "I have full authority to sign on her behalf."

"Okay, explain that to me. I sign a contract with an individual, not with a company. Are you Brigitte's trustee?"

"Jesus Christ, Jameson, what do you want?"

Jens had enough of Schöteldreier's arrogance. "I trust Brigitte Friends and she trusts me. I have yet to trust you, Mr. Schöteldreier. I'm sorry."

Alarmed, Schöteldreier jumped up. Apparently it had been a long time since anyone had called him by that name. He seemed to realize he was in trouble. "Apparently you have already begun, if you know my real name," he said churlishly.

"It only makes sense to look into someone you do business with. Didn't you do the same—have someone run a background check on me?"

Schöteldreier only growled. He slid the contract across the table toward Jens, placing the pen next to it. Jens skimmed it to make sure it was the same contract he had sent. Then he initialed the first page and signed the second. At the bottom of the second page he added, "*In complete trust.*"

He slid the contract back and when Schöteldreier looked at it and grinned, he said without much conviction, "You will provide the signature?"

"Yeah, sure." Onkel Gerard's German accent came through.

Jens rose and shook his hand. "Don't worry; it's going to be a great book."

Schöteldreier scowled.

3.

Jens had made reservations at Joop's Hotel, which offered studio apartments at a reduced price on the Internet. He got an apartment with three beds, a kitchenette and a dining room table he could use as a desk. He threw his luggage on one of the twin beds and threw himself on the king. It was 10 a.m. He had taken the overnight flight from JFK to Schiphol Airport in Amsterdam. He never managed to sleep on planes. With his height of six-four and the ever-shrinking legroom in economy class, he always felt like Houdini locked in a box for too long.

Brigitte had offered him the use of her private jet service. Just out of curiosity Jens had looked it up to see what that would cost. He could get a one-way ticket from New York to Amsterdam for $72,500.

"Very funny," he had replied. "I could live off that amount for two years."

When she had wanted to arrange a first-class ticket for him instead, he had refused that too. She had seemed puzzled but eventually nodded that she understood.

Jens's second meeting with Brigitte had been in a simple restaurant in SoHo. It was his idea to take her out to dinner. At first she had laughed, saying she seldom left her apartment, let alone without security to keep away pesky fans. Jens reassured her. He instructed her to dress just as inconspicuously as that morning they first met. She was to put on her glasses, have her hair in a ponytail and skip the make-up. Nobody would recognize her. He had made reservations at the Broom St. Bar, a good no-frills American bistro. He picked her up in a cab and gave her an approving look when she hopped in sporting a cheap denim jacket. Nora stood on the sidewalk and stuck her head through the window to ask where they were going.

"Just out," Jens said, and he instructed the driver to go.

"This is scary but fun, too," exclaimed Brigitte. "Why do I never do this?" she said, gazing out the window as if she were in a strange city. She commented on the people she saw, the chaotic traffic and the Iranian cab driver's ID. She was happy.

Entering the restaurant, she nervously tried to hide behind Jens but he held the door open for her, insisting she go first. Inside, the hostess paid more attention to the reservations ledger than to her new guests' faces. The further they got into the restaurant, the more Brigitte relaxed. No one recognized Friends the superstar. She loved it.

"This is truly the first time in ages that I have been on a date," she said enthusiastically once they were seated and given the menu.

Jens laughed awkwardly.

"Not a real date, of course," she added quickly.

She accepted the glass of house champagne and sipped cautiously. The second sip was bigger and within no time her first glass was empty. She took out the contract Schöteldreier had given her and handed it to Jens.

"He made a few changes but I printed your version and signed it. Here you go."

Jens took it and without further checking, he initialed and signed one of the two copies and gave it back to Brigitte.

She was astounded. "Don't you want to check it?"

"Whatever," he exclaimed, and they both burst out laughing.

When they recovered he said, "I would like to just tear this contract up and throw it in the trash. The problem is: I can't work without an advance from my publisher. As your detective can tell you, I need money, and if I want to pay for this project myself, I need a contract."

"I could finance it," Brigitte said cautiously.

"I know, but it wouldn't be the same."

"Nobody needs to know."

"That's not it. I would know that you're paying for the project. And you would know. You asked me because you wanted an honest story and that's why I'm paying for this myself."

"Well, let me pay for dinner."

"Don't be silly. I invited you."

"Split the bill then?"

25

"That must be your background showing—going Dutch. It's not going to happen."

It was a pleasant evening. They talked politics, love, ambitions, parents and their talents, in short, everything two people discuss on their first date. Brigitte was slowly getting drunk, ordering one champagne after another. Jens kept pouring water for her, encouraging her to drink it. Finally he refused to order any more champagne for her. He kept drinking himself but with his threshold it had little or no effect.

On the way out she greeted all the diners and told them how much she had enjoyed herself. Jens steered her to the exit and apologized for her behavior.

He took her home in a cab. In her apartment he carried her to her gigantic bed and undressed her except for her underwear. He quickly covered her beautiful body with the comforter. Brigitte put her arms around him, saying he was a wonderful man and did he want to stay for breakfast? Jens told her he would definitely come back for breakfast, since tomorrow was their first interview session, which would last all day. But now he was going home to get some sleep. He kissed her forehead and quietly left the apartment.

The next morning at ten he rang the doorbell, carrying fresh donuts, buns, eggs and bacon. Nora opened the door and informed him he wasn't welcome; Brigitte was still asleep. He looked at Nora and asked if he could speak with her in private. She was surprised but let him in.

"Listen, Nora," he said just inside the door, "I get that you love Brigitte a lot. I only met her a few days ago and I think she's pretty amazing, too. I'm going to write a book about her and to do that I have to spend time with her, whether you like it or not. I also like to have fun and yesterday Brigitte had a wonderful evening. I wish I had a personal assistant like you—I really mean that. Please don't make this difficult. I'm here and I'm not leaving until the book is finished or until Brigitte tells me to go."

Nora tried in vain to break off his monologue. When Jens was done she was momentarily quiet. Then they both heard Brigitte calling from her bedroom.

"Jens? Are you finally here? Where's my breakfast?" This morning her voice was definitely not Emmy-worthy.

Nora and Jens looked at each other and laughed. Jens extended his hand and Nora shook it. The peace treaty was signed.

"It's coming, it's coming. Are you decent?" Jens scoured the kitchen for a skillet so he could fry the eggs. The kitchen was roughly the size of Jens's entire apartment but it didn't have a simple skillet. Brigitte entered wearing only a t-shirt. She poured a glass of water and drank it with two ibuprofen.

"You were a real gentleman." Her voice betrayed neither admiration nor letdown.

"Is that good or bad?"

"You decide. Any other man would have joined me in bed."

"Except you weren't really there."

"Are you sure?"

Jens smiled. He was positive Brigitte hadn't experienced the last hour of the evening. He continued to fry the bacon and eggs. Brigitte peeked in the broiler he was using and the sight obviously made her stomach churn.

"Well, I believe I was still in high school the last time someone was that nervous taking off my pants."

Jens dropped the fork in the pan and looked at her.

"And then there was my warm embrace with a cool kiss on my forehead in reply. In the restaurant you apologized for my behavior and referred to me as your wife."

"Jesus, Brigitte, I could have dumped you at the front door. I just assumed you wouldn't remember any of it the next day."

Brigitte looked at him and burst out laughing. "I haven't had such a great evening in years, and . . ." She pushed away her hair and struck a challenging pose, "Ta-da! Nobody recognized Brigitte Friends."

Although Jens pushed the English breakfast, Brigitte only took a few nibbles. Then they began the interview. Jens turned on his digital recorder, which could hold 186 hours. He also took notes in a small Moleskin notebook. An hour into it Brigitte was already complaining that she'd had enough but Jens persisted until, six and a half hours later, she refused to give him any more answers.

Now he was lying on his hotel bed in Haarlem, the Netherlands—a city that perhaps still had some connection to Harlem, New York, although he hadn't been able to detect any similarities on his way to the hotel. He was bushed. The seven-hour time difference, the many alcoholic beverages on the plane and the lack of sleep made him feel like he was in a vacuum.

Haarlem was a provincial town twelve miles from Amsterdam and only four miles or so from the beach town of Zandvoort, where—Jens had already discovered—Brigitte's mother lived. He had decided not to take a hotel in the little town itself. It was May, off-season, and an American in such a village would be conspicuous.

Jens had rented a Smart, the cheapest wheels he could find. It was just over four feet long, so he could park it in any of Haarlem's narrow parking spaces.

The next day he would have his first appointment with the private detective who had kicked off the search for Brigitte's father. He was confident the man could give him some interesting pointers.

Although he would have preferred to go straight to sleep, Jens got up and took a shower. He unpacked, brushed his teeth and walked to the reception desk, where a friendly, blond, and above all large woman named Karla, who spoke perfect English with a British accent, was very helpful when he bent over the brochure stand to find out where he could get a decent, inexpensive hamburger. His jet lag made him crave one. She told him he would probably like McDonald's or Burger King best. He gave her a disapproving look and said that he hadn't flown more than three thousand miles to go straight to his own junk-food embassy. So she had suggested that he surrender to the food of this country. What should he eat, then, he asked her. Karla mentioned several healthy dishes. There was the soup factory, a place where you could put together your own soup, with wonderful whole-grain bread on the side.

Yuck, soup for lunch? And brown bread—way too healthy. Then there was the sushi bar where the sashimi was delicious. *Ugh, raw fish rolled in sticky rice.* And then there was the *snack bar.* Fries, *frikandel,* or a ham or cheese sandwich. Karla advised against ordering the burger, because they cook it in the frying pan. *Gross! Fried hamburgers, how could they!*

He thanked Karla for her friendly advice and walked outside to where his Smart was parked on the corner. Driving aimlessly, he suddenly found himself on the freeway. Cities weren't big in Holland. Haarlem was the country's tenth largest city population-wise, yet it was only a fraction of the average smaller city in the States. About ten minutes later he saw a sign to Zandvoort, and his curiosity got the better of him. He took the exit.

First, he drove through a high-end neighborhood in a wooded area with charming houses and small mansions. The landscape abruptly became bare and he was surrounded by endless dunes. Before he knew it, he was on the boulevard where the spring sun was attracting the first beach walkers. He parked and took a path down to a beach pavilion where a blackboard announced that homemade *erwtensoep* was still available. Jens had no idea what he had ordered, until he was presented with a bowl of peas boiled to mush with pieces of bacon and smoked sausage. It came with a side of sticky black bread with boiled bacon. He considered that Brigitte had probably been made to eat this winter sludge, and that made him curious. After a few spoonfuls he began to appreciate the strange dish. The wine he ordered and the heat from the stove in the center of the pavilion made him pleasantly rosy.

"On vacation?" asked an older gentleman, also dining alone at an adjacent table.

"No, I'm in Haarlem for business." *How convenient that almost everyone here speaks perfect English*, Jens thought.

"Ah, interesting. Are you in bulbs?"

Jens immediately questioned his own assumption. "Bulbs" confused him.

"Flowers. Flower bulbs. Tulips," the man clarified. His English was perfect and so dignified he could be mistaken for an English aristocrat.

"Ah, flower bulbs. No, I don't know anything about them. What made you think so?"

"Haarlem. The flower capital of Holland." He took a sip of his lemonade and extended his hand. "Ben. Ben Vervoort. But call me Ben."

"Jens Jameson." Jens shook the friendly old man's hand. "I'm a writer. I'm working on a book."

"Aha, here in Haarlem. Interesting. Not about the city's history, obviously, or you would have known about bulbs and flowers. Ha, ha, ha!"

His laugh was friendly, contagious, yet dignified. Jens took an immediate liking to him. Ben was tall, gray and impeccably dressed in a slightly worn suit. There was something cheerful and at the same time melancholy in his eyes. He was obviously from old money and despite his age and retirement, had maintained that sophistication.

"No, it's about an American pop star."

"Oh dear, I don't know anything about pop music. I don't have any children or grandchildren, so it wasn't part of my upbringing, so to speak. Ha, ha, ha!" After a pause, "So what are you doing in the Netherlands?"

"She was born here—the pop star. I'm looking for her roots. This *erwtensoep* is quite something." Jens did his best to pronounce the word correctly in an attempt to change the subject.

"*Erwtensoep.*" Ben articulated clearly and slowly. He repeated it a few more times until Jens finally pronounced it so a receptive Dutch person would be able to recognize it.

"If there's anything I can help you with," Ben continued, "I'd be happy to, young man. I'm almost eighty-five and I was the director of the local bank for years. So I know quite a few people in the area."

"Well, I might take you up on that. Do you have a card?"

"A card? No, dear boy." He made a dismissive gesture and rapidly mentioned ten digits. "That's my telephone number. Do call me. Can you remember it? Would you prefer to write it down?"

Jens repeated the number and said he had a good memory for numbers.

"Aha, I like that—someone who can remember numbers."

While chatting with Ben about the village and the local culture, Jens wondered if he should have booked a hotel here after all. He liked Ben and he offered to drive him home.

Ben laughed when he saw the Smart. "Your knees must be almost on the street." But once he got in, he was delighted. "From the inside it doesn't feel at all like you're in a covered shopping cart."

Jens dropped him off at a grand house with a solarium of wood and glass. He passed on a cup of coffee, claiming jet lag. He told Ben he had an appointment with a private detective the next day.

"You don't need a detective, Jens. You have me!" the man said jovially as they parted. "I know everything."

4.

Esther crossed the newsroom to the fishbowl, as the chief editor's glass office was called. It was in the center of the more than six-thousand-square-foot floor, surrounded by more than a hundred desks. The newsroom was located above the press in a complex surrounded by empty fields just outside the city. The editorial staff had moaned and groaned when they had to leave downtown Rotterdam. Newspapers belong in the city center, preferably near one another, the way they used to be in London's Fleet Street. Traditionally reporters spent a large part of their lives in bars. That's where they could share the news with one another and hone their opinions. In the port city of Rotterdam, the Witte de With Street had been the Dutch Fleet Street. Nevertheless the newspapers had moved out, and for years the street was plagued by brothels, strip clubs and cheap Chinese and Middle-Eastern restaurants. Now it was trendy—home to boutiques, art galleries and creative entrepreneurial companies. Esther had an apartment on this street. It took her thirty minutes on the subway to get to her desk in the ugly building along the freeway. Once there, she tried to tune out the thousands of telephone calls and conversations taking place around her.

She worked for a quality newspaper, the last newspaper, in fact, that could afford a number of investigative reporters. At the other Dutch newspapers, investigative journalism had fallen by the wayside during the numerous mergers, downsizings and budget cuts. Esther was one of the youngest reporters at the economic desk, so her job was constantly at risk. Fortunately, Frederick Winkler was fond of her. The elderly editor in chief had been having a midlife crisis for the past five years. He had a strangely irregular hairdo with odd tufts that had been surgically implanted, he wore loud shirts with the top buttons open and he walked around in one of twenty pairs of glitzy cowboy boots. He drove a Porsche, even though his height and lack of flexibility made getting in and out a challenge.

Esther was in her mid-twenties. She listened to everyone with a direct gaze and when she talked, she did so with big gestures, clear articulation and an overwhelming smile. She was tall and usually wore her hair in a chaotic updo.

Everyone loved Esther, especially the men. She showed an interest and they were flattered by her frank open gaze and charming manner. She had entered as an intern and never left. Because she was one of the youngest employees, everyone was ready to help her and she could approach anyone with questions.

Lately Winkler was less friendly toward Esther. She had turned him down. One evening, when Esther had been working late, Winkler offered to drive her home so she could avoid riding the subway late in the evening. At Witte de With Street he had suggested getting a bite to eat. The kitchen at Hung Kee, a pretty good Chinese restaurant, was open until the early hours of the morning. Winkler had clearly been drinking heavily and after an elaborate Indonesian rice table — with ten or twelve side dishes—he had proclaimed his love for her. Esther, who didn't drink, smoke or use drugs, looked at him directly and explained she did really like him, but that she saw him more as a father figure than a lover. For another hour and a half, Winkler tried to convince her that he couldn't have been her father. He told her how young he actually was, how lonely he felt, how much he enjoyed her company, that a thirty-five-year age difference wasn't a big deal, and more such incoherent arguments.

Around four in the morning Esther thanked him, kissed him on the forehead and headed home. He called after her but she was already walking away, happy to be liberated from one of those countless little dramas in her life. Too many men fell in love with Esther.

"First of all, congratulations with Fokke Stevensma. You were right. Dutch Federal Reserve has forced FSB into receivership. It's just been announced."

33

Esther glowed with pride and regarded Winkler amiably. She sat down at the conference table across from his desk.

"That's not why I called you in, though." He used the term "called you in" as a sign of his power over her.

Nevertheless, Esther was cheerful, expecting him to give her a new assignment. The newspaper had been the first to discover the foundering of the small private bank. Together with the news editor, Esther had written a meaty article that—it was claimed—had accelerated the bank's downfall. More experienced reporters had taken over the job.

"It's about this." Winkler threw a newspaper clipping on the table. It was about the death of an English pop singer—murder or suicide. The man had a rock and roll band that had become world famous with a few hits. They performed in Europe, Japan and the United States until late in the past century, thanks to a large but aging fan base.

"A murder! But Frederick, I'm on the economic desk."

He ignored her protest. "No, this is more complex. I got a tip. Steve Demood died flat broke while the people around him thought he had a fortune. But it's not so much about Demood's death. It's about the company that had him under contract."

"I was kind of looking forward to a week in London but I suppose it's a Dutch company?"

"Well, it's a multinational—The Music Company. When I checked it out, I saw that it has several famous artists. I was thinking we could work out the details of the assignment over dinner. I smell a story."

Esther sighed sweetly and cocked her head. "Do you think that's wise, Frederick? You know how I drive you crazy and all."

"I can control myself, Esther. I'm not an animal!"

"I know. That's not what worries me. You have feelings for me and I don't want to hurt you. We can discuss it right here."

But Winkler persisted, so they drove into town. She felt uneasy when he turned off at a park and drove onto a dark, unlit road. There were no cars—just a pedestrian or two walking their dogs. Winkler could have parked his car here and tried to rape her, but Esther wasn't worried. After roughly half a mile an illuminated flying saucer of sorts loomed and she knew her boss had brought her to the most expensive restaurant in town. It boasted two Michelin stars and was competing for a third.

34

Winkler took charge of the menu. Esther was awestruck by the waiter who solicitously rattled the whole thing off, using such weird literary descriptions that she had to suppress her giggles. She asked if the chef could prepare something vegetarian.

The chef could do anything.

"The music industry is a strange business. Once you understand how it all works, you can't help being flabbergasted," Winkler began. Esther looked at him, thinking this was a weak opening for the promised briefing. She felt cheated but remembered that at least the evening would result in a new assignment. And if little was known, the more she could shine with what she found out. Winkler had probably spent thirty minutes googling, since it was sufficient for many reporters nowadays to write an entire article, complete with conspiracy theories, arguments and jokes they had often stolen from the Internet. Esther had been taught by old professionals. Back in the day they had to travel sixty miles by train to request information from a Chamber of Commerce in order to find a connection between two companies. Nowadays you could download it all within three minutes from an electronic database.

Esther was proficient in so-called computer-assisted research. Hers was the new generation of reporters. She went a step further than basic Internet proficiency. She had a knack for imagining all the different ways one could phrase something—words and terminology someone would use—so she could arrive at the relevant sources more quickly with advanced searches. In addition, she had found ways of pretty accurately categorizing the reliability and quality—the DIY or the I'm-just-writing-whatever value—of the various self-made websites, blogs and other social media. Some people in these environments did have something valuable to say. It was a matter of being able to distinguish fluff from substance. People were often more open than they should be in the media.

And Esther was not only an accomplished Internet researcher. She realized the Internet was merely the entrée to what you could uncover in the real world. That's where her dazzling appearance came in handy. No one could deny her access. People couldn't keep their mouths shut once she started probing. She knew where she got that attribute. She didn't consider it a talent. She just had what sets reporters apart from the rest of humanity: an insatiable curiosity.

She admired the tiny asparagus, a plover egg and other small edibles on her plate. "Frederick, I did a bit of research. The issue is more complicated than you think. I found out that all performances in Europe are arranged by a limited number of companies who allow one another a certain area. Regional monopolies. No one can compete with them. These event organizers and agencies have formed partnerships and I wouldn't be surprised if there was some price-fixing involved."

Winkler dropped his napkin, dumbfounded. "How can you already know all that?"

"It's not exactly news."

"I never read anything about it."

"There are reasons you haven't. It isn't that interesting for the economy pages and it's taboo for the culture pages—pop journalists don't write about these matters. The artists don't want to talk about them, and neither do the concert venues. Reporters who do write about them no longer get access anywhere. It's not that different from parliamentary journalism."

"Come, come," said Winkler, leader of an independent newspaper. "Parliamentary reporters can write freely."

Esther just looked at him with pity. She almost laughed and quickly bent over her food and took a sip of her water.

"Too bad you don't drink."

"I just don't like it."

5.

To Jens, Amsterdam felt like an open-air museum. He didn't really care for those hyped-up environments. Amsterdam was built in the Middle Ages as a port city, with canals dug in semi-circles across it, connecting it with the river. The patricians' houses lining the canals of Amsterdam were some of the most expensive real estate in Europe. The river led to the Zuiderzee, an almost completely inland sea that had been closed in by a nineteen-mile long dam before World War II. Part of it had since been reclaimed into hundreds of square acres of land. The remaining sea was now a recreational fresh-water lake.

Amsterdam is a collection of vistas, pretty gables, canals full of houseboats, rowboats, motorboats, old bicycles and other garbage real Amsterdam citizens dump there. The citizens of Amsterdam are a bit blasé; they are convinced they are the center of the world.

The company Jens was visiting was part of an American bureau. However, on their website they distanced themselves from their parent company. They were *very* Dutch and respected the country's values. Their offices were situated in a large building along a less prestigious stretch of one of the canals. Many people walked around there, busily doing their secret and discreet business.

Jens had immediately figured out that Jan Dijkgraaf, who held Brigitte Friends in his portfolio, was an absolute dud. The slim, gray-haired, sixty-something looked so lethargic it made Jens sleepy. Dijkgraaf had declared 142 hours at two hundred dollars per hour, and all he had to show for it was a twelve-page report that didn't say much more than what he had done during those hours. His conclusion had been that he had found nothing. The bill totaled almost twenty-five thousand euro, including expenses and tax.

Dijkgraaf had no compunctions with the bill accompanying the report. In hopelessly broken English he told Jens, "I won't charge for this meeting, Mr. Jameson. But if there's going to be a follow-up, shall I send the bill to Ms. Vermeer or to you? If it's the latter, I will have to take down your particulars."

Jens managed to stay calm, even though he already knew his appointment with this man was a waste of time. Dijkgraaf began to leaf through the file on Brigitte Vermeer, also known as Brigitte Friends.

"No, I don't believe a follow-up visit will be necessary. If it is, I will give you my information for the bill. But I do have a few questions in regards the report you sent me."

Dijkgraaf closed the file. "Shoot."

"I understand you never personally spoke with Mrs. Vermeer—Brigitte's mother?"

"No, well, not in person. I did talk to her over the phone, three times. The first time was a bit longer; the next two times she hung up on me."

"That first time, did she indicate why she didn't want to talk with you?"

"I have a transcript of that conversation . . . somewhere." Dijkgraaf turned around and searched for it on his computer. He found it almost instantly. The printer began to hum and a single sheet of paper emerged. He looked uncomfortable as he handed the paper to Jens. He had translated the conversation into English for his client, although he hadn't included it in the file Brigitte had received.

> "Good morning, Mrs. Vermeer. I'm Jan Dijkgraaf with Bureau FMI. We're conducting an investigation on behalf of your daughter."
> "Excuse me? Dijkgraaf? I know no one by that name. What is FMI?"
> "We're an investigation bureau, ma'am."
> "I don't do surveys, especially not those that call me out of the blue and bother me."
> "Ma'am, we're not a survey company. We have an assignment from your daughter."
> "I don't have a daughter."
> "Yes you do, Mrs. Vermeer. Your daughter's name is Brigitte."
> "Sir, I'm telling you I have no daughter."
> "I'm sure you do. She asked us to find out a few things about her past."

38

Jens couldn't believe his eyes. This guy was a complete idiot. He wasn't even halfway through the transcript and could hardly believe how incompetent this man was. And it got worse.

> "I'm telling you I have no daughter. And if you're referring to that woman who calls herself Brigitte Friends, I have nothing more to say to you."
> "Maybe you could tell me something that would help us both understand it."
> "I could but I won't. She left. I'm at peace with that—end of story."
> "Could you tell me who her father is?"
> "Oh, she wants to know who her father is, does she? (Mean laugh) She'll never know, never, do you hear me?"
> "I hear you but..."
> (Connection lost.)

Jens now knew two things: Jan Dijkgraaf was a complete idiot and he could forget about approaching Brigitte's mother directly. Dijkgraaf looked at him expectantly.

"How about the other two conversations?"

"Those really weren't worth transcribing. She got pretty angry that I contacted her again." He moved his mouse back and forth across his desktop.

Jens tried in vain to catch his eye. The man was incredibly insecure.

The brevity of the report stood in shrill contrast with the 142 hours that Dijkgraaf had declared for it. Jens had already read the report. Dijkgraaf had plotted Brigitte's mother's social network in detail, focusing on the most recent people. Her name was Dora, she was sixty-two and in addition to being independently wealthy, she was married to a rich man. His name was Jan Vandenbroeke. He had acquired his fortune in *haute finance*. They had a beautiful house in Bentveld, which was part of Zandvoort, though not on the coast. They also owned a luxurious apartment in Amsterdam as well as a large villa in Aruba and another apartment in Cyprus—something related to Vandebroeke's business. The clippings in the report indicated that Dijkgraaf had gotten this information from Dutch periodicals. Dora and her husband moved in the "better circles," which would make it a lot harder to access her.

She was friends with other members of the Quote 500—the Dutch equivalent of the Forbes 400—as well as with some Famous Dutch People: artists and actors who liked to hang out in their circle. It was a virtually impenetrable little world where reporters and paparazzi typically weren't welcome.

The report included a summary of Dora Vermeer's past. It offered a concise overview of where she had lived and when. However, Jens had already acquired most of those facts himself.

In the late sixties, at age twenty, she lived in Amsterdam. She was married to a 45-year-old Canadian—William Buxton—who had made a fortune in the wood industry at a young age. He was a prominent figure, both in politics and in business. He was less loved in the Dutch colony Surinam, where he obtained his tropical hardwood. He sometimes spent more on one dinner than his workers made in a year. The marriage had lasted quite a while. At age twenty-seven Dora was given a nice alimony and traded in for a younger model. She almost immediately got remarried to a hairy Italian singer about six years younger than she. She supported him with her substantial bank account while trying to make him famous. After a year the virile chap was bored with her, though he did live off her money for a while longer.

The following period was poorly covered in Dijkgraaf's report. Dora disappeared from the news. For several years, the entertainment pages and the tabloids barely mentioned her. Only Brigitte's birth was news— there was speculation about the father.

At the registrar's office, Dijkgraaf had found Dora's addresses during those years. She had moved from city to city—she had homes in Brussels, Milan, The Hague and London.

In 1980, Dora married H.W. Telford, the CEO of a large oil company. The hard-working man of over fifty deeply loved the 33-year-old Dora. The media described her as Telford's trophy wife. By now Dora was less wild; her daughter was two. Despite a large domestic staff including a nanny, she had dedicated herself fully to motherhood. However, that didn't last long. There was a drinking problem; her departure to the first detox clinic was amply covered in the media. Cocaine entered her life, along with a number of private clinics that were supposed to get her off it.

In 1989, it got to be too much for H.W. All the negative publicity cost him his job and he became bitter. Again, her marriage was on the rocks and Dora obtained the next big payoff.

She didn't stay single for long. Within a year she had a new man, 67-year-old playboy Duncan French. She had insisted on a grandiose million-dollar wedding. She married in white and the couple seemed very happy. After playing around his entire life with girls under twenty-five, Dora was an entirely new ballgame for French. The tabloids described her as a nymphomaniac whose sexual desires had been the death of Duncan; he had a heart condition and high blood pressure. French did in fact die during the act and Dora inherited part of the family fortune, after fighting her husband's siblings in court for years.

No mention of Brigitte during this time, as if the child never existed. In 1994, 15-year-old Brigitte ran away from home. More precisely, she never returned from the boarding school to which her mother had sent her. It would be years before Dora mentioned anything about it in an interview.

It was published in a society magazine. She spoke of her "great sorrow" and asked her daughter to come home. The report didn't mention what came of it, if anything. It didn't matter, though, since Jens had heard enough about it from Brigitte.

The report mentioned very little about the time when Dora lived as a relative recluse in Monaco, apart from some problems selling her yachts and the lawsuits that left her with a small part of the French family fortune. This small part was still almost twenty million Swiss francs and along with her other carefully compiled alimonies and payoffs she was worth quite a bit.

Only in 1999, when she married Vandenbroeke, had her life quieted down.

Jens couldn't help asking where Dora lived when she became pregnant with Brigitte, even though he had done the math himself. Brigitte's date of birth was November 16, 1979. Dora must have slept with the father around mid-February, and knowing where she lived at the time might help.

The question seemed to confuse Dijkgraaf at first. "Ah, yes, the date of Miss Vermeer's conception. Dora Vermeer was living in The Hague at the time. That is also where she met H.W. Telford, whom she married in 1980. But he isn't the father." Dijkgraaf was resolute.

"Because?"

"He didn't meet Dora until later."

"You're sure about that?"

"Mr. Jameson, you must understand that a limit was placed on our expenses. After this report, we weren't able to continue our investigation. Apparently Miss Friends has now hired you...."

"Yes, yes, okay." Jens asked if he could borrow the electronic copy as well as the paper version to make copies. That wasn't customary. The report wasn't allowed to leave the building. But Jens persisted and eventually he was allowed to take the report to the copy room while Dijkgraaf copied the electronic document onto a disc.

Jens drove his Smart from the canal into the town center. At the Rembrandtplein he found a café with free Wi-Fi where he could check his email.

Other than some spam, a message from his agent and another from his publisher, there was only one short email from Brigitte, who had the funny address BBforever@hotmail.com. She wrote:

> Dear Jens,
> How was your trip? Did your tall body survive economy class? I had so much fun that evening on Broom Street and I hope you'll be back soon so we can do it again. Next time I'll drink less. Who knows what will happen. :-O
> Take your time with the investigation, though. I'm curious how it's going. Will you keep me up to date? I enjoy receiving mail from you.
> Kisses,
> Brigitte

Jens stared at the email for a while. He was used to analyzing and parsing texts, reading between the lines. *Oh dear, she's falling in love*, he realized, uneasily stirring his coffee.

He had imagined what it would be like, having a relationship with a star. In no time his face would also be in the tabloids. With his vague background and even vaguer bank account he would be vilified. And Brigitte wasn't really his type. She was a little too shallow to his liking. Her songwriting demonstrated some engagement and depth, but the lyrics didn't do much for him. She was beautiful, yet her eyes contained something he didn't find appealing. She would be a good friend and he would have fun introducing her to the world. He wouldn't mind a one-night-stand, if only it wouldn't complicate matters. He thought long and hard before answering:

Hi Brigitte,
I emerged from the belly of the plane broken but alive. I'm staying at a butt-ugly two-star hotel with a friendly receptionist who is teaching me my way around this weird country. I've found out where your mother lives but she refuses to talk about you. I'm working on a strategy. Can you tell me anything about your former stepfather H.W. Telford? We didn't talk much about him in our conversations. If you know anything that can help, I'd appreciate it.
When I'm back, I'll show you a few of New York's other well-kept secrets. It will be fun.
Greetings,
Jens

He searched for Telford on the Internet. It seemed the man vanished from the face of the earth after 1989, when he left as CEO of the oil company at age sixty-one. After endless surfing, he came across an official website with a brief report on a Harry W. Telford who had received a medal on his eightieth birthday for his contribution to the establishment of a special library collection. Telford had donated his private book collection about the oil industry to the Geology Department at the university of his hometown Rotterdam.

There weren't many Telfords in the phone book of the world's largest port city, and only one with the initials H.W. It mentioned the address and Jens glanced at his watch. He had plenty of time to look up the old man after a nap.

6.

With her wristband Esther could go almost anywhere. The organizers of this concert had very strict rules and eighty security employees who enforced them. A white wristband gave access to no more than the VIP lounge. A red band got you backstage. It was meant for the roadies, the caterers and other support staff. With a blue band, you could enter the artist lounge but if you wanted to meet the main act, you needed a yellow band.

Esther had a blue band and she was thrilled to watch all the people walking by. Brad Brittain, a Scottish rocker associated with The Music Company, had given quite a performance with his band Face Job. He played guitar and sang. He had had a few hits and was famous for his work with War Child, an organization that worked with former child soldiers.

An acquaintance that catered for the crew and the security had given Esther the wristband that brought her so close to her target, Brad Brittain. He seemed like an intelligent man who would surely give her more dirt about the company she had been investigating for the past week.

The Music Company was unusual. She had never dealt with such a secretive business. It had entire departments with PR people, press agents and informative websites about all its artists. As a reporter, it was hard to come up with any original questions. But there were plenty of questions TMC didn't want to answer. Esther had asked their London bureau about the late Steve Demood. Did he still own the copyright to his songs? Did they still sell his albums? Why did he die penniless when he had made a fortune? It seemed TMC only gave information about its artists to the tax collectors, and even that only grudgingly. This piqued her curiosity and stimulated her nose for conspiracies. When simple questions weren't answered with simple answers, there was usually a lot to hide.

Esther intentionally wore quite a risqué outfit. Tight, glittery, bright blue pants, a low-cut top, some loud necklaces, and high-heeled boots. When she saw the bass player of Brittain's band at the artist bar, she went to stand next to him. The man was several inches shorter than she. He looked at her in surprise, immediately struck by her artless expression.

"Hello darling." His "R" rolled across the room. "My name is Dave. Who are you with?"

"I'm not with anybody. I'm all alone," Esther answered dramatically.

The man sniffed and smacked his lips, a sign that he probably used cocaine liberally. "Come with me. We'll have some fun."

"I'm actually here to see Brad."

"And what, may I ask, does he have that I don't?"

"Information."

"I know just as much as he does."

Nothing ventured, nothing gained, Esther thought. *Here's my chance.*

"I'm a reporter. I'm new in the business and my editor in chief has me investigating Steve Demood's death. I want to know more about the firm that manages your band, The Music Company."

Dave's eyes widened over as he was taken aback by the flood of words. "If I take you to see Brad, will you and me have some fun tonight?"

"What do you mean by fun?"

"A bit of making out."

Esther's sweet expression briefly iced over. "Listen Dave, I only kiss men when I feel like it, not to get something."

Her remark sobered him. He looked at her with regret, not because he was rejected but because Esther's sweet eyes were suddenly shooting lightning.

"Sorry, sorry. I was just joking. I'll take you to Brad. Follow me."

He took her by the hand and walked toward a hall that was blocked by a stocky young man with a V on his lapel. He glanced at Esther's wristband but he said nothing because Dave dismissed him.

Brad was in his dressing room, seated bare-chested on a couch with his boots on the table. He held a bottle half full of beer. When Esther came in, he sat up and put down the bottle.

"Hello, Dave." He nodded at Esther and the moment he saw her expression he changed from tired and indifferent to surprised and energetic.

"Who's the beautiful lady, Dave?" he asked, extending his hand. Brad was different offstage, much more restrained and civilized than the bouncy guy who wildly handled the microphone stand. His English was impeccable, almost completely hiding his Scottish accent. Esther shook his hand and introduced herself.

"Are you a fan of Face Job?" asked Brad.

"To be honest, no. Although the music isn't bad."

Astonished, Brad looked at her and burst out laughing. "Isn't bad," he repeated as he went to the fridge. "Would you like a drink, Esther?"

She stood there, confounded. "Just water is fine."

Brad bent his knees to look for water in the fridge. He grabbed a small bottle, shook it and gazed groggily at the bubbles. "It seems we only have water with bubbles," he said, defeated.

"Tap water is fine, too." Esther shrugged innocently when Brad burst out laughing again.

With a glass of water in her hand, she explained why she was there.

"Well, well, that's pretty clever, you being here. There's a three-month waiting list for interviews."

"I don't want an interview, don't worry."

Again Brad laughed uncontrollably. "What the hell kind of reporter are you?" he asked, when he recovered. "An interview with me is worth a lot of money."

"I don't know enough about you to do an interview," said Esther timidly.

"Well we can definitely fix that. Have dinner with us."

"I've already eaten." Now Esther joined Brad in laughing at herself. "I'll join you for a small bite, though," she said to make up.

The restaurant of the luxury Park Hotel where Face Job was staying remained open just for them. They were the only diners—ten at the table. The five band members, four groupies and Esther. While Esther was talking to Brad, Dave had picked up another girl at the artist entrance. She was petite and probably chosen for her cup size. She kept chirping, giggling and making incredibly dumb remarks.

"Rumor has it that Steve Demood was killed."

"You think the Company did it?"

"I'm not investigating the murder. That isn't my job. I'm interested in The Music Company. It's a multinational. They have artists under contract, they organize concerts, but they also have connections to the record companies. Three weeks ago Demood filed a complaint against them."

"Is that so?" Brad exclaimed. "That's news to me."

"I discovered it. It isn't general knowledge yet."

"Holy shit!" Brad had just been served a huge T-bone steak so it wasn't clear whether his exclamation referred to the news or the size of the meat. "Complaint about what?"

"Swindle, fraud, forgery and reckless endangerment."

"Where did you get this?"

"I can't name sources."

Brad cut the steak from the bone and grabbed a handful of fries. Not exactly standard fare in this establishment. A menu that had *iberico filet poached in bock beer, with roasted parsnips*, couldn't very well include steak and fries.

"We'll talk about it later—in private," said Brad.

Esther beheld the *Bombe of marinated courgette stuffed with grilled oyster mushrooms and crème brulee de trompette de la mort* she had ordered. She wasn't that hungry. She had taken only two sips from the wine that had been placed in front of her, and only after Brad disclosed that a bottle cost 250 euro. She couldn't really tell. *He's about to tell me something new*, she thought. *Gotcha!*

7.

Jens drove his Smart up the driveway to the mansion. It was situated on a broad lane in the middle of the city, facing a large pond that was as meticulously maintained as the lawn and various gazebos. The main building counted three floors divided into fourteen luxury apartments. The residents had all imaginable services: meals supplied by a central kitchen, twenty-four-hour nursing service, full household support, and yet complete privacy from the other residents.

His watch told him it was 4:30, an excellent time to surprise an old man with a visit. The doorman approaching Jens was of a different mind. The size of his vehicle and his standard outfit of faded jeans and t-shirt didn't contribute to an easy entry.

"What is your business here—do you have an appointment with anyone?" The man translated his question to English once Jens indicated that he didn't speak Dutch.

"I'd like to speak with Mr. Telford. I expect he'll want to see me."

"What makes you think that? Who are you?"

"My name is Jens Jameson. I'm here on behalf of his stepdaughter Brigitte."

The man grumbled that he should wait on the terrace and went inside.

Five minutes later a woman emerged and introduced herself as the head nurse. She asked Jens for the reason for his visit and he explained he was writing a book about the famous Brigitte Friends, and that he had come all the way from America to speak with Mr. Telford. After all, Telford had been Brigitte's stepfather for eight years. To Jens's surprise, the woman spewed all manner of medical facts about her charge.

He had a heart condition and diabetes and was easily fatigued. Therefore, it wasn't recommended that he have visitors. Jens let her finish, nodding semi-sympathetically. Then he tilted his head in a charming manner, like a little dog thinking. The woman couldn't withstand and went back inside to see if Mr. Telford would see him.

Five minutes later Jens was allowed to enter. He followed the nurse along an enormous hallway with a grand staircase. The building was eighteenth century, with gorgeous plaster ceilings and dark oak paneling. The walls were linen-covered and hung with eight-foot-tall paintings depicting various people, probably residents from past centuries.

They ascended the staircase and the woman knocked on an apartment door. A maid opened and asked Jens to come with her. Telford's apartment, too, gave the impression of a museum. There was little to indicate that it was being lived in, until Jens smelled a strong cigar scent in what must have been the library. It looked run-down. The wood trim was perfectly maintained, as were the elaborately decorated plaster ceilings. However, half the shelves were empty or only held a single toppled book. Jens let his eyes glide over the remaining collection. It was a wild medley of books about psychology and photography, as well as world literature in various languages.

He heard a soft coughing behind him and turned to face a giant of a man, who was snipping his cigar with a special pair of cutters. Telford appraised Jens, and a mild smile appeared on his face.

"I hope you or Brigitte don't require money. I don't do that anymore."

"Absolutely not, sir."

"You see, I haven't heard from Brigitte in at least twelve years. And the last time she called me, she needed money."

"It's highly unlikely that she would ask you for money now."

"Proud?"

"Maybe that, too. According to Forbes she's worth a small hundred million dollars, so she doesn't need anyone else's money."

"Well, well, that's quite a sum. Brigitte Vermeer. Forbes, you said?"

"Yes, although you won't find her under that name. She uses the artist name Brigitte Friends. She's world famous."

"Friends? What a funny name. How did she decide on it?"

"How does anyone decide on an artist name? You just choose one."

"Not married?"

"No. She's had several relationships but she isn't married."

"And you're her friend?"

"I'm her biographer—I'm writing a book about her. Jens Jameson."

"You must forgive me but I've never heard of you either."

The man had been holding his cigar all this time, sniffing it occasionally. Now he finally lit it. "I assume you don't smoke."

"Only cigarettes."

"Have a seat." Telford motioned to two chairs standing by the balcony door. "How is Brigitte? Doing fine, of course, if she's that wealthy. Although money isn't everything." Telford opened the door and sat down as well. He blew a big cloud out toward the balcony.

"Brigitte's doing well. I just spoke to her and she's extremely curious about you. She's trying to come to terms with her past. She's searching for her roots. My book is part of it."

"What an unusual way of studying one's roots. To send a friend and have him write a book. How amusing."

"I think she's shy."

Telford began to talk. He spoke slowly and didn't allow Jens to interrupt him with any questions. He spoke of his marriage to Dora. She was a beautiful woman, vivacious and fun loving, while he, on the other hand, had worked all his life. They met in the summer of 1980 in the bar of Hotel des Indes, a prestigious hotel in The Hague. Dora was staying there and Telford often went there in the evenings to have a drink and to escape the loneliness of his apartment.

He was a widower. He had three children who were now all over fifty. He had deeply mourned his wife's death and had lost interest in the other sex. But Dora changed that. She sat at a nearby table with a man who behaved rather boorishly and she made a scene. The man got up. Telford assumed he wanted to hurt her so he tactfully inserted himself into the situation. He asked Dora if he knew her from the golf club, and when she was taken aback and answered evasively, he rattled off a long story about something trivial that had happened at the club that afternoon. Although neither of them invited him, he sat down at their table and offered them a drink. Dora appreciated the save and a few minutes later her escort left.

She said she was worried he would hurt her, so Telford had taken her to his apartment. Sex with Dora was unlike any he had ever experienced before or since. To her it was no more than a one-night stand but Telford was smitten. His dormant libido was reawakened and he did everything he could to win the younger Dora. They married in 1980 and he unexpectedly became the stepfather of a baby.

A year later they had moved into a mansion on a lake just outside Amsterdam, with a houseboat and other boats the couple never used. Telford told one anecdote after another. Brigitte had been a difficult child who was getting into the kind of mischief at age four that you would expect from a 12-year-old. He was a strict father but it didn't make any difference. The child was destined for trouble.

He blamed Dora. The first year she was the ideal wife and mother but then she got bored and had her first lover. She was gone a lot, so she hired an elderly nanny who despised children. The nanny didn't like Brigitte and couldn't stand Telford either. She saw him as a rich bastard who had married a trophy wife. Only Dora could give her instructions but she was never home. She went to every party, grand opening and reception, always in search of beautiful men, champagne and cocaine.

Telford had been Brigitte's father for nine years and he didn't have fond memories of that period. He had spent most of it working eighty-hour weeks to make money for Dora. Because even though she had plenty of her own money, she wasn't about to eat into her personal bank account to pay for her extravagant lifestyle. In the eighties, even for a CEO, a monthly stipend of tens of thousands of guilders wasn't that easy to maintain.

Telford was mild. He spoke with a certain cynicism but the disappointing turn his life had taken was ancient history to him.

"I regret that I let Brigitte disappear from my life," he said at the end of his monologue. "Sure, I sent her money when she lived in Hamburg. I knew something was wrong. Drugs, sex and other terrible things. I didn't want to know. I eased my conscience by sending her thousands of guilders. She sent me Christmas cards, briefly thanking me for the money."

Jens interrupted him. "She's become a very sweet, beautiful and kind young woman." He was snappy, because the old man rubbed him the wrong way. Telford's arrogance, his contemptuous disinterest and self-pity irked him. So it surprised him that the man got a twinkle in his eye when he defended Brigitte.

"So you love her."

51

"I sure do. She's my friend. And she speaks kindly of you. She doesn't blame you for anything. She's . . ." Jens hesitated, wondering how to formulate it. "She would also really like to find out who her biological father is."

Telford's face dropped and he became thoughtful. He gazed out the glass door, silently, unconsciously sucking at the cigar that had gone out a while ago. The sun was almost down and lights came on in the street. "That is a problem, my dear Mr. Jameson. A big problem."

"Why's that?"

"No one knows who her father is. Except of course Dora and possibly the man himself, although I'm not so sure about that."

"She was a public figure...."

"She was indeed. But when she became pregnant with Brigitte, there was also a mystery man in her life. I never knew who Brigitte's father was—I didn't care either."

"You never asked?"

"Sure, quite often actually. I was curious about her genes. She was absolutely gorgeous and at times she was really sweet, but she turned into a little devil!"

"She really has changed," said Jens glumly. "What about the man she was with when the two of you met?"

"He wasn't Brigitte's father. He was an idiot lowlife," Telford raised his voice. "His name was Peter Kruger, a professional con man. He was out to get Dora's fortune. If I hadn't stopped him, he would've disappeared with quite a chunk of it."

Telford jerked, as if he were literally thrown back in time. "He may have known more about Brigitte's biological father. At the time I suspected he blackmailed Dora, though I could never be sure. She never told me what it was about."

He was lost in thought for a while and only resurfaced to show Jens the door, cordially but decisively. "But it was related to Brigitte's origins."

8.

The fish may be biting but Esther realized that getting it into the boat was a completely different matter. Brad suggested going to his hotel room for their private conversation. Once in the room, he dove directly into the minibar and took out a maxi-sized bottle of whiskey. *A predator with primal instincts*, thought Esther, a confirmed vegetarian. She was on guard. Probably all the stories about this pop legend were exaggerated but he obviously did love beautiful women. She declined his offer of a drink.

Brad noticed how gracefully she moved across the suite to take a seat at a small desk.

"Join me on the sofa." He slumped down with a water glass full of whiskey.

Esther was just fine where she was.

"Are you going to tape this or take notes? My publicity agent would kill me if he saw me now."

Esther pointed to her temple. "This recorder is playing." She was able to reconstruct a conversation word for word without taking notes or recording it. Transcribing recordings was time-consuming. Also, the literal text often stood in the way of the proper reflection of the conversation. She didn't want to interview Brad about the intentions of his new album, about his broken relationship with the mother of his two children, his ideas on life, sex, food or whatever usually came up in interviews. Esther wanted to know more about his money.

Did he have a good grasp of his finances? How much was he worth? What did he make off a concert? What happened to the rights to the lyrics he wrote? Where did he pay taxes? How much did the Company make off him?

When he had asked her what she wanted he hadn't expected this barrage of questions. His eyes glazed over.

"I've worked hard tonight, Esther." He stretched and shrugged. "I don't really know much about my finances."

"You don't do it for the money?" Esther was cynical.

"Oh, sure. But I don't keep exact track of the money, no. I do know that I made around thirty thousand euro tonight."

"And where does the rest of the money go?"

"To expenses, committees, technical, support, catering, publicity."

"But do they keep you up to date? I figured out that approximately five hundred thousand euro worth of tickets were sold tonight, after taxes."

"That much?"

"Yes, it's pretty easy to calculate. There are posters in all the big cities, a few ads—say twenty thousand euro—stadium rent, technical, support, security and catering. I asked someone who knows about this—it would come out to roughly a hundred and sixty thousand euro. And TMC has shares in many of the companies involved. Let's say the band and the opening act get another hundred thousand."

"No," Brad interrupted her. "The band gets a total of forty thou and the opening band pays us to play."

"Okay." Esther stared at the ceiling, where she did some subtraction. "Then half of the proceeds disappear into the Company's pockets."

"That's unlikely. They get at most fifteen percent. That's what they tell me."

"So you only start paying attention when they inform you that the money is gone. Just like Steve Demood when all of a sudden he turned out to be broke."

Brad put the glass on the coffee table with a bang. "You know, I'm going to check it out first thing tomorrow."

"Whoa! I wouldn't do that. I mean, what if something's wrong, I wouldn't take such a direct approach."

"But if they're stealing from me…."

"That hasn't been determined." Esther got up and sat beside Brad. "First we've got to find out more and decide on a strategy for determining what really happens to your money."

"How do we do that?" Brad was pretty drunk from the wine and the whiskey and he looked defeated.

"Well, listen, I'm no accountant but we can get to the truth bit by bit. Who has signing authority in regards to your money?"

"The Company—my A&R manager, Jonathan Foucault. He's a nice, dorky sort of guy. He seems reliable. He tells me what I can spend and stuff like that. And then there's my account manager."

"Have you ever seen a copy of your tax return? Do you have a copy here? You could show it to a specialist."

Brad shrugged. "I probably have one somewhere." He looked at Esther. And immediately put his hand on the thigh of her glittery pants. "Are you going to help me with this?" With his other hand he touched her cheek. "I just wish you weren't so damned attractive. Here I am with the most gorgeous broad of the evening and all we do is whine about numbers and money."

Esther took both his hands and put them in his own lap. "I have a boyfriend," she lied and when that didn't seem to make much of an impression on Brad, she added "And I'm monogamous."

"Shit happens," said Brad.

They exchanged cell phone numbers and email addresses and Esther gave him three friendly kisses on his cheeks, Dutch style. She placed another kiss on his forehead as consolation, because he had prepared himself to kiss her on the mouth.

9.

As Esther walked across the newsroom, she saw Winkler sitting in his cage. He couldn't help waving at her, even though he had company. Esther sat down and opened her laptop. She made a copy of her work documents so at least she'd have a backup of all the materials she had collected.

Brad had already emailed her. She was proud of her source and would have loved to inform Winkler about her progress. That would be better than going to the editor of the economic desk, Fred Voorwaarts. He held his important position in spite of being so seriously ADHD, he had acquired the nickname Fast Forward. Forward had hit on the entire female editorial staff as well as those in layout. It worked with almost twenty percent of women, because he was handsome and his chatter was irresistible. In addition, he had the annoying habit of knowing everything, really knowing everything.

Fred hung over her as he eyed her screen.

"How are you getting on with the story?" he asked. She could smell his aftershave.

"I'm making progress. I've got a good source."

"Any idea yet when you'll be done?"

"Not really. It's complex material."

"We need to come to some agreement. Since we merged, we've only been downsizing." His breath blew past her ear.

Much was happening in the media world. Not only Europe was suffering from mergers and takeovers of television stations, newspapers and other publishers—in the Netherlands media frequently changed owners as well.

"Was it fun with Frederick?" asked Fast Forward.

"What do you mean?"

"Well, you two were seen."

"Huh?"

"Yes, I heard it on the grapevine."

"We had a business dinner."

"Oh sure. In the number one restaurant in town. I don't mean to suggest anything," though his tone indicated that was exactly what he meant. He got up and went back to his own desk.

Her chat box beeped and Winkler announced himself. *Hello gorgeous. Can you come to my office?* She sighed, relieved that it had been that easy to get rid of Fast Forward. *I'm on my way, ugly*, she typed.

She entered, shook the visitor's hand and placed a notepad on the table with her pen next to it. Winkler's English was terrible—he was the only one who didn't realize it.

"This American gentleman requires our help. He's searching for someone called Peter Kruger. Didn't you research him once?"

Esther had a good look at Jens Jameson for the first time. She saw a handsome man, shoddily dressed and unshaven, but with a fresh appearance nonetheless. Jens saw something else. *Oh no, they're fobbing me off with an intern*, he thought. *They don't want to waste their time on me.* Still, he was happy he was getting any help at all. In order to find anything in the archives you had to know your way around nondigital files *and* know that bizarre Dutch language. Esther didn't seem that bad.

Jens had sent the request via newspapers in New York that regularly published his book reviews. He'd had to promise his editor to write an article about Friends and about his experiences as soon as the book was published. He was immediately and hospitably received by Winkler, who was thrilled to have a "well-known pop journalist and author" sitting at his desk. Jens and Esther began to sound each other out in a conversation and Winkler soon had enough. He shooed them from his office, grumbling as he watched them go.

Esther led the way to the elevator. It was a strange parade, with the graceful, hip-swinging Esther, followed by a badly dressed, shuffling American. She was clad in black jeans, a black silk blouse and her usual high heels. Everyone stopped for a moment, watching the miniature procession. In the elevator their eyes met and Esther gave him a broad smile.

"You're probably used to everyone eyeballing you." Jens was amused. He hadn't figured out yet whether Esther was a friendly, innocent girl or the type that makes men lose their minds just because she can.

"Yes, but I ignore it. Otherwise it would drive me crazy."

"Do you get hit on a lot?"

"I can't complain but it always comes from the wrong men."

"Do you have a boyfriend, married?"

"Not even that. Single. A lot of men can't stand that."

She stiffened briefly. She didn't feel that it was unprofessional to discuss these things; it was just that she wasn't usually this forthcoming about them. She sighed. "This feels like an interview."

"No, not at all. Just interested," said Jens as the elevator door opened.

The restaurant—still almost empty—was situated on the ground floor of the enormous building. The staff was busy preparing lunch in an open kitchen behind the self-service counter.

They got a table by the window and ordered coffee. Jens watched Esther's shapely hands as she stirred sugar into her cup.

"Did you see Face Job yesterday?"

"How could you possibly know that?" She lifted her arm with the blue band still attached but it didn't have a name.

"It was the only large concert last night. I know those wristbands. I hung out here last night and I was looking for anything going on. So I was just guessing."

"And did you go?"

"No, I don't care for that English guitar rock."

"Me neither."

"Ah, so you were working? Do you do reviews?"

"No, I work at the economic desk. That's how I got your Peter Kruger. So you're a pop journalist?"

"Occasionally. I mostly write books about pop stars."

"Tell me!"

"My most successful book was about Jenna Long, the singer who went to Africa . . ."

He glanced at her, hoping that maybe she had read it.

"Long. Yeah, I heard about her. And now?" She was evidently more interested in the present and his research on Peter Kruger.

"I'm writing a book about Brigitte Friends, heard of her?" Jens teased.

"I know Long, as well. I know Friends from the tabloids," Esther came back cynically.

Jens kind of liked her. Maybe he had underestimated her. He gazed in her guileless face again and laughed. *You're fast on your feet, lady*, he thought.

"Brigitte Friends is actually Dutch. She ran away from home when she was fifteen and was discovered in Germany by a shady café owner. She emigrated to the States, where she made it to the top within ten years. I'm writing her biography." When Esther laughed again, he added, "That's it in a nutshell."

"Will it be an authorized biography?"

"I hope so."

"I mean, have you talked to her yet?"

"Yes, I know her. We became friends." Jens sounded almost childishly proud.

Esther looked at him searchingly. "Friends as in boyfriend-girlfriend or just friends?"

"Ah, now *I'm* the subject of *your* interview."

"Well, we're both reporters, aren't we?"

"No, she called me and asked me to write the book. I was getting pretty desperate for something that pays the bills."

"Okay, fair enough. And what does this Kruger have to do with Friends?"

"Can we make a deal?"

"About what?"

"About what I tell you?"

"We can talk about it."

Jens was taken aback. Of course, it wasn't in his interest to give her all the details about Friends's past at this time. On the other hand, some Dutch publicity would be beneficial once the book was published. It seemed that everyone here spoke English so it should be good for a couple thousand copies. Maybe even a Dutch translation, since Brigitte was born here.

"Maybe we should get to know each other better first," said Jens.

Some people whose workday apparently started early were walking in to have an early lunch. They were rowdy. Dutch has a lot of hard G's. During the war, when the Germans occupied the country, resistance members could spot German spies by having them say words with that

G, like "Scheveningen" or "Dordrecht." It was all Chinese to Jens, apart from the occasional English expression he heard in conversations.

Esther stared off into space for a while when he talked about getting to know each other better. Evidently this man, too, wanted something from her. Yet she didn't want to discourage him too much. She was definitely no tease, although many men expected her to be, based on her cheerful, frank yet enticing appearance. She actually would like a man in her life but she never met anyone interesting. Besides, she hated the testosterone-driven behavior of most men. Maybe it had to do with her past, maybe because she was tired of all those fools who had tried her out for a night, a month, a year. She loved her work. That was compensation enough for all those complicated relationships she kept ending up in a few years ago. She had tried for a while to dress as unattractively as possible. In that time she wore oversized sweaters, didn't use makeup, cut her hair short and didn't move as gracefully. Within a few months, she had slid into isolation and she was terribly unhappy. She missed men's eyes on her and women's envy of her appearance. After a while she was done with the experiment. She rued her short hair; the rest was undone within a day.

The experiment did make it crystal clear that the attention she received from the male part of society was relative, and that it had nothing to do with her personally. She was also better able to gauge women's reactions. Some saw right through the outer layer and were pleasant company.

She wasn't completely happy with herself. She loved people and was interested in them. She liked being talked to, by either sex. She discovered things by listening and she was genuinely interested. Take this Jens. He was sort of cute, even though he was as fanatic about journalism as she was.

"What are you thinking?" asked Jens, certain she was brooding over something.

"My mind was drifting, nothing important." She expected him to ask more but he looked at her as if he got it.

"Okay. Let's get to know each other better. Tell me what you've got. I promise I won't use it. Honest. Off the record. Professional code. Then I'll tell you what I'm working on. Deal?"

"I trust you." Jens drank the rest of his now cold coffee. "Let's get out of here. Or do you have to stay?"

"No, I don't think my editor will mind if I entertain his foreign guest. Although he is the jealous type."

"You two have something going on?" he asked cautiously and intentionally with much disbelief in his voice.

"No, Jens. Maybe he'd like to but I'm not attracted to older men."

Too bad Jens didn't get the suggestion—he just agreed completely. After all, he was thirteen years her senior and seeing him sit there, you could easily add a few years.

They left the lounge and went to the parking garage.

Esther was cheerful when she saw Jens's Smart. "Oh, I've always wanted to drive in one of those!"

Once she was seated, she turned all the buttons in reach, opened all the little compartments and tried in vain to change the seat's position.

Jens was going for a spiffy takeoff in this thing that could barely be called an automobile, fully intending to tear out of the parking garage with gusto, but the motor stalled and took a while to restart.

They drove along the highway to Hoek van Holland, a cute name for the geographic corner where the two provinces Noord-Holland and Zuid-Holland met. They overshadowed the other nine provinces in population density and economy, so foreigners still often spoke of Holland when they actually referred to all eleven provinces, together called the Netherlands.

Hoek wasn't a terribly attractive coastal town. One benefit was that you could park on the beach and have lunch year round in one of the modest pavilions.

Esther chose a family-owned place called the Sea Breeze, a cozy wooden structure where they served *erwtensoep*, fries and fried hamburgers. During the drive Esther had told Jens a ton about Holland, the Netherlands, Rotterdam and all the customs Americans would never fathom. She also talked about her love for journalism and she constantly apologized for her endless rambling.

"I like you, Esther," Jens finally said, sitting opposite her at a table. He had ordered a hamburger—he couldn't resist trying the fried hamburger phenomenon. She had a goat cheese salad which she nibbled and chewed at length. "I'm really glad that guy Winkler got us together."

Esther nodded, smiling at the awkward way he said it.

"I'm digging into Brigitte's past. I especially want to find out who her father is. She's never met him. For the past seventeen years, since she was fifteen, she has been estranged from her mother and now she wants to know who her father is."

Jens told Esther everything he had learned from the private detective and Brigitte's stepfather, Telford. He also told her about the tip Telford had given him: Kruger probably knows more about who Friends's father is.

Esther had been listening closely. "Exciting. You have a great angle if you can find that out. The father of the famous Brigitte Friends."

"She's really quite different from what you see in those MTV clips."

"Tell me!" was obviously a catch phrase for Esther.

"She's really sweet. She's only five-two, which surprised me. If you saw her sitting on her couch at home, you wouldn't recognize her. She's quite damaged. I don't know the half of what happened in her youth but I strongly suspect it wasn't pleasant."

"What do you mean with 'damaged'?"

"Well, I'm still researching it but I just feel it. Sometimes I can tell just by looking at people."

Esther glanced at him briefly. That was a strong statement. But she found it interesting that Jens could see things like that. When Jens tried to qualify his statement, she asked, "Do you think I'm damaged?"

"Yes," he answered immediately and intuitively. "Of course I wouldn't know if you really are, so maybe you think I'm a jerk."

Esther bit her lip and looked away. "No, you're not a jerk. But you're very American."

"Oh dear, what does that mean? We can't really compare ourselves to others. We never go anywhere."

"Yes . . . well . . . hmm." Esther thought about it. "Americans are very vocal in the way they present their opinions. They also have this 'out of sight, out of mind' attitude. They're often overweight. Badly dressed. And they're convinced that world peace relies entirely on them."

Jens's jaw dropped in his attempt to process all this information.

"Well, yes," he began, "you're right. Apart from being overweight. And as far as world peace is concerned, we're gradually quitting that conviction."

"Oh, well, I didn't mean it personally," Esther justified her criticism.

"Just say something nasty about the Dutch so we're even."

"Huh?"

"Surely you have certain flaws?"

"Yes. The Dutch are incredibly stubborn. Often suspicious. Very moralizing where work is concerned, but also in other trivial matters. The Dutch don't give one another much slack. As soon as someone's successful, they're cut down. If someone's rich, he must not have come by it honestly. If someone's helpful, he must have ulterior motives. I'll rub your back if you rub mine."

"Oh boy, it doesn't sound like a great country to live in."

"It's all because of the climate." Esther nodded toward the beach where a couple of warmly dressed people were battling against the wind.

"Kruger," she said suddenly. Recess was over and they were back to business. "Peter Kruger. If I remember correctly, he was born in Cape Town, South Africa. He immigrated in the sixties and got his Dutch citizenship. He's the only child of a couple that had him when they were older. His father was a wine farmer who emigrated in 1962 so he could have a quiet retirement, away from the dawning struggle against apartheid. His parents died within one day of each other in 1973, and the 25-year-old Kruger inherited several million guilders. He studied economics in Amsterdam but dropped out rather quickly. He began to deal in all sorts of things: stocks, future trade, gold, silver and oil, and he was never successful in any of those ventures. The family fortune slowly evaporated and in 1977 his company went bankrupt. During the proceedings he was accused of fraud. He allegedly hid money but the court couldn't prove it. However, he continued to live in style. He drove an expensive sports car and had a luxury apartment in Amsterdam. Kruger is attractive, so in the eighties he aimed his efforts at rich women who were looking for a financial advisor. Someone who could both manage their fortune and entertain them in bed. In 1988 that led to a few lawsuits. Three separate women accused him of embezzlement. Allegedly, he had made several million guilders disappear. He claimed that he gambled it all on Black Monday on stock options. He supposedly speculated that the market would go up but the next day it crashed. It turned out to be a lie and he was sentenced to six years in prison. He was released four years later. That's the way it is in Holland—light sentences, and even then you only have to do two-thirds if you behave yourself."

Jens's jaw dropped during this story. He couldn't believe Esther had all this at the ready. She hadn't looked in her reports or on the Internet once.

She continued, "When he got out, he disappeared to South Africa. That was in 1992. Mandela had been freed only two years earlier and would become president two years later. South Africa was in turmoil; apartheid was being abolished. At that time, many whites took off. It turned out later that Kruger also left a path of destruction in Johannesburg. He was dealing in minerals. Sometimes the loads he was shipping didn't actually exist, and payments and advances disappeared. South Africa was in chaos, so he was never prosecuted. Back in the Netherlands, he established an insurance agency and quickly expanded it to eighty employees. It seemed like he had finally straightened out. However, in 2004 it appeared he was closing more insurance policies than he took to insurance companies. Through fraud with policies and registrations, he managed to get the insurance companies to pay up in big damage claims cases. When he attracted the attention of the FIOD in 2004—let's say the Dutch equivalent of the IRS—he quickly acquired policies for all his customers and renewed others with other insurance companies. That way he got enormous bonuses. Then his office burned down, along with his entire archives.

"Kruger was in jail for two years. The FIOD could prove fraud in a few cases but they weren't enough for prosecution. He was released in 2006 and he hasn't been active in the financial world since, at least not that anyone can tell. He lives in a small castle along the river Vecht, near Amsterdam. I watched the place once, for a few days, to see what was going on. I stole his mail and followed his visitors but I didn't get a thing."

"Boy, you have an impressive memory." Jens had been scribbling pages full of notes in his Moleskine notebook.

"Yes, once I start following someone, I don't forget any details."

"Photographic memory?"

"Interested memory. Anything that doesn't interest me goes in one ear and out the other. What was your name again?"

Jens was shocked, then laughed when he got that she was joking.

"I suppose you still remember his address and phone number?"

"Absolutely." She gave him both Kruger's cell and home phone numbers and an address, adding that he should consult GPS for directions.

"I'm mainly interested in finding out where he was in February of 1979. Telford told me Dora was with Peter Kruger when they met in 1980. She and Kruger were having an argument and Telford intervened. He claimed Kruger probably knew more about Brigitte's father. He may have been blackmailing Dora."

"Aha," was Esther's only reaction. "Interesting. Let's see. February 1979. His holding went bankrupt in 1977. He disappeared for a while but in 1979 he had an office on the Herengracht. This was when he was an investment advisor and had his rich clients in south Amsterdam. He was thirty-one and a real playboy, very popular with older women. He was also a regular in the tabloids. I seem to remember he was with a woman in her sixties at that time. She had inherited a chain of optician stores from her husband. She sold them and Kruger probably advised her on investing the money.

"Dora was living all over the place at the time. I don't have much information about that period. She had an affair with Bruno Ravalli before that."

"The Italian singer?"

"Yes, the pop star from the eighties. But according to the tabloids he was only interested in her money. Afterwards she was out of the picture for a while. She moved a lot. She was registered in Amsterdam, along one of the canals."

Jens took the folder with his papers on Dora from his briefcase. He leafed through it and asked, "Herengracht 344? Was that Kruger's address?"

"Oh boy, now you're asking too much of my memory. Let's go back to the newspaper so I can look it up. I'll also make copies of a few articles about Kruger. They could come in handy when you're researching that period."

Jens gazed at her in admiration. "You're great."

Esther gave him a brief suspicious look again.

"No, I mean it. I didn't expect this much cooperation."

"I want to go to the States soon; then you can return the favor."

"Aha, the Dutch moral—I'll scratch your back, you scratch mine?"

"I told you so." She laughed and Jens noticed she was blushing. "I've always wanted to go to America. To New York."

"There's America and then there's New York. They're two different places."

"If you continue being nice and you behave yourself, you can show me New York."

Jens laughed at the remark. "And I was just going to make an indecent proposal."

"Let's hear it," she said, curious.

"Have dinner with me in a restaurant of your choice."

"Oh, that's quite innocent in the Netherlands. I believe that in America you have to sleep with a guy if he treats you to dinner?"

Jens grinned tartly. He felt something for the girl standing before him. She was intelligent, attractive, had a sense of humor and was pretty good at her job. Of course, it was out of the question that he would begin a complicated relationship with her, and a casual affair didn't seem right.

"I wouldn't expect you to want to begin anything with a fat, badly dressed, out-of-sight-out-of-mind guy like me." She blushed again. Jens found it the most appealing part of her. "Besides, people do occasionally have dinner in New York without immediately making arrangements for breakfast."

Brigitte and the breakfast he brought her in New York flashed through his mind. Smart, charming, intelligent and good-looking. Weren't those Kruger's attributes? Why couldn't he be her father?

10.

Ina van den Boogaard was a graceful nonagenarian. She lived in a modest room in a modest, modern retirement home in Delft. Her picture window looked out on a lawn and beyond to a quiet street where the occasional car passed by. Now and then children from a neighborhood school livened things up. Ina didn't care much for all the quiet. She couldn't stand the whining of the old folks in the lounge any longer. The subject was always the food. Other than that, the quality of care in the retirement home wasn't bad at all. She could think of two women at most with whom she could converse at a decent level. They had coffee together. They usually talked of the past; only if a worldwide disaster were to happen, would they discuss anything they had read in a newspaper or seen on the news.

In her younger years, Ina had been quite wealthy and her children loved her dearly. But once she was financially ruined they no longer came to visit. Her late husband's fortune was largely gone and she had spent her last penny trying to get the perpetrator behind bars. She had been successful but eighteen years ago he was released. She had made a few additional attempts to make life difficult for him but she didn't want to talk about them. In order to finance this she had had to sell the family jewels.

Ina told Jens he reminded her a little of Peter Kruger. He was also handsome, with a friendly smile and a bunch of flowers in his hand when he knocked on her door. She had opened the door for Jens, asking him to come in without any reservations, breaking all house rules and security instructions.

"I realize I'm probably going to spoil your day by bringing up a nasty event from the past. I'm a reporter and I'm working on a story that involves the nightmare called Peter Kruger."

Ina had hesitated a long time. She peered deep into Jens's eyes and tried to sniff his odor. That had become a habit long ago. She was convinced that, in order to judge someone, she should trust her other senses rather than listen to a spiel. He handed her a letter, which she opened silently.

Dear Mrs. Van den Boogaard,
The carrier of this letter, Jens Jameson, is an American author doing
research on Peter Kruger, among other things. He will inform you
about his exact assignment. Although I can't claim your time, I
would ask you to meet with him and shine some light on the period
of the late seventies.
With kind regards,
Esther Lejeune

Jens and Esther had gone back to the newspaper earlier and leafed through old ledgers of all the quality newspapers. They mainly found articles Esther had contributed to. Next they went to her house, where her personal files offered a ton of information. Jens meticulously typed everything into his laptop while Esther translated. Dora was only mentioned once, in an article about a herring fest in an upscale restaurant. Jens learned that herring was one of the strangest eating habits of the Dutch. The fish were gutted at little stalls on the street, and then stuffed with finely chopped onion. You had to throw back your head and hold the herring up by its tail in order to let the fish slide into your mouth. Jens shuddered at the idea and couldn't imagine that a bunch of the super-rich at a party would indulge in this odd custom. Dora was portrayed as the sad ex-wife of Italian pop star Bruno Ravalli. It was revealed that she had had a baby in a Swiss private clinic four months earlier. Two or three men were mentioned as the possible father. Jens had taken care to write their names down so he could check them out later. Ina van den Boogaard seemed to him the person to begin with.

The dinner he had offered Esther ended up being at a Chinese restaurant on her street; they were that busy. They had beer with dinner and more later, then red wine and finally rum cokes. He was too drunk and tired to go back to his hotel, so she let him sleep on her couch. He had treated her kindly and correctly, although he had indicated that he liked her a lot. She wasn't at all how she had described the Dutch.

"Just wait," she had called as she retreated into her bedroom.

He had waited in suspense, wondering if she was coming back out, but after a while he heard the steady little snore she had warned him about.

Ina stepped back from the door and motioned Jens to come in. There were three chairs and she indicated where he should sit. She asked if he wanted anything to drink and if he would mind getting it himself. Jens declined but offered to get her something.

"Well, at least you are a gentleman. You must excuse me. I am suspicious of the whole world."

"Has it made you bitter?"

The woman looked up in surprise. He saw her think, *how cheeky of him to immediately assume I'm bitter.*

"Well," she said, "it does something to you, watching your entire fortune disappear like melting snow. Would you not be bitter?"

"I beg your pardon, ma'am. Maybe I put it clumsily. I didn't mean to pigeonhole you. I don't have a fortune and probably never will, so I can't imagine it."

"Well, that can be a blessing. When you have nothing, you cannot lose anything." She grinned. "No, I am not really bitter. I have what I need. I was just foolish and it had quite a few consequences in my life."

Ina described Peter Kruger as a charlatan with the gift of gab. As the conversation progressed, something changed in her. Her bitterness was replaced with a strange longing to go back in time. A time in which Kruger swept her off her feet with fun surprises and wonderful presents. She had met Kruger in a restaurant she used to frequent with her husband. He sat at a table nearby with another gentleman and they talked about stocks all night. The figures, names and percentages dizzied her. Her companion was twenty years younger and she was flirting with Kruger. After his friend left, Kruger stayed a while longer, savoring his coffee and a large cognac. Ina's friend invited him to join them at their table and after declining a few times he moved his chair over.

Kruger talked animatedly about opera, theater, ballet—exactly the things Ina and her husband had loved so much. Ina was surprised, not only because Peter didn't say another word about stocks, but also because he focused more on her than on her friend.

He asked her out to dinner the next day. Later he invited her to a birthday party at friends' of his, really nice people out in the country. He shanghaied her for a weekend in Paris, where they had wonderful nights in a beautiful hotel. She was sixty and Kruger was in his early thirties. Ina must still have been beautiful at that time. Even now, in her nineties, she was attractive.

Kruger refused to take her on as a client. He gave her free advice. He looked over her accountant's shoulder and often gave him lucrative tips. When the accountant gave her such a hard time about her spending that he made her cry, she had begged Kruger to manage her fortune. She didn't want to hear about it anymore. He had her complete trust. She wanted to talk about the money no more than once a year. That way being his client wouldn't interfere with their relationship.

The annual reports were complicated and incomprehensible. Kruger never gave her a straightforward answer when she asked what she was worth, and whether it was more or less than the year before. The accountant had always been able to tell her exactly. But Kruger told her those numbers didn't mean much. Those bookkeepers could only add and subtract. Such a fortune was merely numbers on paper.

After a while his interest in her diminished. He kept postponing moving in with her. He worked across the country and took frequent trips abroad. "Eventually he told me he had fallen in love with another woman. A certain Dora Vermeer. In reality he had several, almost all of them his clients. He claimed he had got Dora pregnant and had decided to take his responsibility. That was not true either. I fell for everything he said."

Ina went on, giving Jens all manner of details, which he wrote down at length, even though he didn't know what to do with them. He was extremely curious about her contact with Dora but asking about it would betray the true reason for his visit.

Still he asked, "How can you be so sure Dora Vermeer's child isn't his?"

"I looked her up and she denied ever having had anything with Kruger. They only had a business relationship. She was engaged and it was inconceivable that she would have an affair with such a fool—her exact words."

"A fiancé?"

"Yes, from old money. She was extremely secretive about him. He was an important figure who did not like publicity. At least not with her, and not in the type of magazines that only wrote vile nonsense about public figures."

"But he must have intended to marry her if they were engaged."

"Yes, but something happened when he got her pregnant. He disappeared from her life."

"Really? How do you know?"

"She told me. I spoke to her again much later, when I was suing Kruger. I tried for years to get justice or at least part of my fortune back. Neither ever happened."

"How did that conversation go?"

"That young lady, Esther Lejeune, she wrote that you had an assignment? May I ask what it is?" Ina spoke a sophisticated English pronounced so beautifully it warmed his heart.

"Of course, ma'am." Jens did his best to hide his raw New York accent. "Dora Vermeer's daughter is a friend of mine. The child she was pregnant with is now a grown woman living in America."

"Truly? You are friends with Brigitte?"

"Yes, do you know her?"

"Well, not really. I held her on my lap the second time I visited Dora. A beautiful baby. Beautiful blond curls. What became of her?"

"That's a whole book," Jens joked. Ina seemed annoyed, so he continued. "She ran away from home at age fifteen, ended up in the music world and has a career as a singer. She's quite famous."

"Well, well. Does she make beautiful music?"

"I'm not sure you'd appreciate it. She's not a classical singer. She sings pop music."

"Well, music is music. If it is infused with the proper emotion, even popular music can be enjoyable."

"You know about art." Jens attempted to be charming. "Brigitte erased her past when she ran away. That means she knows little about her parents. She knows who her mother is but her mother wants nothing to do with her. She has no idea who her father is."

"Very well, I will tell you all I can about Dora Vermeer, although I am afraid it will disappoint you."

The amount of detail she provided in her account of Peter Kruger paled in comparison to what she told Jens about Dora Vermeer. But among the barrage of gossip, a few remarkable facts and impressions did surface. Dora had been much savvier than Ina, and Ina had the impression Dora conned Kruger rather than the other way around. Jens also learned a thing or two about the mysterious fiancé. He was a powerful political figure who also had a prominent position in the business community. Ina had figured this out from a few remarks Dora made about their travels together. He was eight years her senior, married and English. Apart from a house in London, the man also had an estate in Spain and an apartment in The Hague. An interesting set of real estate that could end up betraying someone's identity. Jens now knew he was looking for a 71-year-old Englishman, rich and influential, who had had these three homes thirty years ago. It was a start.

She also told him she had followed Dora for years in the news and had wondered if she wasn't a charlatan herself, like Kruger.

Ina had come to the end of her story. "She said something I never quite understood." She seemed tired, glad she had purged it all. "She told me Kruger had the key to all the mysteries in her life."

11.

Esther's cell phone told her that Brad had called four times. It was eleven on Sunday morning and she was having breakfast—home-baked croissants with jelly and a big mug of coffee. The first call had been yesterday evening at seven, the second at eleven, two more at 12:20 and two a.m. She had looked on the Internet to see where Face Job was playing. They were in Paris for two days. The calls were made right before and after the performance. They seemed urgent but she didn't want to wake Brad.

She had turned off her phone because she went out to dinner with Jens. For the promised dinner he had chosen a restaurant with a view of the harbor. It was a bit shabby but they served French food and had a good choice in vegetarian dishes for Esther and tasty wines for Jens.

Esther had told Jens at length about the suspicions she had concerning Steve Demood's death. She recounted proudly how she had ended up in Brad Brittain's dressing room and later in his hotel room. Jens had looked at her searchingly when she told him about Brad's lack of financial insight. She told him about his income per event and which steps they had agreed—later, via email—to take in order to find out more about his personal fortune.

"Did he come on to you?" Jens asked. That interested him more than the rest of the story.

"I informed him I already have a boyfriend—and that I'm monogamous."

"So you do have a boyfriend?"

"Little white lie."

Jens subsequently wanted to know all about her love life and she had been quite open about it. She had also gotten drunk for the first time in a while. Afterward Jens had taken her home. He had given her a chaste kiss on her forehead at the front door and asked if she was sure she could make it up the stairs by herself. She found it strange that he hadn't asked to sleep on her couch again. He had a room at the Home Hotel, a hotel with a reception desk in a café and rooms in six different buildings. It was even on her street. They could practically shout to each other from their windows.

Esther hadn't had any male friends for a long time. She had a best friend and several female colleagues with whom she occasionally went out to eat. For some time now men figured in her life only as guys to have an exciting evening with, occasionally followed by less exciting sex.

Within days, Jens had become a good friend. She didn't intend to have anything more with him than that, especially since he lived in New York. They had a professional relationship and he would leave within a week. Yet she was strangely disappointed that he hadn't tried anything.

At last she could no longer contain her curiosity and she called Brad. She heard a lot of stumbling and coughing before he said his name and asked what the bloody time was.

"This is Esther. You called me," she said timidly.

"Hey, Esther! *I called you yesterday.*"

"Yes, I saw that, so I'm returning your call."

"Sorry, I was still asleep. I was up late last night." She heard a woman's voice in the background, speaking French. "That's the maid."

"Oh sure." Esther laughed. "Does she make your bed from the inside out?" Brad didn't get the joke.

"I've been thinking only of you since last week," he chuckled.

"I hope you mean thinking about our story. That you're thinking about my story."

"Yeah, that too. I have lots of news for you."

"Tell me!" Esther automatically searched for a pen.

"No, come to Hamburg. We're playing there tomorrow."

"No, I can't do that . . ." she wanted to say I have to work. But that was nonsense of course. "I'm not sure my boss would let me. Or if he would pay for it."

"Then call him. You want your story, don't you? I'll pay for your ticket and your hotel room. Or even better, you could sleep with me." He said the last bit ironically.

"I'm bringing my boyfriend," Esther joked.

Brad moaned.

"I'll call my boss and get back to you, okay?"

She called Winkler. When she asked him if she could go to Hamburg, the first thing he said was, "Do you and Brad have a thing going on?"

"No, of course not."

"And that Jens guy, what about him?"

"We've become friends, that's all. What's it to you, anyway?"

"I have to look out for my girl."

"I'm not your girl, Frederick. I could have been your daughter."

"Are you starting that again?"

"Frederick!"

"I only have sons. And I started late on fatherhood. I'm practically a teenager."

After badgering him a bit more, he gave her permission. He did add, "Don't make this a pleasure trip, or I'll take it out of your vacation days."

"Whatever you say, boss. I'll bring you a bratwurst."

She called Jens. He was also still asleep. He blamed it on jet lag. He asked if she had slept well and if she had a hangover, and he thanked her for a wonderful evening. Esther felt bad having to tell him she'd be getting on a train tomorrow.

"I have to go meet Brad Brittain. He says he has important news that he won't discuss over the phone. He's playing in Hamburg tomorrow night."

"That's a coincidence."

"What?"

"I have to be in Hamburg, too. That's where Brigitte began her career. Didn't I tell you it's where her Onkel Gerard's from? I can move the trip up."

Esther was caught off guard. She had joked to Brad about bringing her boyfriend along, not thinking of Jens at all. Now they were practically getting on the train together.

"I don't think that's such a great idea. He might want to speak to me alone."

"Hey, I'm only carrying your suitcase. I have my own things to do. But it would be fun. And it would be easier for me, language-wise. I've heard Germans don't speak foreign languages as well as the Dutch do. German and Dutch are pretty much the same."

"Go rinse your mouth out with soap. They're two completely different languages." Esther deliberated. *It would be handy to have a travel companion. Especially since I have no idea what I'm getting myself into.* "Okay, you can come. I'll book the train tickets."

12.

They had made reservations at the Monopol hotel on the Reeperbahn—a
mere three-star hotel, since they were both on a budget. They had taken the
train that same afternoon and arrived at the Hauptbahnhof Hamburg early
in the evening. Esther could have had a room in the Grand Elysée, the best
five-star hotel in the city, where Face Job was staying, but she didn't want to
be in the same hotel as Brad. In any case, the newspaper didn't allow its
reporters to accept trips or dinners from people or companies they were writing about. The newspaper valued independence more than anything; therefore either the reporters themselves or the newspaper paid for this sort of trip.
    At the check-in counter Esther briefly debated getting one room with
twin beds, to save another hundred euro a night, but Jens held up his
credit card in a grand gesture, saying the hotel was on him. Esther was
simultaneously relieved and disappointed. She protested perfunctorily—
Jens had also paid for her train ticket.
    "You can pay for dinner tonight," Jens had said.

    They checked into their rooms and Esther changed into a short dress
before stepping out onto the Reeperbahn. Flashing female silhouette
lights dominated the sea of neon signs. Jens checked the street numbers
visible here and there next to the inviting doors of clubs and cafes. Soon
they arrived at the building that housed Musik Café Das Schwere
Hertz. It offered a menu of bockwurst and beer for less than ten euro.
Esther grimaced. She had expected more of dinner. Jens suggested
going in anyway. That was a lucky decision.

    Das Schwere Hertz wasn't at all how he had pictured it. Maybe it was
different when Brigitte was handing out beer mugs seventeen years

ago, at age fifteen. She had told him about it extensively. Sometimes she would have to change to belt out a few *schlagers*. Onkel Gerard had stood behind the bar here in his suspenders to keep an eye on the money, to make sure no one ripped him off.

The interior consisted of tables with Persian table rugs and kitschy battery-powered candles. The walls were covered in dark wooden paneling. Cupids hunting falling hearts with bow and arrow were painted on the ceiling. The bar was copper-plated. The staff walked around in semi-traditional dress. Jens had a hard time keeping a straight face. The women wore bright white blouses and push-up bras that practically forced their breasts out of the low décolleté. The men wore leather shorts and white knee socks with cheerful tassels. He couldn't figure out if it was meant seriously—genuine German folklore or a parody.

They sat down at a table near a low stage, where a sign announced the next performance time. Apparently they had just missed one. A blond girl of around twenty came to their table with two enormous menus and asked them what they wanted to drink. Jens ordered a bottle of chardonnay and asked if the owner was in.

A few minutes later, a corpulent man appeared at their table with a suspicious look in his eyes and asked how he could be of service. Jens invited him to join them but he remained standing. His English was terrible and now and then Esther had to help. Her German was fluent.

"I'm writing a book about Brigitte Vermeer. She worked here fifteen years ago."

"Sir, do you have any idea how many people have worked for me in all those years?"

"None of them became world famous singers later on."

"Oh, that Brigitte. Didn't she have a different name?"

"Her name is now Brigitte Friends." The man signaled to a waiter, ordered a beer and sat down.

"Yes, but back in the day she also had a different name, an artist name." Jens adopted Esther's favorite phrase. "Tell me."

The man got up and walked to the wall, which was covered in photos. He took one of them down and returned to the table.

"She was my former partner Gerard Schöteldreier's protégé. He's a con artist. If you're his friend, I have nothing to say to you." He held out the photo and pointed out a blond girl in traditional dress standing at the microphone on the stage.

"No, I've had nothing but trouble with him. And he won't be happy I found you," said Jens.

Esther added to it in German, "They're archenemies."

"But Brigitte has become a really nice person," said Jens.

"Brigitte was always a nice person. She was everyone's favorite. Schöteldreier exploited her."

"Tell me," said Esther, while Jens placed his pocket recorder on the table.

The man's name was Weintraub. He had owned the business for over thirty years. Twenty years ago, Das Schwere Hertz was suffering. One day Schöteldreier walked in and offered to help save it. He would invest in the business, provided he became equal partner. Weintraub was desperate so he took the offer. Everything was arranged with a lawyer. Half the real estate and the business went to Schöteldreier. The promised investments turned out to be only a cosmetic remodeling and a few smart changes that resulted in firing half the staff, which still upset Weintraub twenty years later. Schöteldreier took over the management. Since the staff was drastically cut, Weintraub ended up bartending. Schöteldreier put one of his girls at the cash register so he controlled all the incoming money.

It had been the unhappiest time of Weintraub's life. The sales went up, true. But the quality of the food went down. The entertainment program became increasingly seedy. Poles appeared on the stage where the waitresses danced at night. When that didn't attract enough people, strippers were hired and after eleven the prices were tripled. All the money went to Schöteldreier, who talked Weintraub into taking out a second mortgage on the place in order to do a big remodeling, after which the business could become once again a "quality café." The second mortgage was taken out but the remodeling cost less than a tenth of that.

In addition to his activities for Das Schwere Hertz, Schöteldreier had established an agency where he coached young girls "on their road to fame." Brigitte wasn't the only one for whom he arranged performances in the various clubs in St. Pauli, Hamburg's entertainment district.

"Many of those girls had no talent at all. They were drawn in by his spiel, had to sleep with the bastard, performed once or twice, only to be

79

dumped. Brigitte was the only one with real talent and she refused Schöteldreier's advances. No, I don't imagine that one ever took her clothes off for anything but love."

Jens was amazed. He hadn't been in Hamburg three hours and already he had a valuable source. He did realize, now that he had Weintraub's story on tape, that he had the potential of really becoming Schöteldreier's archenemy. He also realized Brigitte hadn't disclosed everything.

Weintraub didn't want to be mentioned by name. Once he got that promise from Jens, he spoke very clearly at the tape recorder, afraid his words might not be captured properly. He had sought publicity before, but before the story was even published both he and the magazine had been sued. The story couldn't be published because there wasn't enough evidence. Schöteldreier had taken it all with him when he left.

For a while afterward, several Yugoslavs would pay visits to the café. They weren't the respectable types either, like the immigrant workers with jobs in the harbor. They were the murder-for-hire types who constantly threatened Weintraub verbally. When he wasn't intimidated, they picked fights in Das Schwere Hertz. The furniture would end up in shambles. At some point, Weintraub hired a group of Chinese who fought dirty and they eventually got rid of the Yugoslavs. He had had to pay the Chinese mafia protection money for years after that.

Brigitte had a boyfriend. He was a big, strong bar man who stood up for her every time Onkel Gerard tried to rip her off or bothered her. His name was Hans and eventually Weintraub was also able to remember his last name: Johanson. He worked at the Kaiserkeller at the time. Later he started his own café. When Schöteldreier decided the wait staff would work topless, Brigitte refused. That created quite a stir, because as a result the other girls didn't want to comply with the new "dress code" either. Schöteldreier ended up having to fire five of the fifteen girls, because Das Schwere Hertz would be a topless bar. But he couldn't get rid of Brigitte. She was bringing in money with her performances on the Hamburg scene. There was even talk of a record contract.

When she got the contract, Schöteldreier allowed Weintraub to buy him out. He asked an outrageous sum. Weintraub ended up agreeing to it, only to be rid of the bastard. When he left, Schöteldreier emptied the safe and even the small change was gone from the cash registers. Weintraub had to start over. It took him more than ten years to get out of debt.

Jens arranged to come back the next day to take down further details. He also wanted to get directions to the bar where Brigitte's former boyfriend had started. It turned out to be a minor place on the edge of St. Pauli.

Finding a halfway decent restaurant was tricky. Jens and Esther ended up in a fancy, modern café where they didn't serve bockwurst or potato soup. Jens had wanted a hamburger—he was convinced the world famous bun with a patty of ground beef originated in this city. He settled for a tuna carpaccio and Esther ordered vegetarian sushi after asking if Jens's dish had the right type of tuna. She was okay with yellow fin but the others were threatened with extinction. Jens was amazed and felt a little silly that he didn't know this.

"Well, that was quite a story," said Jens.

"It sure was. Our stories are beginning to overlap."

"Schöteldreier won't make this easy for me. He watches my every move. I'm beginning to see why he wasn't too thrilled with Brigitte's desire to rake up her past."

Esther grinned. "Well, if you're not going to use the story, you can give it to me."

"It's not a story just yet."

"Because we only have one source so far?"

"Yes. And maybe Hans, who experienced it all close up. Tomorrow I'll ask Weintraub about others who were there at the time. The girls Schöteldreier fired, for instance. Staff that was beaten up by the Yugoslavs." Jens drew circles on the tablecloth with his knife.

"Even so, how can you prove Schöteldreier was behind it?"

"I'm afraid I would have to find some of those Yugoslavs . . ."

"If they're not in jail by now."

They glanced around as if they would be able to find the Yugoslavs among the restaurant's clientele. Then they both burst out laughing.

"If I can't use it I'll finish it for you. I like you, Esther. I'm glad we met."

"Yes, it's a pity we live so far apart. We would make a perfect team."

"You mean . . . professionally."

"That too." She smiled and briefly touched the back of his hand with hers. "Fortunately we're both adults."

"Now, what does that mean? Do you mean you no longer fall in love?"

"Not that quickly anymore, no. I didn't tell you everything that evening, about all the affairs I've had."

"You left out your biggest heartbreak?"

"You noticed that?"

"Yes. You were quite candid that evening but I did get the impression you were leaving that out."

"Are you psychic?"

"No, not at all. I've learned to listen. Maybe it's a professional tic. You don't have to tell me everything. I keep a lot to myself as well."

They were quiet for a while. The main course was served. Jens had no idea what he had ordered. He liked that: just pointing to something random on a German menu. But when he got his plate, he still had no idea what it was. It tasted fishy, with potatoes, melted cheese and over-cooked, unidentifiable vegetables. It wasn't that appetizing but he started on it in good spirit.

"You haven't actually told me anything yet. About your love life, I mean." She looked at him curiously. "Only that you almost slept with Brigitte Friends once."

"Well, there isn't much to tell. I was married and I have a daughter. After that I fooled around a bit. Nothing serious."

"Really? You have a daughter?"

"Yes. Barbora—she's fifteen. Her mother's parents are from the Czech Republic—that's why it isn't Barbara. They live in St. Augustine, a town on the Florida coast. I met Tereza in high school in Provincetown, where we lived at the time, so we were high-school sweethearts. I was twenty-two when we had Barbora. We divorced when I was thirty. There wasn't anyone else; we were just fed up with each other."

"So you've been single for eight years now?"

"That's right."

"Disappointed in women?"

"No. I've met plenty of interesting women but they're either already taken or disillusioned or so hard to get that I didn't have the patience to pursue them."

"And I fall in the middle category?"

"Or the last," said Jens.

"You haven't even begun pursuing me." Esther herself was taken aback by the remark. She tried to correct herself. "So you do find me interesting?"

"I sure do. Interesting, sweet, beautiful and sexy."

Esther was blushing again. She took a sip of her wine, a brief look of concern on her face. She was thinking of the hangover she had had that morning.

"I had found the ideal man. He was tall, strong and handsome. He had a great job, a car and his own home. He was considerate, charming, caring and wonderful in bed. I was madly in love. I was twenty and completely smitten. When we had lived together for two years, he proposed and I said yes. Then one evening two police officers were at our door. He had crashed into a tree; death was instantaneous. There was a girl in the passenger seat. I didn't know her. She was dead, too. No one knew who the girl was, so I wanted to find out. That's how I got into this profession, three years ago. "She paused and looked at Jens.

"And who was she?"

"She was his other girlfriend. He had been with her for five years; when he claimed he had to travel for his work he was actually living with her."

"Jesus, that sucks." Jens was shocked. "I'm sorry. I don't know what to say."

"Don't say anything. But maybe you get why I'm wary."

"Disillusioned."

"Quite a cliché, isn't it?"

"You'll get over it. I'm sure of it. When I look into your eyes, I can see that time will heal your wounds."

"That's sweet of you, Jens."

They walked back to the hotel. She took his arm and together they avoided the crowds ambling along the Reeperbahn. They picked up their keys at the reception desk and took the elevator to the second floor. When they got to her door, Jens hugged Esther and kissed her on the lips. She made a soft sound and broke off the kiss. "We're going to have sex, aren't we? Very unprofessional. Awful consequences in the future. But we're going to do it anyway, right?"

"Yes," said Jens, "are you psychic?" He pushed her over the threshold.

13.

Brad was waiting for Esther at the reception desk of the Hamburg Grand Elysée. With five-hundred-eleven rooms and suites, three restaurants, an oyster bar, a gallery with terribly ugly art, large conference rooms, a gym, an enormous swimming pool, a massage parlor and an atrium with a waterfall, it was almost a village. Everything was five-star quality, though the highly respectable waiting staff's training had evidently not included anything like humor or informal friendliness. The interior decorating was lackluster, as befits a hotel that caters mainly to seniors and spoiled young people living it up with their fathers' credit cards.

Brad had a penthouse suite on the seventh floor but his suitcases were still on the cart in the lounge. He had called Esther on her cell phone to ask her how long it would take her to get there. The trip to Hamburg had been terrible; the night before he had performed in Lyon. The plane was delayed, first class was overbooked and half the band had had to fly economy. Brad had joined them in solidarity. To make matters worse, they missed their connection and had to get up at nine in the morning. Just when cities were farther apart and they had no downtime in between.

When they were at their peak, the band had the use of a small Learjet. Management had given it up now because it took up too much of the touring budget.

"You look great," said Brad as Esther approached him gracefully across the red carpet.

She greeted him impassively and kissed him three times on the cheeks. Clad in a short leather skirt, blouse, tight-fitting leather jacket and high boots, she came across as a woman in the rock scene. Exactly the kind of outfit Brad wanted to see, she figured when she got dressed this morning.

Esther was a whiz in choosing her outfits. She had a large wardrobe, having had the same size since she was sixteen. Since she took good care of her clothing, she just had to wait for something to come back in fashion. Both men and women unconsciously judge people by their clothing and Esther had fun with that. She loved clothes and the effect they had on the people around her. Every morning she considered whom she'd be meeting that day, whom she had to wheedle information from, whom she had to shock, or whom she had to be careful not to shock, or how she could distract attention from herself. Her outfits varied from extremely sexy to very modest, from sporty to gala dresses. Now that she stood before Brad, she wondered if she had overdone it.

"Let's go to the bar, so we can talk," said Brad and led the way.

They sat in a booth in the darkest part of the bar. Brad looked at her for a long time. "It's lovely to see you again."

"It's good to be here. Hamburg is a great city."

"Are you coming to the concert tonight?"

"Of course."

"And we'll have dinner afterward?"

"No. I'm having dinner with my boyfriend."

"Shit, Esther, you brought him along?"

"He had business here as well."

"In Hamburg? Sure he did."

"No, really. He's a writer. He's doing some research here."

"You're just scared of my charms. And your boyfriend? Is he jealous?"

"Not at all. He's writing a book about Brigitte Friends."

"Hell, that rock bitch!"

"You know her?"

"I've met her once or twice. She's a diva."

"He says she's really sweet, a cute girl."

"Well, good for him. So you might be rid of him soon?"

"No, she's not his type."

Brad sank back in his seat. Evidently he had pictured this meeting differently. He usually had more success with women. If they didn't fall for him right away, they did within a few days.

"Did you get my flowers?" he asked.

"No. You sent me flowers?"

"Yeah. Three times, from different cities."

"Where did you have them delivered?"

"To the address you gave me."

Esther blushed. "That's the newspaper's address, silly." She could just picture it: three big flower arrangements on her desk with intimate messages written on the cards. She envisioned Winkler seeing them, cursing because a rock star was taking liberties with his "girl." "I haven't been there in days."

"I'm sorry. I assumed it was your home address."

"Well, thanks anyway—for the flowers."

"I even wrote a couple of declarations of my love for you."

"I was afraid you would."

"So when you said you were willing to come to Hamburg, I was looking forward to it."

Esther blushed again. She realized Brad had mainly made her come to Hamburg because he believed she was finally responding to his advances. *Shit, I came here all for nothing*, she thought.

"I'm sorry, Brad. I think you're cool but that's all. I came here because you had news for me. I hope that's true?" She said it as sweetly as possible; she didn't want to hurt his feelings.

"Of course it is but I'm in love. You're so beautiful—so independent. I haven't met a woman like you in years."

"You must not get around much. You just have to get out of that stuffy scene of yours. I'm not that special."

"That's what you think. Okay, let's go out tonight, and you can point out all the women who are just as cute as you."

"Hey, I'm not a matchmaker for overeager rock stars." It just slipped out.

"You see, that's what I like about you. Anyone else would be honored to show Brad Brittain the Hamburg nightlife. 'No matchmaker for overeager rock stars.' Wonderful. May I use that in my lyrics?"

"Of course. There's no copyright on it."

They shook hands. When she tried to let go Brad held her firmly.

"I'm going to help you with your story, Esther. You're totally awesome."

She turned on her tape recorder. "Tell me."

Brad cleared his throat, looking at Esther again. "You were right about Demood. He did want to file a complaint against TMC. I talked to his widow. She wants to talk to you."

"I already talked with her, Brad. I need better than that."

Brad was aggravated. "Okay. So I began to inquire where my money is. That really rubbed my manager and my account manager at TMC the wrong way. The latter immediately adopted evasive tactics. He gave me a whole lot of incomprehensible material."

He handed her a memory stick. "It's all here. Do something with it before we speak again."

Esther took the stick and put it in her purse. She gave Brad a grateful look.

"There's stuff there about Demood as well. I have a friend who's a computer whiz. I helped him get a job at The Music Company, so he owed me a favor. At the end of his career, Steve Demood was completely broke. Something to do with his investments. Demood was a nitwit when it came to finances. So am I, so whether I'm looking at his finances or my own, I wouldn't even be able to come up with a useful question."

"You could ask what your assets are."

"I did. They gave me a list of my real estate, stocks I purportedly own. They say they bought them for me because the bank offers such low interest rates. I also have a bank account without much in it. When I add it all up, it's nowhere near what I thought I was worth, but I'm not broke like Demood—not yet at least."

"And what stocks do you have?"

"They're those funds whose names I recognize: oil companies, Coca-Cola, American Express, Microsoft—stuff like that. But also unknown companies. I can't figure out how much I have of each. I need you to find out for me. That's your profession. It drives me crazy that I'm playing my ass off every night for Jack Shit."

"You didn't ask about that?"

"About what?"

"That you get paid so little for a performance."

"They say they keep my income low to avoid paying too much in taxes. They keep the expenses high and incomes low."

"Their expenses."

"Yeah, well, that's for you to go tell them."

Brad felt defeated. In one afternoon he was rejected and he had to admit he was probably being ripped off big time.

"I can't figure out The Music Company itself, either—who's behind it, who owns it, what their management structure is. And I don't have the ability to find out. I don't know anything about this stuff but it could be a terrific story for you."

"Is it possible Demood was killed?"

"No, I don't think so. They're regular business people, not the mafia; they're not murderers."

"I hope you're right. But be careful."

"Are you worried about me?"

"I would hate it if anything happened to you."

"How much would you hate it?"

Again Esther's frank expression mesmerized him, just like that evening in Rotterdam. He had watched her walk away and he had stayed behind in his hotel room. Depressed and lonely, he watched sentimental movies and cried. He had no one to talk to, no one who ever said anything that mattered. The next day he had written a beautiful love song, both the music and the lyrics, which he sent along with flowers to her address. He hadn't heard anything back. He left for Brussels and got so drunk he had the hardest time remembering his lyrics on stage. The situation was hopeless. He knew he would only see her again if he could give her the information she was looking for.

So he made phone calls. In the car on the way to the airport. On the plane. In the hotel room. In the dressing room. He was even making calls behind the curtain. He spoke with Demood's widow several times, with relatives who allegedly profited from his fortune, and with partners in businesses in which he supposedly participated. No one had ever actually seen him in these companies. He even called Demood's account manager, pretending to be someone else, and asked him a few pointed questions about the vanished fortune. Halfway through the conversation the man had hung up and hadn't answered the phone since.

He had demanded his own account manager send him all kinds of annual reports but he couldn't figure them out. When he asked for clarification, his account manager got angry.

He also called other musicians who were managed by The Music Company. Some were surprised by his suspicions; others told him they discovered years ago that the division of profits wasn't too kosher, so they had taken on external accountants. One musician had left after an argument—John Stevenson, a singer-songwriter with one gold record to his name. He hadn't performed for four years and no one could tell Brad where he was.

Brad was rattling off a lot of extremely detailed facts, so Esther wrote as fast as she could. When she asked him to spell names, he rattled those off as well. The information was rife with loose ends and assumptions but she could tell he had done his utmost to put together a good story for her.

"And for this you won't even have dinner with me tonight?" he had asked when she thanked him for all his work. He looked at her hopefully.

"In the Netherlands they would call that tying the cat to the bacon."

"The cat to the bacon?"

"It's an expression."

"So I'm the bacon and you're the cat?"

"No, it's the other way around. The cat will eat the bacon because he's tied to it. A person would be stupid to do that."

Brad thought for a while but couldn't make sense of it.

"You're not fat! And besides, I don't like bacon. But if you mean that I'll be better off without you tonight because of what I feel for you, you're wrong. I want to have dinner with you. A broken heart is beneficial to a musician."

"Huh?"

"Where do you suppose all those beautiful love songs come from? Not from being lucky in love."

"Okay, I suppose I can have two dinners."

Esther stayed in the bar while Brad went upstairs to freshen up. He had invited her to come up to his suite to wait for him there but she had declined, feeling it would be too intimate.

Last night's events had her on cloud nine all day. She wasn't sure what to make of the new situation. Jens had been very gentle and careful with her, and incredibly patient. She didn't expect that—disenchantment would have been more convenient. She felt three problems weighing on her. *Unwise, unprofessional, and the prospect of a long-distance relationship.* Yet at the same time she had butterflies in her belly and she finally felt like a woman again.

They had studiously avoided making eye contact during breakfast. Jens was doing his best to put the night into perspective with cynical jokes. Esther tried to reconstruct the story of the day before and they came up with a strategy to get it all together.

Only once they were seated across from Weintraub for the second time did they feel at ease again. The poor guy got a barrage of questions, which they had composed over breakfast. Weintraub himself hadn't been idle either. He had brought along two women who had worked for him for twenty years. These respectable, slightly chubby middle-aged women had a lot to say about Onkel Gerard's sexual harassment, his temper tantrums if things weren't going his way, and the period of the Yugoslav invasion. They were among the girls who hadn't opposed going topless and that's why they weren't fired.

They were both bothered by what happened with Brigitte. She was like a younger sister to them.

"That child was damaged," said one of the women.

"The girl had a father complex," the other claimed.

The anecdotes rapidly followed one another. Before her departure from Das Schwere Hertz, Brigitte had been a mediator between the girls and Onkel Gerard.

Weintraub had also found Hans Johanson's phone number. Johanson had reacted rather uninterested when they called him. But sure, if they bought him lunch he'd be willing to tell them a few things about his ex-girlfriend.

Hans had been drinking when they met him an hour later in the Alster Pavilion, a café at the edge of the Aussenalster, that strange lake in the center of Hamburg. A ferry connected different warehouses along the water, functioning as public transport and an almost-free boat tour around the entire city.

Jens had described himself and Esther to Hans, but Jens figured Hans would wait passively until they recognized him. And Jens guessed correctly. Hans was still muscular, with a bodybuilder's thick neck. His face was lined and he wore dark glasses—to hide bloodshot eyes, it turned out.

"So, what do you want to know? I should never have let that girl go. I would've had it made if we stayed together."

Esther immediately disliked this unsympathetic weakling. "You have a café downtown, don't you?"

"A small café, yes. And it's hard work. I barely make minimum wage if I work really hard and don't hire too much staff."

"But the drinks are free," Esther remarked drily.

"Yes. Speaking of which," he bit back, "I wouldn't mind a double whiskey, straight. Make it a malt."

Jens looked accusingly at Esther. When she looked back indignantly, he laughed. He beckoned the waiter and asked for a malt whiskey. Esther wanted water and Jens ordered a dry white wine. Lunch was a steak for Hans, salad for Esther and two bockwurst sandwiches for Jens.

"Bockwurst?" said Hans. "My God. Why don't you order something decent?"

"To be honest, this is my first German bockwurst. I'm quite excited. So tell me about your relationship with Brigitte."

"She dumped me."

"Really?" Esther said it just a little too emphatically.

"I protected her for years and then she dumped me."

"You were her bodyguard."

"No. We were in love. We had fun at first. She was sixteen and I was already twenty-eight. She was good to me and helped me through a difficult period."

Hans recounted how he had met Brigitte. She had been the opening act once in the Kaiserkeller with her band Keine Einfahrt (No Entry in English). It was hard guitar rock and she could barely make herself heard with her high voice. He was the bouncer, and after closing time he had to make sure the band left the dressing room and he helped Brigitte clean up. They had sex that very first night on a sofa in the dressing room and a month later Brigitte moved in with him. He had countless conflicts with Onkel Gerard, "that first-class gangster." But occasionally Schöteldreier hired him as a bodyguard. Although he really didn't like him and he wasn't the fighting type, he did like the jobs because he made fifty Deutsch Mark in one hour, going along on two occasions. All he had to do was be present when Schöteldreier closed a deal with a business owner. Hans wasn't sure what was discussed during those visits.

"You could tell those people weren't happy with the deals he made with them."

Hans had many juicy stories about Brigitte, describing her more fondly as he consumed more malt whiskey. He'd like to get back in touch with her. It had actually been his fault she dumped him. He was snorting a lot of coke at the time, and he did speed as well. Brigitte tried to stop him. She had stayed with him against all odds, until he beat her up. Then she had packed her few possessions and walked out. He said it with admiration in his voice.

Hans couldn't tell them much about the conflicts with the Yugoslavs, since that was after his time at Das Schwere Hertz. He did know those types were for hire cheaply at the time. He knew about a restaurant called Sarajevo in a suburb where only fools went nowadays. The real hard core was in jail, or back in Serbia or Croatia, raising hell in the war.

It took a while for Brad to come back down. Esther had tried to get hold of Jens a few times. She had decided to cancel her dinner date with him because they had done almost nothing but eat and drink since he had come into her life. She really didn't want to eat out twice today. She felt like a pig, although nobody who saw her would have shared that view.

Esther was curious what Jens thought of their discoveries of that afternoon, because he was going to go to the Sarajevo restaurant. She had tried to talk him into going the next day, when she could go with him. Jens didn't think that was a good idea. It could be dangerous, so he wanted to go alone. She hadn't said anything—she thought it was sweet that he was worried about her.

Brad emerged from the elevator with the other members of Face Job. They carried their black guitar cases and were all dressed up for the concert. Six o'clock—three hours to go. Brad headed straight for her and put his arm around her. They walked outside, where two stretch limos waited to take them to the Color Line Arena. It was one of Face Job's biggest concerts. It was sold out with standing room only. Hamburg was the rock and roll capital of Europe. This is where The Beatles began their career, and Janis Joplin, the Doors and Jimi Hendrix had played in obscure venues around the Reeperbahn.

Brad Brittain was proud to have Esther on his arm when they went to the limo. Approximately thirty girls were waiting outside. A red crowd-control rope and a few security guards held them at bay. Brad approached them and handed out a few autographs.

When they were inside the car, he apologized. "I'm sorry to keep you waiting. Some of those girls had been waiting for three hours. It's crazy but you can't just ignore them."

"No problem. It's very nice of you."

Of course Brad knew that; he had been fishing for the compliment.

"That French girl had been waiting for you for hours as well, I'm sure."

"Which French girl?" Brad tried.

"The one lying next to you in bed during our phone call."

"Oh, that one." He tried to remember what he had said about it. "The maid!" He laughed grimly. "She was an old girlfriend from *la France*. Oh la-la, you just can't ignore those girls. I was sad that you didn't call, so I sought consolation."

"Your morals aren't for me, Brad. I like you but I'd hate to fall in love with you."

"Why?"

"Well, I'm monogamous, for one…"

"I would be monogamous, too, if I were with you."

Esther sighed deeply, sinking back into the leather of the limousine.

14.

Jens was happy. He had had a wonderful night with Esther, slept well and woke up content. And he had made tremendous progress on his story through his conversations with Weintraub, the two women and the drunken Hans. He realized he had hadn't been in touch with Brigitte in days.

When Esther left for Brad's hotel, Jens went to his hotel room, checked his email and found three messages from Brigitte. The first was calm, but by the third it was clear she was quite worried.

> *Dear Jens,*
> *This is the third email. I know firsthand that Europe isn't the Third*
> *World, so I don't understand why I'm not hearing from you. I'm*
> *thrilled that you're working on my past but maybe you've found all*
> *kinds of nasty stuff that you don't want to tell me. Of course that*
> *makes me even more nervous. Onkel Gerard has come by three*
> *times already to ask if we can't get out of this deal. Of course I don't*
> *want to! Please call or mail me a.s.a.p.*
> *Kisses and love,*
> *Brigitte*

Kisses, no less! And is this a covert threat with Schöteldreier? Jens wondered and he replied.

> *Dear Brigitte,*
> *Everything's fine here. I had an interesting conversation with your*
> *stepfather Telford in the Netherlands. I also found out your mother*
> *was seeing a guy called Peter Kruger around the time of your birth. He*
> *was a con man. My sources claim he's not your father but apparently he*
> *was close friends with your mother, so there's a chance he knows who is.*

I'm still figuring out the right way to approach him.
Right now I'm in Hamburg. I hear nothing but good things about
you here. Weintraub, Angela, Martha and Hans said to say hi. I'm
hearing strange stories about Onkel Gerard, though, and I'm not
sure what to make of them. It seems he wasn't exactly pure as the
driven snow. Well, we'll see.
I'll probably be back in a week or two, three. By then I'll be done
with this part of it, at least for now. I might have to come back here
at some point but in between we can catch up.
Greetings,
Jens Jameson

He read the mail and pressed send. For the first time he wondered
what all this must be like for Brigitte. Her memories of Weintraub, the
girls of Das Schwere Hertz and her ex-boyfriend Hans Johanson were
ten, twelve years old. She would have known about the whole mess
involving the decline of the café and Onkel Gerard's actions, so she
also knew a researcher like himself would dig up all this shit. Was that
her intention? Was anything wrong between her and Schöteldreier and
did she want to get it out in the open in this indirect way?

He dozed off on his still-made bed until he heard a ping indicating a
new email. Brigitte had already replied.

Hi Jens,
It sounds like you're making great progress. In Hamburg already!
How is that old Telford doing? He's a nice guy but he never had any
balls in his life or mine. I've never heard of Kruger. And how is Hans
doing? Did he turn out all right? At the time he was a fool because he
was on dope. Is he clean? Weintraub is also a fool. I hope the book is
going to be good, Jens. Or is it going to be all doom and gloom?
Fools, con men, junkies. Perhaps you should keep Gerard out of it.
What do you think? That's not what the book is about, is it?
Love,
Brigitte

He detected a different tone in her reply. She was becoming more
reserved. Maybe he should put off answering this one. He closed his

laptop and decided to head out to the Sarajevo restaurant. The first three cab drivers in front of the Monopol didn't know it. Finally an Iranian whose English was terrible thought he knew where it was. He made a call on his cell phone, speaking in rapid Arabic, using his free arm to give himself directions.

After a long drive, they arrived at the restaurant that was actually more a café, in a desolate suburb near the harbor. It didn't seem likely that Jens would be able to get a cab from here but the Iranian absolutely refused to wait.

"Bad neighborhood," he said curtly.

The interior was exactly what Jens had imagined it to be. Lots of dark wood paneling; several cartwheels, fishnets, balalaikas and obscure agricultural tools were screwed to the walls, as well as photos of the war in the former Yugoslavia. No photos of the atrocities or mass murders, but plenty of photos of the committers of the atrocities and the mass murders, in manly poses with their weapons.

It didn't look like the food would be any good, so Jens took a seat at the bar. He was the only customer. The only other person was a rough-looking character standing in front of the bar, though he apparently belonged behind it. He wasn't tall. He had a monobrow, his face was unshaven and his teeth were yellow. Not the type of person you would want to order food from.

"What do you want?" the man asked. Since he was being addressed in German, Jens assumed the man was asking what he wanted to drink.

"Just give me something strong," he answered in English.

Apparently the man didn't understand him—he poured him a beer. Jens pointed to a bottle resembling whiskey. It turned out to be slivovitz, which contained roughly fifty percent alcohol and made his eyes water when he took a sip. Luckily, he had the beer to put out the fire.

"You don't speak English?" Jens asked when he recovered.

The man looked blandly at Jens. "English. No." Perhaps the only words he knew.

Jens shrugged, regretting his decision not to bring Esther. The man turned on the music—a kind of Balkan pop Jens had never heard before.

"What do you want?" Jens suddenly heard in broken English, coming from behind a dividing wall.

"Information." Jens had no idea who he was talking to.

"Are you police?"

"No."

"Intelligence? Interpol? What are you?"

"I'm a writer."

"Reporter?"

"No, I write books."

The man appeared—a carbon copy of the man behind the counter. A twin who did speak English? Or was this just the standard Yugoslav look?

"Buy me a drink and tell me what you want to know."

Jens took the bottle of slivovitz, two shot glasses and his beer to the man's table.

Without saying a word, the man first took several shots of the swill. Jens sipped from his and washed it down with beer. When he felt the silence had lasted long enough, he decided to get straight to the point.

"You used to be able to get a certain type of help for hire here. For convincing someone to do something for you."

The man gazed at him, dumbfounded. He clearly hadn't expected such a direct approach. Then he laughed.

"So you want to know the names of assassins?"

Now Jens was shocked—he hadn't expected this. *Yes, I suppose it is a rather direct question for murderers*, he thought.

"No, not assassins. More the type of guy who can rough someone up a little."

"Ha, ha, rough someone up a little," the man repeated. "And you think I can provide you with a name and address?"

"Well, roughly ten years ago some guys were recruited here to destroy a café. Das Schwere Hertz. Because the owner at the time threatened to sue someone."

"Aha." The man rapidly threw back a few more shots. Was he unable or unwilling to answer?

"Well?"

"What do I get out of it?"

"A hundred dollars?"

The man laughed loudly and threw back another shot.

"Give me two hundred euro and I'll give you a name," the man grinned. "No more. One name and I never gave it to you."

97

"Okay, two hundred for a name and an address."

The man laughed again. Meanwhile Jens wondered if he had enough money on him. He had one hundred and fifty euro in his shoe—a habit left over from South Africa. He used to put part of his money in a secret place so he could still get home if he were mugged. Of course, shoes were the first place muggers looked in South Africa but perhaps not here at the Sarajevo.

The man held up his hand, indicating he didn't plan on saying another word until he was paid. Jens pulled the money from his shoe and neatly unfolded the bills. He had just enough left to pay for the drinks.

"His name is Mikulas Danitsha. I'm not saying he's in that business but he knows a lot," he whispered.

Jens handed him a notepad and a pen so he could write down the name. The man scowled at the notepad, as if he might implicate himself if he wrote Danitsha's name in his own handwriting, but he did it anyway. Jens read it and smiled.

"Where can I find him?"

"In prison, ha, ha. He's been there for the past four years—for murder."

Jens looked the man in the eye to determine if he was being fooled. He shrugged. Either way it was a shot in the dark, trying to get evidence this way. And for what? *Perhaps you should leave Gerard out of it. What do you think? That's not what the book is about, is it?* Brigitte had written in her email. So why should he work so hard to expose Onkel Gerard? And maybe he would have left it at that if the evening had ended differently.

Jens found a bus stop and waited for a bus to take him back downtown. He had a good view of the Sarajevo from the bare wharf. A few people had entered and left again. His informant also stepped outside at some point, glanced around and went back in. Jens didn't feel completely safe, so after waiting for nearly ten minutes he took off toward the next stop. It was just a feeling but he had learned to pay attention to those feelings.

He was the only passenger on the bus, which was reassuring. A message came in on his cell phone. Esther was canceling dinner and apologized. To be honest he had completely forgotten he had to be back in town at seven to meet her for dinner.

He got it. She must be on to something with Brad. He wouldn't allow himself to be disappointed. He didn't feel like letdowns so he kept his expectations low.

He decided to go to the hotel bar. His waitress resembled Annie Lennox—blond hair in a short ponytail and clear blue eyes. Her narrow face was amiable enough when they had eye contact but she went through the motions rather sullenly.

He ordered steak, fries and salad and washed it down with a carafe of Australian white chardonnay. He wanted to go back to the Netherlands, to look up Peter Kruger and other connections, such as Brigitte's nanny. And of course he eventually wanted to approach Dora Vermeer, although he still didn't know how he would go about it.

After his steak, he got another text message from Esther.

I'm having supper with B.B. in Oyster Bar
in hotel Grand Elysee Rothenbaum Chaussee.
Can you come and save me around midnight?
XXX E.L.

He smiled, texted back that he would be there, paid his bill and went back to his room. He tried in vain to sleep. He racked his brains, wondering how he could fit Schöteldreier's story into the book without ignoring Brigitte's request and still make it a *good book*. He wrote out his notes and made online backups of all his recordings and files.

Around eleven he went out again. It was a warm night for the time of year and lots of people were ambling along the sidewalks of St. Pauli. The flashing neon signs and the broad-shouldered bouncers were strangely alluring. He took some money from the ATM and walked into a joint that promised *showgirls* and *lap dance*. A sign informed him that drinks cost around twenty euro, about ten euro less than average. *I couldn't care less if you'd rather have dinner with that flaky Glasgow rocker. I'm not going to fall in love with you, girl. I...* He was taken aback by his own thoughts. The cover charge was fifteen euro. The cashier was a rough type who would have been more at home in the Sarajevo than on the Reeperbahn. Jens paid him no further attention, even though the man behaved suspiciously by turning around immediately.

It was quiet inside, probably because it was still early. The girls jumped up; apparently they were paid by the customer. A few uninspired topless girls did something vaguely resembling dancing to David Bowie's "Let's Dance." They weren't much good. A girl of about twenty sat down next to him and asked if she could have a drink.

Jens looked at her. "I don't speak German."

"I speak English," she said. "Can I have a drink? A piccolo."

"And how much does that cost?" Jens felt like teasing her.

"Thirty-five euro."

"Can't you just order a coke or a beer?"

"Are you Dutch or something?"

"How's that?"

"The Dutch are stingy."

"Well, I'm just wondering why I should buy a complete stranger a piccolo. Anyway, you probably earn in a week what I earn in a month. Why don't *you* offer *me* a drink?"

The girl stared at him, dumbfounded. She was kind of cute. She wore a silver top and tight, golden silk pants. Her stilettos were so high she could barely walk on them. But she did have a Catholic cross on a necklace. In any case, she had no more one-liners after Jens's smart remark, so she hobbled away on her too-high heels without saying goodbye.

An older woman, who had observed it all, approached Jens. She was probably the girls' supervisor. She was also dressed provocatively but the years and the pounds made the tight clothing more comic than titillating.

"Feel like having some fun?" she asked bluntly, and not like she meant it.

"Well, no, I'm just here to watch the show for a while and then I'm leaving."

"Who's that other guy?" Evidently she had more than entertainment on her program. Her age and her serenity suggested she was management.

"Which guy?"

"You know who I mean." She nodded toward a man who had entered at the same time as Jens, sitting at a table in a corner.

"Oh, that one. He's my personal bodyguard. Always one step ahead." He wasn't sure why he said that but it worked.

"Ah, so you're a VIP." The woman was suddenly a lot friendlier. "At first I thought you were police but you're obviously a native English speaker, so I suppose you're not a cop. Where are you staying?"

"At the Grand Elysée," Jens lied.

He tried to size up the man, who was retreating even more. *Is he a Yugoslav? Am I being followed? Am I in danger?* He was getting cocky from all the alcohol he had consumed that evening. The slivovitz in the Sarajevo, the chardonnay with dinner and now a screwdriver. He glanced at his watch. It was still too early to pick up Esther.

The woman made a few more attempts to keep him focused on her but once it became clear that Jens wasn't going to buy her a drink she wandered off. A little later he paid and walked out. As soon as he was outside he ran to the opposite side of the street and waited around a corner to see if his "bodyguard" would follow him. He waited about four minutes but didn't see anyone emerge. He ambled along the Reeperbahn and asked someone for directions to the Grand Elysée.

He walked along the Holstenwall, past a tenebrous park, along the Forch-Fock-Wall, also with an unlit park to his left. Then along the Dammtordamm toward the Dammtor train station. He took pleasure in the street names, which spoke to his imagination since he was only accustomed to English.

He walked along the edge of the park across from the station. From there he could see the hotel and he stepped up his pace. It was close to midnight.

He didn't see or hear it coming. He only felt a hard object slamming into the back of his head and a sharp pain in his side before he fell. Everything turned black.

15.

Face Job's performance drove the crowd in the Color Line Arena crazy. Brad Brittain was in top form, a Hamburg reviewer would later write about the more than two-hour performance. Esther had a spot in the VIP area, with a spectacular view of the stage. Not until the second encore did Esther get why Brad had explained so nervously exactly where she should sit.

For the first encore they sang their latest hit, a song everyone had been waiting for all evening. For the second encore Brad entered the stage alone with his guitar. He announced a new song, inspired recently by a girl for whom he had fallen completely. Esther liked the band's ballads but unfortunately the sensitive intros usually morphed into rock-hard refrains. Now that Brad got to work with just his guitar, it looked promising. She could even make out the lyrics:

> *She kept her open eyes closed for me*
> *That should be a clear alarm*
> *Cool distance she exposed for me*
> *While killing me with charm*

The words didn't impress her. However, the refrain had the effect Brad intended.

> *Can't you feel the beat*
> *Of a Dutch girl's treat*

"Oh dear," Esther blurted out spontaneously. Since they could hear one another for the first time now that the volume on stage was so civilized, people in her vicinity looked over in surprise.

Brad continued to sing about Esther's wonderful traits but also about her beautiful, honest eyes, her full lips, and her graceful movements. Esther began to doubt this song was about her. But when he reached the last refrain, he clearly added her name to the lyrics. Esther felt her face pull into a nervous grimace and she turned beet red. Fortunately no one was looking at her; no one had any idea this was about her.

That anonymity didn't last long. Brad signaled. One of the spotlights that had been shining on him on an otherwise completely dark stage was turned to shine on Esther. It was no use trying to duck; the back of the chair in front of her was too low. She was fixed in a blinding light before she could think of an alternate escape. The other seventeen thousand people saw her, looking like a deer in the headlights.

"Oh, Brad, no," she hissed under her breath, while trying to smile at the same time. The song was over. Brad received the applause, pointed at Esther, and shouted in the microphone:

"Ladies and gentlemen. My inspiration! Esther Lejeune! Give her a big round of applause."

Esther waved weakly at the audience and waited for the spotlight to swivel back to Brad. The band joined him for a last song and Esther silently prayed this one wouldn't also be about her.

The people around her now observed her with interest. Clearly this girl was the famous singer's new love interest. She saw both pity for Brad and jealousy in the eyes of the women around her. They were all wondering if his infatuation was reciprocal and many no doubt were more than willing to console him tonight if it wasn't.

After a lengthy final applause the place slowly emptied. Esther wondered if she could sneak out but Brad had either thought she might or he was just attentive: A security guard appeared—a Neanderthal-like giant whose back could easily block two Esthers from view. He was quite friendly and he politely asked Esther to follow him.

They took all sorts of sly routes backstage and past several security checkpoints to the dressing room where Brad was completely ready. He had showered and put on a sweater, a leather jacket and snake leather Tony Mora boots.

"That was fast. Didn't you have to catch your breath?"

103

"Nah, I'm done here." He was evidently disappointed that she hadn't immediately commented on his song.

"That was a beautiful song, Brad."

"Well, you inspire me tremendously."

"It's a good thing I'm not responding to your advances. Otherwise you would never have written such a wonderful song."

Brad looked sheepish. He hadn't expected this reaction. How many people could withstand the sound of applause? He had thought that being thrown unexpectedly into the spotlight would have weakened her defenses a bit. But even the VIP treatment—with almost more attention than he himself got—didn't impress her.

"I would appreciate it if you left me in the dark in future."

"Didn't you like it?" he asked with the last remnants of surprise.

"No, I don't like being the center of attention. I prefer to stay in the shadows."

She accepted his arm, to console him. She knew she shouldn't go on with this too long. It would certainly end badly sooner or later. They walked toward the entrance, where close to a hundred girls had gathered. They shouted all sorts of things while Brad ushered her to the limo.

"Hey, *I'm* Dutch, baby! I'm a Dutch girl, too!" Esther heard one of them yell.

The Oyster Bar was reserved for Brad and his band, and the doors were blocked by two hotel security guards who were definitely less into rock and roll than those at the concert. Right now it was just the two of them, because, as Brad explained, the other band members still had to score someone for the night.

"It's pretty lonely on tour. Most of the boys are married and their wives do come along, but toward the end they fight so much and the women are so homesick that they all leave."

"And you've never been married?"

"Never."

"Why not?"

"Why not? Why do you think? It's hard to find someone who isn't out to get my money or who's only turned on by all the fame." He grinned. "Or they dream that I'll write a nice song about them."

"Ah, that brings us back to us."

"I wouldn't mind marrying *you*."

"Come on, Brad. You're just infatuated. If you got me in bed, the novelty would quickly wear off."

"No, I really don't think so."

"You don't have to deny it. I like you but we're not getting married."

"I haven't proposed yet, I haven't even proposed yet!"

"And you won't."

"No, you're right," he acceded. "You're so damn sensible."

"And I'm the one who got away. Isn't that great?"

While the staff at the bar was busy preparing the Oyster Bar specialty, Brad talked about his youth in Glasgow. The Chablis—the other specialty—was already empty by the time a large bowl of ice was brought to their table. Two halves of a large Canadian lobster, langoustines, crawfish, oysters on the half shell and jumbo shrimp were all staring up at Esther. She didn't have the heart to tell Brad she was a vegetarian. And she didn't eat lobster out of principle. She felt it was inhumane to boil them alive.

Brad was from a working class family. He hadn't finished the technical school where he had trained to be a steel worker. Music was his passion; he formed his first band at age twelve. Esther had already read the full story on Internet, so she focused on things that weren't common knowledge, such as his first girlfriend, his first sexual experience and his criminal record. *How did she know he had a criminal record?* Lucky guess. Brad talked and talked about himself and Esther managed to distract him from the fact that she wasn't eating any of the seafood on ice.

She had told Brad her boyfriend Jens would pick her up around midnight. But her prince didn't show up when the clock struck twelve. Around 12:15 Esther sent him a text message, asking him where he was. About 12:30 she went to the restroom to call him but she got his voice mail. Around 12:45 she admitted she was getting worried. Brad didn't understand her anxiety.

"This isn't Naples or Bucharest."

"Still, I have a bad feeling about this."

Esther called the hotel. The receptionist had last seen Brad around ten. When she hung up, she got the scare of her life.

Like a bloody zombie, a figure fell against the glass entry door of the Oyster Bar and hung there with its cheek stuck against the glass. Esther recognized the bleeding face immediately. Jens! She screamed and pointed at the door past Brad's shoulder.

The waiter walked to the door and glared disapprovingly at the man pressed against the glass on the other side. He motioned to another door but Esther pushed him aside and pressed the emergency button. The door opened out but Jens collapsed around it and fell inside. He lay motionless on the floor. Esther pulled him completely inside and tried to determine the source of all the blood. His clothes were torn on one side and blood was seeping out. Jens was deathly pale and babbling incomprehensibly. Brad called to one of his security guards.

"Brian, do something! You have your first-aid certificate, dammit! Do something, man! Call an ambulance!"

The waiter was standing in a daze. Brad yelled so loudly that the customers in the hotel restaurant stood up in a panic to see what was going on in the Oyster Bar.

Esther had put Jens's head in her lap taken and taken his hand. Teary-eyed, she looked gratefully over at Brad, who was busy directing traffic. He motioned to the band members, who had just arrived, to go back outside. Brad and the second security guard kept the other employees at a distance. In the meantime, the first security guard tore open Jens's shirt and pressed a clean dishcloth to the bleeding wound. The restaurant was in chaos.

Brad bent over Esther and tried to console her by patting her head. She took his hand, pressed it against her cheek, and cried.

"Well, this is my boyfriend, Jens," she said through her tears.

16

"What day is it?"

Esther jumped up and walked to the bed. The sterile surroundings of the Hamburg Academic Hospital had put her in a kind of trance the last couple of days. Jens's weak voice seemed to wake her from a white dream. She took his hand and sighed in relief. It was Thursday. Jens had been in a coma for almost three days.

His attacker had hit him good. A whack from a hammer had created several hairline fractures in his skull. The police found the hammer in the park. He was also stabbed twice in his side with a knife. One of the stab wounds was superficial; the other had ruptured his spleen. He had lost a lot of blood—it was a miracle he had made it to the Oyster Bar by himself. Had no one seen him while he lay bleeding a hundred yards from the street?

The spleen surgery had taken seven hours. When the anesthetic wore off, Jens stayed unconscious. Evidently he had slipped into a coma during the operation.

Esther had kept guard for three days and tears of joy sprang to her eyes when he finally came to. She kissed his hand since his head was completely covered in bandages. A tangle of intravenous and oxygen tubes lay on his bed.

"It's Thursday."

"Jesus, what happened?" asked Jens with a raspy voice.

"You tell me. You fell into the Oyster Bar cursing and mumbling. Were you mugged? Do you think it has anything to do with the case?"

"I have no idea." Jens thought long and hard, trying to recall the moment in the park when he was attacked. He hadn't seen a thing. He had only felt a whack on the back of his head and then he fell forward. He felt the pain in his side and then nothing.

"I was hit and everything went black."

"He stabbed you with a knife."

"Interesting. What about my laptop?"

"In your spleen. He stabbed you in your spleen and you're asking about your laptop? Did you have it with you?"

"Yes, I always have my laptop with me."

"Shit, so you lost all your work. No backup?"

"Of course I backed it up."

"Aren't you interested in hearing how you balanced on the edge?"

"What edge?"

"Of death."

"Oh, that edge." Jens felt woozy. "Did they manage to put me back together again?"

"Acting the tough guy?" She wanted to jab his ribs but stopped herself just in time.

"What I don't get," Jens said suddenly, "is how I ended up at the Oyster Bar."

"What do you mean? You crawled there. It was closest to the park. You just went to the light."

"I really can't remember doing that. It's almost as if . . ."

"What?"

"As if someone took me there."

"But you were conscious. You were cursing."

"I don't remember any of that. I only remember looking into your eyes."

"You must be mistaken. Who would pick up a half-dead guy and drop him off at a restaurant door?"

"I don't know."

They sat looking at each other for a while. It was a bizarre situation. A few days ago they had lain in each other's arms and made love until the sun came up. Next thing Esther knew, her meeting with Brad was harshly interrupted by Jens falling into the door, half-dead. She had sat at his bedside for three days, hoping he would regain consciousness. She had jumped up at every little sigh, to see if he was waking up. She had stared for hours at the heart-rate monitor, the regular rhythm of the machine connecting her to his heart.

At night she used a guest room meant for relatives of ICU patients. It was a bland hospital room with a small television where she watched

108

the broadcast of the local news station on Monday about "the American writer Jens Jameson who had been seriously injured during a mugging" and "who was hospitalized in serious condition." The newscast also mentioned that the police suspected a mugging and that nothing was known about the book the author was presently working on.

In the meantime, she had used Jens's telephone to inform a few people of what happened. She had opened his address book and saw a lot of first names slide by on the display. She recognized one of them: Barbora, Jens's fifteen-year-old daughter. She couldn't remember his ex-wife's name. She called the number.

"Yes, Dad, what is it?" asked an adolescent voice.

"This is Esther, a friend of your father's. Is your mother home?"

"I'm not at home. Neither is my mother. What do you mean, a friend of my father's? Who are you?"

"My name is Esther Lejeune. I'm Dutch."

"But why are you calling?"

"I want to speak to your mother."

"I'm not sure my mother would want to speak to you. Tereza doesn't care much for my father's girlfriends."

"I'm sure she doesn't. Thanks for the information. Take care."

"Hey, don't you want to speak to my mother?"

"Yes. I didn't know her name. You just told me, so I can call her myself."

"But..."

"Bye."

Esther had been acutely aware of the age situation. She was twelve years younger than Jens and only eleven years older than his daughter. She had a strong urge to quarrel with the little punk but that hadn't seemed appropriate at the bedside of her half-dead father.

Tereza seemed nicer.

"Hey, Jens, how's it going?"

"This is Esther Lejeune. Are you Jens Jameson's ex-wife?"

"Yes, I am. I see you're calling from his cell."

"I'm a friend of his. I'm calling because he had an accident."

"Oh no, God, no..."

Jens had evidently portrayed his relationship with Tereza as a little more distant than it actually was.

"He's in intensive care. He was unconscious for two days. The doctor says he'll make it."

"Oh, that's terrible. What happened?"

Esther told her about the mugging and the injuries. Tereza was terribly upset. She apologized for her strong reaction, explaining that they had known each other for a long time. Esther said she understood. She wasn't the jealous type but she found herself in a surreal vacuum between Jens and his unfamiliar circle of friends.

Brigitte was also listed in the phone. Another enthusiastic female reaction.

"Hey Jens, I'm so glad you finally called. How's it going? How are you?"

The flood abruptly ended when Esther made herself known. She wanted to say, *Yes, I'm sorry it's just me, his new squeeze*, but she restrained herself. After wary introductions, she told Brigitte that Jens lay in a semi coma in intensive care after being hit over the head and stabbed. Brigitte screamed, invoking God and sundry to help express her shock.

Esther gave her the details and the promise she would keep her posted.

Brigitte said, "I *told* him to be careful in Hamburg."

As a true reporter, Esther couldn't let that remark pass. "Do you think it has to do with the book he's working on?"

"No, no, that's not what I'm saying. Hamburg is a dangerous city."

"But a lot less dangerous than New York."

"I suppose."

"So maybe it does have to do with the story. Jens was looking for a few Yugoslavs."

"Oh God, no!"

"Do you know them?"

"Hey, who are you anyway? Are you a cop or something? How did you get his phone?"

"I've been at his bedside for the past twenty-four hours. I'm a colleague. I'm helping him with his work."

"He never said anything about an assistant."

"It doesn't matter. It's none of my business. But Jens was seriously hurt and he would like to know who's behind it."

"So would I. I'm sorry I'm so suspicious. Oh, this is terrible!"

110

Then the phone calls to Esther began. At the most random times—day and night—because Americans are not very aware of time zones. Ellen was the first to call. She immediately explained her relationship with Jens. On the one hand Esther appreciated that. On the other hand it made her jealous to hear about her having been his "best friend for years."

Winkler called almost every hour to cheer her up. Of course his intentions were ambivalent—he wanted to hear all about her room and whether she was wearing a nightie. She had called him a dirty old man.

"Old maybe, but not dirty and still sprightly," he had answered.

The publisher, two friends, a sister and finally Jens's mother called, extremely upset by the news.

For two days Esther kept them all posted and she was relieved she could now send them a text message with good news.

"What are you doing?"

"I'm sending a few people a text message to tell them you emerged from your coma."

"Jesus, was it really a coma?"

"Well, you were pretty unconscious."

"What did you write?"

"Jens conscious / big mouth again / getting better / more news later. Greetings Esther."

Jens was amazed at the reactions Esther had gotten when she called everyone. Brigitte's reaction especially raised his suspicions.

"So she thinks this is connected?"

"Jens, you still had your wallet but your computer is gone. I think it's connected, too. This wasn't just a random mugging."

"Well, it still seems unlikely Schöteldreier or these Yugoslavs have already taken steps. If they were even going to."

"What sort of mugger would attack someone in the middle of the city ...?"

"... in a park ..."

"Two hundred yards from a road where people drive by ..."

"And another shady character drops the victim off at the door of a restaurant thirty minutes later."

"Well," said Esther, "all the data can be retrieved, even if the computer is gone. The investigative report, the conversations with Telford, with Ina, etc. There weren't any exclusive conversations or comments that couldn't be repeated."

"Except for the last conversation with the Yugoslav."

"Tell me," said Esther.

Jens told her about the bar and the one patron who had given him a name. Mikulas Danitsha. He had immediately memorized the name, as he always did with key parts of his stories.

"We'll have to pay him a visit." Esther was decisive.

"We?"

"Yes, I'm not about to let you go on any more of those dangerous expeditions by yourself."

17.

Well, things didn't go as planned. Esther didn't need to join him on his expedition. Jens felt sufficiently protected by the maximum-security prison where Danitsha was housed. The man was also chained hand and foot when he was brought in, and he was then chained to the chair opposite Jens. His first impression was of a quiet, not unsympathetic man of around forty—rough, with broad shoulders. The prisoner asked for the cigarettes he had made Jens promise in return for the interview. He spoke English fairly well. Jens handed him a carton and took a second one from his bag and placed it on the table.

"What do you want, Mr. Whiskey," said the man, referring to Jens's last name.

"I want to talk to you about something that happened in Hamburg years ago."

Jens had had to stay in the hospital for two more weeks and even then they didn't want to release him. Risk of infections is substantial after spleen surgery and possibly lethal within twenty-four hours.

The upside was that he had had time to mull everything over at his leisure. Esther had bought him a new laptop. Within two days he had all his software reinstalled and in thirty minutes the online backup was in place. The first few days he couldn't work much because he tired easily and got splitting headaches. Still, he was able to write a first draft of a few chapters, based on the information he had gathered so far.

The assault had kept him busy, too. Two detectives from the German Polizei Kriminalamt had visited him and asked him lots of questions, but they couldn't tell him anything new about the crime scene or about the perpetrator. They had combed the park and eventually found the hammer with Jens's blood still on it but no fingerprints. They were still following up on leads. For instance, some skin tissue from the hammer could provide a DNA profile but only if the DNA was in a database. They had canvassed the neighborhood but there were no witnesses.

Even an appeal in the local paper didn't get any results. The perpetrator's *modus operandi* was unique. Hamburg had never experienced an attack with both a hammer and a knife. A couple in Turkey had once been killed with a hammer, and it was a popular weapon for attacking spouses in numerous soap operas. But muggers always used a knife, never a hammer. The detectives suspected it was a reprisal. They wanted to know all about the story Jens was working on. Jens didn't feel like letting these two gentlemen broadcast to the public that he was writing a book about Brigitte Friends and her past in Hamburg. In no time his story would be on the desks of the likes of Frank Johnson. Wouldn't they love it in New York if they could get all that in the entertainment pages?

So Jens told them he was working on a story about the Hamburg music scene in the sixties, when The Beatles began their career here.

He had discussed the matter with Esther as well. It could have been a regular mugger who had seen him walking with his laptop bag, thinking he'd be an easy target. However, he had been carrying his laptop in a simple canvas shoulder bag, nothing like a real laptop bag. It also seemed unlikely that a regular mugger would kill for such minor spoils. It was also strange that the perpetrator hadn't searched Jens's pockets; ninety-nine percent of men don't carry their wallet in their bag while ninety-nine percent of women do. It could have been a totally psychotic person who therefore couldn't be held accountable, but the completely silent approach made that unlikely as well. It seemed more like a professional attack, since Jens had been alert yet heard nothing.

Either someone wanted to get at Jens's information, or he wanted to discourage him from continuing his research. In which case it had to be the Yugoslavs. But Jens was convinced he hadn't been followed by anyone from the Sarajevo. He hadn't told them which hotel he was staying at or where he was going. He was the only passenger on the bus and he sat in the back so he could see if a car was following him. The man in the topless bar hadn't come outside when Jens left. And in any case, the bouncer would have stopped him if he had had a hammer hidden under his coat.

And why would the Yugoslavs want to rough him up, anyway?

Because he asked a question about something that happened fifteen years ago, something that hadn't been prosecuted at the time and likely could not be prosecuted now? The statute of limitations probably passed a long time ago. Or could the Yugoslavs still be in touch with Schöteldreier? Maybe they called him and he was so angry he ordered Jens killed? Too far-fetched.

So it had to be from even longer ago. Telford, maybe? He probably didn't have anything to do with this but perhaps he had talked to someone about Jens's visit. Perhaps Ina van den Boogaard had called Peter Kruger to get him all riled up about his murky ventures being scrutinized again? That was too far-fetched as well. Brigitte's father? He could be a factor, of course, but only if Jens had already met him without realizing it. He went over all the people he had met in his mind. The private investigator Jan Dijkgraaf, the banker Ben Vervoort from Zandvoort, and Frederick Winkler. The last two made no sense but Dijkgraaf could have had a double role. Jens and Esther now saw the way he bungled the investigation in a completely different light. What if Schöteldreier had bribed the man to do nothing? Or what if he had actually hit upon some interesting facts and was bribed by either Schöteldreier or Brigitte's father?

What had been the intention of the perpetrator or whoever paid him to do it? Had they really wanted to kill him and was it bungled because the fool had stabbed Jens in the wrong spot? That seemed impossible. Jens had blacked out and was a powerless victim for several minutes. He could have been stabbed all over. Maybe a passerby had interrupted the attacker, causing him to flee? But that person would have called the police, right?

Was it merely a warning? And if so, how was Jens supposed to know? And a warning for what? What was it that he wasn't allowed to publish? Did the fact that his wallet wasn't taken mean it was a warning? Did they want his laptop to see where his story was headed? In that case they should have attacked him later. It would be hard to make sense of the transcriptions of a bunch of interviews and a stack of notes. In any case, the material wasn't unique—nothing that couldn't be acquired again.

The three most logical explanations seemed to be that either a lunatic or a junkie committed a completely random mugging, or an attacker mistook him for someone else, or someone had heard from Dijkgraaf that Jens had been digging into Brigitte Friends's past and wanted to discourage him. So far, only Onkel Gerard and Brigitte's father fit that bill. Dijkgraaf seemed to be the only lead in that scenario, so they decided they should look into it.

Friday and Saturday flew by with all this puzzling. On Sunday, Esther had appeared at Jens's bedside with their suitcases. She put Jens's in the closet and shoved hers under the bed.

"I have to go home. Frederick won't give me any vacation days. He wants me to finish the Demood story." She looked at him sadly. Seven days of hospital visits had only strengthened her feelings for Jens. She was amazed at how tough he was, lying there. He never considered quitting the story, even though she had brought it up a few times. She suggested flying back to New York with him, to spend a cozy summer in Provincetown, his hometown. Schöteldreier and Brigitte could go to hell. And Winkler too.

She hadn't expected Jens to react the way he did. "Jesus, that's a great idea! I wish I could." He had seemed very happy. Really. But then he had found all the reasons why they couldn't. It would be hard for her to find a new job. He would have to pay back his advance. He wouldn't be able to pay his alimony. He would have to leave his apartment. And they would both be letting go of a great story.

Were they reporters or weren't they? She had looked him in the eye and concluded that he wasn't really in love with her. She should keep her feelings in check.

But not right away, she thought. They growled at each other and Esther did what she had taken pains not to do all week. She climbed onto his bed and gave him an unforgettable goodbye.

And so here he was a week later, sitting alone opposite Mikulas Danitsha.

"What do you want from me, Mr. Whiskey?" the man asked, opening the first pack of cigarettes. He looked thoughtfully at the second carton.

Jens put a water bottle on the table. The guard at the door stepped toward them while Jens took more things from his bag: a tape recorder, a Moleskin notebook and two pens.

The man was aloof. "I'm not going to say much. You don't need that many pens."

116

"I don't need to know much. Just one thing. Water?" Jens nodded at the bottle and smiled.

The man hesitated before taking the bottle. He moved it from his left to his right hand and put it back in front of Jens.

"I was in a restaurant bar called the Sarajevo in Hamburg. They had the same wonderful mineral water there."

Danitsha gave him an incredulous look, took the bottle and waited until the guard was distracted. He inhaled deeply and his rigid face relaxed somewhat. Then he took a swig of the slivovitz. He gave the bottle back to Jens and nodded.

"So you come all the way from America to ask me one thing?"

"Well, it concerns only a small part of the book I'm writing."

"And what's the book about?"

"About the Hamburg nightclub scene, among other things. About pop artists, impresarios, record companies—that sort of thing."

"Boring." Danitsha took another drink from the "water." Jens had intentionally brought a small bottle and decided to join in himself, so he wouldn't be held later for smuggling alcohol.

"It wouldn't hurt you to tell me about it, since the statute of limitations has already passed, and it would help me to publish my story. If you don't tell me, there's still no harm done. You've enjoyed a drink of water and I'll be back on a train in thirty minutes."

The barrage of words confused Danitsha. He obviously wasn't in the habit, here in prison, of rapidly drinking that much strong liquor.

"How is the Sarajevo?"

"Not much to eat in that restaurant. It was really quiet. I was there around dinner time and I never saw the chef."

"They fucked up my business."

"I'm sorry."

Danitsha gazed somberly at the wall, taking another drink from the bottle. Jens tried to keep up with him but he took smaller sips because he immediately felt the stuff go to his legs. He posed his question. What did Danitsha remember about Das Schwere Hertz and the fights that took place there several times between Yugoslavs? They had flared up about nothing at all and the damage was considerable. Danitsha was debating how candid he could be about that job. His eyes shifted back and forth while he thought. Then he shrugged. Jens was in luck yet again.

"Gerard Shitbuyer, that's the asshole who ordered the fights. He paid well for them. Overall we probably made around ten thousand marks off that guy. Three, four fights. We trashed the place."

"Schöteldreier, was he called Gerard Schöteldreier?"

"Yeah, yeah, that's his name. So was that your one question?"

"How did you meet him?"

"Everyone knew you could just sit in the Sarajevo and wait until someone asked you what you wanted."

"Anything, or just those types of jobs?"

"That's enough, Whiskey, or should I call you Slivovitz?" He was openly exasperated.

"I'm asking because the night I went to the Sarajevo, I was hit on the head with a hammer and stabbed in my side, in my spleen." Jens sounded relaxed as he lifted his shirt and revealed the dressing.

Danitsha looked thoughtfully at the white gauze and grinned, reveling in it.

"So that's why you really came?"

"No, I don't think a Yugoslav did it."

"Yugoslavs," he scoffed. "They don't exist anymore, pinhead. A Serb maybe. But no, they don't use carpenters' tools. That would be too embarrassing. A hammer. Ha, ha, ha!"

"No, I came for Schöteldreier. Did he tell you why you had to trash the place?"

"He might have, but we didn't give a shit. Someone told us what he wanted and paid half in advance. That was it." He nodded at Jens. "There's not too much of that stuff for sale in Hamburg anymore. It's been cleaned up, you know. So it must have been an outside job. That makes your search a lot harder, doesn't it?"

They talked a while longer, about the prison, about the German prison guards, whom he called fascists they had already fought in World War Two, about the beauty of Serbia, where it was safe enough to go on vacation again. But Jens should avoid backward places like Croatia and Bosnia.

Jens gave him the second carton of cigarettes and they finished the bottle. Then he took out a roll of peppermints. He gave Danitsha two and took two himself.

The Serbian murderer grinned broadly as they parted. "If I ever need to get rid of someone for you, just give me a call. And do drop by if you're in the neighborhood. Ha, ha, ha!"

When Jens got up, he noticed the few sips he had taken were just a little too much in his condition. The visitor lounge suddenly seemed like the inside of a ship in a serious ocean storm. He held the table for quite a while before cautiously walking to the door. He heard Danitsha laughing loudly but he could no longer determine where the sound was coming from. The hallways seemed endless. He bit his tongue until he was outside and the warm June wind caressed his face.

Gotcha, Mr. Schöteldreier, a.k.a. Onkel Gerard. If you're behind this, that's the end of your career.

18.

Esther was waiting on the corner. She was thirty minutes early. She made it a point to always arrive ten to twenty minutes early with some excuse. Often people prepare themselves in the last ten minutes before an interview. They build up tension, getting defensive even before their guest arrives. Arriving early always made for a relaxed atmosphere. And she herself was anxious about the appointment, too.

For eighty euro she had bought a two-way ticket from Rotterdam to London and she had found a room in the single-star Central Hotel for thirty-five pounds a night. Though the name suggested a downtown location, it wasn't. It was close to London's Central Park but it was quite different from New York's park of the same name. It was in a suburb where one wouldn't want to walk alone at night. Her room was above the pub. Fortunately it closed at eleven. The Underground connection with downtown was excellent.

A lot had changed in her life when she returned home from Hamburg. She had reported to Fred, also known as Fast Forward, on Monday morning and heard that an editor had been assigned to her story. She had to give him all her information and other material on Brad.

"No way," she told Fred. "I worked hard to get that information and I have an agreement with Brad about how it will be used."

"This is way over your head," said Fred. "I insist you hand over the material so we can look at it. It goes without saying that we will respect your sources when we publish it."

"I can't do that. I really have to do this story myself."

"Esther, you're a researcher, not a reporter. Someone has to write the story."

"I already have a writer for it."

"Surely not that crazy American who was reckless enough to get himself stabbed?" asked Forward.

He walked off, exasperated and feeling he had spent more than enough time on the conversation. Five minutes later Esther was called in to Winkler's office. He sat back, with his feet on the table, but rose slightly to give his "girl" the once-over.

"You look divine, as usual," was the first thing he said.

"I could sue you for sexual harassment." Esther was joking but because her boss had called her into his office she was out of sorts and it came out differently.

"Well, well, so we're on the warpath. Listen Esther, I have to agree with Voorwaarts. You can't handle this story. And I really don't need an American co-writer."

"I've got explosive material, Frederick. I have an agreement about how I'm going to use it, and I'm not going to bicker with some smart-ass from the economic desk. Jens Jameson helped me with the story. His book and my story are connected. And I get the Dutch exclusive on the exposés in his book."

"What exposés?"

"I can't tell you. But think front page of The New York Times."

"Is that stabbing connected?"

"We still have to prove it," said Esther, because, with her guileless face, trying to lie would have been pointless.

"Can't you compromise? You can choose your own editor, how about that? Or you can do it with Sarah Verdonck."

Esther went over her co-workers in her mind. The old guard was out. One guy was even grayer than the next. If Esther were to play music by Face Job, they would crawl under their desks in shock. The younger guys would immediately take her story from her and put her on the sidelines. She didn't trust them with her sources. They wouldn't be conscientious. She had had an argument with each of them about that before, especially with Sarah Verdonck.

Esther had worked for months on unraveling the tangle of corporations owned by the biggest private bank in the Netherlands, FSB. But Sarah's name had been at the top of the stories, with "in cooperation with Esther Lejeune" somewhere at the end. Sarah had been invited to television shows; she was interviewed and she was already nominated for a journalism prize.

"I'm sorry. I'm with Forward, eh, Voorwaarts on this one. He's right—you're still too inexperienced for this."

"Then I quit."

"Excuse me?"

"You heard me. Look, Frederick, I appreciate you giving me a chance by hiring me, but I have to take care of myself. I have a great story. When it's finished, you can buy it from me."

"Now, now, you can't do that. Just do your work. The work you already did is ours—just be a good girl and hand it over."

Esther was dumbfounded. This was one of those situations she had maneuvered herself into. She turned around, walked out the door, slamming it shut behind her.

She went home and threw herself on the bed, spending a few hours ranting and raving. Then she made two phone calls: one to call in sick and one to her union. The lawyer who spoke with her was helpful and told her she wasn't obligated to hand over information she had acquired in confidence. She also had the right to refuse work if she had conscientious objections. And she could resign with notice without going back to work; she still had seven weeks' worth of vacation coming. The lawyer said she would call Winkler. She knew him and was willing to mediate.

Finally I get something in return for the union dues I've been paying for the last three years, thought Esther, and she called Jens in Hamburg.

"I'm in the garden," he called cheerfully, when he picked up.

"I'm in trouble."

Jens was serious right away. "Tell me."

She was glad he was immediately attentive. She related the complete story, including what the union did.

"Good," said Jens. "I'll write your story. Or better yet, I'll help you write it. Writing for a newspaper is just a trick, it's easy. Don't let those bureaucrats get to you. I've got your back."

But no one had her back here on the street corner of this affluent London suburb. She had an appointment with Marcus Jackson. He was a former TMC employee who was willing to answer some questions about his former boss. Esther was having a harder time than Jens. After all, events of fifteen years ago are easier to discuss than the shady dealings of the impenetrable TMC.

She had applied one of her hallmark tricks. Through the Internet and the newspaper archives of the Chamber of Commerce, she collected as many names as possible of company employees. Then she called the company and asked to speak to those people. She pretended to sell magazine subscriptions and usually she didn't get further than the secretary. But that was okay—she wasn't out to talk to current employees; she wanted to learn about the people who no longer worked there. She had collected names of forty TMC employees, and six former employees. Three of those had found better jobs elsewhere, two turned out to be a dead end after several telephone conversations, and one of them—Marcus Jackson—she thought might be a bull's eye.

According to his Facebook profile he had worked in the company's accounting department. He was Orthodox Catholic, trained guide dogs for the blind in his spare time and chaired a foundation that had built a small school in Mali. He seemed to be sincere, so he may have left TMC as a conscientious objector. Or he was fired because he was about to blow the whistle on a bookkeeping scandal. In any case, he was at home, unemployed.

Brad Brittain had told her he didn't know any M. Jackson, except for his late colleague Michael Jackson, who hadn't worked with TMC. But Jackson did know Brad, though not personally. And since Esther had said she was looking for information on behalf of Brad, he finally agreed to an interview, after first declining several times over the phone. She hadn't needed to lie, because she was no longer employed by the paper where she had worked her tail off for three years.

Esther had been called to the editorial office for a conversation, initiated by the union lawyer, who apparently intended to placate both parties—she tried to be a mediator. Esther didn't appreciate that. Twice she snapped at the woman, "Hey, you're here for me, lady."

The lawyer said that two issues needed to be resolved. Esther wasn't sure what she meant.

Voorwaarts and Winkler sat ten feet away from the two women, at the head of the large conference table. Voorwaarts had a notepad and pen so he could take minutes of this meeting. Winkler was nervously playing with his iPhone.

Esther had a folder containing copies of her research. She had omitted the interesting details, so it wasn't much. During the negotiations, the folder moved from Esther to Winkler.

He took it with an indifferent grin. "Well, that's not much for ten days' work."

"As you know, I focused on a specific source who gave me a lot of details but I need to protect him."

"That information is ours," said Voorwaarts.

"I don't think so," said Esther.

"Theoretically the information is indeed yours," said the lawyer. "But Ms. Lejeune is the only one who can decide, in concert with her source, how it is to be used."

"Let's see it, so we can determine what it's worth," said Voorwaarts.

Esther noticed that Winkler was very quiet. For some reason he wasn't engaged in the conversation and was gazing outside in a detached manner.

"Come on, Fred. Give me a chance, damn it. I was here for three years, putting together stories for others, sharing my sources—no problem. But this is different. I have to do this myself."

"Go ahead, but not as an employee of this newspaper."

"You mean you're firing me?"

Voorwaarts looked at Winkler who continued to stare out the window. He didn't dare push this.

"That's up to the editor in chief," he growled, not looking at Esther. "What was the other issue?"

"Sexual harassment," said the union woman.

Voorwaarts flinched. Obviously Winkler had seen it coming. Still his broad shoulders sagged and his mouth did the same. The large man was bracing himself. He put his elbows on the table.

"Wait a minute," said Esther to the lawyer. "No way. What are you thinking?"

Winkler sat up.

"During our preliminary meeting..."

"I trusted you with information. You're a lawyer. You didn't tell me you intended to mention this."

"Could I speak to you in private for a moment?" the lawyer asked timidly.

"That's not necessary. We were discussing whether you men wanted to fire me or not."

"No, no, I don't really want to do that," said Winkler.

"But..." bristled Voorwaarts.

Winkler looked at Esther, feeling he couldn't win this dilemma. When he was thinking, he usually took a tuft of hair at the back of his semi-bald head and twisted it into a little ponytail. He would twist it and twist it, as if he could pull the solution to a problem from his brain that way.

"Esther, I'm sorry. There's nothing I can do." He put his head in his hands. "You will be honorably let go as of September first, due to reorganization. In addition, I will pay you for three more months. Until then you're dismissed from your immediate responsibilities."

Voorwaarts was breathing again, visibly satisfied. "What about the story?"

"I will buy it from her if it amounts to anything—freelance." He handed the folder with clippings back to her.

Voorwaarts sputtered some more but Winkler gave him a stern look. The whole business was ugly enough.

Esther hadn't seen Winkler since.

These last few days she had felt terribly lonely. She hadn't anticipated the enormous change leaving the newspaper would be in her life. The idea that she was on her own, without the security of employment, benefits, a pension, co-workers who asked how her story was going, parties where everyone got drunk—suddenly she missed those things she had never valued. Her safety net was gone. Of course, she still had her income until December, she could apply for unemployment and she had savings. Financially she was all right. Maybe this was the career opportunity she had missed by alienating Fast Forward and Frederick Winkler. A job at a quality newspaper like that was hard to find.

And after all, what did all her "exposés" amount to? Jens's story that might never go anywhere. Vague files on Brad Brittain, value as yet undetermined. Hard to prove insinuations by Steve Demood's widow. In short, she really didn't have anything. She had left with a folder full of clippings and a memory stick that might contain an angle but that could just as easily contain nothing.

And that wasn't all. Her existence as a single, emotionally independent woman had been thrown off balance. Although she didn't want to admit

125

it, she had strong feelings for Jens. She wanted to lie in his arms but at the same time she preferred to be alone. She wanted to speak with him over the phone all the time but every time she hung up, she felt so lonely that she told herself it would be better not to call him again.

She wanted to make it through all this—stay independent, bring this story to a conclusion and prove that she absolutely did have talent as a reporter.

Jackson's home was a respectable townhouse in one of London's suburbs. The front yard was a bit neglected but the house itself was well maintained. Jackson opened the door himself. He reached to about Esther's chin and seemed edgy and timid. He led her to the living room, which smelled strongly of cat piss. The curtains were half drawn.

Jackson's wife had left him and he wasn't shy about it. He motioned to a seat at the dining-room table.

"She didn't agree with me. She never agreed with me on anything. She was a nice woman but she was terribly self-involved."

When Esther put her digital recorder on the table, he said, "We have to come to some agreement before I say anything, and that tape recorder stays off."

"No problem." Esther picked up the recorder, with her thumb on the record button, and turned it on as she placed it in her purse.

"Anything I say is confidential, so nothing I say can be traced back to me."

"But you left TMC quite a while ago."

"First of all, they're still paying me. For two years, as severance pay. Secondly, I signed a non-disclosure agreement. They could litigate my house out from under me if I said anything. Thirdly—and this is also important for your own safety—someone has already died."

A brief, dramatic silence hung in the dusky room. Esther decided to say nothing. She knew he was referring to Demood but Jackson had to say it himself.

Jackson pulled out a sheet of paper and handed it solemnly to Esther. "This is a contract between you and me."

She took it and read. It guaranteed that the man's name wouldn't be mentioned in any publication and that Esther and the entity which published the story would be responsible for any and all damage claims—legal and lawyer expenses Jackson would owe due to breaking his non-disclosure agreement.

Esther read the document meticulously. She did have some comments and questions about it, but she decided to just sign.

"Good," said Jackson. "Now let's talk about payment."

"Payment?"

"Of course. There has to something in it for me—not even so much for me as for my foundation. We built a school in Mali; it requires a lot of money."

"Sir, I have nothing. I'm doing this research on a freelance basis. I don't have any money."

"But you could . . ." The man really saw Esther for the first time. The big, innocent eyes that were gazing at him in amazement took him aback. "Can I rely on a contribution if you sell your story?"

"Well, I can commit to doing my best. I'll talk Brad Brittain into contributing."

"Fair enough."

Then Jackson told his story. Esther wrote it down with a strong hand and never stopped being astonished.

Three hours later she was lying on the bed in her hotel room, listening to Jens's voice over the phone. It was almost four in the afternoon and she was puzzled by his slurred speech. He had thrown up so much that he was still catching his breath, so his voice sounded as if he had inhaled helium and was impersonating Donald Duck.

"Drunk already," Esther said cynically.

"I just came back from the prison. It's going well. That Serb just admitted to it. I'm so lucky. First Weintraub, then that Johanson and now the Serb, just like that."

"Yes, you're so lucky. A hammer to the back of your head, stabbed in your spleen," she joked. "So you went to Danitsha alone after all?"

"Of course, honey. You know me. Completely irresponsible. Besides, you're in London and I'm in, in… Damn, where am I again?"

"Aachen, Germany."

"Whatever. Anyway, your trick with the slivovitz worked like a charm. He drank it all."

"Except the portion you threw back yourself. Did he confirm everything? Because if he did, you've got yourself quite a problem with Schöteldreier."

"Well, at least I have something to hold against him if he wants to stop me. How did your interview with Jackson go?"

"I was lucky, too. The man's a veritable flash flood of information."

"Tell me."

"I'll tell you when you're sober."

"Okay, okay, I'll go sleep it off. When will you be back in the Netherlands?"

"When I'm done here."

"I want to see you. Do you want me to fly over there?"

"Absence makes the heart grow fonder."

"Excuse me?"

She said goodbye sweetly and hung up.

19.

"Have a seat, my dear man. I chose this place at the table so I can see you properly. You're in the spotlight, as it were, while I'm merely a silhouette to you, sitting by the window, ha, ha, ha!"

Ben Vervoort's characteristic laughter burst across the golf-club restaurant—a beautiful mansion with an English-thatched roof on a dead end street at the edge of Zandvoort. The Kennemer Golf Club was more than a hundred years old and was one of the hundred best golf courses in the world. The vast green lawns with three nine-holes stretched out among the bare dunes behind the sea.

"You look paler than the last time I saw you," Ben remarked.

"Yes, I probably do. I just got out of the hospital."

"Oh dear, oh dear, nothing serious, I hope?" Ben seemed genuinely worried.

"A severe concussion and a spleen surgery."

"Huh." Ben thought, moved the silverware, the wine and the wine glasses in a perfect position and lightly shook his head. "I don't quite see the connection between your skull and your spleen."

"It was either a mugging or an attempt on my life—we're not sure. I was stabbed in Hamburg."

"Oh heavens, Mr. Jameson, surely not? Why would anyone in his right mind attack a nice man like you?"

The waitress used the ensuing silence to approach the table. She greeted Ben as an old acquaintance and asked if he was having the usual. That turned out to be a glass of port wine. Ben flirted a little with the young lady. Jens didn't understand a word but the girl obviously appreciated it.

"Does that assault have any connection to our story?" said Ben in his perfect English.

Jens looked at him sharply. *Our story*, he thought. *That would be good news.* "I believe it does. Maybe you could help me."

"I will help you as much as I can," Ben said firmly.

"A man called Dijkgraaf is the connection. He works for a private investigation company. The company itself is rather large and seems pretty honest—as far as that's possible in that line of work, anyway. He also happens to live in Zandvoort."

"Dijkgraaf, Dijkgraaf—it doesn't ring a bell."

After visiting Danitsha in the maximum-security prison in Aachen, Jens had returned to Rotterdam. He had picked up his car and driven to Amsterdam. There he staked out the company's office. He had intended to confront Dijkgraaf but once the man emerged, he had walked so hurriedly along the canal that Jens had no choice but to follow him. He barely made it onto the streetcar Dijkgraaf jumped onto and he decided to follow the man for a while longer. He got off at Centraal Station and took the train to Zandvoort. Jens got on as well and went in search of the ticket collector, to purchase a ticket. Once that was taken care of he chose a strategic spot in a booth behind Dijkgraaf and waited for him to get off the train. In Zandvoort he followed Dijkgraaf from the station to his house. He had hung around the street for a while. He noticed that Dijkgraaf had a brand new BMW 5 Series in his driveway and a contractor's sign on his lawn. From the front Jens couldn't see exactly what was being remodeled.

In the train back to Amsterdam he started to sweat, he got sharp pains in his side and a panic attack. *What the hell am I doing? I have a child I have to take care of. I was writing a book and now I'm mixed up in a crime story. I've got to stop this.* The notion that he could stop immediately with this part of Brigitte's story calmed him down. He sank back on the bench and the tingling left his fingers. Then he thought, *Sure, I could stop this any time. But maybe I should keep going just a little longer.*

He told Ben about following Dijkgraaf, about his new car and his home remodeling.

"You think he's been bribed," said Ben firmly. "But he could simply have come into a small inheritance or received an annual bonus. Maybe it's time you told me the complete story."

That did seem like a good idea. Jens did his best to summarize his findings, from meeting Brigitte to his shadowing Dijkgraaf. Only Ben's eyes betrayed that he was overwhelmed at times. He remained quiet until the whole story was told.

"Mrs. Vermeer—yes, I do know her. A nasty woman, Mr. Jameson. Unlike her spouse—Mr. Vandenbroeke—a specialist in financial products and a fervent golfer. He could walk in any minute," claimed Ben.

"In what way is she nasty?" asked Jens.

"Well, Mr. Jameson, I would compare her to a hyena. You see, hyenas are dogs that attack weak or injured animals and eat them. She has a soft spot for older men with large bank accounts."

"Do you know her personally?"

"I do indeed. I know her like the back of my hand but of course I can't tell you about any of that. Our bank secrecy may not be as complete as in Switzerland but we do have a strict code about giving out information about clients."

"Yes, I understand. It's just that I could locate the man who almost killed me if I knew who had paid Dijkgraaf."

"Yes." Ben was momentarily quiet. He drank pensively from his port and grabbed a few nuts from a small silver bowl. "You do understand that that is impossible for a man in my position."

20.

Jens was pouring over the printed papers on the floor of his suite in Hotel Central. He was looking for connections, trying to determine a timeline. He put everything in neat piles and walked to the wall, where he had made a large white area by sticking printer paper on the wall with tape. He had written names, drawn lines and arrows in black and red marker. There were two organograms that vaguely resembled Christmas trees. In one treetop he had written the name Brad Brittain and in the other the letters TMC.

Jens constantly walked back and forth from the piles of paper to the wall, now and then drawing a new box or writing in a new name. Esther was on her knees on the floor. From time to time she raised a piece of paper, called out a number and Jens would scratch out something and write on the paper on the wall.

At the end of an exhausting day they examined what they had. TMC was a holding, based in Amsterdam. The Netherlands is one of the most popular tax havens in the world. Many multinationals have their headquarters in Amsterdam, The Hague or Rotterdam. The headquarters of such a company, that often employs tens of thousands of people, is no more than a single desk and sometimes just a post office box.

Big companies like Microsoft, Ikea and Coca-Cola all have the same address. The address is an administration office that does the honors in the Netherlands. Those offices represent thousands of large companies with a combined cash flow of billions of euros.

Rock and roll also discovered the Netherlands as a place to establish their parent companies. The Irish band U2 and the Rolling Stones were located along one of the canals of the Dutch city for years. In the Netherlands they paid two percent taxes on all their earnings, at least ten times less than in their home countries. For those who have the wherewithal to have someone set up a smart structure, the Dutch saying "paying is for the stupid" is a reality.

Jens was overwhelmed. Since his surgery he tired easily and sometimes he had a high fever in the evenings, leaving him weak and nauseous. Every time they found another piece of the puzzle, it gave them an adrenaline rush. Esther promised to get drinks from the pub downstairs. When she came back to the room Jens was lying on his back amid the papers. That gave her a terrible scare. She fell to her knees and slapped his cheek. Jens jerked, which made them both laugh.

Jens and Esther's reunion had been quite awkward. Jens told her over the phone that he was tired of waiting for her. And when she was quiet for a long time and had drawn a deep breath to process her disillusionment, he said he was getting onto the first plane to London and hung up.

He booked an early flight from Rotterdam to London Gatwick. From there he took the bus downtown and then the tube to Central Park. Esther was just having breakfast and, despite his announcement that he was coming, she was surprised he was already there.

They had embraced and given each other three kisses on the cheeks. Then they looked at each other in disappointment, followed by a cautious kiss on the lips.

"I'm so glad to see you again."

"Yes, me too," said Esther, though she wanted to say I missed you so much. Jens looked different, too. Still shoddily dressed but he had also lost a lot of weight during his hospital stay. Less handsome than in the picture standing on the top of her computer desk.

On the other hand, Jens was immediately mesmerized by Esther again. He had courteously held open doors for her and held her hand. They went to her apartment and sat on the sofa until they were reacquainted enough to touch.

"So," said Jens, once he had come back to life among annual report printouts and bank transfers. "TMC is a holding based in the tax haven called the Netherlands. We don't know exactly who owns the business because the stockholder is a company in Barbados, which is also a tax haven. However, that company has stocks in three other companies they invest in: TMC-Investment, TMC-Events and TMC-Venues. TMC-Holding in the Netherlands has four more companies where the real money is made: TMC-Agency, TMC-Concerts, TMC-Transports and TMC-Sound & Light Equipment. They all have their headquarters in Amsterdam."

"Yes. Brad pays those last four enormous amounts to have his concerts. Because TMC-Agency organizes the concerts and TMC-Transports transports the band. And the décor and equipment is provided by TMC-Sound & Light. But Brad's holding is also located in the Netherlands, with at least three subsidiaries. One where his royalties go, one for the income from his concerts and one with which he invests."

"Nothing special so far," said Jens.

"What do you mean, nothing special? It's a huge tax-evasion network."

"All the world's largest companies do it. Do you have any idea how much companies such as Shell, Philips and Microsoft pay in income tax?"

"Yes, I'm familiar with the story. But they're not in Barbados."

"They pay at most two percent income tax on a profit that is probably already skimmed to various corporations that own copyrights and receive royalties."

"But…?"

"It's not illegal to avoid paying taxes. It's morally wrong, maybe, but not illegal. Big business has no conscience and therefore no moral guilt."

"You have a hidden leftist streak."

"That's verbal abuse in America."

"Well, liberal democrat then?"

"The question is how the structure is used to rip off the artists."

"Aha, now we're getting somewhere. How do we prove that?"

"Well, I write about pop music and you're the economic editor."

"Not anymore," said Esther glumly.

She lay down beside Jens and they stared at the ceiling. Nothing special to be seen there. But their heads were reeling with research, diagrams, printer paper with numbers and red and white lines on the wall.

"I've got it," said Jens.

"Tell me." Esther got up.

21.

The small cottage smelled pleasantly of lemon, lavender and various other scents from Martha Demood's cleaning solutions. There were flowers everywhere, simple field bouquets of flowers Jens and Esther had seen along the side of the road when they drove their rented Toyota from London to Little Horwood. The village wasn't much more than a crossroads with a church and some houses in the Aylesbury Vale district of Buckinghamshire. Steve Demood and his wife spent the beginning of their retirement in a small rental home adjacent to a small garage. According to the police report, the cluttered garage was where Steve had committed suicide in the classic tradition: He had attached a big garden hose to his exhaust pipe. He had purchased the hose a week earlier at the local hardware store in Buckingham, six miles away.

Fingerprints were found on the exhaust pipe, the hose and the door handle of the car. An autopsy was deemed unnecessary. At Martha's insistence they did take blood and sent it to the forensic lab for tests but that hadn't led to any unambiguous conclusions. Steve drank and had taken sleeping pills, but not a lethal dose. Not even enough to lose consciousness completely.

And he had a motive. He had declared personal bankruptcy. He owed the tax collector tens of thousands of pounds, his bank account was empty and his attempts to organize a comeback tour had all failed.

Martha was special. She was almost fifty. Her life with a rock star and the hard life in the country had left their marks but she was still a beautiful woman. She was also impressive because she stood over six feet and had the build of a swimmer in training. She had friendly eyes when she shook hands with Jens and clumsily embraced the fragile Esther.

"I feel like we've known each other a long time," Martha apologized, when Esther didn't return the embrace.

Esther and Martha had talked for hours on the phone, so Esther already knew the story before coming here. But Jens had insisted on driving to Little Horwood to interview the widow himself. He claimed it was good to get context for the story, and also to see if the information Jackson had given Esther would help them learn more about Demood's financial management.

First Martha showed them where Steve had been found in his twenty-year-old Jaguar. Esther found it harder than she had expected. The Jaguar was parked outside. Martha no longer wanted to drive it. She rode her bike to the village and took the bus for longer trips.

It had been two months since she had found Steve in the garage with the motor still running. The police determined that Steve had died three hours earlier of carbon-monoxide poisoning.

"I just know Steve didn't kill himself," said Martha, once they were in the living room, where tea was steeping in a pot on the table. The teacups and cookies were put out as well.

"Do you have any clues?" asked Jens.

"We discussed how we would take care of our problems. He was furious at TMC when it turned out they would no longer do anything for him, apart from forwarding his tax assessments."

"What did he want to do?" asked Jens.

Martha spilled it out with a passion, as if she had never told the story before.

"He wanted to sue them because he was convinced they had cheated him. He was never interested in numbers; he always left that to others. But he did have a pretty good idea of what he was worth. We received small payments from the royalties and his investments. About 1,600 pounds a month, enough to live off down here. He had planned to move to a warm island—he had calculated that he should have enough money to buy a small home in one of the Caribbean islands so we could spend the rest of our retirement there. But all of a sudden there was nothing left. Wrong investments that evaporated during the crisis, they said at headquarters. Putting his eggs in the wrong baskets.

"The royalty checks also stopped coming. Those were used to pay his back taxes. Steve was convinced he was being bamboozled. He never invested in high-risk funds. And he could weather the depreciations of the exchange rates because he had never borrowed any money. When he asked for a clarification and a report of what exactly had happened, they asked him if he was sure he could afford an accountant's report. It's an outrage."

When she was finished, she inhaled deeply, as if she had said everything in one long breath. Then she calmly poured the tea and studied Esther closely. Esther was seized with emotion. She couldn't stop thinking about the Jaguar outside and the black garden hose in the garage. What a terrible notion that someone would simply attach a hose to his exhaust pipe, lead the other end into the car through a window, get behind the wheel and start the engine. She hadn't thought about death since her fiancé's terrible car accident. She was able to compartmentalize it. Until that awful assault on Jens. And now this. The past was catching up to her.

Steve Demood was sixty-three when he died. In the sixties he made his name as a singer-songwriter who protested in his songs against violence, injustice and poverty. He also wrote songs about all the loves he "consumed" in his younger years. He worked hard. Over the years there were periods where he was deeply involved in global problems. Other times he got lost and surrendered to alcohol and drugs. One song had been a number one hit in England and ten other European countries. Most of his songs were considered classics. Record sales and concerts had been profitable.

At fifty-three Demood began to suffer from acute rheumatoid arthritis, which made playing his guitar increasingly difficult. A farewell tour temporarily increased record sales and Steve retreated to the English countryside to dedicate himself to his vegetable garden, a few sheep and living off the interest of his accumulated wealth.

His songs were still being played by other artists and on jukeboxes in cafes and diners across the world.

"The police said they investigated everything. There were no signs of violence. And they only found alcohol and sedatives in his blood," Esther said.

"That was strange in itself. Those sedatives are one thing. He did suffer from insomnia those last months because of all the problems. But he hadn't touched alcohol in four years. They found a bottle of whiskey next to him. *Irish* whiskey. As a red-blooded Scotsman he would never buy Irish whiskey and no fan of his would send it to him. According to the police report, they investigated where the hose was bought but not where the whiskey came from. I checked all the off-licenses and pubs myself. They didn't sell him the stuff."

"And there was no suicide note," said Esther, to underline Martha's story.

"No, he would've left a note. We were awfully close. He wouldn't just do that without any explanation."

Steve's bookkeeping of the past few years, a few binders with all manner of papers, lay on the table. In addition, Martha had a handwritten report by Steve: his elaborate analysis of what had happened to his money, the basis for the lawsuit he had been preparing. The original was stored on his computer, which was stolen during a burglary four weeks before his death and three weeks before his personal bankruptcy. They had driven to London in his Jaguar that day to give TMC one last chance to provide clarity.

"Okay." Jens tried to get the story back on track. "That hose. It bothers me. Why did he buy that hose?"

"I don't know."

"It's too wide for watering the vegetable garden. But much longer than necessary for committing suicide."

"What do you mean?" asked Martha.

"That hose is at least thirty feet long. The distance from the exhaust to the window is at most eight feet. Why would he buy a thirty-foot hose?"

"He did mention an irrigation system at times, but that was too expensive. Maybe he wanted to put something together himself."

In the car to Buckingham, Esther and Martha were both staring tensely out the window. Esther hoped their sudden new insight would lead to a new opening in the case. Martha was blaming herself. She had never wondered about the long garden hose before, since she was so sure Steve hadn't killed himself.

They had walked out to the garage. Jens had taken the hose and rolled it out in the vegetable garden while Esther held one end by the garden faucet. This strange exercise showed that the hose fit perfectly.

"He bought the hose to irrigate the garden."

"Then he would need a drip system," Esther had said.

Once in Buckingham, Martha gave them directions to the hardware store. The friendly owner recognized Martha right away and came toward her.

"Hello, Mrs. Demood. How have you been?"

"Good, good," said Martha hurriedly. "I want to ask you something, Mr. Harris. When Steve died I canceled all his orders. Do you remember that?"

"Of course I remember, Mrs. Demood. I take it this is important, since you're invading my shop with three people?" The man was trying to make a joke to break the tension.

"Did Steve order a drip system?"

"A drip system?" asked Harris. He blanched. "I would have to look it up, Mrs. Demood."

Jens was a definite believer in conspiracy theories. History was riddled with conspiracies which either were or were not exposed by writers, historians, lawyers and reporters, and which had sometimes changed world history. Whether it was the murder of President Kennedy, the destruction of the Twin Towers, or the actually exposed conspiracies of the 1973 oil crisis or the Watergate scandal, Jens loved them and read everything he could about them. That Mr. Harris was involved in the conspiracy surrounding Steve Demood's death was too far-fetched. The skinny man in his too-tight dustcoat, who had made an honest living all his life just outside of London, couldn't possibly be an accomplice to murder.

Harris opened a large ledger and ran his finger down a few pages. "Drip system!" He looked at Martha, defeated.

"Mr. Harris, I'm Jens Jameson from The New York Times. Could you tell me if this drip system, together with the forty-five-foot hose Steve purchased here, could be used for an irrigation system?"

"Yes." Harris looked down. He pointed to the book and tapped it twice. "Especially since he also bought a timer for the tap."

Tears sprang to Martha's eyes. She finally had support for her claim that Steve didn't commit suicide.

They went to the pub where Jens ordered three glasses of Scotch and three pints of weak English beer. He casually leafed through his Moleskin while Esther and Martha stared numbly. Okay, so new evidence meant the police investigation could be reopened, but the chance of catching a suspect this late in the game was small. Any trails would be gone by now and apparently the murder was carried out so perfectly that it would be virtually impossible to catch the killers. Nevertheless, Jens was optimistic.

"We're getting somewhere," he said cheerfully. "All the evidence can be called into question. The Irish whiskey, the sleeping tablets, the garden hose—none of it is undisputable evidence, on the contrary. And there's a motive. We have to prove it based on the papers. We have to get a lawyer with the guts to sue TMC. How does that work here? Can you pay a lawyer on commission?"

"I have no idea. Maybe we should discuss it with Brad."

"Who is Brad?" asked Martha.

"Brad Brittain, of Face Job."

"I believe I've heard of them. They play guitar rock, don't they?"

"Yes, he has several platinum albums," said Esther.

"Honestly, I only liked Steve's music. The rest was rubbish. Silly, isn't it? And now that you mention it, I haven't played his records since his death."

"Was nothing released upon his death?"

"There was, yes. They released a 'Best Of' CD. It was in the shops a week after he died."

"With which company?"

"BMR Records."

"Shit. But you inherited his copyright," Jens replied.

"I inherited everything from him. His debts as well."

"So who signed the contract for that album?"

"TMC. According to the agreement, they manage everything."

"And was there no say, didn't he have any input at all?" asked Jens.

"Yes, he did."

"And you didn't sign anything?"

"No."

Jens grinned widely. "Then we need to find out who gave permission. Because if it's not legally watertight, at least you can afford a lawyer."

They dropped Martha off at her home and drove to the police station in Buckinghamshire. They put their press cards on the counter and asked to speak to the detectives who had been in charge of the investigation into Steve Demood's death. A young woman came down the stairs. She wore a leather jacket, jeans and bright white tennis shoes.

"Hello," she said cheerfully. "Of course I can't talk to you. You will have to get in touch with our public-relations officer. Or with the chief constable but he's out for the day."

Jens held her hand just a little too long. "You don't have to talk with us."

She had clear blue eyes and blond hair and she laughed impishly at Jens, who realized she was interpreting his behavior as flirting.

"It's just that we have made an important discovery that calls your entire investigation into Steve Demood's death into question."

"Oh!" The woman looked at Esther, who won her over with her famous gaze. "Of course I'm not at all curious as to what that might be."

"I could tell you," said Jens, "but we did come to get a comment. And if you refer us to your boss, we'll get the usual useless bullshit. Newspapers have printing deadlines. Deadlines aren't called that for nothing."

During that last sentence Inspector Preston led them toward a hall away from the front desk and the sergeant who had first spoken with them.

"Okay," she said, once they were halfway down the hall. "My curiosity has won over my sense of duty. I won't say anything. I will have to refer you to my boss for an official answer." She ended her remark with a big fat wink.

"What was the main evidence for suicide?"

"The hose he bought, the alcohol, the pills."

"Okay, he bought the hose to irrigate his garden. The accessory drip system and the timer were on back order when he was killed."

"Proof?"

"Mr. Harris's ledger at the hardware store in Buckingham with the same name."

"Golly," said Inspector Preston.

"The booze—Steve hadn't had a drop in four years, not even after he heard he was bankrupt. On top of that, he hated drinking Irish whiskey and guess what kind of bottle they found?"

"Irish whiskey. What about the sleeping tablets?"

"He had those because he couldn't sleep worrying about the lawsuit he was preparing against the managers of his fortune."

141

"But the dose was too small to drug him."

"And that's the missing link. How did they knock him out so they could put his fingerprints on everything and let him asphyxiate, powerless to help himself?"

"There was never a comprehensive autopsy." Preston let it slip out and gave the reporters a concerned look. "I didn't say this on the record."

"Then it seems to me one should still be done," said Esther. She continued, "He was preparing a lawsuit but the charges disappeared after his home was burglarized. How many burglaries do you have per year in this district?"

"Oh, quite a few."

"But a burglar who breaks into an old cottage that's obviously not inhabited by rich people and then steals a ten-year-old computer?"

"Yes, I suppose that is unlikely."

"So where do we go from here?" asked Jens.

"I will discuss it with my boss. Could you put off publication?"

"Yes, I'm sure that's possible." Esther could be generous since she knew a lot still had to happen before she had a real story.

22.

"We would like to know who TMC's stockholders are. Why did you choose such an opaque structure? How much of the tax break from being in tax havens such as the Netherlands goes to the artists? And where did Steve Demood's fortune go?" Esther spoke clearly. Her voice was emotionless. She never got stuck, never repeated herself and she didn't sound rehearsed.

Jens observed her proudly, though she didn't notice. Her voice reflected the confidence acquired by long and complicated research—research that had led to some uncomfortable conclusions.

The lawyers of the upscale firm of Smith, Wensworth, Brown & Harewood all looked unimpressed, as if none of the questions was relevant. Wensworth evidently believed he was in charge. He was the only one of the four partners who participated in the conversation. The other three were yes-men who moved around fat files, occasionally leafing through them. Jens had noticed straight away that the files were of varying size and filled with colored paper. It was unlikely they had anything to do with their case. *This is pure intimidation*, he thought.

Wensworth cleared his throat before he began, to get everyone's attention. Just as he was about to say something, Jens added to Esther's questions. He often did that to overconfident people to knock them off balance.

"Why would a respectable law firm such as yours want to be involved in a case that caused negative publicity in the world media within weeks, I wonder?"

"Mr. Jameson, you're a reviewer at The New York Times, and Ms. Lejeune has recently been fired from the Dutch newspaper where she worked. Please define 'world media' for me."

"Perhaps you're not fully aware how the world media works." Jens not only imitated Wensworth's strangled English accent but also said it with so much venom that Wensworth was caught off guard. "If it's in the community's interest, reporters can point out facts, draw conclusions and ask questions. Regardless of what their job description is with a newspaper, and regardless of whether they're working freelance or in the employ of a major newspaper."

"Are you going to tell me anything I don't know, Mr. Jameson?" asked Wensworth, who seemed to have recovered. But Jens could tell he got the message.

"The fact that you're all here with your fat files makes me wonder." Jens felt confident. "Are you trying to intimidate us with overkill, or do you actually have complicated files about this case?"

Wensworth was a third-generation lawyer. He grew up in the sixties and seventies, he had used soft drugs abundantly, he had enjoyed Demood's music and that of his contemporaries, and he had been rebellious right up to taking the bar. Afterward he became an obedient follower in his father and grandfather's footsteps. Perhaps the man still had some nostalgic feelings for guys like Demood but he wouldn't show them during this discussion.

"Mr. Jameson, Ms. Lejeune, we are aware that you have looked into the miserable situation in which Mr. Demood found himself before he took his own life. Naturally we're willing to answer any questions that we deem ourselves competent and authorized to answer. However, we do ask that you formulate your questions carefully."

Esther jumped up, turning red. Jens wasn't sure what was making her blush, the criticism or Wensworth's infuriating arrogance. He wanted to step in but Esther beat him to it.

"These are simple questions. They're clear, unambiguous and if you wish, I can also tell you why I'm asking them. If you don't answer me, I will record 'no comment.' Perhaps you couldn't keep up since I asked all my questions at once, so I'll start over. First question: Who are the stockholders in TMC?"

"TMC has many stockholders," Wensworth replied irritably.

"Of course that's possible. But I'm interested in the stockholders who own more than five percent. In my country, where TMC is located, that's public information. So I can also tell you the majority of TMC stock is held by a limited private company in Guernsey. When I inquired about names of stockholders, they gave me no answers."

"That's the law. Everything according to the law. We as representatives of TMC have no reason to disclose more than is legally necessary."

"So we can record," said Jens, "that TMC, one of the biggest companies in the rock and roll business, representative of a large number of famous artists, is owned by a group of anonymous businessmen who aren't prepared to come forward to answer questions concerning the practices of their company."

"Someone who has stock in Shell or Microsoft isn't personally held to account when an oil spill occurs in Nigeria or when monopoly abuse in web browsers is discovered." A smart reference to two international affairs concerning the two companies. But not enough to get rid of Esther and Jens.

"Mr. Wensworth, ninety-five percent of the stock is owned by a company in Guernsey with the illustrious name WLM Ltd. Further investigation has shown that those initials don't stand for We Love Music, as is suggested in several publications. It stands for We Love Money."

"You are well-informed, Mr. Jameson," said Wensworth.

"And we know more," said Esther.

Wensworth immediately turned to her. He thought he no longer had to answer questions about the situation concerning WLM Ltd. And that Esther was an easy prey.

"Tell me," said the man.

And before Jens could get angry with Esther for messing up his intro, she said, "But Mr. Wensworth, could you first tell us which people are behind WLM?"

"It's perfectly normal that a company is represented by the CEO and the commissioners, not by the stockholders."

Esther slowly began to feel comfortable in the distinguished firm's glass conference room, overlooking Canary Wharf, London's business district.

"The CEO of TMC holding is a certain Ton Pastoors. He's also CEO of seven-hundred and eighty-nine other small, mid-sized and large holdings. We would like to have a talk with Mr. Pastoors but we both know Mr. Pastoors has no idea what really happens at TMC. Then there's the London bureau's highest boss, Jenny Davis. Thirty-four years old. She was a secretary

145

at a concrete drilling company until she was thirty. Clearly other people behind the scenes run everything, not Ton Pastoors or Jenny Davis."

"Well, it's all you're getting." Wensworth clearly felt cornered and frustrated.

Jens saw what was coming. "Before you end this meeting, I would like to say something. First of all, you will need to give us more than 'no comment' soon. Perhaps you should talk to the concrete driller's secretary. The investigation into Steve Demood's death has been reopened. The police suspect he was killed. The widow is suing TMC for swindle, embezzlement and fraud. Brad Brittain is demanding full transparency regarding his earnings and his fortune, both now and in the past. We have a story but we're willing to hold on to it for comments—let's say twenty-four hours, no more."

"You do realize we will have the judge block any untrue stories."

Jens laughed. "Mister, go ahead and try. We can all bluff."

There was a momentary silence in the conference room. Wensworth realized he was cornered. He had underestimated his opponents. His research had revealed that Jens Jameson was a minor writer of books about pop music, not this eloquent tiger sitting opposite him. And Esther Lejeune was a bookworm and avid googler who may have been able to find a lot in archives but other than that she was a nerd who belonged at a desk. Not this hard-bitten yet sparkling personality who had dumbfounded all his colleagues so that he had to do all the talking.

Okay, so he was faced with two international reporters who had apparently been researching the firm's ins and outs for months. The company he represented, the company that always paid its bills on time, the company that called his expensive office for every little thing, the company that had never had any criticism of what he had done for them and certainly had never complained about the generous number of hours they had billed.

This wasn't going well. In the end this would reflect negatively on his clients and seriously damage his firm.

"Mr. Jameson, Ms. Lejeune, I understand your confusion about the company's structure and that the stockholders would like to remain anonymous. And I can understand that you have questions about the events surrounding Steve Demood's death. We all regret it very much but I'm convinced TMC played absolutely no part in it. We're as saddened by his death as his fans and his loved ones. TMC represents the interests of its artists completely and unconditionally, and if any questions arise, they will be answered in detail. But we will answer to the artists, since their finances are confidential."

"Finally the right answer," said Jens. "That is the kind of 'no comment' that satisfies us."

Wensworth was taken aback again.

Oh man, you're such an easy target, Jens thought. *You're pretty useless to TMC.*

Jens and Esther began to gather their papers and put them in their briefcases.

"But…"

"Surely you didn't expect us to discuss this with you," said Jens. "We only wanted to ensure that you were heard, and evidently this is the best you have to offer."

"Nevertheless, you will be sued if…"

"If what? We have tried to present our story to the accused party but they refuse to come forward; instead they send a whole law firm after us, threatening us with lawsuits."

Jens and Esther glanced triumphantly at each other and got up. The lawyers with Wensworth, holding their big files, did the same.

23.

Winkler turned the pages calmly. He was reading excruciatingly slowly, taking occasional notes. No less than seventeen sheets of printer paper
lay before him, the text neatly double-spaced, written in coherent Dutch.
Or rather, neatly translated by Esther into coherent Dutch. A story in
three episodes. A series about TMC, Brad Brittain and Steve Demood.
Esther sat restlessly on the chair in front of Winkler's desk. Jens was
reading the Herald Tribune he had purchased at the bookstore, but to his
frustration it contained mainly European news. He was glad the story
about Demood was finally getting published; he was homesick for New
York. He was itching to continue with his book about Brigitte, to be in
his apartment for a few days, to catch up with his friends, to visit with his
daughter and to leave the hectic search behind him.

A lot had happened during the past weeks, all of it perfectly docu-
mented in the story Winkler was reading. Jens's boss at The Times had
already approved the story; a good fee had been arranged and he would
also make sure other European newspapers and magazines would buy
the rights. Eighty percent for Jens and Esther. Winkler also had to pay
quite a price for the story. Because apart from the series of stories there
was also an article that could be front-page news in any paper.

TMC's lawyers were able to bill quite a few hours, because they got the
story yesterday as well. But their payment wasn't a sure thing. TMC had
issued a press release this morning. The CEO of TMC was requesting a
suspension of payments. The problem was that several artists, Brad Brittain among them, had called TMC to account and demanded their money. A lawyer representing Brittain, Demood's widow and thirteen other
artists had had TMC's accounts in the Netherlands frozen, as well as all

its subsidiaries. Brad had just finished his European tour but for three other artists the rest of their world tour was up in the air.

So the story had to be published today. At The New York Times the presses were already running. Winkler would put it in the evening paper. That is, if they could agree on the price. When he finally turned the last page, he gazed at Esther with a certain melancholy. He raised his arms and gave her a small applause.

"A top story. I told Fred he would be amazed when you delivered it. Look at him sitting there," he said scornfully, while he pointed at Fast Forward, who had also received the story but hadn't been invited to the fishbowl.

"By gosh, I'd like to kiss you but of course that union woman wouldn't let me. And the fellow sitting next to you probably wouldn't either."

"Come on, Frederick, let's keep it professional. Are you going to pay us the honorarium we requested or do we have to take it to another paper?"

"It's a lot of money. Can't you give me a discount? Since I gave you such a generous exit payment?"

"You're already getting a discount. If you had to buy it through The New York Times, it would cost you more. Especially if you also want first dibs."

"Very well." He waved at Voorwaarts, who got up and sped to the fishbowl in his familiar trot.

"Page one and opening second section? The language has to be edited here and there but content-wise it's good."

"Hello Fred."

"Hello Esther." With that he was gone.

"Fred won't be with the paper much longer. He's a candidate for early retirement and although he doesn't really want to, he's going to have to bite the bullet."

"Poor thing," said Esther sarcastically.

"I can understand that you have little sympathy for the man but he was competent. A sexist and a bit of a dork but that's why he fit well in my team."

He laughed at his own joke, though his heart wasn't in it.

The series opened with the description of the graveyard in Little Horwood, where the remains of Demood were exhumed under supervision of Inspector Preston. Demood was transferred to the forensic lab. A thorough autopsy proved that suicide was not the cause of death. The initial blood tests had been routine—the only thing they were looking for was alcohol. The police had added the sedatives themselves, because they found them at the scene. There had been no tests for anything else. Now it seemed Steve's blood contained the date rape drug GHB. They also discovered how he ingested it. Extensive research showed trace amounts of the tea Demood had drunk that afternoon. The thermos had been rinsed and stood on the workbench in the garage. A new and more elaborate canvas had been carried out, and a farmer remembered a blue Ford Cortina parked out front for quite a while. The same Ford Cortina had been spotted by another watchful Little Horwood citizen at a crossing near Buckingham. She had seen an Asian man and a blond woman inside. In short, all the pieces came together. An indictment against a large corporation, a staged suicide, a deferred payment and roughly fifteen famous and lesser known artists who could forget about ever seeing their money. Now that was news. The background story gave quite a few juicy details, varying from secret informants who exposed the complicated structure of the international companies, to speculations about who was behind these dubious transactions.

But for all the research into the tax havens and international routes the money had taken, so far the whereabouts of the people behind WLM Ltd., which owned TMC-Holding, hadn't been determined. Scotland Yard was looking into it because murder should trump bank privacy even in the most obscure countries.

Jens and Esther went downtown after leaving the newspaper. Brad had called Esther four times. He had even called Jens. He had left a message on Esther's voicemail:

"You're not talking to me anymore? Are you done with Brad Brittain? Am I being dumped? You no longer need me?"

Esther called him back while they were still in the car. Several television stations and other newspapers had called them, requesting an interview. Esther had met them all at a café near her apartment, one at a time. She really just wanted to sleep.

"Hello Brad," she cried when he picked up. "Are you doing okay?"

"Since you came into my life, I'm not so sure, Esther."

"Why, what do you mean?"

"I'm in love, I've been rejected, and now I'm also destitute."

"But you're still healthy, right?"

"I suppose. I have enough food 'til the end of the week. I thought maybe I could crash with you for a few days."

"You're exaggerating, Brad. You have enough to survive."

Two days later they had Martha on the phone. She had been busy answering all the phone calls and emails she had received since the story had made the front page of The New York Times and since the British media had also published the revelations. The media had then sought out Brad and Martha to add their reactions to the story. Martha was happy. She spoke of "we" when she talked about the victory, and she wasn't referring to Esther or Jens.

"We deserve this. We may not see a penny of our honest earnings but at least I'm certain those murderers won't enjoy it either."

"When are we continuing with the story?" asked Esther when she ended the call with Martha.

"What do you mean?"

"Well, we still don't know who killed Steve or who ordered the murder."

"No, but we triggered an international police investigation. There's no way the two of us would get more than Scotland Yard and a horde of Interpol detectives would with all their leverage. We just have to wait and see."

"So are we finished?"

"I still have a whole book to go. Because of this story I haven't made much progress on Brigitte Friends and her past."

"You sound as if you resent it."

"No, of course not."

"We made good money with the story. Don't we deserve a vacation?"

"I'm behind schedule."

"I could help you catch up."

"Maybe," said Jens absentmindedly.

"You don't sound too enthusiastic."

"No, I am, Esther. Let's figure out how we're going to do this."

Esther was quite for a moment. She stared out the window sadly while they drove through town at a lazy pace, searching for a parking spot. She had pictured this milestone differently. They hadn't really solved anything. The owners of TMC and WLM were unknown. The killers had disappeared without a trace. Those who had put out the contract remained untouched. And where Steve, Brad, and the others' money had gone remained a mystery. Esther wasn't sure she could leave this alone.

PART 2

24.

Brigitte was thrilled that Jens was visiting her in Miami. A uniformed driver stood at the airport exit, holding a sign. He took Jens's bag, led the way to a stretch limo and held the door open. Brigitte embraced him so clumsily that he fell to his knees on the car floor. On the way home she talked his ears off. She always talked too much when she was nervous, she said. She showed him all the rooms of the house, a beautiful mansion on North Bay Road. This is where she lived when she was sick of New York. The small palace counted eight bedrooms, as many bathrooms and a living room where she could easily fit a hundred-person party. It had beautiful views, indoor and outdoor pools, and a boathouse with a large speedboat.

The other rooms were those of the maid (*my only employee*), the billiard room (*I've never touched a cue*), her home theater (*I love old classics*), her office with an impressive desk and a bookcase full of neatly arranged books (*I have yet to read most of them*). The basement housed a small recording studio (*this is where I spend most of my time, writing songs and stuff like that*).

Everything was white. The furniture, the walls, the rugs—even accessories such as vases, ashtrays and lamps. It was so sleek and modern that Jens felt uneasy putting his black backpack down anywhere. Brigitte was also dressed all in white. Wide harem pants, a wide blouse and white Nikes.

She insisted on taking the boat to give Jens a tour of the famous North Bay Road residents and those of Star Island. Her house was modest compared to those of J.Lo, Springsteen or Beyoncé. Why would you have twenty guest bedrooms if you don't require more than six? Evidently Brigitte had planned her "little tour" carefully, because the behemoth had to be manned by a crew of two. Brigitte apologized: *The boat came with the house—I thought you might enjoy it.* To be honest, she didn't really care much for the water, she said when she noticed Jens didn't either. She had put the boat up for sale.

Brigitte imagined Jens would be handy with the barbecue, and once he finally managed to get an even fire going, she appeared with a plate stacked with meat, enough to feed an average family for a week. *I didn't know what you like*, she explained. The maid brought a big silver-plated bowl of ice and a few bottles of expensive French white wine and a bottle of Bollinger. The little singer had really outdone herself for her guest.

She raised her glass as the first sirloin hit the grill.

"It's great to have you visit me, Jens. I don't really have many friends here. I'm always bored to death in Miami."

"That's unusual. Normally money and fame are a magnet for friends. More friends than you can handle."

"Yes, but I'm picky. I hardly ever go to parties, and if I give a party myself, I invite the guests myself. People I know and like. Everyone else around here has a party organizer who asks you who you'd like to see. So you choose. Doesn't matter whether you know them or not."

"Funny." Jens had read about such practices in the tabloids.

"I don't like it. I like the people in my band but they all live in New York. Every now and then they come for a week to practice but that's not always that much fun. I prefer to put them up in a hotel to having them stay here. My producer is in L.A. He's nice but he never comes here. And there's Onkel Gerard, of course, but he's always busy. He's not that much fun."

There was a momentary silence at the mention of his name. It brought them both out of the cozy and relaxed mood and threw them back into reality.

Jens kicked off his shoes and asked if he could take off his shirt. After being in the chilly Netherlands and an only slightly warmer New York, he wasn't adjusted yet to Florida's tropical temperatures. She looked closely at his upper body. His upper arms weren't big—he was pale with a small tuft of hair on his chest and a bit of a belly. Suddenly Brigitte saw the scars on his side and they shocked her. The stitches hadn't been removed yet, so they were quite gruesome. She got closer and studied the wounds carefully.

155

"I never asked you directly. Do you think Onkel Gerard had anything to do with the assault in Hamburg?"

"No. Although he won't be too happy with the shit I dug up."

"Is it important for the story?"

"I don't know. The mood in that place, what Gerard did to your co-workers, to Weintraub—it wouldn't feel right if I left that out or if I distorted the facts."

"He told me he wouldn't allow you to vilify him."

"He doesn't have a say in the matter."

"I've thought about it, Jens. I'm sticking to the contract."

"I'm glad. I'll handle it with care. At least if I don't discover any more shit. Or if I find out he still does the same stuff."

"He wouldn't, would he?"

"I should tell you something. I'm on my way to Barbados."

"Yes, you told me. It's a pleasure trip."

Ben had invited Jens to have some port wine with him. He lived in a three-room luxury apartment in a building that stood perpendicular to the coastline. He had a view of the village, the sea and hundreds of square acres of dunes. Ben's home was like a museum. The walls were hung with priceless paintings by Dutch masters, a Rembrandt etch and a few lithographs. The furniture was a medley of styles and periods. An ugly sofa from the fifties stood next to an expensive desk from the nineteenth century. The carpet smelled stuffy, the windows were dull from the sea wind, which also provided a whistling sound.

Ben had put out two glasses and a bottle of old port that was already a quarter empty. "My dear man, I gave myself a head start. I need it, because today I'm going to do something that is completely against my principles." He spoke in his distinguished, deliberate, beautiful high-society English accent. "I'm going to help you, my dear Mr. Jameson, in a way that goes against every Dutch banker's code. But this is how I see it…"

He sat down and stood again. He was noticeably uncomfortable with his decision. Jens remained quiet.

"During the past couple of weeks I have come to see you as my friend and when a friend is in need, one must help. You're a friend in need, Mr. Jameson, because certain individuals are out to kill you. That is why I did some research. I still had a few favors I could cash in."

Jens's heart was racing. He sipped his port and waited tensely for Ben to continue.

"Mr. Dijkgraaf did indeed receive two large sums of money. Approximately six months ago he received sixty thousand euro and three weeks ago he received twenty-five thousand euro, right after your arrival in the Netherlands. Unfortunately the money came from an account at the Barbados National Bank in Bridgetown. It's a tax haven in the Caribbean so they will probably handle bank privacy better than yours truly."

Ben sat down and sighed. He seemed defeated and stared out beyond the dull windows to the sea and the dunes.

"Ben, I thank you from the bottom of my heart. My research was going nowhere and I wasn't feeling at all safe after the attempt on my life. Now I have a clue and I can carry on the search." Jens stood and shook his hand.

"Surely you're not leaving yet?" Ben was confused.

"No." Jens still held the old man's hand between his two. "But I want to thank you. It takes courage to do what you did."

"We'll drink to that. And that you do the right thing with the information. Look, I wrote everything on this piece of paper. The name and the bank account. The amounts are in dollars but at today's exchange rate they come out to the rounded amounts in euros that I mentioned."

They had continued to sip the old port for hours. Then Ben opened an expensive bottle of red wine. He had received it twenty years ago at the annual meeting of a multinational where he had stock. The wine had matured well, as had the stock.

The next encounter was with Dijkgraaf, because Jens soon realized it would be hopeless to try to find the person behind the bank account. The company behind the account was Stonewater Enterprises. According to the Chamber of Commerce in Bridgetown its mission was so general it was probably a front. The CEO worked for an accounting firm and was possibly CEO of another three hundred companies.

Jens was amazed how a simple biographer of pop musicians such as himself had ended up in the complicated world of tax havens. These practices were perfectly legal. But it did mean that the more money you had, the lower your taxes were. You could hire first-rate advisors who would make sure you paid little or no taxes. This was true for both rich retirees who called the many paradisiac islands of the Caribbean or the smaller European countries home, and for big corporations with tens of thousands of employees. People who all use the facilities in the countries where they live, facilities for which their company should be paying taxes. The employees themselves do pay taxes. In all, they pay many times more than the company does.

Dijkgraaf was quite taken aback when Jens rang his doorbell. Over his shoulder Jens could see the remodeling in full swing. He was looking straight at a gleaming designer kitchen and a beautiful, newly sanded parquet floor.

Dijkgraaf didn't invite Jens in. "How can I help you, Mr. Jameson?"

"I'd like to speak to you in private for a minute."

"You can make an appointment to see me at my office, through my secretary." Dijkgraaf threw him a scornful look. "Of course you must be thinking it will cost you. But I'm willing to answer a few more questions for nothing, if that's necessary."

"I don't think you will want to answer these questions in your office. They're rather personal."

"Ah." Dijkgraaf was losing confidence.

"I get the impression you have seriously thwarted my research into Brigitte Friends's past. You purposely omitted a few matters you knew about from your report."

Dijkgraaf was palpably alarmed.

"That's quite a statement, Mr. Jameson. What makes you think so?"

"I have my sources. Good sources."

"I have no idea what you're talking about, Mr. Jameson. This conversation is over."

"That's fine, Mr. Dijkgraaf. I will be discussing it with your boss." He bluffed by turning around and walking away.

"Wait a moment, Mr. Jameson."

Dijkgraaf slammed the door. Ten seconds later he came outside with a dog on a leash. Jens asked what breed it was, to ease the tension. Dijkgraaf growled that it was a mutt.

They walked to the end of the street and turned a corner onto a lane with big front lawns and large houses where people were visible through large windows eating at their dinner tables.

When they had been walking in silence for about five minutes, Jens began, "Mr. Dijkgraaf, I realize you can't speak freely. Perhaps you haven't heard that there was an attempt on my life while I was working on this research."

Again Dijkgraaf was taken aback. He swore in English under his breath, though still loud enough that it would be bleeped in a movie or television broadcast. The f-word sounded strange coming from this respectable man who looked more like a civil servant than a detective.

"I already know Peter Kruger, whom you had left out of your report, but I would like you to give me another name."

Dijkgraaf slowed down and said firmly, "Kruger is the only name I know."

Jens smiled in satisfaction, careful not to show that he had been bluffing about Kruger.

"And you had contact with Gerard Schöteldreier."

"Yes, but that was in reference to something else."

"Tell me."

"That man threatened me."

"And Kruger paid you."

"Paid me?"

"Yes, he paid you."

"I don't know what you're talking about."

"Two amounts, Mr. Dijkgraaf. One six months ago when you finished your so-called investigation and one recently, when you put certain people on my trail."

"I don't know what you're talking about," repeated Dijkgraaf, but with much less conviction.

The men stood still and Dijkgraaf took on an aggressive posture. The dog only looked confused and wagged his tail, thinking something was expected of him. Shake or fetch, maybe.

"I don't mind mentioning the exact amounts, if you'd like."

"Which amounts?" Dijkgraaf looked at him in disbelief.

"For that twenty-five thousand euro you're probably an accomplice to attempted murder, Mr. Dijkgraaf. And for that sixty thousand euro you thwarted Brigitte Friends's assignment. That will directly or indirectly damage your firm."

"But how..." Dijkgraaf clearly wanted to ask Jens how he had gotten that information. He changed the sentence awkwardly. "How did you get that idea?"

"I can't imagine you carried out an assignment for Stonewater Offshore in Barbados in your spare time. I could ask your boss if that is customary."

Jan Dijkgraaf resumed his walk. He pulled up his shoulders and thought. Jens gave him another little verbal push.

"I'm not interested in your moonlighting activities, Mr. Dijkgraaf."

"I have to think about this." Dijkgraaf stepped up his pace.

"I can imagine. But if you tell Mr. Kruger about our conversation, you'll be sorry. I'm sure you understand that I have taken precautions. This conversation is taped and along with other evidence it will be on a desk at The New York Times. I'm willing to protect you as my source but only if you help me along with my investigation."

"Yes, yes, I understand." Dijkgraaf walked so fast that Jens had to trot to keep up with him.

"I'll be at pavilion Take Five at the beach at noon tomorrow. I'll expect you there on time and alone," Jens called after him.

"I should tell you something," he had said to Brigitte while the first slab of meat was turning black. "I'm on my way to Barbados." And Brigitte had teased him with the number of pleasure trips involved in the project. She had looked at him sweetly.

"I don't know, Jens. Sometimes I feel I should ask you to stop the investigation of my father."

Jens flipped the black piece of meat onto a plate and cut it in half. "It's a bit late for that, don't you think?"

"I have this premonition. I sometimes dream that you're killed."

"That's not so strange. And it's more of a post-monition."

"I get you. But what if it was a warning. I mean, they can't say it out loud or pin a note to your body. You have to see it yourself. Stop your investigation or we will really kill you."

"We examined it from every angle and a warning does seem the most likely."

"So you should stop. Let my father go to hell. You're my friend. I can't let anything happen to you."

"That's sweet of you, Brigitte, but I was born lucky, so nothing will happen to me."

"You're a bluffer, Jens." She sat down beside Jens on the large white couch on the enormous patio with her plate in her lap. "And you can't grill to save your life. Jesus, just let me do it. It's all burnt."

"Aren't you curious about what I have to tell you?"

"I'm scared, honey. I'm getting really scared." She sounded so sincere. For a moment Jens debated keeping quiet about what he had found out over the past two weeks. But that was no longer an option.

"I need to discuss it with you, Brigitte. It's pretty big stuff."

"Okay, my curiosity wins."

Jens shrugged at her cynicism and told her about the false results of Dijkgraaf's investigation and about the cover-ups. That Dijkgraaf was paid to omit any details that could lead to identifying her father.

Brigitte was unimpressed that she was ripped off to the tune of thirty-five thousand dollars, which Jens couldn't fathom. About Ben's move she said:

"Oh, that poor man, what a sacrifice. So good of him to do that for you."

She had gotten a bit drunk. Jens remembered the first evening they went out to dinner, so he was paying attention. "You still know exactly what you see, say and think, Brigitte Vermeer," he said. "Tonight I'm really not going to undress you."

She leaned lightly against him. "But Jens, we can be friends, can't we?"

"Of course."

"And friends can keep each other company if they're lonely, can't they?"

Jens got up to try again with a few simple hamburgers. The fire had slowed down; the flames had retreated to a red glow in the charcoal briquettes. The sun had gone down and the mosquitoes were on the prowl.

25.

The green, hilly island of Barbados slid away under the wing of the American Airlines jet, which had started its descent fifteen minutes earlier. The flight attendants were collecting the headphones and Jens gave up his plastic glass. A flight attendant with whom he got along well had kept it filled with whiskey the entire trip.

He claimed the whiskey was necessary to keep the circulation going in his calves, since legroom wasn't a major priority for the average airline company.

Jens had never been to Barbados. The only time he went to the Caribbean was twelve years ago. He and Tereza had still been together and Barbora was only two. They had gone in the middle of winter and he had always remembered the constant tropical temperature and the lovely sea breeze. Unfortunately, Caribbean vacations had become financially impossible. So he had decided to make the most of this business trip.

This time Brigitte had taken him to his bedroom. He had declined her offer to undress him. Jens had no romantic intentions with her. He had kept his distance the entire evening, saying he needed it in order to write a good book about her, and how complicated it would be if they got involved. He thought it better to leave his affair with Esther out of it for now. But Brigitte did ask. She asked what Esther looked like and how they were professionally connected. She devoured the story about Steve Demood and Brad Brittain. When Jens asked her if she was sure her money was safe with Onkel Gerard, she said she would bet her life on it.

The next day they had had another interview session, lasting almost six hours. Then they had dinner at Nobu, a high-end Japanese restaurant at the Shore Club. They had a table in the back, hidden from the rest of Miami's jet set by white veils. They let the chef surprise them and Brigitte and the waiter were entirely of the same mind when it came to the wine choices. When they were presented with the bill, Jens wanted to take it but Brigitte had already put her black American Express card on the platter. She claimed it was her turn.

Jens blanched when he saw the amount at the bottom of the bill. He had just raised his limit recently, otherwise he wouldn't even have been able to pay this. His financial situation wasn't bad. He still had most of the advance and together with Esther he had made decent money with the TMC story. Still, if it were up to him, he wouldn't have splurged like this. He told Brigitte he had never had such an expensive meal in his life.

"Neither have I. All the expensive wine adds up," Brigitte had replied.

Barbados brought Jens back down to the world of the not so rich and famous. He didn't want to spend thirty dollars on a cab from Barbados International Airport to downtown Bridgetown, so he took a bus, and from there he took a second bus to Holetown. That cost him three Barbados dollars, or $1.50.

The rickety bus drove past expansive sugarcane fields. More people got on as it got further from the airport, and it gradually filled up. The population of Barbados is mainly black, their ancestors having been potential slaves who ended up on the island on their way to the United States. Most of the whites are British descendants, who exploited the island for three hundred years as a colony.

Officially Barbados is still part of the British Commonwealth, with Queen Elizabeth II as its head of state, but since their independence in 1966, most Bajans are done with British rule.

Jens noticed right away that the Bajans were incredibly friendly. Everyone greeted one another and asked how they were doing. He was the only white person on the squeaky bus, so they all wanted to know where he was from and where he was headed.

An intoxicated blind man briefly dominated the mood by cursing everything and everyone in practically incomprehensible English, but he did get a laugh when he loudly intoned the Lord's Prayer.

The road to Holetown was lined with hundreds of small wooden houses, painted in bright Caribbean colors. The traditional building structure consists of three small houses with steep gables, connected along one side, thus forming a three-room house. In the poorer areas the faded blue, red and yellow paint was peeling off the houses and unemployed Bajans sat staring at the traffic.

A Rastafarian seated next to Jens told him the entire history and demography of the island. He talked non-stop and pointed out a monument erected for the victims of the plane crash of 1976, when terrorists blew up a Cuban plane. Motioning broadly, he described the way pieces of the plane, chairs and dead bodies had been spread out over the sea and beaches. Next he talked about his seven children and fourteen grandchildren, and about his high-quality genes—one of his sons was the top DJ of the island and another played for the national soccer team. At some point the houses abruptly disappeared behind tall fences and hedges. The Rastafarian, Iowa, told him that was where the rich lived. They passed by Sandy Lane Hotel, where stars like Mick Jagger, Victoria and David Beckham and Hugh Grant had stayed.

Jens felt like he was in a surreal movie. First he had been on a tour of the rich and famous in Miami, and now, more than a thousand miles further south, he was experiencing something similar. Iowa got off before he did. He gave him his phone number. He told him he was a cab driver but that he had lost his license. He was willing to drive him around for thirty Bajan dollars a day and the price of gas.

Jens had made reservations in the All Season Europe Resort, a modestly priced place with forty-eight cabins, each with refrigerator and stove, so he wasn't dependent on the restaurant.

However, the first evening he did go there and ordered a meal. Flying fish salad as an appetizer and Mahi Mahi as the main dish. That was dolphin. "No Flipper, though," said the friendly waiter. This particular dolphin was no more than two and a half feet long and didn't resemble the darling of the sea at all. Jens enjoyed the wonderful tropical temperature, the strong cheap wine and the fresh catch of the day.

He had been looking forward to his return to New York but it was a disappointment. Coming from sunny Amsterdam he landed at a rainy JFK and the rain continued for the next five days. The refrigerator in his apartment had turned into a science project with beautiful molds and other living organisms. Cleaning it all up had taken hours. His friends hadn't changed. Some of them hadn't even read his stories in The Times or they didn't realize he was one of the two people who uncovered the whole thing. He had gone to the hospital for a follow-up appointment. It had been crowded and the medical staff was rushed and unfriendly. A week later he had fled the Big Apple.

He flew to St. Augustine and stayed with Tereza, trying to do some father-daughter bonding with Barbora. She was only interested in his exciting stories about Europe and his encounters with Brad Brittain and Brigitte Friends and the presents he had brought her. His inquiries about her school, her boyfriend and her ideas on college remained unanswered. It had been a tiring two days. Tereza had bugged him about the regular stuff: the roof was leaking again, Barbora needed money for the school trip to the Rocky Mountains and a few other things she couldn't pay for out of her monthly child support.

Tereza lost her job as a realtor when the housing market crashed and her attempts to start her own business had failed. In short, nothing but doom and gloom. The days with Brigitte were a lot sunnier. It had been hard work. They needed to fill the gaps in the information from the Netherlands and Hamburg and he also wanted to include her personal impressions in those chapters.

Brigitte had three qualities that made her special, aside from her musical talent. She was humble and didn't have a diva attitude. She didn't flaunt her name and fame, she didn't have excessive houses or if she did, she was too embarrassed to brag about them.

She was also sweet. Not the fake type of sweetness some women apply when they want to be liked; she was innocent, empathetic, warm, and extremely friendly.

Finally, she had a keen business sense, which made her get exactly what she wanted. One might call it peasant cunning; it wasn't sly or polished. She already had that cunning when she had to negotiate things she was or wasn't going to take from her mother and later from Onkel Gerard in her Hamburg period, when she absolutely refused to serve topless in Das Schwere Hertz. Even when she had played Jens with her trust and the strange contract they had both signed—on the one hand it gave him tremendous freedom; on the other hand she also had him on a leash. After all, he had promised not to publish anything she didn't want him to.

Jens sort of fell for Brigitte. She made him feel like he wanted to protect her, like a real man. He was her guide in a world full of threats.

And she was deliciously American, very different from Esther. Esther's Dutch common sense was quite a culture shock. On the other hand the intellectual challenge Esther provided was on a completely different level than the talks he had with Brigitte.

During dinner, the owner of the All Season Europe Resort came to introduce her husband and daughter. Jens had noticed that the women in Barbados were either very fat and short or very tall and thin. The owner stood over six feet and she was slim. Her husband wore an impressive uniform with a row of medals on the left side of his chest. Jens was too polite to see if he had stars or stripes on his shoulders. He also couldn't quite read the text on the man's upper sleeve. He guessed he was a general in the Bajan army. It turned out he was the leader of the island's Christian Boy Scouts.

Like the owner, the general, their daughter, the cook, and the waiter, all the visitors in the resort were unbelievably relaxed. Jens, however, wasn't relaxed at all. He had made a lot of progress but the real work still lay ahead of him. He didn't even really like fieldwork, especially when he had to use improper methods.

26.

The plan was simple, maybe too simple. It was a sunny day and most of the English tourists were already poolside. Jens had donned khakis, even though it was almost thirty degrees. He had his laptop and recorder in his bag. He had called Iowa and hired him for the day. At seven the cheerful Rastafarian was waiting in the hotel parking lot with a small Toyota station car. He explained that he wasn't a morning person. He used to work the night shift with his cab, so he decided to stay up the night before, afraid he might miss his appointment with Jens.

Dijkgraaf had been at the Take Five beach pavilion promptly at noon. He was terribly nervous and had been looking around as if he were being followed by several spies or assassins. Jens was also tense. He didn't want to walk into a trap again.

Dijkgraaf told him Dora had called several times. He had given Jens the transcription of the first call. The next conversations had indeed been short and Dijkgraaf suggested that she had only brushed him off. What he hadn't told Jens was that Dora had demanded Dijkgraaf's cell phone number and said someone would be in touch and that he should never bother her again. Two weeks later he got a call and was instructed to go to the upscale hotel L'Europe in Amsterdam and ask for Mr. Kruger at the desk.

Kruger had met with Dijkgraaf in his suite. The man had a sob story about Dora. That he was her friend and needed to protect her. He didn't know who Brigitte's father was and he sympathized with her attempts to find out, but it would be impossible without Dora's help and she had sworn to take the secret to the grave. So there was no point continuing the investigation.

Naturally Kruger recognized that this would hurt Dijkgraaf's reputation as a competent investigator, but could he also make sure his own name stayed out of the report? Dijkgraaf would be paid for this. He had immediately refused. The whole idea insulted him. He had gotten up and threatened to leave.

When Kruger had mentioned an amount of thirty thousand euro, Dijkgraaf had sat back down, flabbergasted, although he was against receiving bribes. Kruger told him to consider it a freelance assignment for a foreign company. Dijkgraaf could send a bill and even pay regular taxes on the income. Dijkgraaf had said that half would then go to the treasury, and Kruger responded without blinking by doubling his fee. Dijkgraaf felt he had no choice.

The assignment wasn't much. Dijkgraaf had to find out what was public knowledge about Dora Vermeer and Peter Kruger's past. He had been able to simply copy it from the existing report, but since it would be a conflict of interest, he had accepted the assignment in private, not as an FMI employee.

Kruger had given him an address in Barbados, the address of a large international accounting firm in the capital city Bridgetown. He had also received the phone number of a contact, in case Brigitte asked for a follow-up of the investigation. Dijkgraaf had called that number when Jens called him from America to make an appointment. He had found out Jens was a writer of integrity who had a reputation as a thorough investigator. He doubted this man could be bribed.

Over coffee at the beach he asked if he was right about that.

"Whether or not you can bribe me? Is that what you're asking?"

"Heavens, no," cried Dijkgraaf with a start. "I just mean…"

"You should be careful what you say, Mr. Dijkgraaf," Jens said angrily.

That it had been so easy to find an address to go with the phone number was probably just plain luck. Jens had googled the Barbados white pages and typed in the number. Then he had looked up the matching address. He chose the hotel based on its proximity to the address. The All Season Europe Resort was located in Sunset Crest, a relatively secure neighborhood with vacation cottages and permanent residents. According to the white pages, the contact for the development was Jennifer. No last name, just Jennifer.

For the past few days Jens had staked out the address, a wooden bungalow. During the weekend a small green American mid-class car was parked out front. Jens had walked by about twenty times, hoping to see someone in the yard, maybe Jennifer herself. On Monday morning he had donned his running clothes and ran around the neighborhood. At seven the car was suddenly gone and late in the afternoon it was back. If the car belonged to Jennifer, maybe she would go to work at the same time tomorrow.

He directed Iowa to Jennifer's street and instructed him to wait. The car had no air-conditioning so all the windows were open. Iowa wanted Jens to hear his entire collection of reggae music but Jens wanted absolute silence. Iowa's enormous flood of words was also impossible to curb. During their fifteen-minute wait, he had talked as much as a normal person would in an hour.

"We're going to follow that woman," said Iowa, as the bright green car drove onto the street. "We'll follow that woman to where she's going. And we'll continue watching that woman like we're two detectives of the worst law enforcement in the world: the Barbados police."

Iowa would have liked to tailgate Jennifer in his old clunker, but Jens told him repeatedly to keep his distance.

"This is dangerous. Is this illegal? Are we going to get in trouble with the police? Oh man, I'm still on probation—I don't want to do anything illegal."

"You're just driving behind a car, man. Relax. You're not doing anything illegal."

"Good, because I'm not about to do anything illegal. I have seven children and fifteen grandchildren."

"Yesterday you had fourteen grandchildren."

"Yes, they just keep coming. Another little boy was born, and again they didn't name him after me."

"Who would call a child Iowa?"

"That's my nickname, son of James. My real name is Marcus Winston but none of my children want to name their children Winston or Marcus. Children are so stubborn. It makes me wonder: Do they even love their father?"

169

Jennifer drove toward Bridgetown. It became harder to keep up with her in the chaotic morning rush hour. Cars, buses and motorbikes threw themselves left and right across the two-lane road. Iowa had turned up the music so loud that the speaker cones almost burst from their frames. The car was all over the road, barely missing the curbs on each side, and he honked every ten seconds to make other drivers get out of the way.

Jennifer was headed for St. Michael, where Stonewater's accounting offices were located. She parked in a quiet street and Jens jumped from the car to follow her on foot. Iowa also wanted to get out but Jens told him to stay put.

Jennifer was dark-skinned. She wore a light suit and carried a large shoulder purse that seemed to be a mix between a briefcase and a lady's purse. She had a fine figure and walked gracefully ahead of him in high heels. It wasn't a busy street, so Jens kept his distance.

Suddenly she disappeared. Jens continued cautiously and passed a few store windows. A fashion store, a coffee shop and a realtor. He peered in the windows and saw Jennifer in the realtor's office. She was bent over a computer, which she had apparently just turned on. Jens examined the photos of a few mansions and estates in the window and a model of several large houses surrounding a golf course. "Green Monkey Holes" said the sign above it in shiny green letters. Next to it was a neat logo with a cute little monkey whose three-foot long tail formed the name of the development. The same breed of monkey that came by his hotel each morning with its family. The green monkeys had come along with the slaves centuries ago and formed large colonies on the island.

He had a clear view of Jennifer. She was a good-looking woman of around thirty, with a slim waist and substantial hips and buttocks. Two women were already sitting at their desks. Jennifer was gesturing elaborately, perhaps discussing the day's schedule with them. The girls nodded willingly and tapped on their keyboards.

When Jens returned to the car, Iowa was lying on the back seat with his feet over the back of the passenger seat.

"It was early, Son of James. Usually I sleep until four in the afternoon. I'm a night person. When I drove the cab I always had the night shift. I started..."

170

"Yeah, yeah, you're starting to repeat yourself, Son of Marcus or Winston."

Jens sat down in the driver's seat. He took out his phone and called a number in the Netherlands. He glanced at his watch. It was five hours later in the Netherlands, a decent time to call. Dijkgraaf answered and asked nervously if he could hold. It sounded like he was walking out of his office. Jens heard voices and then a door slamming.

"Yes, I'm here." Dijkgraaf sounded breathless.

"Good. We're going to do what we agreed to, Mr. Dijkgraaf. When I hang up, you wait exactly ten minutes and then you call the number you gave me. Tell the person who answers that there has been an important development. You can't say what; you have to speak with Kruger himself. That's it."

"Okay. And when Kruger calls back I tell him you've been back to my office and that you casually mentioned you had been assaulted and you suspect me of leaving out information. That you also insinuated that I had something to do with it. And that you're now after Kruger, and that I told you nothing."

"Correct."

"What if he wants to know how you got his name?"

"You tell him I got it from Telford."

"That's it?"

"That's it. I lost part of my data during the assault, so I came back to make new copies. You didn't give me anything new."

"Okay. But why..."

"No questions, Mr. Dijkgraaf. Just tell the lady there's been a new development in the case. Wait ten minutes after I hang up and then make the call."

Jens hung up and glanced at his watch, a simple Seiko that he bought for himself when he left Tereza. He had made the decision after two years of fighting and he was so happy that he wanted to buy himself something nice.

He told Iowa to wait. The dear man started talking again about his work, his spare time, being a cab driver, what it's like having a soccer player and a DJ as a son, until Jens interrupted him and walked back to the office.

Now his good trousers and shirt came in handy. He turned on his recorder before entering the office. The three ladies all looked up in surprise when their first client came in without an appointment. They were all very friendly, greeting him and asking him how he was doing.

Jens was undecided where he should sit until Jennifer gestured to a chair. He sat down and placed his briefcase on the desk. Jennifer's cell phone lay on the desk between them.

Jens got right to the point. He told her he was a realtor himself, looking for a large home on a golf course for an American client whose name he didn't want to mention.

"You came to the right place. What's your price range?"

"The price isn't that important, the details are. My client wants at least a four-bedroom-four-bath with a sizable office. A swimming pool is a must. The golf course must be well rated—my client is an avid golfer. And privacy is important. The house has to be somewhat secluded and the club should be exclusive. Closed membership is a must."

"We have several golf course homes in our portfolio but perhaps our Green Monkey Holes development is an interesting option."

"Can I see it already or is it still just a model in your window?"

"No, the model is old. The first and second phase are finished and the third is under construction. "

"What does that mean? Construction noise?"

"No, absolutely not."

She was about to continue but her phone rang. At first she wanted to dismiss the call; then she changed her mind and asked if Jens would mind if she took it. Jens nodded amiably. He got up and walked to the wall, supposedly studying a map of Green Monkey Holes. He listened closely. Jennifer said "yes" twice and "okay" once. Then she hung up. She was clearly conflicted about whether to give her new client priority or to follow up on Dijkgraaf's call. She chose the latter. Jens closed his eyes and listened carefully. He was lucky. Jennifer had a keypad that beeped. The tones betrayed the number, and the recorder registered it perfectly. He also counted only seven beeps, which meant Kruger was on the island. This conversation was also short. She said that Mr. D. had called. That he should call him back. And she ended the call with something that pleased Jens very much. *I was definitely born lucky*, he thought when Jennifer ended with "See you this afternoon."

After having asked everything about the available homes, whether his client could use his own interior designer and how the bathrooms and kitchen would be finished, he asked a few more questions about the developer's credit rating. What guarantees could she give? Who were the investors and could he get referrals from current residents?

That was a lot of questions at once. She told Jens he could check out the English company, which invested in golf resorts and exclusive hotels all over the world.

"No problem. I'm often in Europe and I have connections all over the world that will be able to help me."

"I'll provide you with all the information you need, if your client is serious."

"I will have a look myself first, perhaps with an architect or a builder."

"That should be no problem," said Jennifer.

"Then there is the matter of the commission."

"Yes." Jennifer sounded surprised.

"Of course you get a commission when you sell one of these homes. I'm the one who has to make the deal. A fee of 1.5% seems appropriate."

As Jens had expected, this was a subject she obviously had no authority over.

"Well, I don't know. I'll have to discuss it with the owner of this office."

"Ah, so it's not your own company?" Jens was being charming as possible.

Jennifer smiled proudly. "No, that would be Mr. Peter Rock."

"Well, that certainly sounds solid."

"I'm seeing him this afternoon. I could arrange a meeting with him if you want to have a look."

"That sounds like a plan." Jens was inwardly jubilant. He had just discovered that Peter Kruger probably had taken on a new name here.

He gave Jennifer his business card. Not the one with his own name. He had a card printed in the name of E. Jacobs, consultant. It was red, black and gold—designed to impress. Ever since the stabbing, an alter ego made him feel he could move around inconspicuously. E. Jacobs sounded good and harmless. That was Ellen's name, his editor at Walker. The Broadway address was her office. Only the cell phone number was correct. So in the future he would have to answer with "Hello" instead of with "Jens."

"Well, Mr. Jacobs, we will be in touch later today."

"That's wonderful. I have to say I'm looking at other options as well. I won't say it's first come, first serve but I won't be on the island for long, so there is some urgency. However, for my client, time is less important than quality."

"I understand. Most of our clients feel the same. It might interest your client that Mary Ball has a home in Green Monkey Holes, as well as the oil baron Hugh Brown, and the author Antony Hutchinson. They also wouldn't like to be bothered by just anyone."

"Well, well," said Jens, "those are interesting names. Mary Ball is of course an icon from antiquity for me, but my client is over sixty-five, so he will definitely be impressed. Hutchinson is the famous thriller writer, isn't he? I don't like his books but he may be an interesting person to meet."

"Well, I don't know him myself."

"What about Hugh Brown, how old is he? I don't know him."

"He's not yet fifty."

"Well, the younger, the better, my client would say."

Jennifer looked embarrassed.

"Perhaps we could discuss it further over a delicious dinner."

She laughed coyly. "Well, Mr. Jacobs, if you're looking for a date, this lady is taken."

"Oh, I didn't have anything dishonorable in mind, Ms. . . ." Jens glanced at the card she had given him. "Eduardo. You were born on the island?"

"I guess I could have a drink with you. Where are you staying?"

"I rented a house somewhere. What would you say to Sandy Lane? That's in my vicinity. Seven o'clock?"

"No, not today or tomorrow."

"The day after tomorrow then."

Jennifer hesitated. "Well, maybe the day after tomorrow for lunch. I could tell you a lot about our island."

"And about Green Monkey Caves," Jens teased.

"Holes," said Jennifer.

"Hole in one. I will see you the day after tomorrow at the Sandy Lane around one o'clock," said Jens cheerfully.

He walked out and could barely contain his sense of victory. He was five thousand miles from home and came here without much of a plan. He had one phone number and he had needed a lot of luck.

Count your blessings, thought Jens. *Don't think you're invincible. You're a reporter, not a detective. Claim your right as an investigative journalist to freedom of information. Establish who you are. Don't hide behind a fake business card.*

A second personality seemed to be talking to him. An angel on his shoulder, like in fairy tales. A Dr. Jekyll and a Mr. Hyde. Where was this coming from? This wasn't like him. He had been a quiet, nerdy teenager who never made waves. He had married young and written books about safe subjects. During the pop concerts he had to review he had always been friendly to everyone. The research he had done for his book about Jenna Long was probably the most far-reaching he had ever done. He had suffered for three months in a shabby hut. But he had been scared to enter the slums without a guide. He had experienced it all from a safe distance and from behind the broad shoulders of Jenna's protectors and bodyguards. What made him go this far now? Pretending to be someone else, going out for drinks with who may be Kruger's lover? Following people with a crazy Rastafarian who could betray him any moment? He didn't know. He had no idea what possessed him.

Back at the parking spot where Iowa was waiting, all those thoughts resulted in a panic attack. He was sweating like a pig; he was dizzy and could scarcely breathe. Iowa came toward him and saw how pale Jens was.

"Hey man, you don't look too hot. I won't nag you about throwing up in my car, since it's already a puke mobile, but how about some pot to calm down?"

"Sure," was the only thing Jens could utter. At that moment it seemed the solution to everything. He would throw up a drink. A cigarette wouldn't help, but maybe a joint would take the edge off.

Iowa got in and motioned to Jens to sit down but he didn't want to get in just yet. He needed fresh air and a joint but Iowa didn't want to light one up in a busy parking lot. So he had another idea for calming down.

"Hey, is that you, Jens?"

"Shit, yeah, Esther. I'm so glad to hear your voice. I'm having a panic attack."

"Oh gosh. What is it? What happened? Why are you panicking?"

"I just threw myself into the lion's den. I'm no longer sure I'm doing the right thing."

175

"Tell me."

That worked better than a joint or a bottle of liquor. He started to talk. Esther knew the background. She had heard everything about Dijkgraaf and his connections to Kruger.

Following their victory parade in the Dutch and international media, which praised their job as investigators, they had gone to Paris for a long weekend to catch their breath. It wasn't quite the romantic weekend they had expected. The cultural differences between the States and the Netherlands had unexpectedly come to the foreground. Esther preferred to go to the Louvre or the Rodin museum while Jens wanted to see the Eifel Tower or the Arc de Triomphe. When Esther wanted to have a romantic dinner in an exciting upscale restaurant, Jens preferred a simple place near the market where they served hamburgers. And because they were both willing to do what the other wanted, they spent most of their time aimlessly wandering the streets of the French capital.

Jens immediately disliked the Parisians. In his eyes they were chauvinists and unfriendly and he had nothing nice to say about their culinary skills. On the other hand Esther loved French cuisine and the culture, and she spoke the language fluently.

They usually made up for the occasional short-fused moments at night, when they discussed how to continue with the TMC story or Jens's book.

After the Paris weekend Jens had begun his search for Kruger. According to Esther's research he lived in a small castle along the Vecht River but they found it empty. The manager, a realtor working for an aged baron, had given them a tour. He wanted to prosecute Kruger because he owed tens of thousands of Euros in back rent. Esther and Jens searched for clues he may have left behind but Kruger had left the building clean. Not even a piece of paper, a knick-knack, nothing.

The realtor said Kruger had claimed to be a former member of parliament from South Africa who made his money in futures trading. Every time the realtor had come by to talk about the back rent, an expensive car had been parked out front—a Bentley or a sports car.

The first year Kruger paid his rent on time. Then the payments became irregular and eventually more than a year in back payments had accumulated. The lease was in the name of a private company that had just gone bankrupt when it was sued. Kruger disappeared after stealing and selling some expensive antique furniture.

The realtor had taken it personally first of all because he had loaned the baron money when Kruger was behind on his payments. But also because all his management bills had been unpaid and he had really believed Kruger. He offered Esther and Jens money to locate Kruger. They had immediately refused—they weren't bounty hunters.

What they did get from the tour was a photo of Kruger, so they knew what he looked like. Just a driver's license photo, but Jens thought that with the realtor's description he could recognize him. Kruger was about the same height as Jens, with balding gray hair, a sharp nose and a receding chin. He had broad shoulders and a beer belly. He usually wore impeccable custom suits and a hat. The realtor had described him as if he were describing a mugger to a police officer.

After stalking Dijkgraaf, Jens told Esther he wanted to go back to the States to take care of business. He had to visit his daughter, have some more sessions with Brigitte and take a trip to Barbados. Esther realized that she couldn't be present during the first two but she didn't understand why she couldn't come with him to the wonderfully sunny Barbados, an island paradise in the Caribbean. They had bickered about it. Did he want to continue the story by himself? He said Barbados was a long shot and he didn't want to spend the money for two.

"I told you I should have come along," said Esther, when Jens was finished. "I'm going to book right now. I have to take care of some loose ends here. I also have a few ideas about how to continue with the TMC story. What's the weather like there? Can you pick me up?"

"Sure," said Jens meekly. "Give me a call before take-off."

Jennifer didn't leave her office until the afternoon. She walked to her car. Jens was in the backseat of Iowa's car and slumped down when the woman passed by. Iowa woke with a jolt when Jens punched him.

"I assume we're following that woman again? Yah man, but nothing illegal, okay?" said Iowa and began anew about his probation. It had to do with a bank robbery that a few men he'd never met had carried out and for whom he had allegedly driven the getaway car. According to Iowa the robbers stopped him in the street because their real getaway car wouldn't start. So he took the three gentlemen in their ski masks like he would any other fare.

Jennifer turned north toward Holetown. She drove quite fast and since Jens didn't want to be noticed, they almost lost her. Then she slowed down and turned into a fenced neighborhood with a sign saying Green Monkey Holes. They gazed at a hotel, mansions and beautiful rolling greens.

Iowa's old car couldn't enter. And this wasn't the moment to confront Kruger anyway. So Jens made Iowa circle the subdivision to get the lay of the land. He saw the phase that was still being developed. There were few workers on this Wednesday, and it wasn't a holiday.

27.

The crash barrier at Green Monkey Holes didn't open for the shiny cab. The guard came outside and asked the driver for his identification. He made Jens lower his window and asked him for his passport.

"I have an appointment with Mrs. Ball and I only give my passport to Customs or the police," barked Jens.

The man eyed him morosely and returned to his booth. He picked up the phone and spent at least five minutes fumbling about before he had the right person on the line. Then he ambled over, gave the driver a map and indicated where Mrs. Ball's home was.

Jens had looked on Wikipedia first, to see if he could find a reason to do a story on Mary Ball. Two months from now the Hollywood star would turn ninety. Jens wasn't even surprised anymore about the lucky coincidence. He had called the editor of the entertainment pages of his newspaper and suggested interviewing Ball so the article would be ready in two months. He read that Mrs. Ball didn't give interviews, and again he counted on luck. He called her, saying he was a fan who had come to Barbados on a whim. He also told her he had written a book about Jenna Long and that he was working on a book about Brigitte Friends. Although Mary Ball had no idea who Brigitte Friends was, she had read the book about Jenna Long. She had found it quite entertaining. She didn't want to give an interview but she would like to meet Jens. He had told her he would be able to convince her, but if not, he was honored nonetheless to meet her.

In 1936, at the age of fourteen, Ball had made her debut in the classic *Vanished Paradise*. That was followed by ninety other comi-dramas. In the seventies she had her own television show. When she was seventy-five she did Shakespeare on Broadway to prove she still existed and could still do serious drama. That was a small drama in itself. The reviewers were brutal, except for the one at The Times. He had written a long piece about Mary, praising her incredible energy, her professionalism and her beautiful voice. He didn't mention the play itself. Later that day Mary Ball would call him a true gentleman who had given her a loving and honest farewell. She bravely finished the agreed-upon thirty performances in half-empty theaters and then said goodbye to acting.

Mary Ball's maid answered the door. She was a large black woman in uniform. She scrutinized Jens before opening the door completely. Speaking with a Creole accent, she said it wasn't really convenient. Mrs. Ball only had one hour until lunchtime and after lunch she had to take her nap.

"Serena, stay out of it," Mary called cheerfully from the living room. "You're not my mother and you're not my nurse either, even though you wear that silly uniform. What must Mr. Jameson think?"

Serena grumbled once more and led him to the living room.

"I don't have many visitors," said Mary. "I don't have children. My old flames are all dead. A few colleagues are still alive but they're all in Hollywood and I wouldn't be found dead there. They're too old to get themselves onto a plane."

Jens was amazed at how alert this 90-year-old woman was. He gazed out the picture window at the rolling green lawns. "You decided to live in heaven on earth." Then he saw that Mary Ball was in a wheelchair and rued his comment. He bent down and kissed her hand politely.

"I was an avid golfer, Mr. Jameson. Single handicap!"

Jens had never grasped the score keeping, so he simply nodded, afraid that Mrs. Ball would try to explain it. He took her word for it.

"But you've lived here a long time."

"No, I lived in another golf subdivision first, until it went downhill economically. At one point they even let in people on a Caribbean cruise, so they would come for a day and whack the sod off the green. Whole crowds would pass by."

"And that's not what you want to see in your front yard, Mrs. Ball," added Jens wittily.

"No, Mr. Jameson, it's not. I lost the use of my legs in a car crash. Otherwise I would invite you to a round."

"I'm honored." Jens had once taken someone up on such an invitation. He had whacked a bit of sod himself.

They spoke of all manner of things and Jens asked if he could turn on his recorder.

"No. If you want to write a story, just remember what I say. I hate those machines."

She hadn't given any more interviews since her embarrassment on Broadway. She resented media that portrayed her as an old woman who insisted on staying on. As if she should just keep her mouth shut and watch what's going on in her front yard once she reached a certain age. Ball had started doing volunteer work. She got involved in a homeless shelter in Los Angeles and *thank god none of those lazy reporters ever noticed*. She worked there until she was eighty and then she moved to Barbados. Three years ago she was in the back seat of her car when her driver crashed into a bus. The good man didn't survive. Mary Ball broke her back and was paralyzed from the waist down.

She invited him to stay for lunch and Serena complained and grumbled that she didn't have enough food for three. Mary suggested that she prepare lunch for them and that she herself go to the village and have a nice lunch somewhere. "At least that will get rid of her," she had whispered to Jens.

A delicious rice dish with vegetables, flying fish and a hot sauce appeared on the table, along with two glasses of mango juice. When Serena had closed the door, Mary asked him if he could make coffee. Next he was asked to go to the sideboard and pour some rum in the juice. She was visibly relishing her own mischievousness.

Jens served the coffee. "You told me you have few visitors. I can't imagine that. I'm sure you have fans here on the island as well. And you have a lot of neighbors. There's a club and a restaurant."

"Yes, I do still have acquaintances but I prefer not to invite them here. I know Hugh Brown, the billionaire. He's a nice guy. Not at all arrogant, despite all his billions. Though his house here at Green Monkey Holes is quite ostentatious. I enjoy a laugh with him every so often. He's lonely—we have that in common." She paused and thought of Hugh, who apparently had a weak spot for this remarkable woman, even though he was forty years younger. "I play bridge with the Darwells. Two nice people but so terribly old. Neither of them has even reached seventy-five but compared to me they've been dead for ages." Mary laughed loudly.

"Do you know a Mr. Rock?" asked Jens.

"Oh yes, that nice man has been here once or twice. What a coincidence. You know him too?"

"Well, no, I just happened to hear he lives here," lied Jens. He didn't like lying to Mary—he liked her. She was a star, someone to envy. With charisma, despite her disability and her age. Anyone would want to live to ninety that way.

"The man is involved with the sale of the new phase on the north side. He promised me he would only admit the most respectable people," said Jens.

"You're right. They don't have to be rich; I don't care about that. Whether you have a billion or a million, it's no indication of class—on the contrary."

"But?"

"When you walk outside and the peace and quiet embraces you or when you're in a restaurant trying to ignore the muted conversations around you, when you open your window and you hear the birds and at most the odd curse from someone whose ball landed in the bunker— that's when you know you're in the right spot."

"Beautifully put. No one would know from all those comedy dramas you played in but you're a true poet."

"Mr. Jameson, you're smooth."

"But not fake. You genuinely fascinate me. I remember your television shows. They always made me laugh."

"You must have seen the reruns. You weren't even born in the fifties."

"No, but I do have videos from that time."

"Ah, video, yes. That's how we live forever."

Jens suggested they take a walk. She loved that. Serena didn't like going on walks. It was usually too hot to walk, the wheelchair was too heavy to push, or she would have some other excuse why it wasn't convenient. He got her sunglasses from the sideboard and a large straw hat from the coat rack.

Once outside, she told him about the course rating of the green surrounding them. At one point she asked him to walk out onto the field toward a group of people who had just driven up with their golf cart.

She spoke with gusto with them about the irons they were using and the best way to hit the ball.

The lengthy walk left Jens sweaty and exhausted. Toward the end, as he pushed the wheelchair back toward Mary's home, they passed a large house. It gave Jens a jolt to see Jennifer's bright green Toyota parked outside.

"This is where Mr. Rock lives."

Mary told Jens about every house—the name of the residents, where they came from and their approximate worth. She didn't know much about Rock. He claimed he was Australian originally but he had an unmistakable South African accent. Rock didn't buy the house; the owner of the subdivision let him live there.

"And who is the owner of this lovely paradise, Mrs. Ball?"

"He's a remarkable man, an Englishman and a gentleman in every way."

"You must have met him when you wanted to buy a home here?"

"Yes indeed, I insisted on it, what with all the scam artists in this world. I want to look someone in the eye and see if I can trust him."

"What was his name?"

"Philip. How English, right?"

"Philip?" Jens was hoping he'd get a last name as well.

"I only know his first name. You know, when you've been in the entertainment business as long as I have, you eventually know who you can trust and who you can't."

"You're a remarkable woman," said Jens and he meant it.

"Philip still sends me a Christmas card every year. He was a big fan. He told me he wasn't involved at all in his investments but he definitely wanted to meet *me*."

While Jens was pulling Mary over the threshold of her front door—hind wheels first—Jennifer's green Toyota drove by. Jens quickly turned his head so he wouldn't be recognized. It caused the wheelchair to lurch and he apologized. Jennifer honked and Mary waved.

"Mr. Rock's mistress," she said. "She often comes in the afternoon and I doubt it's just for lunch." She gave Jens a big wink. "She's a gorgeous girl and I get the impression Mr. Rock is quite virile for his age."

28.

Jens was in a great mood. He had spent the morning at the Bridgetown Chamber of Commerce's land registry and he discovered who owned the almost three-hundred-acre subdivision Green Monkey Holes. He was surprised. The name of the real estate company included the same name as the offshore company that had paid Dijkgraaf hush money: Stonewater Real Estate. The CEO was the same: Jeremy E. Baldwin of the international accounting firm FDMG.

Jens had called the firm and asked for Baldwin but he wasn't in. In fact, he was hardly ever there—he was a former partner. When he asked how Baldwin could be the CEO of two important companies and if this was the correct address, he was told Baldwin could definitely be reached via this office. By now Jens realized that retired accountants or tax consultants of the companies that had set up the tax structure functioned as CEOs of the empty corporations. When he insisted, he finally got Baldwin's phone number but he decided to put off the call.

Jens had learned a lot. Kruger didn't own Stonewater but the company did pay Dijkgraaf hush money. If Mary was to be believed, an Englishman named Philip possibly owned Stonewater. Apparently Kruger had such a good relationship with this Englishman that he had access to large sums of the company's money, and he lived here for free.

Jens had bought a suit. That had taken some doing. Finding a suit for someone with his build on an island like Barbados wasn't easy. He had gone to one store after another, always concluding in front of the mirror that the chosen outfit looked awful. He looked ridiculous in every one. Finally he found a tailor in a side street who pulled a beautiful three-piece white linen suit from his rack and quickly managed to adjust it to Jens's size.

Now he looked like a hero from a seventies television show, so he decided to get his unruly hair cut as well. A completely new Jens walked into the Sandy Lane complex and asked directions to the restaurant. He saw that Jennifer hadn't arrived yet, so he took a table on the ocean side to have a view of the sea, with its crashing waves, and of the beach and all the people sunning there or at the pool.

He opened the menu and saw that lunch here would probably cost him as much as his seven-day stay at the All Season Resort. No wonder stars like Mick Jagger and Beyoncé would eat caviar and lobster here out of boredom, and then take an afternoon nap on their king-size beds in four-thousand-dollars-a-night penthouses. If they didn't rent a beach house, that is, which cost several times more.

The meals varied in price from eighty to two hundred fifty dollars. Jens decided to limit himself to a fresh fish broth and a salad. Maybe he could convince Jennifer to only have one course. He glanced around and saw that the mostly rich people hoping to have lunch with Jagger or Beyoncé so far shared tables with people like themselves.

Jennifer arrived promptly at one. She was dressed elegantly and quite provocatively in a dress with a deep neckline that nevertheless didn't reveal much of her breasts. She walked on heels that most women would have to take a course for, and she wore a necklace that Kruger perhaps stole during one of his scams. It glittered on her dark skin like the crown jewels of England.

"You look gorgeous, Ms. Eduardo. Unfortunately I'm married and I believe in love eternal but you're truly enchanting."

Jennifer was beaming and Jens was convinced he saw her blush. The black-skinned part of humanity had an advantage in that their blushing was less noticeable than that of white people. Jens wasn't just playing Jennifer. She was truly a beauty with enormous sex appeal; he made the comment about being married and believing in eternal love because he knew himself. He could easily lose himself in this woman.

"Call me Jennifer."

She extended her hand. Jens took it, turned it and kissed it. He had learned that from Ben. Or maybe from his father—he had also been a charmer and maybe Jens's bond with Ben had something to do with that. Jens liked charmers who could put women at ease, mainly because he himself was so bad at it. He thought of Esther and was confused.

185

"You know, I'm from New York where it's about sixty-two degrees and rainy. Then American Airlines drops me in a warm bath of about eighty-five degrees, with only sweet, kind, warm, sensitive people around me."

"Yeah, yeah," said Jennifer. "Let's not get carried away. What does the E stand for?"

"What E?"

"The E in E. Jacobs."

"Oh, my name is Jens."

"Ens."

"No, Jens. I traded the E for the nickname 'Jens'. Some parents have no idea what they're doing to a child when they name it." Jens was doing his best to come up with a name to go with that remark.

"You're Edward," Jennifer guessed.

"No, that wouldn't be so bad. I'm not going to tell you."

"Edgar."

"Okay, I'll tell you. It's Ellis."

"A girl's name, I could have known."

"Okay, now that I've told you everything about myself, it's your turn. Tell me your story. Were you born here? What did you do before you were a realtor? How old are you? Who's the lucky guy who shares his life with you? Who are your parents?" Jens paused.

Jennifer was confused. Apparently Jens was interested in her as well as her work. She tried to gauge this strange man in the suit that didn't quite fit, but she couldn't tell whom she was dealing with.

She told him about her life. She was thirty-four and born in northern Barbados. Her father was a laborer on a sugarcane plantation and her mother had managed to raise seven children on her husband's meager wages. Jennifer escaped the hard life on the sugar cane plantation at the age of twelve. She went to Bridgetown, where she got a job at KFC. First as a dishwasher, then as a fry cook and finally as a cashier. *Welcome to Kentucky Fried Chicken. Can I help you?*

Jens was amazed at her forthrightness. She spoke with disdain about the plantation and KFC but she held eye contact with Jens, who listened carefully and never took his eyes off her either.

"I'm a self-made woman. I finished high school, took the realtor's exam, took a course in speaking English without an accent, and a

186

course in high society etiquette. I learned it all. You could say I'm a product of my training from beginning to end."

"Who isn't?" Jens took her hand, because he felt Jennifer was venting. "I'm a fool from New York. I don't have much of an education either. I talk my way into the upper crust and earn my living with bribery and hustling."

Jennifer looked at him in surprise at first. Then he saw a joy in her eyes. "We're all hustlers."

She looked around pulled her hand back. *Maybe she's expecting someone*, Jens thought. *My god, what if Mr. Rock walks in?*

Jens also glanced around. "Are you expecting someone?"

"My boss might join us to discuss Green Monkey Holes."

"Oh." Jens's disappointment wasn't an act.

"You wanted to know about Green Monkey Holes's solvency. He can tell you."

"You don't know?"

"I know a thing or two."

"Stonewater Real Estate owns the development but I can't find the investor behind the company."

"No, that information isn't public."

"Philip Stonewater?"

"His name isn't Stonewater!"

"No?"

"I don't know his last name but it isn't Stonewater."

"Oh come on, secrets don't sell homes."

"Jens, you're a decent guy but I don't trust you completely."

"Why's that?"

"You think I didn't see you this afternoon with Mary Ball?"

"I did think that." Jens felt his face burn. He knew he must be visibly blushing. It disturbed him and he had to breathe deeply because he hadn't thought that Jennifer had seen him.

"What were you doing there?"

"You told me about Mary Ball. I've been a fan since I was little, so I thought this was a good opportunity to talk to her about life at Monkey Caves."

"Holes!"

"Holes!"

187

"You know, Ellis Jacobs, I'm beginning to doubt your story. What are you looking for?" Jennifer seemed relaxed. Jens didn't get the impression she wanted to expose him. She didn't seem to care one way or another who he was. She glanced at her watch and looked around once more.

"I don't really feel like seeing Mr. Rock. Shall we get out of here?"

"No, well, sure, but where to?"

"I don't know, just somewhere else."

"Well, I'm not sure that's a good idea."

"Is Rock your lover?"

"Excuse me?"

"It's plain English, isn't it? Is he your lover?"

Jennifer stared at the first dish that was being placed before them. The plate was beautifully arranged but with hardly anything on it. Jens's broth was as clear as water and almost colorless.

Jennifer thought about what Jens had said. "My relationship with Rock isn't your business, is it?"

"Of course not. I'm just trying to draw you out. Because you're cute."

"Yes, you've made that clear." Jennifer smiled coyly. "He's very nice to me." She hesitated. "We often have lunch together. He's incredibly charming." She glanced at Jens and he sensed some shame in her eyes.

He was deeply unhappy. He didn't want to pretend anymore, not with Jennifer. He just wanted to be a reporter or writer again.

The conversation became awkward. His false moves had confused her. He wanted everything to be over. He spoke of New York, of how special it was compared to America and the rest of the world. He described Cape Cod and the wonderful ocean view three blocks from his ex-wife's house. She wanted to hear about that ex-wife and his child and gradually the pleasant mood returned.

They both had a salad as the main dish. The plate of greens was not worth the astronomical price, even if it did have a great dressing. They both laughed about the cost of all that nonsense on their plates and thought of their backgrounds—she the daughter of a laborer on a sugarcane plantation and he a simple boy from a village on Cape Cod.

They finished the wine and passed on dessert. When the bill came, Jennifer wanted to pay. She said it was business, so she could expense it.

But Jens was firm. He didn't want to have lunch if it was paid for by Kruger. That would be bad luck.

They got up and Jens was reminded of Jennifer's height. Especially in her high heels, their eyes were almost at the same level—that's an unusual experience for a tall man.

He suggested a walk along the beach. That reduced the chance they would encounter Kruger on the way out. Of course it was a ridiculous suggestion since Jennifer was wearing stiletto heels but she immediately agreed. She took her shoes off and held them elegantly in one hand while she offered Jens her other.

It was low tide so the beach was wide. Still they had to cross a rock here and there, and walk between beach chairs or through the calm waves. When they approached a beach bar they looked at each other and smiled while they took a table and ordered a drink.

"You're hitting on me, Ellis Jens Jacobs," said Jennifer, as the waiter brought her a champagne cocktail and Jens a screwdriver. For a brief moment Jens felt dizzy. They had had so little food to go with the wine.

"I couldn't do that, Jennifer."

"Because you're a married man?"

"That was a lie. I'm not married."

"Because we should keep it professional?"

"That's a lie too."

Jens didn't know what possessed him. During the walk he had decided that the bizarre situation he had gotten himself into had to end here. It was time to confront Kruger. It was enough for his story that he worked here under an assumed name for a wealthy person who was maybe called Philip. This Philip could be Brigitte's father. A wealthy Englishman. Jens would confess to Jennifer who he really was.

Using an assumed name was a contentious issue among reporters, just as wiretaps, document theft and other illegal practices. Was it permissible or not, and if so, under which circumstances? In general Jens believed that just about everything was permissible, although he himself never used these methods. It had all been theory for him. Now he was in the middle of it.

Jennifer gave him a resigned look that suggested she knew that already. She was also worried, because she knew that what Jens had to say wasn't anything good.

"Okay, spill it out. You're just a stalker, trying to hit on me in an original way."

"I wish it were that simple, Jennifer. The truth is even more embarrassing."

"Huh?"

Jens deliberated. To what degree could he trust Jennifer and try to win her over to his side? He would have to tell her about Dijkgraaf. But if she went straight to Kruger, Jens would commit a mortal sin. He had promised Dijkgraaf confidentiality, and he strongly believed in that principle.

"You're not here for a rich customer who wants to buy a house. You're here for something else."

"Yes, Jennifer. But that has nothing to do with the fact that I like you and I don't really want to get you involved."

Her shoulders sagged and she stared numbly ahead. "I'm already in up to my ears, Ellis Jens or whatever your name is."

"My name is Jens Jameson and I ..."

Jennifer's jaw dropped. "Oh shit, of course. How incredibly stupid of me!"

"What?" asked Jens.

"Oh my god! I really hope we left in time."

"What's stupid of you?"

"Peter told me a reporter named Jens Jameson might show up. And that I should warn him immediately if he did."

Jens's shoulders sagged. "Well, you should do what you have to."

Jennifer stared into her cocktail. "He told me you were an international con man who has been stalking him for years. That you have murderous tendencies, that you have attacked him several times and that you tried to stab him."

"Interesting. And that I hit him over the head with a hammer?"

Jennifer flinched. Jens had hit the nail on the head. "So it's true?"

"No, but you did just tell me he had something to do with the attempt on my life."

Jens's heart was pounding as he lifted his shirt and revealed the scars from the stab wounds. Jennifer started but instead of turning away or pulling a face, her hand moved to the wound and she gently touched it with her fingertips. That confused him. Esther always regarded his wounds with a grim face and she certainly didn't want to touch them. Even when making love she avoided them, despite his assurances that he couldn't even feel the scars.

He bent over and turned his head.

"Here's the hammer he mentioned."

She moved his hair away in order to see the wound the hammer had made.

Jens was suddenly decisive. "Dear Jennifer. Let's do this: Forget what I told you about who I am. We had lunch today and while we talked it became clear I have several options for my rich client. I promised I would call back if he was serious. That phone call is never going to come. That's it."

"And I know nothing and what . . . ?"

"I want to tell you what's going on. But only if you trust me more than Rock or whatever his real name is."

"Will it hurt me to know more?"

"You could get involved if you don't handle it right."

"And then what?"

"I honestly don't know, Jennifer. This is the first connection I've found between what happened to me in Hamburg and Peter Kruger who's a realtor here."

"Kruger?" Jennifer was astonished.

"Shit, here we go."

"I must say it's a ridiculous name, Peter Rock." Jennifer was cynical, trying to make light of it. "E. Jacobs is much more believable."

"It's Ellen's name; she's the editor with my literary agent."

"You're a writer?"

"Let me first tell you I would definitely hit on you under any other circumstances. That sounds stupid but I don't want you to think I …" Jens felt it sounded too stupid for words, and he had no idea how to finish the sentence.

Jennifer just grinned.

"I'm a writer. I've written a few books. I also write reviews for The New York Times. Two months ago Brigitte Friends invited me to her home and asked me to write her biography. She wants to know more about her past and who her biological father is. I started digging and I'm sinking further and further into the morass that is Brigitte's past."

"*The* Brigitte Friends?"

"Yes. And Peter Kruger is a link to her father. He's covering up—he's protecting the father."

"But how did that bring you to me?"

"You don't want to know."

"Of course I do."

"But maybe it's better you don't."

"Jens." Jennifer was suddenly strict.

"Okay. I had your phone number because it was used as a contact between Dijkgraaf and Kruger."

"Dijkgraaf, Kruger—am I still supposed to know what you're talking about?"

"Mr. D. and Mr. Rock."

"That call had to do with this?"

"Yes, and that he called just as I was sitting at your desk was no coincidence either. When you went to see your boss, I followed you."

Jennifer's shoulders dropped and so did her head. The whole drama suddenly became clear. Mr. D. had called and Jennifer had led Jens straight to Rock, or Kruger. And through Mary Ball he had also managed to make the connection with the owner of Green Monkey Holes.

When Jennifer's shoulders couldn't sag any lower, she sat up and shook it all off.

"Okay, so now what?" She didn't wait for a reply. Somehow, in that short period when she crumpled, she got the whole picture. "Shit. You even know where I live." She remembered seeing Jens running along her street in the early morning, wearing shorts and a t-shirt. "Yes, you were the jogger. Shit, shit, shit!"

Jens suggested getting a cup of coffee somewhere and figuring it all out. They walked to the beach-club parking lot and got into a cab. Jens was about to give the name of the coffee shop in Sunset Crest where he had wonderful Italian coffee every morning but Jennifer gave the driver a different address. Jens sat back and waited for where the trip would lead them.

It led them to her house.

Jennifer entered quickly. She kicked off her heels and put on slippers. She began to fidget elaborately with the coffee maker and then watered the plants while the machine warmed up.

Jens stood behind her. "I'm sorry. I never meant to get you involved in this mess. But you were the only link. Kruger had disappeared from the Netherlands. I had to follow the lead. Looking back it sucks for you but I couldn't have done it any differently."

Jennifer poured the coffee. "Is it that important, what you're doing?"

"It's my job. In itself that isn't important but when they hit you over the head with a hammer and stab you in the side, you only have two choices."

"Two?"

"You're either a coward and you quit, or you get mad and continue."

"And you continued," said Jennifer. "Too bad for me."

"That remains to be seen."

"How's that?"

"You could forget all of this. I can walk back to my hotel. E. Jacobs is never heard from again. I pay Kruger a visit but you don't know me."

"I get it. But I can't ignore the problem of Rock a.k.a. Kruger."

"That's an advantage. You now know he's a con man. He is a con man, Jennifer. It's to your advantage that you're aware of that."

"A win-win situation," Jennifer concluded.

"Yes," said Jens, frustrated.

"Because . . .?"

"How do you mean?"

"You say it as if it's really a lose-lose situation."

Jens looked at her, looked at her longer than he would in any other situation, much longer than the content of their dialog justified. They both knew the signals had been there from the beginning—in her office, during lunch at Sandy Lane, during their beach walk, when they held hands, if only to support each other, enjoying drinks at the beach bar and the candid conversation that followed. He couldn't just leave and let her disappear from his life.

"Okay," said Jennifer. "I know you have to get out of here as soon as possible."

They stood in the kitchen, both holding a cup of coffee and both looking more into their cups than at each other.

Jens put his coffee on the counter and moved toward her. Without any hesitation she put her arms around him. She held his head between her hands and despite his shyness he held her gaze. They kissed intensely.

She wasn't out to secure her position and he didn't try to win her over to his camp so he could find out more. All that may happen, but for now they just surrendered for a stolen moment.

29.

The sunset was breathtaking. The west coast of Barbados is famous for its spectacular view of the setting sun. Dozens of Bajans and a handful of tourists had gathered on the beach and in the bar, sitting in the sand or on chairs on the bleached wooden lanai, watching until the red ball disappeared behind the horizon.

Jens couldn't really concentrate on the event. He had an important meeting and he was nervous. He mashed the lemon slice into his screwdriver with the swizzle stick and looked up anxiously every time someone entered.

Jennifer had cooked for him and they ate the simple rice dish with spicy chicken out on her lanai. They drank a cool red Chilean wine. Jennifer had become guarded. She was serious and a little somber. Jens told her a little about his life, his child and his ex-wife. About his time in South Africa, his apartment and his friends in New York. About his travels through Europe, and about his findings in Germany, France and the Netherlands.

Jennifer said very little. When she finished eating and when the wine was half gone, she suddenly said, "I think its best we stop right here."

Now Jens was the quiet one. Of course that was best. Things could get nasty for her. Kruger didn't assume a false identity in Barbados for nothing. He was working on a project involving tens of millions of dollars and if he did indeed order the assault in Hamburg, she was in serious danger.

"Aren't you going to say anything?" she asked after a while.

"Well, what do you want me to say? You're right. It was my idea. It's better this way. But it does suck. I haven't had such a wonderful afternoon in ages."

"You're a charmer."

"I don't hear that very often but if I am, I'm a sincere charmer." It was something Ben could have said.

"To be honest, I'm more worried about you."

"I can take care of myself."

"Didn't you just tell me they left you for dead and that it's a miracle that you were able to get up and find help?"

"I've become more cautious since."

She just smiled. "I've seen Rock in action for six months now—he's ruthless. He surrounds himself with some strange individuals. Sometimes he deploys them when he has a conflict with one of the subcontractors or the building-supply companies."

"Huh? How do you know that?"

"Well, I'm not directly involved but I hear a thing or two when he makes calls in my presence."

"And you have lunch with a guy like that every day." Jens couldn't disguise the jealousy in his voice.

"I like him. *Liked* him. He's a friendly, charming man; nothing ever happened between us. He's a bit like a father to me."

"But you won't betray me?"

"No. Aren't you convinced of that by now?"

"Of course," Jens said quickly. "I just mean that it must be hard for you."

"Well, of course he's still a stranger to me. And I've often thought he's no good."

They stared out beyond the lanai, aware that the moment was approaching when they would say goodbye forever.

Jens wondered if he had made the right decision to meet with Peter Kruger after dark. The restaurant was emptying out and the personnel were setting the tables for dinner. The bar was still plenty lively; he couldn't get beaten up unnoticed. And Iowa was also standing guard somewhere, at a safe distance. Jens had instructed him to call the police if he saw anything suspicious.

Iowa had explained that it was hard for him to go to the police. Jens had insisted that if he didn't, at least he should stay out of what might happen. In this world, Iowa, with his seven children and fifteen grand-children, was indispensable. Jens wasn't.

To be safe, he had sent all his findings to Esther and asked her to send them in turn to someone she trusted. He didn't need a name. Esther had read everything and called him back, saying he shouldn't meet with Kruger. He promised her he would call the American embassy if there were any trouble but that he couldn't cancel the appointment. The next day he was meeting the cultural attaché but he hadn't told her what the meeting was going to be about.

Two days after he met Jennifer, he had called the Green Monkey Holes office and asked for Mr. Rock. But Peter Rock wasn't interested in an interview with Jeremy Johnson. He should speak to someone else at Green Monkey Holes but that person was out this week, so Jens should call back at a later date. Then Jens had demanded to speak to Rock. He would call back at four and if Rock didn't answer he would publish some embarrassing details without his comments.

Kruger sounded cheerful. "Hello, Mr. Johnson, this is Peter Rock. I heard you have an urgent request for an interview."

"Yes, Mr. Kruger. How about that, huh? This is Jens Jameson."

"Ah, Mr. Jameson." Kruger was taken aback but he recovered quickly. "What can I do for you?"

"I would like to talk with you."

"We *are* talking. Ha, ha, we *are* talking!"

"I would like to meet with you. Do you understand why?"

"But I'm far away, not in Europe, and you're in . . . you're in . . .?"

"I'm in Barbados as well."

Kruger was momentarily quiet on the other end. It seemed he had to process this information, that he couldn't figure out how on earth Jens knew where he was, knew his false name, and knew Green Monkey Holes.

Kruger agreed to a meeting, although he seemed to have a problem with the location.

Jens sat on the balustrade facing the parking lot, so he could see who was coming and going. A silver Mercedes S-Class turned off and stopped near the stairs to the bar. Three men got out—a fourth stayed in the car.

Kruger stepped onto the lanai and looked around. Jens waved to him with the newspaper, which he had said he would have with him. Kru-

197

ger briefly glanced back. The two other men were waiting at the edge of the lanai and sat down without making eye contact.

Jens shook Kruger's hand. "You brought quite an entourage."

Kruger grinned, scanned the parking lot and sat down. "It's not unusual for someone in my position to have a few bodyguards along. There's much poverty here. If you have nothing to lose, it's easier to cross the line."

Jens would've liked to react to that but he decided to stick strictly to his rehearsed scenario.

"So tell me, Mr. Jameson," Kruger continued amiably, "how can I help you?"

"Well, Mr. Kruger, this won't take long. I only have two questions for you."

Kruger laughed. "You came all the way to Barbados for two questions?"

He was indeed charming. He was sixty-three, gray and half-bald but his skin was evenly tanned. His custom suit was spotlessly white, the Panama hat he had placed on the table was an original and he wore expensive-looking alligator-leather boots. His gentle friendliness confused Jens. Maybe this was the allure of a con man who had taken the fortunes of hundreds of women, but could this also be the cold-blooded gangster who gave the order to have someone hit over the head with a hammer?

Jens studied Kruger's companions closely. They seemed rough, Caucasian—probably European. One of them could very well be the man who had followed him when he entered the strip joint on the Reeperbahn. He shuddered at the idea that one of these men could be his attacker.

"So, two questions," said Kruger. "For instance, why do I work under a different name here?"

"No, I already know why." Jens watched Kruger's reaction closely. "By now I know so much about you, I could almost write a book. But even though that is my profession, I don't intend to. You see, I'm working on something more interesting and that's what I have a more important question about."

"Ah, you're a remarkable man. You claim you can expose certain things about me but you won't. After everything I've learned about you, I'd say you're talking nonsense."

"You're aware that I'm working on a book about Brigitte Vermeer, also known as Friends, and that she asked me to look for her father?"

"Is that so? Interesting."

"I also know that aside from Brigitte's mother, you're the only one who knows who he is."

"You may think you have accomplished something but here's how it is: I do know Mrs. Vermeer. It also seems likely that she knows who Miss Brigitte's father is. I, however, do not."

"Unfortunately, I know that's nonsense." Jens's nerves were on edge. He didn't dare pick up his glass with his shaky hands. Luckily the waiter briefly dispersed the tension, asking Kruger what he would like to drink.

"Well, Mr. Jameson," said Kruger, after ordering a mineral water, "That's a rather strong statement."

"I also know Brigitte's father paid you to thwart the attempts of a Dutch investigation agency."

"Such self-assuredness, Mr. Jameson."

"I'm not that interested in your story. The trail you leave is clear enough to be picked up by real reporters later on. Right now I'm working on Brigitte Vermeer's case and I don't want to disappoint her. Still, it wouldn't be hard to inform the local authorities about your background and that you're selling real estate under a false name."

"That sounds like a threat, Mr. Jameson. I don't care much for threats."

"Then help me out." Jens realized the conversation wasn't going at all as planned. And that wouldn't be all.

"You had two questions. Maybe I can answer the second one," said Kruger stonily. He paused while the waiter brought his mineral water. "I'm not entirely deaf to your demands and I really do want to help you."

"Philip, the man living in London who owns Stonewater Offshore and Green Monkey Holes—what's his last name?"

Kruger scratched his temple and deliberated. "Well, well, Mr. Jameson. I really underestimated you. You're quite a competent investigator. Where on earth did you get that information?"

"Unfortunately I can't disclose that. It's confidential. I'm sure you understand that in this business that's a code I can't simply ignore." Jens deliberated. He wanted to leave. This meeting was useless. It might have been better if he had stuck to phone calls but he had been convinced he had to see Kruger in person.

"You wouldn't consider helping me? Would you think about it?"

"Of course," said Kruger. "I suggest you drive with us and we can have dinner somewhere while I make a few phone calls."

"I'm not sure I want to get in a car with those goons of yours."

"You don't seem to be the cowardly type. What could possibly happen to you, Mr. Jameson?"

"I've already been hit over the head and stabbed in the course of this investigation, so I'm cautious."

"Are you suggesting I had anything to do with that?"

"No, I wouldn't dare," said Jens cynically. "I said I'm cautious, Mr. Kruger, not scared."

"Nevertheless, you should ride with me, Mr. Jameson."

"What if I politely decline?"

"I'd have to do something I don't like to do, something not entirely new to you, evidently."

"And what's that?"

"Make threats." Kruger said it casually.

"Because," said Jens, in an attempt at irony, "you have a gun under the table and any moment now your men are going to produce a hammer."

"Mr. Jameson, we're neither cowboys nor carpenters." He took another sip of his water and wiped his mouth with his napkin. "Like me, you have been careless. That's why you will take a ride with us tonight."

Jens wondered where he had gone wrong. "What do you mean, careless?"

"We will take you to an address where you will enjoy my hospitality for a while. If you behave, that is, and if we can come to an agreement."

"Or else?"

"An acquaintance of yours is also staying at said address. How careless of you to follow up your meeting in private with Jennifer right under my nose."

Jens sighed and tried to smile. Apparently they had left the Sandy Lane too late. Kruger had seen them and followed them. He knew everything.

"What if I refuse?"

"You won't, Mr. Jameson. You're a gentleman when it gets down to it. I'm sure you realize that this is that kind of moment. You wouldn't want to get Jennifer in trouble, would you?"

Jens looked down and thought. "You can't do anything to us. I didn't meet with you without taking some safety measures."

"I wouldn't doubt it. But there's no need to make everything so complicated and dramatic. Consider it an evening off from your investigation. Relax, you're in Barbados."

Kruger got up and made an inviting gesture. He threw several dollar bills on the table. Jens rose and walked ahead of him. The two other men also jumped up after leaving a tip.

Jens was forced to sit between the two men in the back of the Mercedes. He recognized the smell of Old Spice—the same aftershave his father always used. But he had smelled it more recently than that. It must have been in Hamburg, during the assault in the park. Strange that he hadn't remembered that.

Kruger sat in the passenger seat. The chauffeur started the car and calmly drove toward the parking lot exit.

Jens broke out in a sweat. Maybe he should've taken a cab to the embassy or the police station. Suppose Kruger's bodyguards weren't as polite as he made them out to be? He didn't check to see if Iowa was following them. In the rear view mirror he looked straight in the driver's face, wanting to come across as perfectly confident.

They drove along the coast, straight to Green Monkey Holes.

"There's no reason to involve Jennifer," said Jens from the back seat.

"Unfortunately she already is involved."

"I didn't tell her anything about you. She believes I'm Ellis Jacobs, a realtor who's looking for a house for his client."

"Is that so?" was all Kruger said.

Jens couldn't tell if it was really a question.

The crash barrier rose immediately when the silver Mercedes approached. Kruger waved at the guard as the car zoomed up the well-lit road. They drove past his house and took another side road that ended in a sandy trail. They passed a few unfinished homes, finally stopping at a sign saying "Model Home."

They got out. Contrary to what Jens had expected, the two bodyguards didn't touch him; they just pointed toward the front door.

"Ellis!" cried Jennifer when Jens entered. She was smart; with this one cry she indicated that she had kept to her story. She had a red welt on her cheek that would probably be a sizeable bruise in a couple of days.

"Hello Jennifer." Jens thought feverishly. How could he get both of them out of this situation?

"Ellis?" Kruger grinned.

"Ellis Jacobs. I met Jennifer when I was looking for a house for a client."

Kruger gauged whether Jens really hadn't told her anything about him. He would like to believe that Jens had hit on her to get more dirt on him without disclosing who he really was. He sent Jennifer upstairs and ordered the driver to stand guard outside her door.

"See? That proves it. She doesn't know anything."

"Shut up and let me think," said Kruger irritably.

"Let her go. You have me. Don't complicate things unnecessarily."

"Shut up, damn it!" Kruger said, getting short-fused.

He went to an adjacent room. The door closed and Jens heard him making a call. He spoke in a low voice and Jens couldn't make out what he was saying but it was obviously a heated conversation in which he was receiving instructions.

Jens asked for a cigarette but neither of the two men in the room reacted. When he put his hand in his inner pocket, they jumped up and took on a threatening stance. Jens calmly took a packet of cigarettes from his pocket. One of the men said smoking wasn't permitted. He spoke English with an accent Jens immediately recognized.

"You two are Dutch!" Jens said as cheerfully as possible.

Astonished, the two men looked at each other and tried to ignore the remark.

"Is it possible I have met one of you before?"

One of the men smiled tepidly.

"Perhaps in Hamburg, on the Reeperbahn?" Jens went on.

Now the smile was gone. The man turned around and puttered about in the kitchen. The heated conversation in the next room came to an abrupt end.

Kruger returned. He sent the two men away. One went to stand guard at the front door; the other headed out back.

"I don't intend to keep you much longer, Jameson. I'd rather be rid of you but you realize I can't just take you back to your hotel. Where are you staying?"

"Sandy Lane." Jens grinned widely.

"That seems a little out of your range."

"Why? I work for the multimillionaire Brigitte Friends. What would you know about my range?"

Kruger hesitated but he still didn't believe Jens. "You don't want to tell me where you're staying?"

"You want to find out who else has my information."

"That's easy enough. May I have your cell phone?"

"Can I refuse?"

"Come on, don't be that way. We on our part are trying to keep this civil."

Jens took the phone from the breast pocket of his jacket. The headphones were still connected and the microphone was also hanging from the jacket.

"So we're here at Green Monkey Holes in a model home in the western phase, which hasn't been built out yet. With me here in the room is Mr. Rock, also known as Peter Kruger. He has his bodyguards standing guard outside. I can't say I'm here completely of my own free will. In fact, this is kidnapping." Jens had taken the microphone and he obviously wasn't talking to Kruger.

Kruger looked aghast. "Alfred, come here immediately!"

The man at the front door came running in.

"Get that phone!"

Alfred yanked the phone from Jens's hand and tore loose the wire that was wrapped partly around his hand, breaking the cord in the process.

"Man, that was an expensive call," said Jens.

Kruger looked at the display on Jens's iPhone. Below "Unknown Caller" a timer indicated the call had lasted an hour and fourteen minutes. That time coincided pretty much with the beginning of their meeting at the restaurant, the drive to Green Monkey Holes and the time spent in the model home.

"Goddammit!" Kruger pressed "Recent Calls" and saw that the unknown number was the only one on the phone—the address book and favorites were also empty. He looked at the text message display and it, too, was empty. The calendar and all other personal information were deleted. He hadn't thought this operation through. The phone call that afternoon had thrown him off balance. He had overestimated his powers of persuasion. This Jens Jameson may seem weak but he had a hard core.

"Who were you talking to?"

"The call is recorded."

"Okay," Kruger thought fast, "you spoke of safety measures. Is this it?"

"It's one of them."

"What else?"

"Tomorrow I have a meeting at the American embassy. If I don't show up, all hell will break loose. The whole story is known in different locations and it's being published as we speak. Your practices here, those in Nieuwersluis, the Hamburg affair and the large file that has already been built against you will all lead to an international arrest warrant in the very near future."

Kruger was furious. "You think all this will help? If my position is that hopeless, then . . ."

". . . you might as well throw me in the Green Monkey Holes pond wearing concrete boots?"

"That seems too much trouble for the likes of you." Kruger was clearly done being polite.

"Swindle isn't murder, Mr. Kruger. My offer still stands. I just want to find out if this Philip of Stonewater Offshore or Onshore is Brigitte's father."

Kruger scowled and gave Alfred an order. The man grabbed Jens by the arm and took him to the garage. In the back of the dimly lit space was a door to an empty storage room without windows. Jens was shoved through and fell against a wall.

"You're an asshole, Alfred," said Jens, when the door slammed and he was left, scrapes and all, in complete darkness.

30.

Esther was feeling sorry for herself. She was staring out the open window of her small apartment at the rain. She was angry with Jens and angry with Winkler. Angry with her father and mother. Her friends, her enemies. She was angry with everyone and most of all she was angry with herself.

Staring at the rain, she wondered *why* she was so angry at the world. She felt Jens was done with her. But wasn't that her fault? When he sent her a long email two days ago, she had been furious. She had kicked her computer, severely damaging the screen. A bar of thin color lines rendered the entire thing unusable.

Jens wrote that he had gotten so carried away with his story, that he had become friends with the person who had led him to Rock. He had gotten drunk and he hadn't been completely true to her. He was very sorry and ensured her it would never happen again.

Became friends? Not completely true? The adrenaline shot through her veins and she had cramps in her heart, stomach and belly, all at once.

But why not? she mused. Hadn't she made it clear their relationship had no future? Professionally maybe, but as lovers they were at each other's throats so often that she herself had decided she should take it slower with Jens.

Of course she could understand what Jens had done. She had answered so guardedly to his questions about their relationship that he evidently no longer took it that seriously. Now *he* was on a treasure island and caved for the first tropical gem to come his way while she had to work her tail off in rainy Holland.

Jens had put her to work finding out everything she could about Dora Vermeer and her husband. She was also looking for a man with real

205

estate in Majorca, London and the Netherlands. The man had to be worth hundreds of millions and his name was probably Philip. *And* she had to find out what Kruger had been doing in Nieuwersluis before he disappeared. *That's all*, Jens had added subtly before he left.

Esther felt betrayed.

Jens had sent her a memo full of his adventurous discoveries about Kruger. She had to send it to someone she trusted. She had chosen Winkler. He had immediately opened the document and called her back.

"This is fantastic! What an angle! Let's go, we're going to hang this guy by his toes," he had cried.

She was furious that he kept pointing out that Jens was far away. He could be in mortal danger. She had trusted Winkler as a colleague and a friend and that's why she had sent it to him, she explained. Only then did Winkler calm down.

"What do you see in that overweight Yank, anyway," he had tried, but then he kept quiet. He did ask her if she wanted her job back but by then she was so thoroughly sick of him that she had immediately said no.

Her father and mother had visited her. They had nagged her an entire Sunday about no longer having a permanent job. When she told them that Winkler said she could always come back, there was no stopping them.

In her windowsill with the rain outside she suddenly had a strange feeling. If she didn't usually feel more like she was from Mars than from Venus, she would have called it female intuition. It could also be telepathy when it involved a loved one, because apart from the infidelity confessions, Jens's message had contained worrying information. Esther began to reconstruct the message that she couldn't retrieve on her damaged computer.

Jens was in Barbados. He had located Kruger, who was operating under the name Rock, selling large homes in a golf-course subdivision called Green Monkey Holes. He had met a woman who worked for Kruger and she had told him Kruger behaved like a criminal. Tonight Jens was going to meet Kruger and she had been given instructions concerning his safety. And she couldn't remember a thing about what she was supposed to do, because Jens's confession of his kissing Jennifer had gotten in the way.

She glanced at her clock. With the time difference it was eight in the evening in Barbados. When did Jens have that meeting? Six in the evening! What was she supposed to do? Something with a server where he recorded conversations. She jumped up, yanked her raincoat from the coat rack and ran downstairs.

At a 24/7 Internet café a few blocks away she sat down behind a computer and called for help. A friendly young man came out from behind the counter and started up the machine for her. Among her other emails she found the message, the files and the link to the server where Jens had sent the conversation via his phone. The mp3 recording had stopped. She looked at the times the conversation began and ended. It had ended only one hour ago. She swore loudly and jumped up. At the counter she rented headphones.

She listened breathlessly to the conversation, which wasn't very clear and sometimes even inaudible, and then decided to transcribe it.

> *"You came with quite an entourage."*
> *"It's not unusual for someone in my position to have a few body-guards along."*

She started at the first sentence. The meeting didn't take place the way Jens had demanded, one on one.

Then came the frustration.

> *"You think you've come far but here's how it is: I do know Mrs. Vermeer. It does seem likely that she knows who Miss Brigitte's father is. I, however, do not."*

She heard Jens spluttering and playing his cards about the Dutch investigation agency. Then he gave Kruger the information about Philip and the Stonewater companies. Her ears were burning, especially when he mentioned the hammer in Hamburg. Next came the threat and Jens asking what would happen if he refused.

> *"You won't, Mr. Jameson. When it comes down to it, you're a gen-tleman. ... You wouldn't want Jennifer to get hurt, would you?"*

Esther growled. For a moment she considered stopping the transcription. What did she care if this Jennifer got hurt? The home wrecker would just have to take care of herself. But, darn it: Of course Jens was a gentleman, so he would go along.

Then Jens mentioned the safety measures and she realized this was where she came in. Her heart was pounding. Despite the inferior sound quality, she heard the tension in his voice. Next she heard them get in the car and drive. Esther could barely restrain herself from fast-forwarding—she was that curious and tense from listening to the recording.

She grumbled again as she listened to the scene with "Ellis" and Jennifer. *They're pretending not to know each other,* Esther thought. She was shocked again when she heard Jens's remark as Kruger was making a phone call:

> "*You two are Dutch! Could it be that I met one of you before? Perhaps in Hamburg, on the Reeperbahn?*"

She almost cheered when Jens gave them the wrong hotel but she also realized she was listening to a downright kidnapping. The recording became even harder to make out and Esther realized the phone had been discovered. She picked up "*Green Monkey Holes*" and "*model home.*" All of a sudden the recording was clear as a bell and spoken right into the microphone:

> "*And I can't say I'm here completely of my free will.*"

She heard someone curse heartily, then nothing. A little later someone breathed into the phone, then yelled "*Hello?*"—and the connection was broken.

Esther took the memory stick on her keychain and made a copy of the mp3 recording. She carefully reread Jens's email and printed it. She started the file again and searched for a comment in which Kruger compromised himself. It was hard to find; the man was guarded and chose his words carefully. Finally she found a useful part and pressed stop so she could replay it. She took her cell phone, turned off the number recognition and connected it to the memo recorder she always had with her. She called Jens's number. The phone rang five times; then she heard his voice telling her to leave a message. She swore and hung up before the beep. She waited a few minutes and called back.

When Esther heard someone on the other end say "Hello?" she turned on the recorder and on the other end Kruger could hear himself loud and clear.

> *"You claim you could expose things about me but you won't. Considering what I've found out about you, I'd say you're talking nonsense."*

It was momentarily quiet on both ends.

"Who's this?" asked Kruger.

"That doesn't matter. But you must release Jens Jameson immediately. If I don't hear from him in fifteen minutes, I'm calling the police."

"Mr. Jameson gave me this phone," said Kruger.

Smart, thought Esther.

"Let's not do anything hasty. A lot could happen to your colleague in fifteen minutes. I assume I'm speaking with Ms. Lejeune?"

That disconcerted her and she thought feverishly.

"Mr. Kruger, I recognize your voice. What's the point of holding Jens when all the facts are already out there? Even the kidnapping is on tape."

"Kidnapping is a big word. We asked Mr. Jens to come with us."

"Can I talk to him?"

"He's not here at the moment."

"I want to talk to him."

"I'll ask him to call you back."

"I don't trust you. What are you going to do?"

"I need some time, Ms. Lejeune. Nothing will happen to your friend. If he still is your friend, after having cheated on you with another woman."

Esther was indignant. "You don't know anything about the two of us!"

"You aren't the only one investigating, Ms. Lejeune."

"What do you suggest?"

"Give me twenty-four hours and everything will be fine."

"That would leave us with no leverage."

"That's true. Then again, you never really had any."

"You're wrong. I could have you picked up."

Kruger laughed. "You sound as if you're CIA, as if you're in a police television series. Barbados is a peace-loving country—everything moves slowly here. You're in the Netherlands, right?"

"Let me speak with Jens. We need to discuss what to do."

"As I said…"

"If I can't speak with him, The New York Times will run a story tomorrow morning about one of their colleagues being kidnapped in Barbados by a con man named Peter Kruger, a.k.a. Peter Rock. In addition, Jens has an appointment at the embassy tomorrow but they will be informed tonight. And think of the damage you'd be doing to your employer in Majorca."

"Ha, Mr. Jameson certainly covered his back."

"I want Jens on the phone."

"I will call you back." And Kruger hung up.

For a moment, Esther didn't know what to do. She ran back outside and headed for a taxi stand. She glanced at her watch: 2 a.m. No cabs were waiting but one drove by, so she jumped in front of it. The car stopped with screaming tires.

"I'm picking up a fare, ma'am," said the cab driver politely.

"This is a matter of life and death. I'll pay double!"

The latter impressed him more than the former. He nodded and Esther got in the back. While the driver called his dispatcher to request another cab for his original fare, she called Winkler.

"Frederick, I have a problem and I need your help. I can't do this alone."

"No problem, poppet. Where are you?"

"I'm in a cab. I'm on my way to your office."

"Good, I'll go there right away."

"Call the editor of The New York Times and tell him Jameson has been kidnapped and that he has to stand by to publish it."

"I'll reserve space in tomorrow's paper."

"It's not a sure thing. We're over a barrel. They're threatening to hurt him."

Jens had been in the dark for about two hours now. He had kicked the door a few times but no one had ordered him to keep quiet. At first he could see a line of light coming from under the door, but after a while that was gone, too. He had no idea if his kidnappers were even still in the model home.

He had systematically felt around the walls, floor and ceiling with his hands. He had explored the entire space; the only thing he had found was a piece of wood with a rusty nail in it, three concrete blocks and a piece of string. The door had a keyhole but the key was in it on the other side, so he couldn't see anything. The walls and ceiling were completely smooth. The floor felt like rough stone, probably concrete. The only thing that deviated was a vent on the bottom of the door and a vent in the wall that Jens suspected was for the return air, since it emitted a soft breeze. And there was a ceiling light in a steel frame.

Jens didn't intend to wait and see what was going to happen, so he got to work with the piece of wood with the nail. Within fifteen minutes he managed to take out the wall vent, which was attached to a sheetrock wall in front of a concrete wall. The opening wasn't big enough to crawl through. He tried to figure out the room's position within the house and he decided the wall to the right was his best chance, since it was an interior wall, and therefore possibly only made of sheetrock.

He got to work, if only because he'd die of thirst if they didn't come back. Two hours later he heard voices again. The light under the door also reappeared. He stood up but was blinded when the door opened.

Alfred and his partner took him to the living room. Kruger wasn't there. He asked for water and they gave him a glass which he emptied right away. Alfred shoved a cell phone in his hand. It wasn't his own.

"This is Kruger. Are you still doing well?"

"Let's just say your hospitality has room for improvement."

"You complain too much. Here's what's going to happen."

"I'm not getting back in that room. I'm claustrophobic."

"You do as I tell you, and we'll see."

"Are you leaving the country already?"

"Mr. Jameson, your questions are really annoying."

"Even though I only had two, neither of which you wanted to answer?"

"If you would really leave me alone afterward, I would give you some information but your word isn't worth much. Not anymore."

"Not anymore?"

Kruger growled. "You're bull-headed. When someone gets in your way, you stop at nothing."

"Maybe. You could take that chance."

"I happen to be very loyal, even though it may seem strange to you to hear someone with my background say that."

"Whatever. What's the plan?"

"Unfortunately your colleague, Ms. Lejeune, has threatened me with rather upsetting actions, so I'm conflicted."

"Tell me."

"You have two options but I only want to discuss one of them over the phone."

"And what would that be?"

"You will enjoy my hospitality tonight and tomorrow. I won't send you back to the storage room. You can use the upstairs bedroom. Around noon tomorrow you'll be free to leave."

"What do I have to do?"

"Nothing."

"And then I'm going to write a shocking article about master con man Kruger who has evaded the law again, and about the elusive owner or Green Monkey Holes."

"Yes and no."

"What do you mean?"

"Maybe I can prevent you from writing that article if I let you speak with Mr. Philip. Let's call him that for now."

"Is he Friends's father?"

"Like I said before, I can't tell you that."

"And if I refuse?"

"Then the story won't end happily for you."

"Those two bullies wouldn't let me leave?"

"That's right."

"So I have no choice."

"The problem is that you need to do something else."

"What's that?"

"You must call your girlfriend Ms. Lejeune and tell her to keep quiet until you're released. Obviously I can't prevent, shall we say, 'stories' coming out about me. But Ms. Lejeune's timing is inconvenient."

"Tomorrow's New York Times."

"Exactly."

"What if I don't call her or I tell her to go ahead and publish it?"

"Then it doesn't bode well for me. But it wouldn't bode well for you either."

"I thought you didn't like making threats."

"Oh, we've been doing that all day, Mr. Jameson."

212

Jens was quiet.

"My colleagues over there will hand you the phone. They have orders to make your stay comfortable."

"I'll think about it," said Jens.

"Take care, Mr. Jameson. I will call you the day after tomorrow if I haven't come across my name in a paper. Then we can talk about the possibility of speaking with Mr. Philip."

"What about Jennifer?" asked Jens.

"You will see her shortly, Mr. Jameson. She's just fine."

"You hit her."

"No, no, she merely bumped her head on a kitchen cabinet." He hung up.

Esther was in the newsroom, in Winkler's fishbowl. She was staring at the cell phone, which was connected to the recorder as well as the charger. She had been staring at the machine for thirty minutes. Winkler had brought her coffee three times and water twice and was gazing groggily at his "girl." He had had a long talk with his colleague at The New York Times. It had been hard to convince him to hold off on the story. A freelance contributor to The New York Times kidnapped— that was front-page news. They couldn't stand the idea that they would miss it and that Winkler would get the premier.

Esther was just about to give up hope when the phone rang. She saw a familiar number and his photo on the display.

"Jens, is that you?"

"None other," Jens sounded casual.

"How are you? Are they treating you all right? Where are you? Still in a model home in Green Monkey Holes?"

"Yes."

"What do you need me to do?"

"They promised to release me tomorrow at noon. Kruger's making a run for it and if he can't, things won't end well for me."

"So . . . ?"

"So I suppose I have to wait until noon tomorrow. Kruger's taking off but I have to wait." It sounded cryptic with the emphasis on "I" like that.

"Can they hear you? Are we on speakerphone?"

"No."

"You want us to go after Kruger?"

"I'd discuss it."

"Discuss it with whom? You can't say, can you? You can't say who we should discuss it with."

"Right."

"Interpol?"

"For instance."

"The CIA, the embassy?"

"Definitely the latter."

"The American embassy in Barbados?"

"Sounds like a plan."

"I love you," said Esther.

"I love you, too."

"Is that Jennifer still around?"

"I wouldn't know," said Jens. A little white lie.

31.

"Ms. Lejeune?"

"Speaking. Kruger?"

"You spoke with Mr. Jameson. Is everything taken care of?"

"That depends on you, doesn't it?"

"I will treat him with the utmost respect. You're getting the wrong idea about me."

"Mr. Kruger, I believe your employees are capable of anything. Certainly if you give the orders."

"I have no idea what you mean." Kruger was cautious, as if he was being interrogated by the police or as if the conversation was being taped.

"How do we proceed? I talked to Jens and he's obviously being held captive. That's kidnapping."

"I realize you're trying to get me to say all sorts of things over the phone, but I strongly deny any kidnapping."

"Okay, I get it. You don't want to incriminate yourself, although I don't think it'll make much difference."

"I invited Mr. Jameson to come with me and he did."

"On the tape he clearly says he's kidnapped."

"He can say whatever he likes. In return for coming with me, I promised him a conversation with someone he'd like to meet."

"Brigitte Friends's father?"

"Ms. Lejeune, that's between Mr. Jameson and me."

"We're writing that book together."

"Well, well. I look forward to reading it once it's published."

"But . . . ?"

"But what?"

"You won't let him go."

"I explained that I need some time."

"To get out of the country."

"The question is: What are you going to do?"

"Well, we've decided to wait 'til noon tomorrow."

"Good." Kruger hung up.

Esther looked at Winkler. She was worried. He answered her frown with a big smile. When he saw that that didn't go over too well, he changed his smile into a look of concern.

"Well?" asked Esther.

"Well what?"

"What are we going to do?"

"The papers—both here and in the States—will state that Jens has been kidnapped. We will also call the embassy in Barbados, so the local police can locate those assholes and arrest them."

"But Jens is in danger," said Esther, concerned.

"But as far as I can tell Kruger is really dangerous. He'd finish what he began in Hamburg. No more Jens."

"But he's a hostage."

"We'll see about that."

The men in the model home were busy transferring Jens's conversation from a digital memo recorder to a laptop. That finally worked and they could listen to the conversation between Jens and Esther at length.

They weren't the brightest stars in the night sky and they couldn't make anything of the cryptic discussion about what Esther and Jens were going to do. They were at a loss, so they emailed Kruger the file and called him, telling him to check his mail.

They offered Jens a sandwich. Fifteen minutes later the phone rang and they talked to Kruger. Alfred swore and hung up. He told his companion to get Jennifer from upstairs. He grabbed Jens by the arm and twisted it onto his back.

"You think you're so smart, huh?"

"I just know you're not, Alfred."

"Shut up and do what I tell you."

"What would that be?"

"We're leaving."

Jennifer came down the stairs. Her eyes were red from crying but she walked down proudly, with her back straight. She flinched when she saw Jens being held so painfully by Alfred.

He shoved Jens outside toward the car. For the first time Jens got a good look at the driver. He was now almost positive he had seen the man in Hamburg, and again he smelled Old Spice. No hard evidence of course but it did mean these men were probably capable of anything.

They were being taken to a different address. He could've been found here but now that they were being taken to a different location the situation was much less favorable. He probably wouldn't get a chance to inform Esther of a new address. At least he *hoped* it was an address and not a hole in the ground, where they'd be dumped after being murdered. However, he didn't think Kruger would do that—at least not straight away. The risk of being arrested was too big, and then he'd have to stand trial for murder as well as for fraud.

Of course Kruger's men were a different story. Jens rued insinuating that he had seen them in Hamburg. That could be a reason to hit him over the head with a hammer again, this time with a lethal blow.

Jens took his chances the moment Alfred let go of his arm. He shoved the man, causing him to lose his balance. Jens didn't have much time but he ran.

After a hundred feet he saw it was futile. He was a smoker, in terrible condition, in a humid climate, and his pursuer was in perfect condition. It wasn't going to work. When he heard Alfred's footsteps getting closer, Jens jumped aside and stuck up his hands.

"Okay, okay, it was worth a try," he gasped.

Alfred wasn't amused. He swung and hit Jens hard on his jaw. Then he punched him twice in the stomach. Jens dropped to the ground, cringing in pain. Alfred kicked him a few times in the stomach and when Jens turned away, he kicked him in the kidneys. He swore and it was clear he had lost it. Fortunately his partner came up from behind and restrained him.

"Remember, no visible injuries!" His English sounded South African.

The kicking stopped. Alfred stomped off and his companion pulled Jens up by his shoulder.

"If you don't stay put, you'll regret it," he whispered.

What a cliché, Jens thought. *Obviously there's still no college for gangsters and other thugs where they learn to come up with more original lines.* And straight away he wondered what on earth made him think that.

He stumbled to the car, where Jennifer was already waiting.

He was shoved onto the backseat next to her.

"Hi Jen," he whispered with a strangled voice. "I'm sorry I got you into all this."

Jennifer's voice was cold. "So am I."

"Are you angry with me?"

"Does it matter?"

"It would make me feel even worse than I already feel."

She ignored his remark. "What are they going to do with us?"

"I have no idea. They're taking us to a different address because they know where we are."

"Who's 'they'?"

"The people at the newspaper I informed."

Alfred, sitting in the passenger seat, snarled at them to shut up. He rubbed his knuckles. Jennifer gazed outside, clearly upset.

Jens could barely sit up. It put him in a foul mood.

"You're the one working with a bunch of gangsters. I can't help that. I only came back because they threatened to hurt you if I didn't."

Jennifer sobbed. "Oh Jens, this is terrible. I don't want to have any more to do with this."

"Calm down. I'm just in pain. I didn't mean to chew you out."

Alfred swung his fist and Jens only barely managed to avoid it.

"I told you to shut up."

"I wasn't finished yet," said Jens. "But I'll be quiet now."

The men drove at high speed across Green Monkey Holes, flashed their lights and the crash barrier was immediately raised. They sped up the road. *Hidden on an island of 166 square miles—how are they ever going to find us*, thought Jens despondently.

Jennifer suddenly realized where they were going. "Shit."

It was her house. Apparently Kruger didn't have any other inconspicuous address where he could hide Jens and Jennifer. The car pulled up on the driveway and everyone was led around the back as quickly as possible. Jennifer was made to unlock the kitchen door and they went inside. The driver got in the car and came back later. Apparently he had parked a few streets further on.

So there they were, all packed into the living room. Jennifer went to the kitchen and asked if anyone wanted coffee.

Iowa was stressed out.

When Jens and the men had emerged from the beach bar and gotten in the Mercedes, Jens hadn't looked around at all. Had he forgotten that Iowa was waiting for him? He had gotten into his clunker and had followed the Mercedes at a safe distance but when they drove past the barrier of Green Monkey Holes, he had panicked. He couldn't continue the tail and he remembered what Jens had said.

"Go to the police and tell them I'm in danger."

But Iowa didn't want to go to the police. If he walked into a police station, he probably wouldn't emerge for the next two years. They had given him the benefit of the doubt, giving him probation for being a cab driver to bank robbers, but if he walked in now, saying he had worked illegally for a foreigner who was being threatened by a prominent resident of Green Monkey Holes, that would almost certainly be the end of his freedom.

He parked his car and walked along the fence. Every so often he had to work his way through thorny bushes and across ditches in the dark. A little over a mile from his car he saw a padlocked gate. It looked like a construction entrance. He shoved the gate open as far as the chain would allow and eventually managed to squeeze his head through, followed by the rest of his body. Halfway he had gotten stuck but he pushed and squirmed until he was through.

Across the unfinished phase of the subdivision Iowa saw lights. He approached cautiously. The first thing he saw was the Mercedes and he knew he was at the right place. It was the only inhabitable house among all the homes still under construction.

He crept up to the house, hoping he could look in the windows. The closer he got, the harder his heart pounded. *I'm a hero, not a coward*, he said to encourage himself, but it had the opposite effect. He retreated.

It was a good thing he did, because at that moment he saw two men come out of the front and back doors and stand watch. He didn't dare move for fear one of the two men would hear him.

He held his breath until he almost burst and couldn't breathe inaudibly. Luckily the men were busy smoking and doing things on their cell phones.

Iowa slowly retreated further and went back to his car. He waited, hesitating again about calling the police. He had no idea what to tell them. He didn't know how to turn off the number recognition on his cell phone so that he could make the call anonymously. He called one of his sons, who immediately began relating such a convoluted story that he soon lost track. So he decided to wait and it didn't take long for him to fall into a restless sleep.

It was either magic, coincidence or luck that Iowa awoke with a jolt just as the Mercedes drove by at high speed. He was wide awake at once. Unfortunately he couldn't see if Jens was in the car but he decided to chance it.

There was barely any traffic—the Mercedes and Iowa's clunker were just about the only ones on the road—so keeping up with the car without being seen wasn't easy. Fortunately they entered the coastal road, where he could get closer than on the quiet roads around the golf course.

About ten minutes later the car turned off at Sunset Crest. Iowa assumed they were bringing Jens back to his hotel but when they turned onto another street, he realized: *Hell, they're going to that woman's house. They're going to the same address where this whole crazy movie began!*

He parked his car in the same spot as a week ago with his dear friend Jens Jameson. He saw Jens get taken out of the car and quickly shoved around the back. The woman followed, also being pushed. Iowa had an idea. He grabbed his phone and called the police emergency number. He was put on hold. Apparently the receptionist had to take a coffee break or go out for a cigarette, because he didn't get to tell his story for another four minutes.

Iowa told him he had taken a friend back to his hotel, and that they were attacked on the way there. His friend was dragged into a house on Sunset Crest. They had to send someone immediately, said Iowa. It was Jens Jameson, the famous foreign reporter. And a woman was being raped as well.

He waited, praying he had done the right thing. That Jens would be happy, pay him triple for today and would listen to all his stories again tomorrow.

Jens heard the sirens. The men were bent over their cold coffee. They hadn't dared to drink it because Jens had jokingly said that Jennifer might have laced it with sedatives. The sirens were turned off a few blocks away and Jens glanced at Jennifer in defeat. It was hopeless. No one could possibly have any idea where they were. It would never occur to anyone to check out Jennifer's address.

For a while nothing happened. Jens looked anxiously at his watch.

The New York Times would be printed by now but he didn't know if they were running the story.

All of a sudden about eight men were in the living room. They had bashed in the front door with a heavy metal object and entered the living room with guns drawn.

Alfred, his partner and the driver were scared stiff. They immediately raised their hands.

One of the men in the SWAT team stepped forward. "Mr. Jens Jameson?"

"That's me," said Jens. "The lady and I were kidnapped by these men."

"Ms. Jennifer Eduardo?"

"That's me."

"But you live here."

"We were held somewhere else first. At Green Monkey Holes," said Jens. "We were held by a man called Peter Kruger but on the island he goes by Peter Rock."

"Yes, yes, we arrived too late to get him. Fortunately your friend called us."

"My friend?"

"We're still finding out who he is. His story was confused but he gave us this address. He said his name was Iowa."

"My God! Iowa!" In the end it was that the crazy Rastafarian who had saved them from this terrible situation. Jens was touched.

Alfred and his men were handcuffed.

Alfred protesting loudly. "Ms. Eduardo invited us here," he tried.

"Liar."

"Then I misunderstood you."

"That's a typical Kruger trick," said Jens. "I suppose I also invited you to punch me in the stomach and kick my kidneys?"

"Accidents happen," said Alfred.

The commander grinned widely.

"I take it you won't tell me where we can find Mr. Kruger?"

Alfred growled. "I would if I could."

Jens wasn't surprised that Alfred didn't want to betray his boss but he wasn't worried; it shouldn't be too hard to locate Kruger.

Alfred's pants pocket rang. The ringtone of an old-fashioned telephone. It made him jump. The SWAT team commander walked over and grabbed it. Jens held out his hand and the man handed the phone to him. The display showed "unknown caller" and Jens growled "Yeah" in Alfred's deep voice.

"The cargo is safe," said Kruger. "Lock them up and come to the arranged place ASAP."

"Where?" Jens tried with the same deep voice.

Kruger swore under his breath and hung up.

PART 3

32.

Charles Rupert Hardford called himself Carlos here and he spoke the language almost without an accent. Not just Spanish but Catalan, the Majorcan version. It was very unusual and incomprehensible for 99.99 percent of the world's population. Charles lived on a large eighteenth-century Majorcan farm, called a *finca*, most of which wasn't in use. It had been remodeled several times. Throughout the years he had brought it back as much as possible to its original state. It had been time-consuming and he had acquired certain skills along the way.

He had learned how to fix old walls with natural stone; he had learned old woodworking methods and how to repair a roof the way it was done a hundred years ago.

The ground floor of the *finca* consisted of an entryway that doubled as a living room with a big open staircase to the top floor, a big eat-in kitchen and a few side rooms furnished as bedroom, office and dining room.

There were four more bedrooms with adjoining bathrooms upstairs. These, too, Charles had meticulously brought back to their original state. Bathtubs with claw legs, beautiful handmade tiles, antique porcelain sinks and toilets with wooden seats.

He spent most of his time in the kitchen, with a large fire in the hearth that kept the space warm and that he also used for cooking and grilling.

If someone from the historical preservation society had been invited to inspect all this work, he would have shaken his head, wondering what the point of all this occupational therapy was. Because despite his efforts, Charles never became a real craftsman. The remodeling was far from perfect but he didn't care. He was happy when he was working with cement and stone.

He had put a similar effort into the garden. When he moved into the *finca*, all the trees were dead. In the summer the dead growth was practically invisible, and in the winter the garden was covered in clover. He had had to learn which trees bore fruit and if they could be brought back to life with proper pruning, or if he should cut them up with a chain saw for firewood.

He had plowed the land with a tractor, planted new fruit trees, sown grass and planted an herb garden, and rabbits had eaten everything. He had found a large palm tree for a decent price and planted it close to the house. He had had to pull it up four times because it kept canting in the soft soil. The tree ended up at a sixty-degree angle but nevertheless it provided excellent shade at certain times of day.

Charles didn't care that the interior of the *finca* looked hopelessly neglected because he didn't like cleaning. Last summer he had fired his cleaning lady. She had stolen from his liquor cabinet, though that wasn't the main reason. She had a big mouth, she treated him like an old man and she threatened to sue him for sexual harassment when he gave her a forceful pat on the butt once. Luckily she was gone and Charles was alone with his animals.

His dog Luna was a perfect mix between a Labrador and a keeshond. If someone asked him what breed Luna was he would reply that she was a Mamutt. And if they weren't familiar with the breed, he would tell them that it was short for Majorcan mutt. As for cats, he didn't even know how many he had. Sometimes a few disappeared and new ones appeared, all preferring the cat food he bought in enormous quantities to catching their own meals. When the rabbits got out of hand, and Charles got sick of hunting them, he would ration the cats. Without supermarket food, they turned into wild tigers within days. They killed more rabbits than Charles would ever manage with his rifle. He just wasn't much of a marksman.

Luna happily joined in. She was a first-rate rabbit catcher. When she got hold of a rabbit, she would play with the animal, which, if it was lucky, would break its neck after a few shakes. Otherwise she was a sweet dog.

Charles was sixty-seven. He had a well-coiffed head of hair and a big mustache, both completely gray. He was stocky, with wide shoulders and a nimble gait. He had big brown eyes and his skin wasn't just tan in the summer; it was year-round weathered. He resembled Charles Bronson in his later years, although he was as much a film star as he was a builder, a farmer or a hunter.

Sir Charles Rupert Philip Hardford was knighted by the Queen of England for his service to his country as an RAF pilot and member of the House of Commons. He was a minister's son from a small town north of London and thanks to the church he had been able to go to university. Charles was a brilliant student; he studied philosophy and economics and then went to the London conservatory where he studied guitar and piano and wrote his thesis about the history of jazz in Europe. A publisher picked up the thesis after several jazz authorities had cited it. It was considered a leading academic text on the subject until well into the nineties.

However, in the long run those things hadn't been important to Charles. Once he made a career of politics and business he had no more time for philosophy or music. Only success had been important, success and lots of money. He had been a respectable father and faithful to his wife Anna Catherine, who, unlike Charles, had inherited her aristocracy effortlessly from her ancestors.

Catherine was the daughter of a duke. According to Charles he was a nobody. To him nobility had to do with being noble, honorable, patriotic and more of those lofty traits. Catherine's father lacked all of them. He was an opportunist.

Charles had never done anything wrong in his life. He had never cheated anyone out of a dime. He had never evaded taxes, never hurt or threatened anyone, never done any business he was ashamed of.

Three years ago, after his wife's death, he had broken with his in-laws. Catherine had been five years younger than Charles. Out of the blue she had begun to complain of headaches but she refused to have herself checked out because "headaches can be caused by so many things." Charles assumed she was referring to his shortcomings as a husband. But the headaches became unbearable and sometimes she was unconscious for several minutes at a time. He forced her to go to the hospital, where they discovered an enormous brain tumor, way beyond surgery or radiation. Catherine was resigned to it and Charles and his wife had spent a few more weeks together. Those weeks were both cleansing for his soul and the saddest of his life.

He had loved that woman.

It was evening. He had fed the chickens, the dog and the cats. He had showered the canaries—which he kept in an aviary—with birdseed. He had fixed some rice and chicken for himself, and he drank a terribly expensive red wine, the only luxury he hadn't given up.

The phone rang. He picked up.

A female voice on the other end: "Hello?"

He recognized her immediately. "Hello," he said tepidly. "It's been a long time."

"I couldn't find your phone number. You seem to be hiding nowadays."

"From people like you, you mean?"

"I don't know."

"Well, I don't. I just change numbers every now and then. You should try it. Without telling everyone about the changes, of course. It saves a lot of walking to the phone."

"Then get a cell phone."

Charles laughed. "That would defeat the purpose entirely. Then I'd never be safe."

"Charles, you're a fossil."

"Still, I bet I look better than you. Country life agrees with me."

"Oh, don't start all that green shit, Charles. We've got to talk."

"Do we? What about?" He was as amiable as possible, though the last thing he wanted was to talk with this woman.

"We can't discuss it over the phone."

"Well, that sounds exciting." Charles didn't sound like he meant it.

"I need to look you in the eye when I talk about this."

"Oh dear, that sounds like a family drama I want no part of."

"Come on, Charles."

"Carlos."

"Huh?"

"I'm a Spaniard among Spaniards."

"Would you stop that nonsense? I'm willing to come to you."

Charles considered it for a moment and sighed. "Still traveling first class and in limousines? Should I book a hotel for you?"

227

"No, darling, I'll do it myself."

Charles was unperturbed. "Send me a telegram when you get there."

"A telegram? They don't even exist anymore."

"Well, let me know."

"I will."

33.

Jeff stood in the bow and threw the line to Esther.

She missed it by a hair. "Yoho!"

Jens laughed and moved her aside while Jeff pulled up the line and threw it again. Esther jumped aside and Jens got the wet rope in his face. Now Esther was laughing.

"A couple of real sailors," said Jeff, walking to the stern and jumping to the pier. He pulled the stern line and tied it to a mooring ring. Then he came toward them, his hand extended.

"Jeff Jansen," he said and looked at Esther. "You must be Esther Lejeune, Frederick's friend."

"Well, friend is a big word. He was my boss but we have been on a better footing since he fired me."

"Funny story," said Jeff, his gaze shifting to Jens. Switching effortlessly from Dutch to English, he said, "You're the unlucky writer who got hit over the head and stabbed while searching for the truth. I recognize you from the photo."

"Fortunately the attackers were incompetent," said Jens, shaking Jeff's hand. "Jens Jameson."

They walked across the dock to the yacht club restaurant. Even though the club wasn't exactly the place for the jet set, a berth for an average-size boat still cost almost a thousand euro a month.

Jeff was wonderfully tanned. He had a muscular upper body which was perfectly visible, thanks to a tank top that ended halfway up his belly. A six-pack. Jens envied him. The only sporty thing he ever did was become a member of a gym. He had paid membership fees for years and kept meaning to go, until he calculated that each visit so far had cost him a hundred and ten dollars.

Jeff was five years younger than Jens. He was flexible, didn't have an ounce of fat on his body and he was attractive in other ways as well. He was friendly, well-spoken and charming. Esther immediately walked alongside him and Jens trudged behind them in his half-soaked shirt.

The restaurant was quiet—it had only just opened for lunch. The season had clearly ended. The islanders went back to taking the time and space for everything they had had to put off for three months. The waiters and kitchen staff were on their last legs. The last tourists weren't really that welcome. But Jeff was. Everyone greeted him in an incomprehensible language.

Two months earlier the Bajan police raided the home of Jennifer Eduardo and arrested three South African men and charged them with unlawful restraint of Jens Jameson. Jens had immediately made contact with the detective who handled the case in Hamburg; the German police were also interested in the detainees. They had discovered that two of the three men had indeed been in Germany at the time of the assault. They even spent the night in a Hamburg hotel. In addition, the forensic lab had derived a DNA profile from some skin tissue they found on the hammer's wooden handle. So the German police had asked the Bajan authorities for DNA samples of the men. Alfred and his men had gotten one of the most expensive lawyers on the island, so it took weeks before the DNA samples were granted. Then they had to be taken again, because in Germany it turned out the samples were useless. In the meantime the men were still in the Bajan prison, while their expensive lawyer came up with something new every day to stall the trial.

Kruger had disappeared into thin air. When news of the kidnapping appeared in the international media, the Bajan police had done everything they could to arrest the fugitive swindler. There wasn't a single Caucasian male above fifty on the island who hadn't been stopped on the street at least once and asked to show his ID. Kruger's passport photo was on posters at all the harbors. Everywhere, from the largest seaport to the smallest marina, officials were on the alert. Extra law enforcement and military were deployed at Grantley Adams International Airport and security was also tightened at smaller airfields. Kruger was wanted for swindle as well as kidnapping. Apparently his realtor's office had collected down payments on contracts without transferring them to the owners of Green Monkey Holes. According to insiders he had embezzled at least 1.2 million dollars. And some of the homes had been sold two or three times.

The local newspaper spoke of The Green Money Hole, because the payments to the realtor's office were taken in cash and probably deposited in a different bank. Since bank secrecy was sacred in Barbados, the money couldn't be traced.

To Jens the whole embezzlement story was a letdown. The connection between Philip and Stonewater Offshore now had a different meaning. He realized that Kruger had actually conned Stonewater. He supposed it was a dead end.

Everyone in Barbados had recognized Jens. Iowa was the media's darling, the hero who had informed the police of the hostages' whereabouts. The police commissioner had even spoken with him personally and promised to do what he could to reinstate his taxi license.

Jens was interviewed on local television. They asked him what kind of book he was working on. He told them he wrote about international con men and that Peter Rock/Peter Kruger was one of the main characters in his book. He didn't mention Brigitte Friends because he didn't want to involve her.

She did that herself by flying to Barbados in a large jet to pick him up. She had driven to the All Season Resort in a big white limousine, where she had found him having dinner.

He was astonished. "Brigitte, what are you doing here?"

"I'm bringing you to safety."

She had brought along two broad-shouldered men who stood at the entrance, looking around, searching for any potentially shady characters around the pool.

He arranged a meal for her, and the bodyguards also got to eat at a small table by the entrance. Brigitte thought the hotel was great and she loved the people. She also loved it that nobody recognized her or bothered her. Even when she sang something for the hotel owner and her husband, the Boy Scout General, they did nothing more than clap politely, saying it was a very nice song.

"You have to quit work on the book," Brigitte said that evening.

"Brigitte, I can't do that. I've escaped death twice. You can't ask me to stop now, that's not fair."

"I don't want you to get hurt."

"I'll be careful."

She said she didn't believe it. He should come with her—he had nothing more to do here. In a way that was true. The whole thing hadn't done his relationship with Esther much good. Jennifer had broken off all contact with him. Like Peter Rock, her job had vanished into thin air. Kruger had stopped paying the rent on her house at Sunset Crest and she had gone back to the northern part of the island to hide out with her parents. She had apologized to Jens and that was it.

So Jens decided to go with Brigitte and take it easy for a few days at her home in Miami. Esther hadn't been too happy about that. Jens had explained that he had to stay in Barbados in case Kruger was arrested. That was why he couldn't take the first plane to Amsterdam, where Esther had hoped to pick him up. But he did let himself get picked up in a large jet by "that blond bombshell with her diva attitude." Although Barbados wasn't that enthusiastic about Brigitte Friends, her arrival in Miami was a media circus. The accounts reached Esther within twelve hours via the entertainment pages: *Brigitte Friends saves her new lover from Pirate Island.* Jens could hear her growl from across the ocean—he didn't need a phone call to do it.

He had stayed with Brigitte for a few days and slept most of that time. Later he flew to Amsterdam and took the train to Rotterdam, where Esther was waiting for him at the station. When they hugged on the rainy plaza in front of the station, Esther forgot everything she had wanted to say. She stopped Jens when he wanted to say how sorry he was.

They got drunk and Jens had fallen asleep beside her in bed with a happy smile on his face.

In the following days he didn't understand what had possessed him that afternoon when he slept with Jennifer. He couldn't remember ever having so much sex and such terrific sex as with Esther. A whole world opened up for him and he became more and more convinced he should never let this woman go. They worked amazingly well together, she was a wonderful conversation partner on any topic he could think of and she taught him things he desperately needed to learn at age thirty-eight.

Without a doubt, Jeff was a competitor. Manly, tanned, and such a charmer that Jens practically had jealousy spouting from his ears. He had to restrain himself constantly from making sarcastic remarks. Jeff chose a table and decided what everyone should order. After all, he knew best what to have for lunch here. Since Jens didn't want to say he didn't like fish, didn't really want a salad and liked french fries for lunch, he surrendered grudgingly to this flamboyant sailor with his perfectly tanned skin. Esther probably noticed Jens's envy but she did nothing to make him feel better.

You're just taking revenge for the thing with Jennifer, dammit, thought Jens, but later he adjusted it: *You're right, I deserve it.*

Jeff gave them a variety of interesting details about Majorca and about the customs and traditions of the Catalan population. Apart from the locals, three hundred thousand foreigners also lived permanently or semi-permanently on the island—the rich and the retired who had managed to buy a nice house or farm at the right time. It had the best climate in Europe; in the past ten years it only snowed one afternoon and even that had melted within hours.

Jens quickly calculated that Majorca was ten times the size of Barbados. That meant finding things here would also be ten times as hard. Especially since, according to Jeff, half the economy was under the counter and registering official data wasn't taken that seriously. But Jeff had done his homework and they would follow up on an interesting lead.

When Jens left, Iowa went back to work as a cab driver. Jens had promised him a three-thousand-dollar interest-free loan, to be paid back over ten years, to buy a new car. In return Jens had asked Iowa to always drive him around for free whenever he was on the island. Iowa had found an adequate car for $1,750 and Jens told him to spend the rest on his family.

Apart from working his night shifts, Iowa was still fascinated by Kruger's disappearance. He was convinced Kruger had left the island by boat, so he visited all the marinas he could find and chatted with the harbormasters. He called Jens daily with new ideas. In order to save him money, Jens always hung up and called him back. He would tell Iowa to give it up. Kruger was supposedly picked up by an aquaplane that had been arranged by a smart international organization with lots of money. Jens didn't really believe that. Kruger and his men were amateurs and Iowa might very well find out how Kruger had left the island but he didn't want him to get into any more trouble.

But Iowa didn't give up. After going to all the marinas, including the really exclusive ones, and getting nowhere, he focused on the fishing villages. At the fifth village he hit pay dirt. Someone told him another fisherman had taken his boat out on the night in question and didn't come back until the following day. Without any fish! So he must have had a passenger. When Iowa questioned said fisherman he immediately became defensive.

So Iowa came back with his sons—all seven of them. They drove to the fisherman's tiny house in his new cab and his old Toyota. They all walked in and told him they would beat him up first, next they would burn down his house, then they'd sink his boat and finally they'd hand him over to the police.

The fisherman had complained that this was overkill. It wasn't logical that they would first abuse him and destroy his home and his boat and then call the police. But after some shouting back and forth he offered a solution. For five hundred Bajan dollars he would tell them what he had done that night. That way Iowa and his sons didn't have to commit a crime and they could also avoid involving the police.

To Iowa the idea sucked. He had already spent a hundred dollars on gas and on food to get his family to come along. When the fisherman said he would settle for four hundred dollars, that did it for Iowa. With full force he threw the cup of tea he had been given at the glass door of a dresser. When the fisherman opened his mouth again, Iowa told him how it was going to be.

"The whole world wants to know where you took that man. You're going to tell me—for free—or else your future won't be rosy."

The fisherman had done odd jobs for Kruger before. He had called him earlier that day, telling him to be ready. He told him they would make a crossing to St. Vincent that night, a smaller island ninety-three miles west of Barbados. And sure enough, that night Kruger and some other people had arrived. They had large suitcases with them—he suspected they were filled with money—as well as a crate.

They had stayed within the mobile network for a few hours but then had to make the crossing to St. Vincent. There they transferred their luggage to a hundred-foot-long yacht with several cabins. It was seaworthy—able to withstand quite an ocean storm.

The fisherman negotiated again when Iowa wanted to know the name of the yacht. For fifty dollars he told him Kruger had left on El Monzón, sailing under a Panamanian flag.

Jens knew that a real con man always had a good escape plan that could be used at any time. He was elated upon hearing the news and promised Iowa a bonus if the story checked out. From then on it got tricky. Anyone who wants to disappear into thin air has only to get on a yacht and leave a marina. Of course he would have to register with the harbormaster and Customs at the next port, but what they write down isn't public information. The only way to locate someone is to personally go through the registers of all the harbors and marinas where the fugitive may have gone.

Still, Jens believed in his luck. He had flown to St. Vincent and found out the crew consisted of two people. The captain was a 55-year-old South African who had been sailing the yacht for years. He had a Facebook page where he occasionally posted news about the yacht or their port of call. The second crewmember was a 23-year-old local kid. El Monzón was the first boat he had signed on.

Jens had looked up the boy's family, together with a colleague from a St. Vincent newspaper. He found out the boy was in regular contact with his mother. Jens had promised the family financial support and in return the colleague would hear about it as soon as the sailor contacted his family again.

The first message came from Cape Verde, which was the closest to the Caribbean. From there you could go to the left to Europe and to the right to southern Africa. The captain posted on Facebook about the Cape Verdean women. The boy called his mother from a public phone in Porto Novo and told her their next destination would be a port in Gibraltar.

Of course Jens and Esther had considered sharing their findings with the police. Interpol would definitely be interested but they had decided to see where Kruger would go, without further investigation into extradition treaties and such. After all, Kruger was the only one who might be able to tell them who Brigitte's father was.

When El Monzón left Porto Novo they had no idea if Kruger was still on board. He could have taken a plane to God knows where. However, that the boat wasn't intercepted and no welcoming committee awaited him in Cape Verde may have made him feel he was safe, at least until the next destination.

Jens had been in Gibraltar himself when El Monzón arrived. But the boat had merely taken on provisions, water and fuel and moved on. The sailor told his mother they were headed for a beautiful vacation island. His mother couldn't remember the name but when Jens mentioned Majorca, she was certain that was what her son had said.

Jeff explained all the dishes that were being placed before them. They varied from grilled green peppers to a dish called *frito Mallorquin*, a mix of potatoes and various organs. They were also served tapas, like sardines, garlic shrimp and chicken livers in hot sauce. Jens's face lit up when the meatballs in tomato sauce arrived. *Albondigas*, Jeff called them. But to Jens it was meatloaf and it saved the day.

El Monzón had registered with the port authorities of Palma, the island's main port as well as its capital. Customs would come on board; however, a thorough inspection wasn't expected. The island's Customs were overextended and even if they hadn't been, they wouldn't be that interested in yachts coming from other Mediterranean ports. Only a harbor in Colombia would have raised their interest.

Once the formalities were taken care of, the yacht would find a slip, but not in Palma itself. Jeff had connections with Customs and he would hear when El Monzón continued to its final destination. Then he would follow El Monzón with Esther. Jens would wait for the boat in the harbor.

"Uh," said Jens, "Why does Esther have to be on board?"

"Well, so she can stay in contact with you."

"Can't you do that?"

"I'll be manning the boat. I need someone I can trust."

"Yeah," said Jens. It sounded like a rock falling from a great height and landing on the table.

Esther had just nodded. Jens had decided she was completely smitten with the six-pack, the thick arms emerging from the tank top, the beautiful brown eyes and the wavy black hair. God, look how happy Jeff was that she had agreed to his proposal!

Never fall in love with an attractive woman, Jens had always told himself, after a fling with a long-legged photo model. He had given up on

236

her—his jealousy couldn't stand more than three weeks of lusty leers from other men.

Jens and Esther stayed in Hotel Jaume III, named after one of the last kings of independent Majorca, before it was annexed by Spain. Despite its name, Jaume III was a modern design hotel with a trendy restaurant that served breakfast, lunch and dinner.

They were going to meet Jeff for a tour of the island that evening but they were quite snappy with each other and it all came out during happy hour. Jens had complained about *that slimy, horny macho* that had his eyes on her and that she—*hopefully being completely naïve*—had taken it all like a *willing young girl*.

Esther had looked at him, mystified. He was unprepared for her frank expression and her friendliness. He had hoped he would finally be punished for what he had done to her with Jennifer.

"You don't seriously believe I'm interested in that guy?" she had said, genuinely indignant.

"Well, I wouldn't rule it out."

"Listen, Jens, . . ."

Here it comes, he thought.

". . . just because you kiss the first slut you meet while under the influence of the booze, the day, the island or the temperature doesn't mean I'm like that, too."

"Touché." Jens searched his mind for a further comeback but all he could say was, "But you're not jealous—I am."

"For your information, Jens Earl Jameson, I almost let you rot during that kidnap because you had written me about that stupid Jennifer. I kicked my laptop—total loss—when I read your 'honest admission'."

Jens struggled not to defend his "stupid adventure." He only just managed.

"How on earth did you find out about 'Earl'? I had totally forgotten I had that name."

"Don't change the subject, Jens."

"You no longer wanted me, Esther. You were fed up with me. You sent me away because you'd had enough."

"So away you went."

"Huh?" was the only thing Jens could utter.

237

Esther was quiet for a moment. She refused to believe he didn't get it. Jens moved his head slowly from side to side, feeling completely hopeless. It wasn't in his nature to say it but that's how he felt.

"Esther, I think I love you. That's a pain but I no longer give a shit. I just love you."

"Oh dear," said Esther.

"Oh dear?" replied Jens.

It was quiet for a painfully long time. Then Esther said, "I love you, too."

So a tour of the island had turned into a tour of each other. It ended up being a wonderful night.

34.

Esther stood in the bow in her bikini, enjoying the subdued waves of the "oh so blue" Mediterranean. Jeff was at the wheel, dressed only in gray shorts, savoring the view. He was quite taken with Esther and he was having a hard time. Certainly, not every woman fell for him. Of course he had no trouble seducing beautiful women, what with this boat and his looks, but that was relative.

This woman roused things in him he hadn't known about himself. She beat him in eloquence, charm and friendliness, but she was genuine. He found in her—in the honest, pure form—everything he had taught himself as tricks, clichés and spiels.

Damn it, he was nowhere near ready for a midlife crisis or penopause. All his flirting and seduction attempts were so obvious that he gave up and resigned himself to just quietly taking pleasure in her appearance. What on earth did she see in that pudgy wimp Jens? He wanted to fight for this woman. Unfortunately that was a sentiment from a different time, a different country, a different life.

El Monzón skimmed along the coast under full sail, so Jeff had to work as well. Not that he didn't like it but he would have preferred turning on the engine so he could stand next to Esther on the bow. But with the engine running he would've quickly passed the yacht, which was sailing close-hauled, and of course that wasn't the plan.

At regular intervals Esther called Jens, who tried to follow the coastline in a rented car. He was quite nervous. Luckily it wasn't a long trip, because the yacht headed for the harbor of Portals Nous, which prominent millionaires and billionaires called home.

Jeff wanted to change course.

Alarmed, Esther cried, "What are you doing? Follow him, Jeff!"

239

"I can't drop anchor here unless I bring a wheelbarrow full of money."

"We'll take care of that," said Esther. "Keep going."

"I really can't, Esther."

"You can always claim engine failure. Or that you're dropping me off. Kruger doesn't know me. But if Jens isn't there on time, we'll lose him."

Grumbling, Jeff surrendered. He told Esther to lower the sails and he turned on the engine.

She didn't want to lower the sails. She didn't want to lose sight of El Monzón for even a second. So Jeff lowered the mainsail, cursing. Then the foresail, and he made no attempt to do it neatly because he also had to watch that he didn't ram a hundred-million-dollar yacht now that he had the engine running.

Esther pointed at the first pier and said he could moor and drop her off. He headed for it and put the engine in reverse. Esther was on the pier before he knew it. Jeff stood there, caught off guard, calling after her to wait for him. He secured the boat and by the time he was done, she was gone.

She had found an excellent position from which to keep an eye on Kruger. She stood on a rise on the dock and saw exactly what was happening once the yacht was moored. In the meantime Jeff was negotiating with the harbormaster and she saw him pull out his wallet. The man was evidently being bribed.

Esther could see the captain and mate of El Monzón two hundred yards away. They had unintentionally left a trail so she and Jens could follow Kruger. No one else seemed to be on board. Had Kruger already disembarked? She cursed inwardly and waited to see what would happen.

Then Jeff was next to her. "I had lost you completely." He said it dramatically and put his arm around her.

"Well, here I am," she said, wriggling free.

"You don't want anything with me, do you?"

Esther met his eyes, perplexed. She didn't expect such a direct approach and this was also about the least logical time for a romantic proposition.

"Honey, this is the most exciting moment in months in this ridiculous continuing story. So right now I'm not in the mood for anything else."

"No, of course not." Jeff was happy that he wasn't directly and rudely rejected. He believed he still had a chance. Esther picked up on that.

"Besides, I already have a man."

"And?" they suddenly heard Jens ask behind them.

Esther felt relieved and pointed at the yacht. "No Kruger. We'll wait and see if his luggage is on board."

They waited well into the evening. Around dinnertime Jeff had gone to his boat and moored closer to El Monzón. He called Esther and invited her to come share his canned-beans dish. She could bring that Jens, if she couldn't lose him.

"I'll bring my lover along," Esther had answered.

The three of them had drunk rum, wine and beer until the lights went out on El Monzón. Jeff had been courteous and hospitable enough to offer Jens and Esther the stateroom, even though the gesture pained him. They took turns keeping watch.

When it was Jens's turn to keep watch, he saw a dark figure approach him on the dock without warning, no more than a hundred and fifty feet away. Jeff had docked so close to El Monzón that Jens couldn't call out without calling attention to himself in the quiet night. The figure stopped at El Monzón and Jens saw the lights inside go on.

In the faint light coming from the cabin, he saw what he had been hoping for. Kruger stood on the pier in a white custom suit. He grabbed two suitcases the captain handed him.

Jens quietly crept into the cabin, opened the door to the stateroom and whispered Esther's name. At first she thought that Casanova Jeff was making another attempt. Fortunately she recognized Jens right before throwing the punch she had in mind.

"Quiet. No lights. Kruger is out on the pier."

Esther crept on deck behind him. They watched as Kruger led the way, followed by the captain and the mate carrying the chest.

This will be your downfall, buster, thought Jens. *As a con man you have to learn to travel light.*

He motioned for Esther to go first, since Kruger only knew her name. They crept onto the pier. At the end they took the stairs to the dock and circled the parking lot to Jens's rental car and hid behind it.

Suddenly they saw a black shadow above their heads. Jens pulled Esther away, his heart beating in his throat. Jeff had followed them.

"Can't I play?"

"We had to be quiet."

"I can be quiet," Jeff whispered angrily.

Someone sitting behind the wheel of a BMW 700 Series opened the trunk from inside, and the chest was loaded in. The two suitcases were placed on the back seat. That meant the captain and the mate wouldn't be coming along.

Jens took stock of the situation. It would be damned tricky to follow the car in the dark without being noticed. And unfortunately the distance was too big to discern the license plate number; they would have to walk by or drive by to take it down, in which case Kruger would definitely recognize him. And that would be a big problem, considering the men he usually had working for him. But he had an idea, which he whispered to Esther and Jeff with pain in his heart.

Jeff put his arm around Esther and lazily ambled along with her from the parking lot toward the BMW on the dock. When the men looked up, Jeff and Esther turned and kissed each other on the lips. Esther wanted to make it a stage kiss but Jeff finally saw his opportunity to really kiss this muse that had crashed into his life out of the blue.

She broke off the kiss both to stop Jeff and because the men were walking back to the pier and Kruger was getting in the car. They walked a little further and were able to read the license plate number as the car left. The captain and the mate passed them and Jeff and Esther continued walking toward the parking lot entrance. There they waited for Jens, who drove his Ford Focus out of the lot as calmly as possible.

"That was just wonderful," Jens growled when they got in.

"It was your own idea," Esther countered.

"Yeah, a really smart one, too," Jeff added cheerfully.

They tore onto the highway and saw the BMW in the distance. The Ford Focus did its best to get up to speed but the BMW's rear lights disappeared over the next rise. It was quiet in the car; everyone was mentally encouraging the little Ford to do better. When the speedometer indicated they were doing over ninety miles an hour and they were passing one car after another, they had unexpected bad luck.

"You just passed a police car," said Esther.

"Yeah, and now he's after you," said Jeff from the backseat.

Jens slowed down. "That's just wonderful."

They were directed to the side of the road. Two Guardia Civil got out. You couldn't do any worse on this island. In Spain the saying went that if you were too dumb to be a garbage collector, you could always join the Guardia. Jeff negotiated in rapid Spanish but to no avail.

They had lost Kruger.

35.

The police station was in chaos. The waiting room was packed and more people waited outside. All nationalities were represented, judging by skin color and appearance. There weren't many white people. Either they had other ways of solving their problems or they just paid their tickets.

Jens wasn't here to pay his ticket. He followed Jeff, who walked straight up to a glass cage where a man with a few stripes on his epaulettes sat behind a desk. Jeff greeted him like an old friend and put a brown paper bag containing a bottle of the local liqueur on the desk. Jeff had explained to Jens that he still owed the man; it wasn't a bribe. They did each other the occasional favor because Spanish bureaucracy was slow. A bottle of booze or a few bills came in handy for oiling the machine. The chief sent away the people who were finally sitting in front of his desk after waiting for three hours, and indicated that Jeff and Jens could sit down.

Once the chief realized Jens was American, he began to talk at length about the difference between European and American football. They discussed the issue for roughly ten minutes, using arms and legs, before coming to the remarkable conclusion that Jens preferred soccer and the chief preferred football.

"They're pansies here, with their sneaky kicking and pulling. At least in America it's honest, straightforward ramming. Ka-Pow! Bang!" To illustrate, the chief jabbed with his fists as if he were discussing boxing.

Jeff came up with an unlikely story: Jens had scratched a dark blue BMW and he had taken down the license plate number. He wanted to stick a note under the windshield wiper but when he got back to the parking lot, the car had left.

The chief rolled his chair to the computer desk and typed in the number. He flinched when he saw the name that went with the registration but he recovered.

"Well, well, you didn't hit just anybody," he grinned. "On the other hand, Mr. Hardford won't be too worried about a little scratch."

"Mr. Hardford?" said Jens.

"Mr. Thomas Hardford," said Jeff. "Owner of one of the biggest estates in Majorca. Almost five hundred acres of fields, hills, forests and mountains. From the highlands to the coast. An enormous gentleman's farm with thirty or forty rooms. He lived there with his parents. Now he lives in a modern mansion on the coast that he had built for at least ten million euro."

Jens turned to the chief. "That's all we need to know. Thanks so much."

Jeff brought up the speeding ticket. He described Jens as a famous American writer who only drove so fast so he could catch up with the BMW in question.

The chief laughed out loud. "His wife was probably driving," he said in terrible English. "That blond beauty." He added a big wink.

Jens just nodded. He wanted to leave as quickly as possible. Back to the Jaume III to find out more about this Hardford and to discuss a strategy with Esther.

Thomas Hardford. So no Philip.

Esther had been asleep when Jens came into the room. The nocturnal chase had exhausted her. She lay on the bed fully dressed and Jens sat beside her with his laptop on his lap.

"Well?"

"The BMW is owned by a Thomas Hardford, a wealthy island resident."

Jens opened his laptop and googled. Hardford's name had quite a few hits. The first disappointment was that the man was forty-five years old. He couldn't possibly be Brigitte's' father. He was a successful businessman with a wide range of property, from a newspaper to an RV plant, from a large cattle ranch in Argentina to a golf course in Majorca. His fortune was difficult to ascertain but it was said his family was worth at least two hundred million euro. He had an office in his mansion, from where he could contact every corner of the world via cable and satellite.

Although Hardford was described as eccentric, it was his wife—twelve years younger—who dominated the tabloids with her provocative behavior. The couple was friends with the king of Spain, who sometimes visited the main building of the estate.

It was actually not his own fortune that he managed but that of his father, Sir Charles Rupert Hardford, a Falklands War hero and former member of parliament. Sir Charles had made his fortune in oil. He had been happily married to Anna Catherine Hardford, who had died three years ago of brain cancer. Charles subsequently withdrew from public life. Apparently he didn't even live in the main building anymore; it was only used for receptions and parties. Charles was older than Dora, Brigitte's mother. His name wasn't Philip but Jens wasn't married to the name. He had a much better chance with Charles.

Esther had put her head on Jens's shoulder, suggesting a keyword from time to time. And so they discovered that Charles had lived in London in the eighties, and that he was also frequently in the Netherlands for the company where he held a senior position. It corresponded with the information that Ina van den Boogaard had given Jens about Dora's mysterious fiancé. He was a well-known figure, both in the business world and in politics.

Jens was willing to bet Charles Rupert Hardford had been Dora's fiancé. Perhaps the engagement was broken off when Dora became pregnant. He closed the laptop and told Esther that they had found Brigitte's father. It felt like a victory but at the same time it was an anti-climax. The solution was so simple that all the effort they had gone to now seemed crazy. He had been discouraged with an assault just to protect someone's honor; he had been kidnapped and he had traveled the world for months to locate a con man.

"Let's see if we can get hold of Kruger," Esther said suddenly.

"Excuse me?"

"He still has your phone, doesn't he?"

"He did but it's probably at the bottom of the ocean somewhere between South America and Africa."

Esther was already punching in the number. "Kind of stupid that you didn't block him."

"Why? If he had used it, I would have been able to trace him through the phone bill."

"That's true."

The phone immediately went to voicemail. So that was a dead end. However, Esther's move did give Jens an idea. When Jennifer was talking to Kruger on the phone in the realtor's office, Jens had recorded his cell phone number. Maybe he still used it.

It took a while to pinpoint the exact moment on the digital recording. When they finally found it, they played the tones on their own phone. Esther called. The tension was palpable. She handed the phone to Jens.

"Hello?" he heard at the other end.

"Hello."

"Who's speaking?"

"This is Jens Jameson, Mr. Kruger."

"I don't know any Kruger."

"Mr. Rock then?" Jens went on stonily.

"I don't know what you're talking about."

"We had a deal, Mr. Kruger. You were going to help me find Brigitte's father."

"Are you trying to trace me through this call?" He sounded tense.

"No need. I know exactly where you are. I saw you get into Mr. Hardford's BMW last night."

He heard Kruger draw a sharp breath, then swallow. "Have you called the police already?" he asked sternly.

"I'm an optimist, Mr. Kruger. What use would it be to me if you're in a Spanish prison?"

"What did you have in mind?"

"A meeting."

Jens recognized the old Kruger when he answered, "Ha, our last meeting had an unfortunate ending. Perhaps we can do better this time."

"I want an act of faith."

"Well, well, Mr. Jameson."

"Tell me where you're staying."

Kruger laughed. "That's asking too much."

"Suit yourself then."

"You're no longer interested?"

"Look, Mr. Kruger, by now one of my questions has already been answered and I'm no longer that interested in Philip's identity."

"Then what do you want to discuss with me?"

"I want you to tell me the whole story. That should no longer be a problem. We can discuss source confidentiality."

"What if I refuse?"

"I'll send the entire Majorcan police force after you. And their first stop will be Mr. Hardford's mansion, to see what you have in that chest and those suitcases."

"You don't have that much leverage, Mr. Jameson."

"Perhaps you didn't hear what the Barbados police did while you were on your way from St. Vincent to Majorca on El Monzón? Kidnapping and brutalizing a reporter—that was front page news in a lot of papers."

"They brutalized you?"

"Alfred wasn't exactly gentle."

"I'm terribly sorry. I didn't give permission for that."

"Your choice of employees leaves much to be desired."

It was momentarily quiet at the other end.

"I'm staying at the Son Antem Resort near Llucmajor. You will come alone and tell no one where I am."

"I will come with Ms. Lejeune."

"Ha, you're a true lady's man. I look forward to meeting her."

"I'll see you in the bar in forty-five minutes."

"That is fast."

"It's better that way." Jens hung up.

He hugged Esther and they rolled across the bed, cheering loudly.

36.

The chambermaid sat on a bench in the hallway, her shoulders shaking. She was crying softly but no one paid any attention. Two medics with a gurney stood nearby but they didn't seem in much of a hurry to save someone's life or rush someone to the hospital. A flash from a camera came from the room. A few police in uniform and some men in civilian clothes were walking around the spacious suite.

Kruger lay on his back on the bed. He was holding a pistol and the pillow beneath his head was red. His head lay in a jelly-like substance, presumably his brains.

The inspector who was bent over Kruger's body studied the clenched fingers closely and indicated to the photographer from which angles he should take his photos. He lifted the sheet with his pen, looking for injuries or other signs that Kruger hadn't voluntarily placed the pistol in his mouth.

In particular Kruger's wrists caught his attention. It seemed they had been tied; he saw light traces of glue or something similar in the hairs above his wrists. He also pulled up Kruger's trousers and pushed down his socks. There wasn't anything out of the ordinary about his ankles.

Jens and Esther stood in the hotel lobby. They weren't allowed on the highest floor, where Kruger's suite was located. They argued with an officer who had escorted them downstairs and who didn't look too bright. They decided to have a drink at the bar and asked the man to inform the investigator in charge that they had arrived.

They were here at the hotel less than 24 hours ago to visit Kruger. Jeff remained in the car. He called them periodically; he was their backup in case things went wrong again. But Kruger was alone. He stepped from the elevator and walked toward Jens and Esther, clearly relaxed.

"Ms. Lejeune. How very nice to meet you. I must say, Mr. Jameson, you have an excellent taste in women."

"You have come far in life with that charm. But I'm afraid that in my case it won't work," said Esther, peeved because she realized that Kruger was also alluding to Jennifer Eduardo.

Kruger was unperturbed. "No woman is impervious to compliments. You have truly beautiful eyes, Ms. Lejeune. I have seldom seen eyes as clear as yours."

"Yes, thank you," she said bluntly and blushed, angry with herself.

"Mr. Jameson, Ms. Lejeune, you are beyond doubt amazing investigators. You followed me all the way here, you simply call me on the phone, you even find out at which hotel I'm staying."

"I suppose you'll be moving to a different hotel today?" Jens guessed.

"See, I trust you so much, that hadn't even occurred to me."

"Let's sit down," Jens said icily.

They sat down in a set of easy chairs around a coffee table.

"I assume you have turned on all manner of equipment? I must say it doesn't make talking any easier."

Esther placed her phone on the table and said it was turned off. Jens placed his new iPhone next to hers. Kruger inspected it closely.

"Okay, I trust you."

He stared blandly for a moment, and then looked intently at Jens. "I suppose you won't tell me how you found me?"

"It's quite simple. I'll tell you if you answer my questions to my satisfaction."

Kruger smiled. "That's reasonable."

"Let's get straight to the point then. Is Charles Rupert Hardford Brigitte Vermeer's biological father?"

"I can't answer that question with yes or no."

"That's not exactly a satisfactory answer."

"It's not as simple as it seems. When is one someone's father? Is it a matter of biology? That can only be proven with DNA testing. Or is it a social and moral issue? That makes yes or no answers complicated."

"Mr. Kruger, stop messing about," said Esther. "We just want an answer. If you won't give it, just say so, but also tell us why not."

"You're observant, Ms. Lejeune. You're right; I'm beating about the bush. The thing is…" He paused. When he spoke, his face and body language were incredibly charming. Esther hung on his every word. She could see how women almost had to believe him, wanted to fall for it, wanted to be conned and swept off their feet.

She had spent more than a year mapping out this man's life—his traces in the Netherlands and South Africa, his fraudulent practices, even the way he had managed to stay out of the prosecutor's hands in 2004, using a super trick—she had unraveled it all. And in the course of her research she learned to admire the man. The incredibly smart way Kruger managed to make tons of money using a combination of legal manipulation and psychology proved his professionalism. That demanded a respect not connected to the ethical side issues.

"Mr. Kruger, I spent a year tracking your history. I was an investigator for Dennis de Bruin, the man who exposed you."

"Aha! So you're the thorn in my side. What an interesting discovery. De Bruin was a first-class fool. I never did figure out how he knew all those minor facts about me."

"Minor facts?" Esther was confounded.

"Sorry," replied Kruger, "I don't mean to trivialize what you have dug up but of course it was only part of the story and not the most positive part at that."

Esther didn't want to react but if she had been alone with him, she would definitely have taken the challenge.

Jens got back to the point. "You were saying you didn't want to beat about the bush. So tell me."

"Mr. Hardford may have had a relationship with Mrs. Vermeer. That may even have resulted in a child. After all, they were both over thirty, adults in love; that is to say *he* was in love. Dora Vermeer was an attractive woman and not so puritanical that nothing could have happened."

"So Dora Vermeer became pregnant and Hardford believed the child was his?"

"Yes. You don't know Mrs. Vermeer. She doesn't get involved with a man without reaping some benefit from it."

"That sounds cryptic," said Esther.

"It does, Ms. Lejeune. You could call the police and they would arrest me but I am who I am. I'm prudent when it comes to matters of honor."

"Matters of honor," scoffed Jens. "Conning people is hardly a matter of honor."

"Mr. Jameson, some people are born to be conned. They have the money and they want to believe they're lucky. Their hunger for more makes them willing subjects in my line of work. Sometimes it's even educational for them to end up in a situation that doesn't end as they expected."

Esther and Jens glanced at each other, their adrenaline rising. But since they both waited for the other to put Kruger in his place, the moment passed.

"I know what you're thinking and you're right. But you must realize that in my business I have to create my own morals."

Jens almost felt powerless in the face of this man's rationalizations. "What about the lives you ruin? The people who never recover?"

"Sometimes it doesn't work out. Then I've really hurt someone. That is an unfortunate side effect of the profession. Things I can't correct, however much I'd want to."

"Ina van den Boogaard," mumbled Esther.

"Ah yes, of course, you met her. A tragic affair. I still regret the way that ended. And I recognize that it doesn't make any difference—the damage is done."

Jens noticed that Kruger was still formulating his sentences with precision, careful never to incriminate himself.

"I could mention more such harrowing cases," said Esther.

"I know, I know. But they aren't a large percentage of the total. Collateral damage, I like to call it. Unfortunate but unavoidable."

"Back to my story," Jens demanded. The conversation had lasted fifteen minutes and Kruger had hardly said anything helpful.

Kruger began his story. Charles Hardford had an affair with Dora Vermeer. He described the trysts in the Hotel des Indes and later in the luxury apartment Kruger had rented for Charles as a *pied-à-terre* in The Hague. He had to arrange those things because Charles was a clueless British aristocrat. Dora had asked for his help. The woman had amassed a sizable fortune from all her marriages and business talent, as demonstrated during divorce proceedings. She was too smart for Kruger. He had intended to make money off her as her advisor but before he knew it, *she* was costing *him* money.

Telford showed up later and Kruger saw it was a *fait accompli* with Dora. Charles Hardford remained the mutual connection. Kruger was to make sure the English lord's paternity remained a secret. Not only for his wife and children but for the public as well. Charles had a reputation to uphold. Kruger didn't want to say whether he and Dora blackmailed him. Just that certain payments and other transactions were carried out.

"Other transactions?" Esther and Jens had cried in unison.

"Yes. For instance, when Mr. Dijkgraaf reached me via Dora, I had to ensure that his investigation failed. That was both Dora and Charles's wish and possibly there were others who would like the same to happen."

"And you paid him from Barbados?"

"Yes. As you know, I had business there."

"Does Stonewater Offshore belong to Charles Hardford?"

"I can't say."

Esther tried to correct him. "You mean you don't want to say."

"Ms. Lejeune, Stonewater is a different subject. I told you where the money came from. Through which channels is irrelevant."

"As irrelevant as you arriving here with a chest and two suitcases which you loaded into Hardford's trunk."

"That has nothing to do with Charles, Dora or Brigitte." Kruger sighed and Jens and Esther did the same. "I'm telling you what you want to know about that case. The rest you can find out for yourselves if it's important to you. Though I strongly advise you to stay away from it."

"Or else a hammer treatment will follow?"

Kruger was suddenly stern. "Mr. Jameson, you must listen carefully. It stands to reason that I—should I even be involved in such a thing—would never admit it to you here. Surely you understand that. But I must say you're barking up the wrong tree. Neither I nor the men who are currently guests of the Barbados justice department had anything to do with that assault."

"I recognized one of the men. He was in Hamburg."

"That's true. But he didn't have an assignment, nor did either of them do anything like that on their own initiative."

"They were just as violent in Barbados."

"They didn't have my permission to use violence. That was something they did on their own initiative."

"They were in Hamburg to follow us?" asked Esther.

"Yes. I wanted to know how your investigation was going so I could avoid discovery of any links to Charles."

"But it was convenient that I was hit over the head," said Jens.

"Mr. Jameson, they may have saved you. They may have driven away your attacker. They may have helped you get back to the hotel."

"Bizarre." For a brief moment Kruger's remark completely confused him. If Kruger's men had followed him, he should have seen them. Maybe they were better and more professional than the person who hit him on the head. After all, there was a thirty-minute gap between the assault and the moment he fell up against the door of the Oyster Bar. Maybe they let him lie unconscious for half an hour and then saved his life.

They tried for another fifteen minutes to convince Kruger to give them more pieces to their puzzle. Any suggestions that he had smuggled drugs angered him. He dismissed any currency smuggling or money laundering. He only said that one acquires a lot of dirty laundry when one is at sea for two months. He listened carefully to Jens's story about the fraudulent practices with the construction at Green Monkey Holes. That homes were sold twice must be a mistake and Kruger shrugged at the down payments not being deposited. He asked if there was a formal complaint and he seemed reassured when he heard there hadn't been sufficient evidence for legal action.

Kruger ended the conversation himself before they got bogged down in too many unanswered questions. "I have spoken with you both in order to be rid of you. You, Mr. Jameson, and maybe you as well, Ms. Lejeune, have the attributes of a dog with an underbite. That sounds less friendly than I intend it. You sink your teeth in and whether you want to or not, you're unable to let go. It's the sort of thing you see in pit bulls or Belgian Malinois. I have surrendered and given you the information you wanted. My role in your play is finished. I will give you one more tidbit you haven't asked for, if you tell me how you found me."

Jens deliberated. It couldn't do any harm and the temptation to find out what else Kruger could tell them was great.

"We just looked for a long time, until we found the fisherman who ferried you to St. Vincent. For a few Bajan dollars he remembered the yacht and that a chest was loaded onto it. Then it was a matter of keeping tabs on the crew and the port registers, and waiting for you here at Customs."

"You do manage to make an exciting adventure of your profession, Mr. Jameson," Kruger said. "And you kept the police out of it all this time?"

"Yes. What would we have found out if they had been involved?"

"I can tell you this one more thing. When Charles had his affair with Dora, it wasn't—how shall I put it—completely exclusive. Charles was not aware of the other man. I don't know the details, only Dora does."

"You know nothing about this man?"

Kruger sighed deeply. "At the time Dora was disillusioned. She was deeply in love."

Esther guessed. "Bruno Ravalli?"

"She was clay in his hands."

"You had an affair with her yourself," said Esther.

Beads of sweat appeared on Kruger's forehead. "Not really. And not in the period relevant to your investigation."

"But you're now suggesting this man could be Brigitte's father."

"This man or perhaps another."

"You kept this from Charles Hardford for thirty years?"

"Charles was convinced the child was his. He believed in her talent."

"And if you want to be conned . . ." said Esther.

"So he did follow her career," said Jens.

"I should stop now. I have disclosed more than I should have. Good luck with your book and as I said before, Ms. Lejeune, I look forward to reading it."

Kruger got up and walked back to the elevator.

They were now waiting for the detective in charge of the investigation to emerge from that same elevator to talk with them. What emerged first was Kruger himself. At least, they assumed it was when two men came out of the elevator with a human shape under a sheet on a gurney. Jens and Esther wanted to jump up and run toward them but that wouldn't have been appropriate.

A long thirty minutes later a young man exited the elevator and walked toward them. "Jameson?"

Jens got up and shook his hand.

The man's English was quite good. "I'm sorry I've kept you waiting. My name is Alejandro Mardavall, chief inspector, homicide. Via your credit card and the hotel staff we found out you had a meeting here yesterday with the deceased. You may have been the last two people to see him alive."

"Was he murdered?"

"The first impression is suicide."

"Suicide?" they cried simultaneously.

"We can't be certain until the pathologist is done. I take it from your reaction you don't believe it was suicide?"

"The man in no way gave the impression he was planning to end his life. On the contrary."

Jens began to talk. He adjusted the story a little, since he may be arrested for helping a fugitive if he told the whole truth. He also left out Brigitte Friends. He and Esther had carefully planned their story so they would both say the same thing.

Jens explained what happened in Barbados: that he had been kidnapped by Kruger, that his assistants were still in custody and that Kruger had fled. That they had gotten an anonymous tip that Kruger may be headed for Majorca and that the anonymous informant had also named the boat Kruger was on. They had waited and seen him load a chest and two suitcases into a car. They had taken down the license-plate number and followed him. Yesterday they called him at his hotel on the phone he had used in Barbados and arranged to meet with him. They had meant to go to the police today to tell them of his whereabouts.

"I don't quite understand, Señor Jameson. You find the person who kidnapped you and instead of going straight to the police, you have a drink with him." Mardavall wrote something on a piece of paper and motioned to an officer, who took the note, walked to the reception desk and made a phone call.

"We're reporters, writers. We're working on a story," said Esther.

"But you're risking a lot of trouble." Mardavall got momentarily lost in Esther's eyes.

"Every profession has its risks," said Esther amiably and smiled.

"So what makes you think this isn't suicide?"

"He planned to move to a different hotel. We promised him a head start in return for his story. He had probably already packed."

"That's correct," said Mardavall. "He even called a cab an hour before his death. That makes no sense. Those are my doubts—what are yours?"

"Kruger wasn't too worried about being accused of kidnapping or fraud. He seemed confident," said Jens. "He was an experienced con man and during our conversation he spoke of his work with pride. He seemed in no way depressed or cornered and his activities in Barbados must have made him more than a million dollars."

The officer returned and handed the note back to Mardavall. He read what was added and raised his eyebrows skeptically. "You're sure you weren't mistaken about the license plate number? What make was the car and what color? Or couldn't you see it in the dark?"

"It was a dark blue BMW 700 Series, a sedan," said Esther. "I walked right by it."

"The number is that of a certain Thomas Hardford, a popular man on the island."

"Oh," said Jens and Esther, feigning surprise.

"Maybe we should pay Mr. Hardford a visit. If he wants to, that is. Junior is a difficult person. I won't be able to get a search warrant. There isn't a judge on the island who would cooperate with such a vague accusation."

A worried hotel manager ran toward them. He spoke in rapid Spanish—Jens could only make out a few words.

Their conversation seemed to have come to an end but when Jens wanted to get up, Mardavall said, "Señor Jameson, you should stick around for the investigation. May I ask where you're staying?"

"Of course. We're staying in the Jaume III." Jens was disappointed. "I had hoped you'd take us to see Hardford."

Mardavall was stunned. "You? The media? Go along on official police business?"

Esther cocked her head seductively. "That way we don't have to bother him twice."

"Besides, we're witnesses. We can tell you if he was the person behind the wheel." Jens was lying, of course; Esther hadn't been able to get a proper look at the driver.

Mardavall shrugged. "Most unusual."

Esther and Jens couldn't believe their luck.

37.

Mardavall got out and spoke into a small box containing a microphone and a camera. He had to hold his badge in front of the camera before the person on the other end opened the remote-operated gate. Apparently they weren't used to unexpected visitors here.

They drove up the well-maintained asphalt driveway onto the estate. It was like entering a nature reserve. The rocky landscape took them high into the hills. The flora changed every three minutes. Fifty years ago someone with excellent taste had planted a varied array of trees and shrubs. Now it was a full-grown collection of everything that was willing and able to grow in this fertile soil. There were orchards, a vineyard on mild slopes, here and there a field of palms and a strange piece of land with hundreds of ancient olive trees.

The first structure they passed was an old *finca*. Mardavall told them that was where the old Hardford lived. He had been a popular figure in the past, but the last three years he had retreated from the outside world.

Higher up the landscape became rougher. They passed the large mansion at the foot of the mountain. A classic gentleman's farmhouse, large enough to easily provide accommodations for ten families.

They entered a pass and then they were on a narrow road going down. The switchbacks were so steep that the driver of the police car had to do an occasional three-point turn because he couldn't make it in one go. The road seemed to have no end but eventually it widened and they saw a parking lot beyond a thick wall. Someone was waiting for them at the open gate, which was closed right after they drove through. Jens spotted the dark blue BMW and felt quite smug.

Mardavall got out and instructed Jens and Esther to follow him, and to say absolutely nothing to Hardford Jr. They followed the man who had opened the gate. He was past his prime but built like a truck. They descended a white marble staircase toward the sea, made a sharp turn and saw an enormous mansion, completely white. The building consisted of eight cubes adjacent and on top of one another. Some exuded soft, friendly light. The square footage of this villa was no less than that of the immense main building they had passed earlier.

The housekeeper opened the door and asked them to wait in the enormous foyer. Large fish swam in a sizeable pond that was kept aerated by a fountain. They resembled miniature sharks—pretty scary but according to Mardavall completely harmless.

They waited a long time and the inspector was getting annoyed. He paced restlessly and spoke in rapid Mallorquin with his colleague. Jens and Esther understood none of it but he was obviously getting angrier.

About five minutes later Thomas Hardford entered. He was short, and clad in a light blue polo shirt, khakis and boat shoes. His thin hair was dyed and neatly combed over his bald spots.

He looked surly but his welcome wasn't so bad. "Welcome gentlemen, madam. What can I do for you?"

"We want to talk to you about an awkward matter," said Mardavall in his best English.

"Well, follow me." Hardford seemed almost disinterested, as if he discussed awkward matters several times a day.

He led them to the library. The books, stacked up to the ceiling in evenly spaced white shelves, seemed fake, as if they had been bought by color, size and by the yard.

They sat down on a large couch offering a view of the sea. The sun was working on one of its better descents.

"Do you know Peter Kruger?" Mardavall began.

"Certainly. He's a friend of my father's."

"A business relation or a private friend?"

"He's an old friend. I don't know if they ever did any business. They certainly don't anymore," grinned Hardford.

When Mardavall, Esther and Jens all looked at him with wide eyes, he clarified. "My father no longer does any business. Except for farming." He laughed, which exposed for the first time a few gold teeth among otherwise unnaturally white teeth.

259

"Do you have any business with him?"

"No. What are you getting at?"

"Where were you Monday morning around two?" asked Mardavall.

"In my bed, I hope." Hardford sat up and raised his voice. "Titsia!"

Almost immediately a blond woman appeared in the doorway. She wore stiletto heels, a miniskirt and a glittery top. She had her hair piled high and she wore an amount of mascara that would last a normal person an entire month.

"Gentlemen," she said in a surprisingly high voice. Then she looked scornfully at Esther, who was wearing jeans, a t-shirt and tennis shoes.

"Oh sorry. Madam."

"Darling, tell these people we went to bed at midnight every night during the past week and that I didn't get up before seven in the morning."

Mardavall interrupted him, visibly annoyed. "I could've asked her that myself. Is it possible your husband left last night without you noticing?"

"No, I'm a light sleeper."

"Does anyone use your car without your permission?"

"No. But you're wondering what my employee was doing in my BMW at Portals Nous harbor," said Hardford.

"Yes," said Mardavall.

"He was helping Mr. Kruger get his luggage off the yacht."

"Off the yacht?"

"Yes. He had just arrived from Gibraltar and he had to get his luggage off the yacht."

"Are you aware of Mr. Kruger's recent actions in Barbados?"

"No, I wouldn't know anything about that. My father asked me to help him, so I sent someone."

"I see plenty of cars in the parking lot. Was your expensive BMW the only one available?" Jens asked.

Mardavall glared at him.

"I saw you in Portals Nous. You were driving," said Esther.

"That's nonsense. I'll give you the name of the man who drove the car. I don't appreciate you coming to my house and accusing me of lying."

Mardavall was standing with his back to Hardford, glaring at Jens and Esther. He raised his finger in warning, and then turned around.

"Where was his luggage was taken?"

"According to my information they drove to his hotel—the Son Antem Golf Resort, if I'm not mistaken."

"Mr. Hardford, Kruger is a criminal who is wanted in several countries for fraud, kidnapping, being a member of a criminal organization and inciting violence—possibly even attempted murder. You say you assisted this man?"

Hardford was visibly shocked. "I think we should continue this conversation with my lawyer present. I don't know anything about Kruger's criminal past."

"Where were you this afternoon around three?"

"I was here. I was here, right, Titsia?"

"Sweetie, how should I know? I was shopping this afternoon." Before Hardford could burst out in anger, she said, "Just kidding." And addressing Mardavall, "He blocked my credit card. He claims it's a crisis."

"Kruger was found dead in his hotel room around that time."

Titsia squealed. "Oh no, that poor man!"

Astonished, Mardavall said, "So you met him?"

"Yes," said Titsia, mystified.

Thomas Hardford looked annoyed at this revelation.

"When?"

"The day before yesterday," said Hardford. "I would like you to end this interrogation now. We will continue with my lawyer present. Would you like me to call him?"

"No, you can come to the station tomorrow."

"That seems a bit heavy-handed, Inspector…"

"Chief Inspector Mardavall."

Hardford was unperturbed. "That's a bit heavy-handed, Mr. Mardavall, but you're welcome to come back here tomorrow."

"I could take you with me." Mardavall was clearly suffering from his Spanish pride.

Hardford merely smiled. "By all means, get an arrest warrant. Either way, this conversation is over."

Mardavall cursed and swore the whole way back. When Jens requested a translation, it turned out the chief inspector was talking in no uncertain terms about *those foreigners who think they can buy immunity here with their euros.*

Esther had been thinking. "It doesn't add up."

"What doesn't?"

"The car didn't go to Kruger's hotel. It went this way. That chest is here."

"Listen, Ms. Lejeune, forget about the chest and the suitcases. If they contained anything illegal, it's long gone now. This estate is almost three hundred acres. Or it's elsewhere on the island, and it's over 1,400 square miles. If you had called us last night, or even earlier, we may have been able to find the contents."

He was right, of course. They didn't have much regarding Kruger's flight. His things were gone and he was dead. They didn't expect Hardford Jr. to cooperate. The only thing left for them was to speak with Senior.

They drove onto the grounds of the old *finca* at dusk. Charles immediately emerged from the front door with a large hunting rifle resting on his arm.

"Get lost," he cried.

"Policia!" called Mardavall.

The man lowered his rifle. "A lousy time to announce yourselves. I'm making dinner." He turned and went inside.

The four of them followed him, straight into the large eat-in kitchen, where a big kettle hung over the fire. It looked like something in a fairy tale and Hardford Sr. resembled a decrepit wizard, somberly skinning a bell pepper.

"If you roast off the skin, the peppers are sweet," he told Mardavall, who shrugged. As if he didn't know. He knew more about the traditional cuisine of the region than anyone else.

"Do you have any questions or are you merely here to see how I make the ultimate *frito Mallorquin?*"

Everyone was standing uneasily around the table.

"Sit down, sit down."

They all grabbed a chair except Esther. She moved to the counter next to Charles and grabbed a bell pepper so she could peel the skin off.

"Ha!" cried Charles. "A beautiful woman in my kitchen again. My wife was the best cook ever—she couldn't keep her hands still for a second."

"We have bad news," said Mardavall. "It's about your friend Kruger. He's dead."

Charles turned to him and grinned faintly. "It's never pleasant when someone dies but in this case I'd say good riddance."

262

"Come now, Mr. Hardford. It seems you were friends for a long time."

"Who says so?"

"Your son."

"Ha! Another swindler!" Hardford turned away and continued peeling the bell pepper. He also examined the pepper Esther had been peeling, to see if it was satisfactory.

"I heard that your son helped Kruger get his luggage off the boat at your request."

"Luggage?"

Hardford sounded like a confused old man, though it could also be that he was covering for his son or that he knew nothing.

"Yes, luggage."

Hardford was silent.

"Well?" asked Mardavall.

"When Kruger asks me something, I refer him to Thomas. He takes care of things with that thug."

"Fair enough. But did you speak to Kruger yourself?"

"No."

"Your son claims you did."

"Maybe I'm mistaken." Hardford didn't seem too interested in the whole affair.

"When did you last have contact with Kruger?"

"Oh, I wouldn't know. I live in a time void. A vacuum of days, seasons, cold and heat. I live with nature and rarely get involved in the outside world anymore."

Esther and Jens glanced at each other. They tried to gauge whether the old man was acting or whether he really was that out of touch.

"I believe Kruger was murdered. Any idea who the killer might be?"

"No. The man had so many enemies."

"Could you name a few?"

"I didn't know him that well. I only know he made a lot of enemies with his fraudulent practices."

"So you knew about those?"

"In a distant past. Distant as in thirty years ago."

"Yet you continued to do business with him."

"Business, that's a big word. I ran into him occasionally and he'd ask me for money."

"And you'd give it to him?"

"Sometimes."

"What did he do in return?"

"Nothing."

"This isn't making any sense."

"No, it's not. I've had enough for today. Come back if you have anything more specific you'd like to ask me."

Mardavall shrugged. He was ambitious. At thirty-five he was already chief inspector. And he had done it without help from his father, who had once been a prominent lawyer and well connected in political and governmental circles. He had solved several spectacular murders and spent the rest of his time on a large number of easily solved family dramas and crimes of passion. He carried the two or three murders he hadn't been able to solve with him like a heavy burden. Every time he found a new lead in one of those cases, he would reopen it and continue to look for the killer.

This could very well turn out to be a similar case, he reflected. It would be easier to just dismiss it as a suicide. Kruger had been a thug who had every reason to kill himself after those reporters had followed him here.

But the facts nagged at him. The duct tape remains on Kruger's wrists, the absence of a suicide note, the fact that Kruger had packed his suitcase and was still wearing his shoes, the strange position of his fingers around the weapon—these were matters he couldn't dismiss.

He wasn't getting anywhere. He walked out and his colleague followed him.

Jens and Esther stayed behind.

"We're not police," said Jens. "We had a meeting with Kruger yesterday."

"Ha, I knew you weren't Spanish police!" Hardford grinned.

"I'm writing a book about your daughter."

"My daughter?" Hardford blanched.

"Brigitte Vermeer."

Charles gazed at Jens without seeing him. He grabbed at his forehead and sat down.

Esther stood so close to Charles that she could almost put her hand on his shoulder. "We would like to come back and discuss it with you. We want to keep the police out of this."

"You're going to reveal that…"

"We want to discuss it with you."

"I'd rather not."

They gave the man a meaningful look. "I understand, but you have to."

"Why?"

"Kruger told us something you should know."

Hardford gazed at Jens with suspicion. His wild hair looked macabre in the light of the fire. He deliberated. "You can come back tomorrow morning, around eleven."

38.

Schöteldreier sat at a neatly laid table in Brigitte's apartment. Ringo Adams, "chef to the stars," was in the kitchen, arranging appetizers on plates. For around $3,500 one could hire Ringo and his staff of three for an evening. He would make a fantastic dinner for two with endless courses using the most unusual ingredients. Ringo was a fan of molecular cooking.

Brigitte was sipping her champagne, a Bollinger from an excellent year. She had already had a few glasses before Schöteldreier arrived, because she was nervous. She had invited him because Jens had sent her the first chapters of the book. She was quite enthusiastic about them.

Jens wrote during the two months he had to wait for Kruger to arrive in Majorca. During this time he and Esther also spent a few weeks in Brigitte's house in Miami. Brigitte herself had come for a weekend to answer some questions. The mood had been different from the first time, without Esther.

The evening she left, Brigitte had told Jens he had conquered a special place in her heart—that she had a hard time seeing him so happy with Esther. She hadn't been difficult or put him on the spot in any way, but it evidently hurt her enough not to want to stay with them on North Bay Road.

"You're drinking a lot nowadays," said Schöteldreier, as the first course was served and Ringo personally poured a white wine.

Brigitte had said she would taste it, although she began to like demi-sec champagne. "Not that much, just often. I like it. It's nice and relaxing after a long day."

"You'll get out of shape and it will affect your concentration and your voice."

She thought before responding to his grumbling. "Shape, concentration, voice. Those things have nothing to do with me personally."

"What do you mean?" Schöteldreier asked sternly. He prodded the four little cubes of food on his plate and examined the test tube in which Ringo had ostentatiously poured the sauce.

"I mean that I'm pretty satisfied with what I've accomplished. And that I want to enjoy life from time to time as well."

Schöteldreier was indignant. "But you like your success, don't you? I wish I were that famous and that I could sing like that, winning the hearts of so many people!"

"Been there, done that—the success, all the people who admire me for my voice. I'd like to really win the heart of one person. Or I'd like someone to really win my heart."

"What is wrong with you, Brigitte? We have come so far."

"Yes, very far." Brigitte was quiet. She emptied the test tube out over the cubes on her plate and seriously tried to experience the taste sensation. It didn't do much for her. She preferred having dinner with Jens. She would rather have a nice juicy steak in a modest restaurant than this exclusive B.S.

Ringo had been Schöteldreier's idea. He had heard that it was a once-in-a-lifetime experience, and, stingy as he was, he would never spend that kind of money on it himself.

After the meal, in the living room, when one of Ringo's assistants poured coffee, Brigitte came to the point.

"Onkel, I have read the first chapters of Jens's book."

"Oh?" Schöteldreier shifted to the edge of his seat. "And?"

"It's really well written. It holds a mirror up to me, and I now see everything extremely clearly—how I've lived my life."

"Hmm." Schöteldreier sat back again.

"But you won't be too happy with the way he portrays you during our time in Hamburg."

"I was afraid of that. I'll put a stop to it, don't worry."

"No Gerard, we won't stop it. It's a good book. Jens wrote it with respect to the way things were done at the time. He even left out certain things at my request, or else he wrote about them in very general terms."

"Such as?" asked Schöteldreier.

"You know exactly what I'm talking about."

"I don't, Brigitte. I have always worked my tail off to provide you with the best of everything. I did all I could to make you a star."

"That's right, Gerard, and he wrote about that. But you also crossed the line a few times."

"Says who?"

"They did their research quite thoroughly."

"You mean they spoke with my enemies."

"It makes no difference. He writes about the whole affair with Weintraub pretty cryptically. And about the girls and the whole argument about going topless."

"Brigitte, this book is going to be disastrous to your image."

"Onkel," she said, more sternly that she had ever been with her manager, "I don't think it's that bad. And even if it was, I would still want it to be published."

"Let me read it. I'll give it to the lawyer. And our publicity people can also analyze it."

"This is my project, Onkel Gerard. I'm not going to involve you."

Schöteldreier was irate. "Then I'll block it based on what you're saying right now! Who do you think you are that you can judge these things? I made you what you are and I deserve some gratitude. I'm not about to have some third-rate snot writer destroy it all!"

He stood up.

"You can't do this to me, Brigitte. I worked my tail off for you all these years. And now you're dropping me. I said from the onset that this would end badly."

Brigitte raised her voice, something she'd never done in front of the man who had been her mentor for more than seventeen years. He had counseled her, cared for her, protected her. He had planned her career from beginning to end.

"Gerard, I've always done what you told me. But it's about time this girl stood on her own two feet. Besides, there's a lot of stuff you didn't tell me. You made a lot of decisions without discussing them with me. You kept things from me."

"I don't know what you're talking about."

Ringo's assistants were doing dishes. They were clearly embarrassed, not knowing where to look in the open kitchen.

Brigitte got up too and drew a deep breath. "Okay, I'll give you one more chance. Tell me about your connection to this Charles Rupert Hardford."

"Who?" Schöteldreier seemed confused.

"Hardford. And Peter Kruger, do you know him?"

"I don't know what you're talking about."

Onkel Gerard had obviously decided to deny everything flat out.

"Brigitte, you're drunk. You're talking nonsense and I'm leaving. We'll talk once you've recovered from your hangover."

"I'm not drunk!"

But Schöteldreier got his coat from the coat closet and left without putting it on, slamming the door behind him.

39.

The conversation with Charles was a breakthrough. Esther and Jens arrived at the gate at eleven in the morning and had to wait for fifteen minutes before they were allowed in. First Thomas Hardford had to approve the visitors, and then Charles himself. Then someone drove up to the gate to inspect their backseat and the trunk.

Charles was picking oranges in the orchard by his house. He stood on a strange triangular ladder above a large fruit basket. Esther and Jens walked toward him and Jens held up the basket so Charles didn't have to go up and down the ladder all the time. Esther began picking oranges as well.

"Only the fruit that are loose," Charles said without greeting them. He seemed distracted, picking the colorful oranges as if in trance.

The odd scene lasted about ten minutes. Everyone was silently working until the basket was full. Then Charles descended the ladder, grabbed in the basket and peeled an orange. He divided the fruit into three pieces and handed each of them a piece. They savored the juice for a moment. Jens had never tasted anything like it. He rarely ate fruit and when he did, it came from a cheap grocery store. That didn't even come close to the juicy, fresh, sweet-and-tart taste he experienced now.

"Well, here we are," said Charles.

Jens and Esther remained quiet, not knowing what to say. What Charles was about to tell them could very well be a milestone in their investigation.

"I couldn't sleep last night." He spoke softly and slowly, pausing after every sentence.

The story gradually became clear through his short sentences and thoughtfully spoken words. Charles had only been unfaithful to his wife once. The woman he fell for was so full of life, so breathtakingly beautiful and sexually uninhibited, so experienced and exciting that everything he believed in had collapsed. All the things that were a part of his life—etiquette, the adoration for his wife, his honor, faithfulness, all the values he had learned, honored and which he later embraced again for the rest of his life—were suddenly gone.

For eighteen months he had been under Dora's spell. He had reorganized his life so he could be with her as often as possible. He had debated leaving his wife and starting a new life with Dora, but in the end he realized his love for Dora was one-sided. Dora liked him and appreciated his company but she didn't truly love him.

At some point she informed him that she was pregnant and that he was the father. That's when he discovered a completely different side to her. She was determined to keep the baby. Not because it was their love child; she was just ready for a baby. But not for a family or a husband. No, she was fed up with Charles, especially when he tried to convince her to have an abortion or to have the child adopted upon birth. She didn't want anything more to do with him.

Charles had been willing to take responsibility for the baby. Dora's daughter was not only a moral obligation to him but also proof that he had once intensely and passionately loved another woman, with a real love that wasn't acceptable or possible, and therefore doomed. The child was living proof of that period of his life. He wasn't proud of the evidence but he grew to love her from a distance. He made it his goal in life to give Brigitte the same chances his other children had, even though he couldn't do it directly.

"But you've always wanted to keep it a secret," said Esther.

"Of course. Sir Charles Rupert Hardford's bastard child would be the news of the year for the tabloids. Certainly since I was a member of parliament at the time, but also later, when I had connections to English royalty and most other European monarchies."

"And now?"

"To be honest, the worst thing of all would have been to put Anna Catherine through it. I suspect she knew, though she never mentioned it. She was a strong woman—I loved her dearly."

"But?"

"But now she's dead and I may not be able to convince you and your pretty assistant to stop your investigation."

271

"Because you tried that."

Charles laughed furtively. "Not really. When I heard that Brigitte wanted to know who her father was, I secretly hoped she'd find me."

He took the basket with oranges from Jens and walked toward the house.

"Thomas arranged everything with Kruger. Thomas does business with the man. He's worried about the family reputation. And that while he does business with that swindler! A swindler who has now shot himself in the head. What a scandal for the family. But I no longer care. I'm sick and tired of all of them. My son, my official daughter and the whole so-called aristocratic lot of them."

Charles spoke of watching Kruger operate on the cusp of what was legal and what wasn't. Dora had rebuffed him when he tried to swindle her but he was the only one who knew about their affair and somehow he had assigned himself as a mediator. Charles didn't want to call it blackmail but he knew a large part of the money he paid to support Brigitte was kept by that terrible Kruger and his partner in crime Schöteldreier after Brigitte ran away from home.

"Onkel Gerard?" Jens cried out in surprise. "You paid Onkel Gerard to support Brigitte's career?"

They had moved to a couch by the front door of the *finca*. A middle-aged woman in an apron brought small cups of extremely strong coffee, and Charles added large spoonfuls of sugar to each of them without asking.

He was taken aback. Evidently he had told the reporters more than they already knew. He deliberated, threw back his small coffee and shrugged.

"Well, I won't give you the details. They don't matter. It seemed she really needed it. She had enough talent to work her own way to the top and she worked hard to do that. I suspect this 'Onkel' mainly enriched himself with the money I sent. He drove expensive cars while Brigitte was drawing beers in that seedy place on the Reeperbahn."

"How much money are we talking about?"

"As I said, I won't give you those details. Let's just say I kept an eye on things." He got that confused expression again. "You're not going to write all this down, are you?"

"We're writing a book about Brigitte and of course we can't omit things about her career."

"My God." Charles put his head in his hands. "My son will kill me."

He shocked himself with that statement. "Of course I don't mean it literally."

"Do you have any idea who killed Kruger?"

"Are you sure it's not suicide? I would shoot myself if I were such a bastard as he was."

"We're not certain but the inspector suspects murder." Esther also threw back her coffee and shuddered. She hated sweetened coffee more than anything.

"I have no idea," said Charles. "And I don't care."

At some point Charles let slip that Dora was on the island. She had summoned him to the Arabella Sheraton, a five-star hotel on the Campo de Golf Son Vida, just outside Palma. But he hadn't gotten around to visiting her. She had called Thomas and sent a car with driver three times to pick him up. Every time he had come up with an excuse. He didn't really feel like seeing her, especially because he had a pretty good idea why she was here. But Jens and Esther mustn't know that.

The woman returned with the coffee carafe. This time Esther smartly evaded the sugar pot.

"Kruger told us something else that might be important to you."

Charles seemed distant. He was pondering Jens's suggestion to meet with Brigitte. They would tell her about him and Jens was sure she would insist on meeting her possible father.

"Possible father?" Charles asked angrily.

"Yes." Esther looked compassionately at him.

His gaze turned inward. For a brief moment something sparkled in his eyes, as if he could picture his daughter sitting here across from him.

"He said Dora was also seeing another man during the time of your affair with her."

It took at least a minute for that to sink in. Then he was startled. They had gradually become used to this man's rhythm. Sometimes the words came gushing as if he were in parliament, giving a speech—at other times he was quiet for minutes on end.

"In hindsight, that wouldn't surprise me," he finally said. He thought back on that period of his life when he and Dora had their secret love affair. The exciting weeks in the Hotel des Indes and their love nest in

273

the luxury apartment. But on the weekends he always flew back to his stately patrician house on the edge of Hyde Park to help Catherine raise their two adolescent children, Thomas and Elizabeth. Of course Dora told him how much she missed him during the weekends and vacation weeks he spent at the estate in Majorca. He was so in love that he never doubted that she was devoutly waiting for his return.

"Who was it?" he asked, after another long pause.

"Kruger implied she was still intimate with an earlier Italian flame."

"Bruno Ravioli. I never met him but I've seen pictures. I can't stand his music."

"His name is Ravalli."

"Ravioli, Spaghetti, Ravalli, whatever. She couldn't get over him."

"He could also be Brigitte's father."

Again a long silence—a silence in which Charles saw history moving past like a film in his mind's eye. He pictured Dora again as she had waited for him in the apartment, but instead of her usual immediate sur-render to lust she had handed him a glass of champagne and said, "Rupert, we have to talk." She never called him Charles. To her it was a ridiculous name that belonged to his life in that backward England with his oh so respectable wife and nuisance children. She told him she was pregnant and that an abortion was out of the question. She wanted to have the baby. So there he was. Passionately in love and torn between leaving her or his wife because a baby changed everything instantly.

When he next came to The Hague she had vanished. Her clothes, jewelry, photos and paintings—anything that indicated they had been together had been painstakingly removed. The only thing that remained was an empty apartment with a couch, a bed, a table, some chairs and a wardrobe containing a tuxedo, a few suits and some *tenues de ville*. He had immediately left the apartment and never returned.

Within a month Kruger made his first appearance. That was the beginning of a long and uncomfortable relationship. He told Charles he was giving him the opportunity to contribute to his child's upbring-ing. Charles did consult Dora to see if Kruger didn't take more than was fair for himself before he sent the money.

Even when Brigitte ran away from home and it became harder to sup-port her unnoticed, he continued to check on Kruger. He had a few private detectives in the Netherlands and Germany whom he hired on a permanent basis. He hadn't had any real contact with Dora until a few years ago. After Catherine's death she called him from time to time, or sent him a Christmas card or a birthday card. Now he would see her again for the first time since that unhappy toast to her pregnancy.

Following their visit to Charles, Jens and Esther drove to the Arabella, where Dora was staying, and had a club sandwich and a glass of wine in the hotel coffee shop. They discussed what they had found out and how to break it to Brigitte, but they were also debating how to approach Dora. They thought they might recognize her from newspaper photos and that simply walking up to her would be their only chance.

Jens had called her a month ago. He had introduced himself and asked her to please not hang up and to listen to what he had to say. He told her he was a friend of her daughter's. That he knew Dijkgraaf and had discovered how Kruger had thwarted the investigation. That Kruger had kidnapped him and had subsequently vanished. That more and more sources were bringing him closer to the goal of his investigation. That he understood she wasn't going to volunteer the identity of Brigitte's father and that he didn't expect her to. But that he did want to talk to her about the first fifteen years of Brigitte's life.

She had only asked him if "that was all" and if he was finished talking. When he confirmed that, she had hung up.

The next day he had called back and Vandenbroeke answered. He told him Dora was very upset by his phone call and didn't want any more contact with him. Vandenbroeke was polite. He didn't give in to the temptation to say anything personal.

They waited the entire afternoon and just when they had decided to call, Dora emerged from the elevator. She glided like a true diva across the lobby toward the bar, where she sat down at a table. Esther waited tactfully until Dora's order had been taken and placed before her. A champagne cocktail by the looks of it. Esther suggested taking the lead, since Jens had been turned down once already. She would let him know if everything was okay.

Dora wore a chic Chanel outfit and she was laden with ostentatious jewelry—pearls, gold and diamonds. She didn't look bad for sixty-five.

275

Her skin was still rather smooth and her hair was thick. She had a lovely figure but especially her graceful movements and her smile made everyone pause when she was near. She took a magazine from a large Vuitton purse and leafed through it while she glanced around. Suddenly she spotted Esther.

"Mrs. Vermeer, I have just been to see Rupert. May I sit down?" said Esther in Dutch.

"Yes, of course. Have a seat Ms....?"

"Esther. Esther Lejeune."

"Funny that that old Rupert still knows anyone from the Netherlands, especially a beautiful young woman like you."

"Well, I haven't known him that long, Mrs. Vermeer."

"And he asked you to give me a message?"

"Well, not exactly. He finds it hard to meet with you after all these years."

Dora raised one of her plucked eyebrows. "You're well-informed for someone who hasn't known him that long."

"He has become more open lately."

"You mean since his wife's death?"

"No, more recently than that."

Dora began to smell a rat. She scrutinized Esther, her make-up, her clothes, her hands, her shoes of course, and she sniffed her scent. Certainly in Dora's world those things were seventy-five percent guaranteed to tell her what kind of person she was dealing with. Esther's blouse was from Dolce & Gabbana but it had been part of the spring fashion four years ago—the cuffs showed some signs of wear. Her shoes were Italian but of an unknown brand. Her hands were raw from peeling bell peppers and picking oranges. But the perfume was Chanel No. 5, a good sign.

"I realize you don't want to talk with us, Mrs. Vermeer, but we have made so much progress with our investigation that you might as well."

"Us?"

"Yes, Mr. Jameson is right over there. I'm assisting him with writing your daughter Brigitte's biography."

"Ah." Dora sat motionless. Her face fell and she blanched, which made her rouge stand out like two strange little islands. "Mr. Jameson. Yes."

"Charles, or Rupert if you wish, suspects you want to talk about Brigitte. But first there's something else."

276

Esther motioned to Jens. He got up and walked toward them.

"I'm not sure I want this."

"I understand. The question is: Which is better—to talk with us or to refuse."

Jens stood before Dora and extended his hand. She didn't shake it.

"Mr. Jameson, you're a nail in my coffin," she said, switching to her perfect English.

"Mrs. Vermeer, it's an honor to finally meet you," said Jens humbly.

"Yes, well, you are aware that it's not reciprocal."

"First let me convince you that this book isn't about you or Mr. Hardford. It's about Brigitte. I didn't suggest writing it. She asked me, and we have become friends."

"A lucrative friendship."

Jens felt an adrenaline rush and at least four comebacks came to mind but he checked himself. "I won't deny that I'll make a tidy sum with this book. That's how it works in this business. Sometimes you have a bestseller, sometimes you work for a few pennies. However, if I didn't write the book, someone else would."

"Perhaps someone who would be satisfied with less and wouldn't dig up issues which others would rather leave hidden."

"Perhaps, but maybe that wouldn't be good enough for your daughter."

"You're aware that we're estranged."

"That's not mutual."

"What do you mean?"

"She would like to talk with you again."

"We have grown too far apart, Mr. Jameson. We have differences in culture, class, milieu—differences that can't be bridged at this point."

"She's in a league of her own. She's sweet, friendly, charming and modest. What differences couldn't be bridged?" That was Esther and it surprised Jens that she would defend Brigitte so passionately.

"We grew apart. Let's just leave it at that."

"I have something else to tell you. A rather painful matter," said Esther.

"Then tell me."

"It's about your friend Peter Kruger."

"Do I know a Peter Kruger?"

"I would think so. And so does Mr. Dijkgraaf of FMI. And so does Charles."

"Okay, so I know Mr. Kruger."

"You're aware he's in Majorca?"

"No," said Dora, though she was clearly more surprised that Jens was aware of it.

"I'm sorry to have to break it to you," said Jens softly, "Peter Kruger died yesterday."

Dora's jaw dropped. She gasped, moved to the edge of her chair, and then slumped back.

"Suicide. So it seems, at least."

Dora was angry. "Suicide? Impossible. He was murdered!"

"By whom?" asked Jens and Esther simultaneously.

"How would I know?" Dora snapped. She recovered quickly from the shock and took a swig from her champagne cocktail, and then another.

"Kruger was quite candid about his role in this whole bizarre affair. About Hardford and his purported daughter."

"Purported?"

"Brigitte," said Jens contemplatively, "has reached a point in her life where she really wants to know who her father is."

"Kruger told us there might be other possibilities."

"Peter dead." Dora began to cry.

Jens and Esther glanced at each other, realizing they wouldn't get much out of this woman.

"How on earth could that be?" Dora asked.

40.

Brigitte was cutting her expenses. She had taken a first-class ticket on a regular flight from New York to Barcelona. But she did rent a private jet to get from Barcelona to Palma de Mallorca. Jens had given her the idea to build a small school in Jenna Long's South African township from the money she saved.

Esther dropped him off at the airport's jet center. She didn't feel like observing Jens and Brigitte's reunion.

So much had happened the last few days that she was happy to go into town by herself and meet up with them later.

The modest-size black limo drove up to the small station building. Jens had to wait outside. Apparently Nora, Brigitte's assistant, hadn't put him down as the one who would be picking up Brigitte.

He didn't really care. He had already started chatting with the driver, who seemed aloof at first but turned out to be a friendly Mallorquin. He didn't care whether Jens was here to pick up the famous Brigitte Friends or whether he was an annoying stalker.

Four people came outside. Along with Brigitte, who led the group, came Nora and two broad-shouldered African-Americans, whom Jens recognized as Brigitte's favorite bodyguards, Jack and Ed. Brigitte gave Jens an enormous bear hug.

"I was afraid you wouldn't be here."

"You should have informed them that I was picking you up. They don't let just anyone in."

She turned around and chastised Nora. Jens extended his hand and greeted Nora amiably. She looked sheepish. Jack and Ed helped the driver with the luggage and everything only just fit. They got in.

"I'm having a terrible argument with Gerard," said Brigitte. "Since that dinner last week he has been sending me incredibly nasty emails."

"I warned you he wouldn't be happy."

"He's going to sue your publisher."

"That doesn't make sense! He hasn't even read the manuscript."

"Do you have a title yet?"

"Yes."

"Well?"

"It isn't *Brigitte Friends: The True Story*. That's what the publisher came up with but it was too cliché for me."

"Come on, tell me."

"Well, I was thinking: This is a book about someone everyone assumes they know but who is completely different in reality, with a completely different history. But because she's famous, it's hard to get at it. She hides behind a *wall of fame*."

Brigitte's phone rang. She was of the generation who couldn't withstand a beeping phone. She looked at the display.

"It's Gerard." She pressed talk and listened closely. "But Gerard, you don't even know yet what's going to be in the book. How can you sue already? . . . Jens is here. You can talk to him yourself . . . Yes, he's here with me . . . No, it's none of your business where I am. I'm a big girl. Stop acting like you're my father."

"Mr. Jameson?" said Schöteldreier.

"Yes, Mr. Schöteldreier." Jens tried to sound upbeat but this sudden confrontation threw him off balance.

"This entire ridiculous business has to stop."

"I don't quite understand what you mean. Ridiculous business? Has to stop?" He repeated it so Brigitte could hear what Schöteldreier was saying.

"Your book will do me irreparable damage."

"I honestly don't think it'll be that bad. Now, if I were to write a book about *you*, that could very well be the case."

It was momentarily quite on the other end.

"But fortunately I'm writing a book about Brigitte and so far she's kindly disposed toward you."

"Still, you will describe things we can't tolerate."

"We? Who is 'we'? You and Mr. Kruger? You and Hardford?"

"We as in Brigitte and I," said Schöteldreier dryly.

"Brigitte will authorize this biography. That's the agreement. I'll scrap anything she doesn't want to share with the world, but so far we pretty much agree on everything."

Schöteldreier exploded on the other end. "If you destroy me, I'll destroy you! I won't say how but you can rest assured I won't have my life ruined by a fucking third-rate writer!"

"That's a serious threat. What do you have in mind?"

"You'll find out. You'll be looking over your shoulder for the rest of your life!" He hung up.

Jens was astounded.

Brigitte eyed him fearfully. "What did he say?"

"That he will destroy me. That I'll be looking over my shoulder for the rest of my life."

"That's pretty strong," said Brigitte, without cynicism. "Maybe we should reconsider his problem."

"What do you mean?"

"Well, maybe we can take it easy on Gerard in the book."

Jens got angry. He didn't say anything but his face said it all. He sat upright and stared out the window. They had taken the highway across a landscape that was gradually turning green again after a dry summer. He wanted to say something but then thought the better of it.

"I didn't mean to upset you," said Brigitte hesitantly.

"I'm not upset. I've just been through too much these past few months to capitulate to a lousy threat."

"No," said Brigitte timidly, "I get it. You're right."

It was quiet in the car after that. They left the highway and drove on a minor road for a while, then turned off on a dirt road. They passed a large gate and the road was paved once more, heading up toward a beautiful old *finca*. The farm was lovingly renovated and surrounded by a lush garden filled with roses, bougainvillea and colorful fruit trees. They were going to stay here—there was plenty of space with fourteen rooms, a large patio, several covered porches and a huge swimming pool.

Brigitte inspected the house immediately upon arrival. She did a high-speed walk-through and had herself shown to the master bed-room. She jumped on the bed and briefly lay down. Then she checked out the bathroom and opened the french doors to the balcony.

Jens followed her leisurely and stood beside her to admire the view. The land before the *finca* was rocky and for the first three hundred feet it sloped gradually downward, ending in a steep cliff, 150 feet high, rising out of the sea. The Mediterranean was as blue as the sky. In the distance they could see a few sailboats and yachts. Compared to New York it was completely silent.

"What is Bruno Ravalli like?" asked Brigitte suddenly. Although Jens had told her the full story of their visit to Italy at length, he understood what she meant.

"He's incredibly charming, a real womanizer. You can still see the twinkle in his eyes that used to floor his fans in that terribly worn-out face."

"Does he look like me…? Somehow I mean…in some way?"

"I couldn't say, Brigitte. I only saw him for one afternoon and he was either drunk or stoned or both."

He and Esther had flown from Majorca via Madrid to Rome, a detour of roughly 900 miles. That had saved them 150 euro each over taking a direct flight. In Rome they had rented a Smart. They had driven to a village some twenty-five miles from Rome and stayed the night in a small hostel.

They had a late breakfast and then went in search of Ravalli's home, somewhere in a narrow alley in the medieval town center. The house had once been a mansion but now it was in disrepair and in need of paint. A woman with a stoic expression opened the door and left them there without a word.

They stepped into the gloom; the only light came from the back of the house. The back door opened onto a courtyard that was covered by clear corrugated fiberglass, which in turn was covered by a grapevine. There was a large couch with the stuffing sticking out in places. In the middle of the couch sat an overweight man who Jens barely recognized as the once extremely successful pop singer Bruno Ravalli. He spoke rapid Italian with Esther—he didn't even notice Jens. He motioned with his hand for her to sit next to him on the couch.

Esther said something in Italian and then switched to English.

"Signor Ravalli, we're reporters. We're looking for the truth in a strange case."

Jens was surprised Esther put it that way. *In search of the truth in a strange case.* Come to think of it, it sounded appropriate and was probably meant as a solemn introduction. Jens knew Italians like that sort of thing from the hundreds of mafia movies he'd seen.

Ravalli made slow gestures with his hands. He seemed drowsy. The glass in his hand contained a clear liquid that could be sambuca or vodka; in any case it definitely had a high alcohol percentage. The stuffy smell in the house indicated there had already been quite a bit of pot smoking going on in the Ravalli residence that morning.

"Di me, bella donna." The singer's voice, once famous for the high notes he managed to reach, was now cracked and squeaky.

"It concerns a very old story. More than thirty years old. Dora Vermeer?"

"Dora Vermeer?"

Jens could tell by his face that he knew what was coming.

"Yes, Dora Vermeer. The Dutch woman you were married to for two years in 1974."

"I vaguely remember." Ravalli smiled broadly.

"Do you know a Peter Kruger?"

"Oh yes, I know him. An asshole. He cost me a lot of money."

"How's that?" Esther was perched on the edge of her seat. Jens was letting her do parts of the interviews more frequently, something she had to learn from scratch. Jens had turned the tape recorder on and took notes of what was said.

"Oh, nothing. Just that he was a con man."

"He blackmailed you."

"Says who?"

"He does."

"Vaffanculo, has he confessed to you? Or is he in prison?"

"He's dead. Murdered, it seems."

"Ah, final justice."

"But he told us you may have had an affair with Dora Vermeer several years after your divorce."

"I don't recall."

"He was blackmailing you about your child with Dora Vermeer."

Ravalli took another drink from his glass, a large swig it seemed; he had trouble swallowing it all at once. Then he told them an incoherent story. He had never really like Dora. They had met at a party in Amsterdam. He was dishwasher at an Italian restaurant and in the evenings he made some extra money singing Italian schlagers with a band in places where Italians tended to go. Dora was out with a few friends and ended up in the tavern where he sang. Although she was quite drunk, it was love at first sight for Dora. For Bruno the night in the beautiful house along the canal, with marble toilets and gold faucets, was a windfall. He had claimed he loved her and a few months later they got married.

Dora was demanding. She arranged auditions for him, hired musicians for a band and set him up with a recording studio. In bed she was also impossible to please. Not that Bruno wasn't potent enough to handle quite a bit but, as he put it, that woman was a wild rabbit in the bedroom. He knew she was truly in love with him but he didn't really go for older women and when his career took off, "appetizing possibilities" presented themselves every evening. Especially when he began performing in Italy, the floodgates opened. Dora caught him in a storage closet of their hotel with a far too young fan and kicked him out.

Later he met her again. He was in the Netherlands for a couple of weeks to record a new album and to reconnect with his friends from his time in Amsterdam. He called Dora and took her out to dinner. She insisted so strongly that they make love, that he succumbed. And not just once. After all those young girls Bruno realized what he had missed—how wonderful it felt to make love to a sexually mature woman.

Eighteen months later Peter Kruger visited him. He stuck a baby photo in his face and said that he had "knocked Dora up.'" He was kind of touched when he saw the little girl but he couldn't imagine she was really his daughter. At the time it had also been really inconvenient to acknowledge a child. Kruger said that was no problem, as long as he was willing to contribute to a trust fund that was set up to ensure the child a secure future. It started off with the reasonable amount of ten million lire, which he made in two weeks at that time. Later the requested amounts were larger. Kruger would come up with all sorts of urgent stories and made Ravalli transfer money. So in a way he owned stock in his daughter. But he gradually began to suspect that Kruger was ripping him off. He called Dora, who was then married to Harry

Telford. She didn't want to see him and referred him to Kruger. That's when he realized she was in on it as well.

Despite his talent Ravalli had no business sense and eventually his fortune was spent on expensive managers, slick, canny financial advisors, and especially on parties, cocaine and high-maintenance women. Three times he started rehearsing for a comeback but he always ended up here on the couch beneath the grapevines, very much under the influence of anything he could get his hands on to numb his mind.

Kruger had looked him up once more but didn't mention money. Ravalli took him out to dinner and they got drunk. That evening Kruger confessed that two other men could also be the father.

"He said *two* men?"

"Yes, two. That swindler really took me for billions of liras."

"But you don't know if you might really be the father?" asked Esther.

"No. I don't even know her name or where she lives. Do you?"

"I do. And it will surprise you." Esther took a folder from her purse and opened it. She took out a glossy color photo with a dedication. *For Esther, in loyalty and friendship, Brigitte Friends.*

Bruno took the photo and tried to focus by squeezing his eyes. He stared at Esther as if she had handed him the wrong picture: "But that's Brigitte Friends."

"Also known as Brigitte Vermeer, Dora's daughter."

It took a while before it all sank in. At first Bruno beamed, then he burst out in an uncontrollable laugh, and he finished off with an enormous crying fit.

The woman entered with pasta that smelled intensely of garlic and bacon. She asked Jens if he could lend her twenty euro so she could buy a good wine with which to wash down the meal. Jens pulled out his wallet and gave her the money.

They got drunk on a five-liter jug of pretty dry white wine, which gave them hangover symptoms after the third glass.

Bruno didn't make much sense anymore, until he remembered something. "About those English. Kruger was drunk as well and when I asked him who the other men were, he gave me their names."

Jens and Esther leaned forward and glanced at each other, doubting very much that the drunk could remember any name at this point.

285

"I remember it had something to do with the royal family." Bruno stood up as if the Queen of England had entered the patio. "One of them was called Charles and the other was Philip, if you can believe that. Father and son. We had a good laugh about that one."

41.

Brigitte was anxiously pacing in front of the *finca*, wondering what to say when her visitor came driving up.

She had a hangover because they had drunk quite a lot the night before. First she had read a few new chapters. Then they had talked for hours about Schöteldreier—why Brigitte still cared so much about him, despite his being involved in Kruger's shady business and keeping her father's identity from her. They had debated what Schöteldreier could have meant with his threats. At some point Esther had discovered that Brigitte also spoke Dutch. That was a shock, both for Esther, who suddenly had an entirely different image of Brigitte, and for Jens. From that moment on he had had to listen to a cacophony of words and glottal sounds that were obviously about him, but without him being able to comprehend a thing.

The new chapters dealt with the period when Brigitte's career started to take off. From the bigger nightclubs in Hamburg she had first conquered the rest of Germany by bus with her band Keine Einfahrt and later with more experienced musicians under the name Friends & Friends. Her first hit was a ballad about the hard life of a runaway—a runaway who has had so many disillusionments in her life that she only has one certainty: to believe in herself.

That became a great hype. Young people of that moment were labeled Generation Nix because they were suffering from a collective identity crisis. Brigitte found that she was extremely lucky because her career took off at a speed that bordered on unbelievable. Soon she was playing in concert halls for more than two thousand people and she had her first tour of Great Britain.

She liked London so much that she got Onkel Gerard to arrange the move to the British capital within six months. In London several record companies were immediately interested in her songs and her voice. They spent a lot of money on the release of her first album: a European tour, a video clip that was played on MTV and TMF all the time, and a media campaign that instantly made her the number one pop singer in the world.

While on a small tour of the American East Coast, she fell in love with New York and wanted to stay there for the rest of her life. It couldn't be compared to any country or city on earth. It was an unparalleled melting pot of people, cultures, art, theater and love. In New York every cab driver was a potential writer and every waitress could soon be on Broadway or in a movie. It was the center of the world and that was where Brigitte wanted to live.

And everything was bigger in America: the recording budgets, the list of famous producers, the media attention, but also the number of people who bought CDs. She was awarded one platinum CD after another. The live performances also took place in increasingly bigger concert halls, until she was doing her first stadium appearance. She toured the country with dozens of semis and then went to Europe and Japan. The money flowed in and at age twenty-four she was at the top of the entertainment industry.

But her isolation grew as well. She began to dislike the speed interviews, where reporters had fifteen minutes to ask her a few foolish questions, three at a time. Sometimes those interview marathons took two days and she had to "work through" more than sixty reporters. She noticed that she got the same questions on talk shows and interviews.

Brigitte decided that she'd had enough; one day she stopped giving interviews altogether. She also stopped going to parties where "everyone" came—the rising stars so they could get attention and stars on their way out because they got paid for their appearance. She worked hard and felt that the public didn't need to get more from her than her music, her clips and her concerts. Onkel Gerard wasn't happy; only at his insistence did she still give the occasional interview.

The past few years she had been doing her best work ever, according to both the media and the public. They accepted that she no longer wanted to be a part of that circus. Brigitte Friends was one of the truly great in pop music.

288

Esther came outside because it was time to meet Charles Hardford. "Are you nervous?"

"Yes, I'm nervous," said Brigitte in Dutch and grinned. She felt she sounded funny in her mother tongue. They had found they got along quite well yesterday while they were talking in Dutch about Jens. Brigitte had told her she was a bit jealous of Esther because she hadn't met a guy like Jens in ages. She thought he was friendly, loving, intelligent, a gentleman, and that he was quite handsome and had an interesting profession. *What more do you want?* she had exclaimed at the end. She had added that she would never try to take him away from Esther. That's not how she was raised, she said and then she had a good laugh at her own expense. *That's not how I raised myself,* she corrected.

Esther told her she was romanticizing Jens. She told her they had almost broken up two months ago and that Jens immediately had sex with Kruger's beautiful assistant. She had to speak in shrouded terms and avoid words like "Jennifer," "Kruger," and "Barbados" so Jens wouldn't figure out what she was saying about him. That had given Brigitte hope again and she had asked if everything was fine between them now. Esther brought her down to earth.

Finally old Charles Rupert Hardford's pick-up truck drove up. Luna sat in the passenger seat, staring straight ahead, even when the truck stopped after a short turn. Charles got down. He had cleaned up for the occasion, wearing a tight dark suit, a white shirt and a bow tie. He walked toward them hesitantly, his head down and his Stetson, which he had taken off when he got out of the truck, in his hands.

Brigitte moved toward him. He extended his hand and Brigitte embraced him and kissed him on both cheeks. Charles clumsily tried to put his arms around her.

"Brigitte," he stammered. "I, eh..." That was all he could manage.

She looked helplessly at Esther. Jens came outside, feeling guilty that he had been talking to his publisher on the phone.

"Welcome to wonderland," said Brigitte and waited until Jens stood beside her.

"Hello Jens," said Charles. "Hello Esther. I'm glad you organized this meeting."

And to Brigitte, "I met you once before. You wouldn't remember; you were only two. After that it was impossible for me to see you. It's a complicated story. I'd like to explain."

"Let's go inside and have a drink." Esther suggested, since Brigitte didn't know what to say.

Brigitte had a glass of white wine and Jens and Esther joined her. Charles just wanted water.

"It's weird, sitting here like this," said Brigitte. Then she decided to skip the small talk. "You say you're my father. Are you sure? Apparently two other men think they are."

"I just know. I asked your mother; she was here last week. She didn't deny it."

"Nowadays it's not that difficult to get certainty about something like that," Esther pointed out.

"What do you mean?"

"Just do a DNA test. We can take samples from you and Brigitte—the test tells you for sure."

"I don't want that." Charles was firm. "You're my child, I just know it. I've followed you for the past thirty-two years. I know you're my daughter."

"Then why wouldn't you want the test?" asked Brigitte.

"What difference would it make? Would it make me feel any less guilty? Would it mean I didn't need to worry as much? Would I be able to forget all the sorrow of not being allowed to see you?"

"You could feel terribly cheated by my mother and Kruger."

"I already felt that before you were born. That didn't make any difference. Maybe I deserved it. Punishment for my cowardice."

"Cowardice? You yourself call it cowardice." Brigitte sounded bitter.

"Yes, certainly, Brigitte. Cowardice. Not indifference, definitely not indifference. I was afraid my wife couldn't bear the scandal. I was afraid I would sink so deep in my colleagues' opinions that I'd never resurface. I was afraid to choose Dora because I was almost certain she'd dump me soon afterward. Afraid, afraid, afraid." Charles was quite emotional. He drank his water in one go and held his head in his hands, crying out the word "afraid" a few more times.

Brigitte shrugged. "Who is Philip? The third man?"

Charles's face was expressionless as he gazed past Brigitte toward the cliff and the sea.

Could it be any more symbolic? Jens thought. They were sitting at the

290

back of the house on a wide porch in low chairs. Jack and Ed were playing badminton down below, which looked funny. Nora had retreated after pouring the wine and water.

"Important interests are at work," said Charles out of the blue. "I can't explain it all—it's damned complicated. I've heard of this Philip but I've never met him. He's an American, a wealthy man. He has stocks in you!"

"Stocks in me?" cried Brigitte. "What do you mean he has stocks in me?"

"You shouldn't take it literally. It's like this..." He drew such a deep breath that it seemed he wanted to tell the whole story in one exhalation.

"Fifteen years ago you walked away from your mother. Dora was relieved that you left—she didn't want to deal with an adolescent. Someone in my inner circle kept me informed, so I knew exactly what was going on. I suggested Dora get someone to locate you so I could have custody. She refused. Instead she sent Kruger again. He took a big sum to spend on private detectives, but in reality he already knew where you were."

Charles grabbed the wine bottle and filled his water glass. He took a big swig and looked Brigitte straight in the eye. His eyes were watery, hers were clear.

"Kruger had arranged for me to meet this guy. I went to Hamburg and visited the bar where you worked. You served me personally. You impressed me, how you were managing, having walked away from your safe nest into the harsh reality of a strange country. I met Schöteldreier, who seemed nice enough at first. Kruger knew you were interested in music, that you could play the guitar and had a lovely voice. Schöteldreier had experience managing musicians and he said he could turn anyone with a bit of talent into a star. He said that of course it was a matter of time, energy and . . . money.

"I didn't care about the money. I had more than enough. Not money I made myself with politics; my business ventures usually cost me more than they made me. But the family fortune is huge and spread over so many funds and bank accounts that I could use large sums without any problem. My wife didn't have a clue about finances anyway."

Everyone shifted in their seats and Charles realized he had strayed from the main story.

"Through Kruger I paid Schöteldreier regular amounts and I was told how you were doing. Sometimes I travelled to a performance and I saw how beautifully you could sing. I would listen to your beautiful but oh so sad lyrics.

"When you were twenty-one and moved to England, I felt you could stand on your own two feet. I stopped paying Kruger, and within a week he was at my doorstep. He was quite friendly and he told me he understood that I felt you could manage on your own from now on. He said I should make some of the money back that I had invested in you. I told him I didn't want to make any money but later I began to wonder. I felt I had handed you to these shady characters because I had done business with the wrong people behind the scenes. So I deemed it best that I stay involved in some way. I invested in a music company that owned the rights to your music."

Brigitte was indignant. She hadn't felt too good about her supposed father's confession so far but now she couldn't keep quiet. "Friends & Friends Ltd.? You have stocks in Friends & Friends? But that's impossible. That's *my* company!"

"Friends & Friends *is* your company. It has several longstanding contracts with a company in Guernsey that owns a portion of your rights. You have stocks in that company yourself."

Esther made a wild guess. "By any chance, is it called WLM Ltd?"

"No, no, but close. WLF—We Love Friends. That's the name of the company. Brigitte, surely you know it?"

"No." Brigitte looked defeated.

"Your author's rights and artist rights for your performances go partly to this company. By now it should hold quite a fortune, because so far nothing has been taken out."

"Nobody ever told me about it. I have to say I always blindly signed everything Gerard put in front of me."

"But there are more stockholders. This Philip—I never met him—he's the mastermind behind the whole structure."

"Could he also be behind WLM Ltd?" Jens asked.

"Well, I suppose that's possible. Businessmen aren't always that creative when it comes to names. WLM . . . Who's the M?"

Esther clarified. "The M stands for several artists. It was called We Love Music initially but later it was changed to We Love Money."

"Or maybe there was originally an M," said Jens.

"Or maybe money from WLF was used to set up WLM?"

Brigitte was exasperated. First of all, she couldn't follow all this stuff about companies and secondly, it was no longer about her.

Charles noticed. "Listen, Brigitte. I stuck with those swindlers so I could stay connected to you. If it turns out they did all this without your knowledge, I will put my lawyers to work tomorrow to set things right."

Brigitte got up and paced. She tried to take stock of what had happened the past week. Onkel Gerard had been found out. Evidently he knew much more about her "fathers'" than he ever admitted. He also had business with this Kruger, who was murdered a few days ago. Maybe he was involved in the murders, just as he was involved in the attempt on Jens's life. Despite the fortune she had managed to get from her exes, her mother, together with Kruger, had blackmailed three men with her pregnancy. She had so wanted to know who her father was, and here she was with a pathetic old man and his hopeless story, with a hopeless alcoholic drug addict in Italy and this Philip somewhere, who was almost certainly no good either. And her career was based on blackmail, albeit maybe only in small part, because Kruger, Schöteldreier and Philip had taken the money for themselves. It was all too much for her. She ran inside, upstairs to her bedroom and slammed the door.

Esther followed her. Jens stayed behind. Jack and Ed had stopped playing badminton. Their last shuttlecock had gone over the cliff. They had hit the thing so hard that the strings were hanging from their rackets and they were laughing as they walked back to the house. Charles had tears in his eyes but he still seemed glad that he had told the story.

"You're relieved," Jens observed.

"Yes, thank you."

"You do realize that now that you have unburdened yourself, Brigitte has an enormous problem."

"Certainly. And I'll do everything I can to help her."

42.

Jens couldn't sleep and that was a good thing. Esther had stayed with Brigitte for a long time. At first all he could hear were big crying fits coming from the room; later he heard muffled voices and finally the occasional laugh or giggle. Then Esther had come down to get a bottle of wine and two glasses.

She had told Charles that Brigitte apologized and that she would call him for another appointment. Right now she was too confused about all these revelations. Charles had understood and left. Esther had come downstairs later to have dinner with Jens and Nora. Brigitte stayed in her room. She had gotten a migraine from all the crying and just wanted to sleep.

Jens had begun transcribing the tape he had recorded when Charles told his story.

Esther sat down beside to him. "Everything we learned only seems to complicate matters. How bizarre that we now have a link between your story and mine."

"Yours and mine? I thought we did everything together?" Jens teased. "Anyway, it might be coincidence that the WL in We Love is the same. Maybe the same accounting agency came up with the names."

"There's no such thing as coincidence," Esther quoted her motto. "We'll never find out who this Philip is, if that's even his real name."

"An open ending doesn't bother me. I'm more concerned that the book can give a very somber image of Brigitte's background and environment if we're not careful."

"What do you mean?"

"Well, just imagine how the tabloids are going to summarize our book. *Disowned daughter of swindler. Began career in topless bar with blackmail money. Protected by third-rate hustler. Blackmail, abuse, kidnapping and attempted murder to prevent revelations."*

"I hadn't considered that." Esther thought for a moment. "Still, she's incredibly tough, having gotten this far with her own music despite everything. Because that much is true. She writes her own lyrics and she's the one who sings and plays them."

"True, but still…" Jens almost automatically continued to type what old Charles had told them. *There's no such thing as coincidence*, he thought, when he arrived at the part about We Love Friends.

The investigation into the Steve Demood murder had run aground. The Scotland Yard inspectors who had been assigned to the case—it was out of the Buckingham inspectors' league—hadn't gotten any further. Nothing was released about the Yard's findings on Guernsey other than that it hadn't resulted in any suspects. Brad Brittain, seven other artists and Demood's widow had sued in an attempt to secure what was left of their money. It was a terrible mess of bureaucratic and legal maneuvering, for which their lawyers claimed hundreds of hours per week. But the names of the stockholders in We Love Money were still not given to the media.

"If we can get Charles to do a DNA test and we're lucky, then at least we can finish this book."

"I don't have much faith in Charles and unfortunately that drunk in Italy isn't her father either."

"Well, I wouldn't have wished it on her, anyway. If those two met, he would probably sexually assault her at first sight."

"Well, DNA doesn't lie. I'll have another talk with Charles."

Jens had finished transcribing the tape and they lay on the bed. Esther had complained that they were so stressed and so busy with their work that they hardly had time for each other. Jens initially responded to that obvious invitation by suggesting a romantic dinner somewhere completely unrelated to the story. But Esther had mounted him and slowly taken off his clothes. They had to be very quiet. Their room was adjacent to Brigitte's and they didn't want to wake her.

Now Jens lay awake. He had to find a way to give the book a positive spin. He listened closely, as usual. Whenever he heard a strange noise, he wanted to know where it came from. Every house had its own sounds, and the first night they slept here, he had already identified the myriad sounds belonging to the old farmhouse. Now the sound of the waves crashing against the rocks was added, the wind was whistling across the land, the windmill was spinning, the shed's shutters were rattling, grass was rustling and a dog barked in the distance. And there were sounds he couldn't place.

He didn't want to get up to check them out because Esther was softly snoring with her head on his chest. But he became more and more curious because out of the blue one familiar sound rose above the wind and the sea. Just for a moment. He tried to place it and it took most of a minute before he did. It sounded like a gas stove turning on with the pilot light: the warm whoosh of fire spreading out across a broad, flammable area. He sat up. Esther grumbled, turned around and slept on.

Now he also heard a crackling sound over the wind. He inhaled deeply. He was thinking fire but he didn't smell anything. He got up, put on his pants and walked to the window. The shutters were closed, so he couldn't immediately see outside. After opening the window, he tried to open the shutter. He couldn't. He went to the second window but its shutter wouldn't budge either. He saw that a piece of wood was lodged in the handles. He pushed against it but it didn't move. He shoved hard—it still wouldn't budge.

Someone blocked the shutters! he realized. Through a gap in the shutter he saw smoke rising.

Jens pulled the blanket away from Esther and yelled that she had to come with him. She sat up, looking around in a daze. She didn't see anything indicating danger, so she asked what was wrong.

"Fire!" yelled Jens and ran to Brigitte's room. He threw open the door and saw her already sitting up, also looking around groggily. He ran to the bed, grabbed her by the arm and shouted that she had to get dressed immediately. He checked the shutters to the terrace. They were jammed as well, even more tightly than those of his own bedroom.

Esther entered and asked what she should do. Jens yelled that she should wake the others sleeping downstairs. When Esther informed him the downstairs was filled with black smoke, he ordered her to help him instead. Together they picked up a heavy, old-fashioned easy chair. They stood by the door to the balcony and Jens counted to three. Then they moved toward the door and rammed the chair against the shutters. They instantly broke from their hinges and clattered onto the balcony. Jens sprang out and looked around. He saw two figures running away.

"Now what?" asked Brigitte.

"We jump from the balcony."

"But it's at least twelve feet high!"

"You can choose between breaking your legs or suffocating in the smoke."

He pushed Brigitte over the balustrade. Esther was already climbing over. Brigitte stood on the ledge and looked fearfully at Jens. He grabbed her by her wrists and instructed her to hold on to the edge of the balustrade. He grabbed on even tighter and told her to let go. He bent over as far as he could, so the distance between her feet and the ground below was no more than six feet.

"Try to land on your feet and bend your knees," he said, then counted down and let go. Next he grabbed Esther's hand and bent over as far as possible with her. He briefly met her eyes. He wanted to say something romantic but he let go before he could come up with anything.

He went back inside and broke a leg off the crushed chair. He looked over the balcony, where Esther and Brigitte were gazing up at him. He threw the chair leg down and flipped over the balustrade. He hung on to the edge, then let himself drop.

A searing pain shot through his left ankle when Esther helped him up. She told him Brigitte was hurt but still able to walk.

"The others," hissed Jens through clenched teeth. He picked up the chair leg and limped to the window of Nora's room. The downstairs shutters were locked with zip strips. He used the chair leg to smash the shutter from its hinges and then smashed the window. A huge cloud of smoke belched out through the broken glass. Jens drew a deep breath, opened the window and climbed in. Nora still lay peacefully in bed and gave no sign of life. He grabbed her under her arms and pulled her body to the window, where Brigitte stood waiting to help him.

In the meantime Esther had taken the chair leg and gone to Jack and Ed's room. The smoke was not as bad in the back of the finca. She battered away and soon the shutters were open and the two sleepy men in their boxers stood outside.

Nora lay on the ground, lifeless, and while Esther was busy calling the emergency number, Jens alternately gave her mouth-to-mouth resuscitation and pressed his hands on her chest to get her heart going again until Ed, who had had to get first-aid training to be a security guard, took over the chest pumps while Jens blew fresh air into Nora's lungs.

Brigitte threatened Nora with everything she could think of if she didn't wake up. After a minute Nora coughed weakly and Ed stopped pumping. Jens jumped up and called to Jack that they should follow the arsonists.

Jack needed no urging. He ran straight to the Range Rover Brigitte had rented and jumped behind the wheel. Jens got into the passenger seat.

The chance was small that they would catch up with the arsonists. But Jens figured from the direction the men had been running that they had parked their car at a scenic overlook half a mile away. That was at least a ten-minute walk across the overgrown terrain, even if they were fast. He used Jack's phone to call the police and asked to speak to Chief Inspector Mardavall. It took two or three minutes before he was put through.

He explained to Mardavall what had happened and told him he was on his way to the spot where the arsonists had probably parked their car. He described exactly where the overlook was.

"Let them go," said Mardavall.

"Excuse me?"

"Let them go. Don't try to stop them. Get the license plate number and the color and make of the car if you can. I'll have all the roads blocked. But don't do anything stupid. Do not try to stop them."

"I know," growled Jens. "You'll be looking for two men stinking of smoke and gas."

"Call me as soon as you see them. Now hang up so I can put out an APB. I'm putting on pants right now and then I'm on my way."

The moon was waning and the road was pitch dark and unpaved, with overhanging trees forming a natural tunnel.

Suddenly a car came from the opposite direction. Apparently he had been driving with the lights off—and turned on his brights right before they would have crashed. The light was blinding. Jack scraped past the oncoming car and they stopped on the shoulder. Jens looked back but he couldn't make out the license plate number because the car had dimmed its lights again. *Smart*, he thought.

Jack threw the Range Rover in reverse and blindly backed up onto the road. He saw a spot further on where he could turn and get going again. Jens put on his seatbelt. Some three minutes later they got a glimpse of the getaway car as it turned onto the main road. Jack gave a satisfied growl. Sweat beaded on his forehead. He was still in his boxers but he didn't seem to care.

"Now he's got me mad," he cried twice and went after the car at full speed. It tried to get away but they were now close enough to see the number. Jens called Mardavall back and told him he should be looking for a black BMW; he gave the license-plate number and told him which road they were on.

The BMW was faster than the Range Rover on the highway and it gradually drove from sight. Jack pushed the pedal to 120 miles per hour but it didn't help. They lost the car.

All of a sudden they saw a sea of blue flashing lights on the horizon. The police had put up a roadblock and the BMW was driving straight toward it. Jens and Jack grinned at each other. They slowed down and saw that the police lights were now moving as well. Near a roundabout they passed a totaled Guardia Civil car and a few dazed officers taking care of a wounded man lying on the ground. The BMW hadn't stopped and had hit the policeman.

They now drove behind a string of police cars toward the next roundabout. Up ahead cars stopped abruptly in the middle of the highway and police officers were running with guns drawn toward the BMW, which was standing on the shoulder with the doors open. Jack and Jens got out and were immediately stopped by an officer who felt they shouldn't be there.

Jens explained that he had called Mardavall and followed the perpetrators. They were ordered to stay behind their vehicle in case shots were fired. Jens hoped the men would be captured alive. With Jack's phone he called Ed and asked for Esther.

"Is Nora okay?"

"Yes, she's in an ambulance on the way to the hospital. Brigitte's with her. They're picking us up later. Ed's fine. So am I. The firefighters are busy but it's a lost cause."

"You should have your feet checked," said Jens.

"Did you find those clowns?"

"Yes, we're here with about ten police cars. They're following them on foot now."

"Then get out of there. You shouldn't be there. They're after you, after us—remember that."

"You're so sweet when you're worried."

"Oh, only when I'm worried?"

"No, you're also sweet when you're romantic."

"Grr. It's easy for you to be tough. It's your third time in real danger. I'm a novice, so my legs are shaking."

"If we're lucky they'll catch those clowns. That would be a breakthrough."

Shots were fired and they heard a lot of shouting. Several police vehicles blocked the lanes on the other side of the road, including Mardavall's little blue Alfa Romeo. He got out of his car and jumped nimbly over the crash barrier along the median.

"I've got to go. Mardavall is here." Jens made a smacking noise that was meant to resemble a kiss and ended the call.

Mardavall headed straight toward him, motioning questioningly with his hands.

"They followed the arsonists and shots are being fired."

Mardavall walked around him to the shoulder and peered into the darkness. When he came back he wanted to know exactly what had happened.

"Amateurs!" he said when Jens finished his report.

"I don't think so," said Jens hotly. "That fire was huge within two minutes. They also managed to jam all the shutters without anyone noticing. It was pure coincidence that I couldn't sleep—that's how I heard the fire. We managed to save Brigitte Friends's assistant with CPR. She no longer had a heartbeat. A few more minutes and we would all have died in the smoke."

Mardavall said nothing. They waited for new signs of life. The tension was high. An ambulance drove up and two medics jumped out. One of them got clothes for Jack. Silver pants and a silver shirt made of thermo fabric. In the headlights he resembled a luminescent superhero.

About five minutes later the first policemen returned. They didn't seem happy but before Jens could begin to swear—thinking the perpetrators had gotten away—a man and a woman, both handcuffed, were shoved onto the road. They were forced to lie on the ground and were searched extra thoroughly. The man looked up and in terrible English claimed to have rights. The commander grinned and gave him a forceful kick in his side.

Mardavall stepped forward and said they were under arrest on suspicion of arson, battery and attempted murder. Jens tried to see their faces but they turned their heads away.

The night was almost over and the first red morning glow appeared in the sky above the mountains in the east.

43.

Schöteldreier took a seat in the first-class compartment and placed his suitcase on the floor next to him. He took his laptop from his brief-case and opened it. Amtrak provided high-speed Internet on this line, so he could open his mail. The subject of the first one was "update." He read it carefully. It was sent by flavio341@hotmail.com and it consisted of two lines:

> *Dear Schöteldreier,*
> *I'm sorry. We had a big slip-up here. Two people are in custody. I'm leaving the island.*
> *Greetings, Flavio*

Schöteldreier had a plan B. He had learned that from Kruger. A skilled con man always has a safe escape planned. Within twelve hours. He had taken care of his alibi by booking a vacation to a Caribbean island where many Americans go for a week or two to relax. Once the storm blew over he would simply have been on vacation, claiming that he had had a physical and his doctor had told him he was stressed. Only yesterday he had sent Brigitte an email, saying he required rest and would be gone to "a warm climate" for an undetermined period of time.

The train would take him to JFK, where he would take a plane to Curacao. He had booked it at a travel agency, along with the hotel.

A slip-up—that was putting it mildly. The slip-up had begun when he had first met that pain-in-the-butt Jens Jameson in his office and caved concerning the contract. Jameson would certainly have quit if he couldn't write what he wanted and had to listen to his instructions.

302

Hiring those fools to get rid of Jameson was also a slip-up. Although he did have to admit that being hindered by the two men who protected Jameson was plain bad luck.

Later he had slipped up by discussing with Kruger that he was responsible for the assault on Jens. Kruger had hit the roof and said *it was a good thing his two men had been around*. But Kruger was dead. Schöteldreier may not know who killed him but it was damned convenient.

It was getting too risky for him. The structures he, Kruger and Philip had come up with, and that at first had unfortunately also involved Charles Hardford and Bruno Ravalli, now threatened to be exposed. The disappearance of a large chunk of Brigitte's earnings would subsequently come to light.

Schöteldreier wasn't even that worried about a court case and an investigation. After all, they had built up an excellent front, and that so much money had disappeared could easily be blamed on the crash of 2008. He was more worried about Kruger's killer, whoever that was.

He knew next to nothing about Philip. He wasn't even convinced that was his real name. Ravalli didn't know anything, Hardford had been sufficiently led astray and Kruger was dead. Dora might still be a risk factor but she had never gotten involved in anything. She had only benefited by getting some of the money in roundabout ways. She was rich and she had put her money God knows where. He had always disliked her. She had gotten rich off dead husbands and husbands she had run off. On top of that she had swindled her disowned daughter.

Schöteldreier had always loved Brigitte as if she were his own daughter. Of course she could be a bitch and was barely kept in check. But families do quarrel and that's why he had stayed loyal to her. Not that it hadn't paid off, but his intentions had always been good.

He typed in the address of the CNN site and got a jolt when he saw a photo of Brigitte in a hospital in Majorca, at her assistant Nora's bedside. He had seen the breaking news on TV but they hadn't known much yet. The perpetrators had obviously failed in their mission. *Assault on Pop Star Brigitte Friends*, it said above the article. He clicked it and read:

Majorca (EFE) – Early Tuesday morning Brigitte Friends barely escaped death. The star and her company were taken by surprise in their sleep by a fire in their vacation villa. The fire was the result of arson. Friends was saved by the watchfulness of writer Jens Jameson, who was accompanying the star. Her personal assistant Nora Page was admitted to the hospital in Palma de Mallorca with heavy smoke inhalation. The arsonists were arrested after a wild police chase. As yet their motives are unknown.

Earlier this year Jens Jameson was the victim of an assault in Hamburg. Sources close to the New York author claim this assault is linked to a biography he is currently writing about Friends.

Schöteldreier was finding it hard to breathe. Sweating, he groped in his briefcase in search of his inhaler. As he inhaled deeply the medicine instantly opened his air sacs.

Outside he saw an enormous cemetery pass by. It had always been there when he took the train from New York to JFK, thrifty as he was. But this time he couldn't keep his eyes off the vast hills with crosses, miniature temples and other grave monuments.

Here he was, as always in an immaculate suit, but his face was deathly pale and his palms were sweaty. He had gone further than he had ever imagined he would. He crossed a line when he hired those two criminals in Hamburg. The idea was that Jens would seem to be the victim of a regular mugging and that he would back off.

Later he regretted it and tried to convince Brigitte that she should have Jens stop. But more and more shit was exposed. Even the link to the untoward practices of Dora, Kruger and the others. He had been forced to take action in order to avoid problems himself. Yes, he had rationalized that it would be best if Brigitte and the two writers would die in an accident. But again he had relied on a couple of clumsy fools who had gotten themselves arrested and might talk in exchange for a reduced sentence. The only thing he could hope for was that Flavio would manage to leave the island on time.

His suitcase was checked in and he shuffled along in line toward Customs. He handed his passport to the customs official, who typed the number in the computer.

"How long do you intend to stay in Curacao?" the man asked.

"Two weeks."

"Okay. You're aware that your passport expires in six weeks?"

Schöteldreier looked steadily at the man, trying to hide the realization that he had slipped up yet again. On the other hand it didn't really matter. He had a second passport in his briefcase. It was fake but it wouldn't expire for four or five years.

"Certainly." He walked off. Once past Customs he breathed a sigh of relief. But his joy would be short-lived.

At the security check-in he placed his briefcase on the conveyor belt, forgetting to take out his laptop. The man behind the computer screen gave the security officer a sign and pointed to Schöteldreier.

"You must not travel much," said the man, still friendly.

"I travel more than enough," said Schöteldreier evenly but with just a little too much animosity.

"Then you know you're required to take out your laptop." The man was now openly irritated.

Schöteldreier heard it but only just. He was being directed to a side table and the security guard slowly unpacked everything. He took the laptop and passed a piece of cardboard with a circle of some type of fabric along it. That cardboard disappeared into a big machine behind him.

"No explosives," he said calmly.

"What's this nonsense?"

Apparently Schöteldreier's German accent triggered something in the security guard, who still held his briefcase. Perhaps his father had fought the Germans in Normandy, or maybe he had merely seen too many war movies, but he emptied the entire briefcase, excruciatingly slowly. Suddenly an American passport fell from one of the folders. Schöteldreier also held a passport in his hand. The man opened the passport from the briefcase and ordered Schöteldreier to hand over the other one. He protested, claiming he *didn't have time for this nonsense; he had a plane to catch.*

The guard motioned to a Border Patrol agent. Two men approached. They motioned another officer to join them. The security guard explained that he had asked for this man's passport. The officer said that wasn't part of his job. Schöteldreier looked up with a grin.

"It's our job," said the officer with an even bigger grin. He took the passport that had fallen from the briefcase and inspected it. The security guard pointed to Schöteldreier's coat pocket and told the officer that he had seen a second American passport.

Schöteldreier was taken into custody for possession of a fake passport. They also found forty thousand-dollar bills in his coat pocket and in America they called that smuggling currency. He was taken to a locked room where he could watch time go by on his watch until his plane took off for Curacao.

44.

The plane taxied the runway. Jack and Ed finally sat down and buck-led their safety belts. The Boeing 727's interior was kitsch but opulent. The chairs were twice as big as the chairs either Jens or Esther had in their small apartments. There were even seats where you could face each other with a coffee table in between that folded out when food was served. Before takeoff they were already given champagne and they toasted to a safe trip home. The luxurious private jet had been under police protection since its arrival, to rule out any sabotage. Mardavall had arranged it with much fanfare. He felt honored that Brigitte was so amiable toward him.

One of the two strict flight attendants checked if everyone had their safety belts securely fastened. Then they sat down, too, watching out the window how the colossus rose off the runway.

All the passengers were dressed in new clothes because nothing was left of the old *finca* or their luggage. Jens was happy that again he had made online backups. His laptop had been transformed into a black, charred waffle iron that he couldn't even open.

Esther had taken this opportunity to improve Jens's personal style. She got him to buy Yohji Yamamoto trousers and jacket, discounted from two thousand to eight hundred euro. Quite a step up for someone who had never spent more than twenty dollars for a pair of jeans. Brigitte had let them all shop with her credit card, since her expensive insurance paid in full for damages in these situations. Esther had taken it easy herself but Jens had a suitcase packed with outrageously expensive clothes. Brigitte was also quite pleased with his new outfit. *Wow, you're turning into a hunk. Clothes make the man*, she had told him admiringly.

The night before, Jens had driven to police headquarters with Marda-vall, where the two detainees had been put in separate interview rooms. The interrogation wasn't gentle. The man was about thirty and looked Asian. His eyes were red and his face was scratched from the branches and thistles he had run through when he was fleeing the scene. His motor skills seemed to have slowed down—according to Mardavall he was a cokehead.

He was tired, discouraged and scared. He kept saying in terrible English that he wanted to talk to his lawyer. When asked who it was, he said he had the right to one phone call. He could forget about the phone call. This wasn't America. The interrogating inspectors each stood at least six feet and more than 220 pounds. The man started about his lawyer again as soon as they had asked their first question, so they kicked the chair out from under him. He fell on the floor and when he wanted to get up, they helped him. But when he was half standing, they pushed him full speed with his head against the wall.

Mardavall turned away and told Jens to do the same. Through the other one-way mirror they saw a man and a woman interrogating the dark-haired female suspect. She was slim and wore a cat-burglar suit. She had blackened her face with soot and she hadn't had a chance to take off her gloves. Behind him, Jens heard the man being beaten up. He was sur-prised he didn't feel the urge to stop the violence. Usually he would have protested immediately or at least questioned the inspector's methods. But something in him had swung to the other side. *Beat it out of him*, he thought, *anything goes. We have to find out who set these two criminals on to us.* Once he realized what he was thinking he burned with shame.

When he decided the beating had gone on long enough, Mardavall went inside. One of the inspectors remained by the door and folded his arms over his chest. Now Mardavall was the good cop who suggested a deal. By testifying against the other and by naming the person who put out the contract, the man could expect a reduced sentence. He described the local prison: no privacy, vermin and terrible food. The sentence for attempted murder wouldn't be less than twenty years. Then he got up and left the room.

He told the woman the same thing. She stared blindly, with disbelief in her eyes. Her shoulders were sagging lower and lower. In her case, too, he left without waiting for an answer.

The moment Mardavall entered the room behind the mirrors with two cups of coffee and a big grin on his face, Jens understood his intention. Both suspects supposed the inspector was with the other and the longer it took, the more they'd think the other was talking and getting off with a lesser sentence.

"They're deliberating," said Mardavall. "Just look at their faces. They're amateurs. They're both going to cave."

"The way they set the fire was pretty professional, though."

"That may be but they took great risks. First by blocking all those shutters with a ladder and then hoping no one would hear them lighting over three hundred square feet of oil and gas. The chance of failure was big."

"I don't know. The wind was loud. I lay listening till the last moment and if I hadn't been so wide awake, I would never have checked it out. And they did get Nora. She was as dead as dead can be."

"They're still a bunch of fools. Look, she's almost ready."

Mardavall went back and forth between the suspects two more times, asking seemingly stupid questions, until the woman said she was ready to make a deal. Too late, Mardavall said. Her partner had already spilled the beans. He only needed some passport information from her. Then the woman began to talk. She told him she worked for a certain Flavio Danitsha, who had taken the job from an American with a German name. She didn't know anything else. Danitsha should still be in Majorca. She wanted to know if her partner had told him the same thing, and if they couldn't both get a reduced sentence. She had never meant to kill anyone. They were just supposed to intimidate those people—they would've woken them up if that guy hadn't appeared on the balcony.

"Nonsense," Mardavall had said. "You're going down for attempted murder." Then he had gone to the other suspect. When he heard that his partner had talked, he dug in his heels. But when the inspector pointed out that it would be better for him if the person he worked for was also caught, he talked, too.

Three people were supposed to die. The blond singer, the American writer and his girlfriend. The others were collateral damage. They had watched the area for forty-eight hours before they decided to strike. They had waited for a sign from Flavio until the last moment.

He couldn't identify the American who ordered the job either, but he did know he was a German who was somehow involved with the singer. When Jens heard that, he had to sit down because his knees were shaking.

Mardavall had entered the room Jens was in. He made a triumphant phone call to get an arrest warrant for Flavio Danitsha. *If that man wants to leave the island, he'll have to swim*, the chief inspector had said. This was his chance. If he solved the assault within twenty-four hours, he would be internationally famous and since his professional vanity knew no limits, he appointed himself leader of the search team at six in the morning.

That had been a good choice, even if all the effort and trouble he had gone to were sort of unnecessary in hindsight. Flavio Danitsha showed up for an eight o'clock flight to New York via Barcelona. He had noticed the heavy security everywhere but assumed the ETA had made a threat or the king of Spain was on the island. Not suspecting a thing, he had walked straight into the trap, suddenly faced with dozens of policemen and soldiers with machine guns.

Danitsha was taken to police headquarters. Because Mardavall was a modern policeman, he had turned on Danitsha's laptop before beginning the interrogation. Danitsha wasn't exactly the smartest criminal on the planet either. His computer remembered his Hotmail password and even though he regularly deleted his old mail, the last couple of messages were still there.

Mardavall had asked him if the name Schöteldreier rang a bell.

Jens was badly shaken. He was dreading the coming meeting with Brigitte, because he would have to tell her what was going on. Schöteldreier's exposure was an emotional event. Of course Jens had always kept in mind that he could be behind the violence. He had already suspected it in Hamburg and after his threats he had decided he would indeed keep looking over his shoulder. He absolutely didn't believe in anything spiritual or supernatural but maybe some small angel had made sure he didn't sleep last night.

Brigitte and Esther had gone shopping that morning. Over the newly acquired cell phone Jens told Brigitte that he had important news. They arranged to meet at the hotel around noon. Armed policemen stood on the steps and a small armored vehicle of the Guardia Civil stood at the street corner. When Esther and Brigitte arrived they insisted on first showing Jens what they had bought. Then Jack and Ed took the new clothes to the bedroom. Brigitte was restless but she did notice that Jens was having a hard time with what he was about to tell her.

"Okay, out with it. You had something important to say."

"You'll find it hard to hear."

"Well, spit it out. I'm a big girl."

"We were able to interrogate the detainees last night. They ended up giving us their boss's name. A certain Flavio Danitsha."

"That doesn't ring a bell." Brigitte was relieved but she still looked hesitantly at Jens.

"Danitsha was taken into custody this morning when he tried to leave the country. His computer contained information about the man he was working for."

"Yes?" Brigitte was getting impatient.

"Brigitte, I wouldn't tell you this if I hadn't seen the evidence myself in black and white. I'm afraid Onkel Gerard ordered the arson."

Brigitte blanched. She didn't breathe and crashed to the floor, taking along some dishes and two chairs. Jack jumped up. An armed policeman ran in with his machine gun at the ready.

Jens held his hands in the air and shouted that everything was fine. Brigitte had fainted.

She came to in her room when they lightly slapped her cheek. They all sat around the bed. Esther and Jens each at one side and Jack and Ed at the foot. In the elevator Brigitte had started sobbing and that had developed into an enormous crying fit. Jens held her hand and Brigitte sat up to use his shoulder.

"I'm so sorry, Brigitte. This is terrible."

The comforting words only made things worse. Brigitte said something along the lines of being all alone in the world. Jens tried to reassure her by saying she had Esther and him.

When she had recovered somewhat, doubt hit. "But Gerard would never hurt me."

"I couldn't believe it either but there were two messages in Danitsha's mailbox. One of them was addressed to Gerard's email address. It said that *it's going to happen tonight and all the subjects will be in the finca.* The second one said *I'm sorry. We had a huge slip-up. Two people are taken into custody. I'm leaving the island.* And he admitted it when he was confronted with the confessions of the two arsonists."

"But why?"

"I think it had to do with what Charles Hardford told us. You should get a lawyer right away and find out how Gerard managed your money. Look what happened to Brad Brittain."

"I don't care about the money." Brigitte sobbed again and once more collapsed automatically into Jens's arms, which made Esther nervous.

"That may be, but losing it in that way is no fun. Just call a lawyer first thing and have him get in touch with your accountant."

The homicide division of the New York Police Department had to prepare a lot of paperwork before an arrest warrant could be issued. First Mardavall needed to arrange an international arrest warrant. A prosecutor and a judge in New York had to be involved to approve the arrest warrant and a search warrant for Schöteldreier.

By the time they arrived at Onkel Gerard's house, no one was there. It had been cleaned out and no personal papers were found. There had been some burnt documents in the garbage chute but apparently they had been burned and shredded before being thrown away. The hard drive had been screwed from Schöteldreier's desktop computer. Very neatly, without leaving a scratch. Other than that there were no clues.

The detective in charge sent out an APB. By now it was four o'clock eastern time. In the meantime Schöteldreier had been taken from JFK to the city, where he was brought before the judge and released at three after posting bail. By the time the detectives realized they had had Schöteldreier for almost a whole day, he was gone.

Jens had suggested they fly back to Miami as soon as possible, because Brigitte would be safest there. He had had to charter a plane, because Brigitte wasn't fully functional after hearing the bad news. Nora had to stay in the hospital. She had probably been dead for several minutes and

312

the doctors worried about brain damage. Also, her condition was still critical from the smoke inhalation.

Nora had been conscious briefly and had been confused to see Esther and Brigitte by her bedside. She had no idea what had happened—she probably suffocated in her sleep.

When they reached cruising altitude, Brigitte retreated to the elegant bedroom in the back of the plane. It was the only bedroom and she had offered it to Jens and Esther, since they *were together.* They had politely declined. Anyway, they were too wired to sleep. Besides, their chairs reclined into beds of sorts with the press of a button. Jack and Ed had already found those buttons and in no time they were both snoring up a storm. Esther and Jens went to the lounge where they sat down on a large couch. The flight attendant brought them a bottle of Chablis and two glasses.

Esther curled up against Jens and cried softly. Jens kissed her and held her tightly. He felt nauseous and realized they had been taking care of others since the fire started. Now the tension was being released. Fear, pain, anxiety, relief, anger—it all came together in their bodies. They had never felt so close and yet so distant from each other.

EPILOGUE

The murder and the fire had thrown Hardford completely off balance. He left his *finca* and traveled to London, in suit and tie, to find out what was going on. In the meantime he was willing to do everything Brigitte asked of him. And that was to take a DNA test.

It turned out to be a match. Brigitte was elated. She could now stop worrying about being the progeny of the elusive Philip or the has-been Ravalli.

Once it became clear that WLF had ripped Brigitte off to the tune of tens of millions of dollars, and that Hardford still had stock in the company, he guaranteed his daughter's losses. Even though his son, Thomas, who under no circumstances wanted to meet his half-sister, was against it.

Esther and Jens's book got a lot of publicity. Their three-part story was also sold to several prominent international papers. Research into the roots of pop singer Brigitte Friends had turned into an exciting hunt in the world of rock and roll and the international underworld. The book flew off the shelves and translators in various countries went to work to get it published outside England and America. Frederick Winkler personally traveled to New York to attend the release party. He begged Esther to return as star reporter.

Gerard Schöteldreier seemed to have vanished. His description was broadcast by the national television stations, but with no results. An international search warrant was issued, but Gerard Schöteldreier was gone. Philip also wasn't found or charged, because it was impossible to find a last name to match this "third man." The lawyers and CEOs of WLF were waiting to see if any legal action would be taken.

Brigitte's nervous breakdown lasted several weeks, but she snapped out of it after Jens and Esther stayed with her for a week. It had been a week of swimming, boating, barbecues and much expensive white wine and champagne. Even Nora ended up relaxing a little, showing a whole new side of her personality. It was as though a different person had come back from the dead. Jens never let an opportunity go by to point out that he had saved her life, and that her life, therefore, belonged to him.

Nora was much more cheerful and took care of Jens and Esther now, as well as Brigitte, as if they were also her employers.

Dora Vermeer met with Brigitte right before the book was published. She flew to Miami with her husband, Jan Vandenbroeke, and stayed at a golf resort. Brigitte liked her umpteenth stepfather. He was a sweet, quiet man who worried a lot about her mother. Dora herself only worried about the role she played in the book. Vandenbroeke was quite shocked at all the facts that emerged. "She also has better qualities," he whispered to Jens and Esther when Dora left briefly to powder her nose one night when they were all having dinner. Later Dora threatened to sue Brigitte into poverty. Brigitte was furious and confronted her mother with everything she had done wrong. They almost came to blows.

Esther moved to New York. She and Jens found a larger apartment, so they could each have their own office. Their financial future looked rosy, thanks to the publicity for their book. They both felt they had finished one chapter of their lives, but that it would inevitably lead to the beginning of another.

End of Part One

Also by Dif Books:

The Five-Woman Theory, novel by Fons Burger

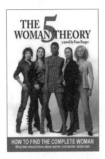

52 Easy ways to change the world from your workplace,
by Fons and Jacqui Burger

Tephran, The Secret of the Volcano, by Paula King

More information on www.difbooks.com